RUINOUS CREATURES

A NOVEL

JESSI COLE JACKSON

ATRIA BOOKS
New York   Amsterdam/Antwerp   London
Toronto   Sydney/Melbourne   New Delhi

ATRIA BOOKS

An Imprint of Simon & Schuster, LLC
1230 Avenue of the Americas
New York, NY 10020

For more than 100 years, Simon & Schuster has championed authors and the stories they create. By respecting the copyright of an author's intellectual property, you enable Simon & Schuster and the author to continue publishing exceptional books for years to come. We thank you for supporting the author's copyright by purchasing an authorized edition of this book.

No amount of this book may be reproduced or stored in any format, nor may it be uploaded to any website, database, language-learning model, or other repository, retrieval, or artificial intelligence system without express permission. All rights reserved. Inquiries may be directed to Simon & Schuster, 1230 Avenue of the Americas, New York, NY 10020 or permissions@simonandschuster.com.

This book is a work of fiction. Any references to historical events, real people, or real places are used fictitiously. Other names, characters, places, and events are products of the author's imagination, and any resemblance to actual events or places or persons, living or dead, is entirely coincidental.

Copyright © 2026 by Jessica Jackson

All rights reserved, including the right to reproduce this book or portions thereof in any form whatsoever. For information, address Atria Books Subsidiary Rights Department, 1230 Avenue of the Americas, New York, NY 10020.

First Atria Books hardcover edition March 2026

ATRIA BOOKS and colophon are registered trademarks of Simon & Schuster, LLC

Simon & Schuster strongly believes in freedom of expression and stands against censorship in all its forms. For more information, visit BooksBelong.com.

For information about special discounts for bulk purchases, please contact Simon & Schuster Special Sales at 1-866-506-1949 or business@simonandschuster.com.

The Simon & Schuster Speakers Bureau can bring authors to your live event. For more information or to book an event, contact the Simon & Schuster Speakers Bureau at 1-866-248-3049 or visit our website at www.simonspeakers.com.

Interior design by Jill Putorti

Manufactured in the United States of America

1 3 5 7 9 10 8 6 4 2

Library of Congress Control Number: 2025949689

ISBN 978-1-6680-9289-7
ISBN 978-1-6680-9291-0 (ebook)

Let's stay in touch! Scan here to get book recommendations, exclusive offers, and more delivered to your inbox.

*For those facing ruin,
carrying the flame of hope.*

RUINOUS CREATURES

Chapter One

ADELA

I polish the bones, rubbing small swipes of scented oils and soothing ointments into the pale, craggy surfaces of the creatures' skulls. Their insistent whispered wants echo through my head. I repress a shiver of revulsion.

I remind myself of the honor of my position. Communing with the skulls is a sacred calling. I shouldn't hate the feeling of their wants flowing through me or be relieved that their voices have grown softer over the years.

Behind me, I hear the cruel scoff of my mentor. "Seventeen years in, and squeamish as ever. The Spinner save us. The day you become matcher will be a bleak one for us all."

"Especially for you," I mumble in reply as I rub rosemary and safflower oil along the edge of a long-dead jackalope's empty eye socket.

After all, Bartholomew isn't yet an old man, and matchers don't have the luxury of retirement. We die. If we're both lucky, I'll have another thirty years as his assistant before I have to take over being head matcher.

If you could call it luck.

"What was that, girl?"

"Do we have more salted lotus wax?" I make my voice light, glad for the matching hut's muddled light and the solid silver mask hiding my face.

He grunts and points to the jar at my elbow.

"Ah, of course." I use it on the broad, angular skull of the gryphon with the chipped beak, then move to another jackalope, my hands and mind finding a rhythm in the work as I polish its twisted antlers. Most jackalopes choose oil imbued with bright cranberries, mint, or lemon verbena. The sharp-beaked gryphon skulls are finicky, preferring first an earthy, autumnal leaf ointment, then vibrating in quick, harsh bursts halfway through my efforts, only settling back into their pleased rumbles when I switch to spicy peppermint or myrrh and repeat the ministrations.

I take down the three gytrash and polish all their canine-like skulls with the musky scent of oakmoss. Gytrash always match in triples. And while any skull can match with any of the three orders, gytrash usually pair only with members of the Huntress order. I wonder if these skulls who assist priestesses with death rites will find their matches during the upcoming ceremony.

On and on I go, trying to sink into the repetition of the work and ignore the scraping murmurs of their voices as well as I can. Not that the skulls speak with actual voices. My best friend, Cecelia, is constantly trying to get me to describe the sensation of communing with the skulls while I polish them. She can hear them too—most keepers can—but they're faint to her, muffled. She's fascinated by the depth of my understanding of their wants and wishes. But I have no words to explain; for me it's as undefinable as any other sense.

I just . . . hear them. Inside my head, or perhaps some deeper part of me. The skulls tell me, without words, their wants, needs, and secret desires. Some are sharp and buzzing; some are gentle and tinkling.

No matter the volume or nature of their voices, I hate hearing them. I oughtn't. I am a keeper, from a long line of well-respected keepers—with one notable exception. And as assistant matcher, I am destined for greatness.

And yet.

Wishing I were doing almost anything else, I reach up on tiptoe and hook a jaw with my finger, scooting our only dragon skull off one of the top shelves.

"Take care!" Bartholomew snaps, and I nearly drop the skull. His voice softens when he says, "That was Psecilious. One of my first . . . charges."

I dust the tips of Psecilious's horns with a tiny bit of rare golden mica, and gently file away a bump from an otherwise smooth incisor the size of my thumb. Inside me, the dragon sounds raspy, and so much quieter than he ought to be. I twist with guilt for my relief.

To distract myself from the complexity of my feelings, I blurt, "He must've been large for a dragon."

Bartholomew will welcome the chance to expound upon the noble nature of dragons. He clears his throat. "Dragons once were massive beasts. Large enough to eat a deer in one great gulp. But where they once bred for size and strength, now they make more civilized choices for mates. Females will choose cleverer, more domesticated matches, and over the centuries it has led to a decline. . . ."

He talks on and on, telling me things I've heard a hundred times before. His love for them runs deep—the two he keeps as pets, more wild ones he watches over from afar, even the skulls of dead dragons— all more cherished than his community.

Particularly me.

While he talks, I toil. Grinding herbs and seeds for scents, pressing ingredients for their essence, emulsifying lectin with water and oil for thick, rich lotions. Plus, of course, cleaning all of Bartholomew's tools.

"It serves them well as a species."

I chose the wrong strategy. Rather than distracting me, Bartholomew's high, persistent droning seems to somehow intensify the creatures' voices until there is a discordant tumult in my head. At least his golden aspen mask muffles him a bit. As keepers, we wear masks whenever we work directly with the skulls of the creatures, to protect us from accidentally matching ourselves.

Keepers serve the orders and care for the living creatures; we do not wield magic.

"No more hungering between hunts or nesting in rocks to raise their young. No, dragons are smart. And loyal. The greatest of all creatures."

When Bartholomew begins to compare dragons to the other types of creatures, I wonder if he'd notice me stuffing bits of my polishing cloth in my ears. Not that it'd help mute the skulls that echo inside me, but at least then their voices wouldn't be fighting with his for my attention.

I finish working with the horsey skull of a nearly silent pegasus and turn back to the shelves. I place the last skull on the shelf and press my hands into my lower back. I arch, hearing the popping protests of my stiff bones. With that, I believe I am done.

Finally.

My eyes skim over to the rows of skulls that glow in the suns' rays through the large windows of the matching hut. Their magic hums with keen anticipation after their polishing, as if they know what's to come. And perhaps they do. The depth of a dead creature's sentience has only been speculated about. But I believe most of the skulls anticipate the upcoming matching ceremony with something like glee, as if they desire nothing more than to be paired with the novitiates and used for their unique magics.

I shiver at the very idea of having to wear a dead creature on my face every time I stepped into public for the rest of my life; for its wants—its voice—to constantly be in my mind, in my heart. No magic, no matter how powerful or useful, would be worth that.

The sun dips slightly lower, following its inevitable path across the valley, and hits a small shelf that sits above all the others. It's so high and small I always thought it was practically useless and, therefore, empty. But something must be up there, based on the sharp glint of sunshine.

I step back and go on my tiptoes to see better. There, pushed so far back that I can make out only the edges of two curved yellow beaks, are skulls. Based on the beaks, they must be gryphons. But why would Bartholomew shove them up there?

I count the other gryphons on the shelves. Six. The exact amount there should be. Have we missed these two in years past? Or are they new? But no. They're so discolored they look as if they have begun to fossilize. Skulls tend to lighten as they age, bleached by the valley sun streaming in through the matching hut's wide windows. But that would make them hundreds of years old.

I get the ladder—no amount of stretching on my toes will help me reach these two. Bartholomew waves me off. "Don't bother. We don't polish the phoenixes. There's no magic within them to awaken, or match. They're just . . ." He searches for a word, but whatever he's looking for, he doesn't find. With a shrug, he finishes with "decoration."

"'Decoration'?" I can't hide the horror of my tone, even when it makes him scowl so hard I can tell despite his mask, just by the tightening of the skin of his eyes. But to call any skull a mere decoration is surely sacrilege, even if they have no magic left in them.

And then the creature he's named registers in my tired brain. "Wait. Did you say 'phoenixes'? They've been extinct for centuries, at least. We don't have phoenix skulls."

"Obviously we do," he scoffs. "The skulls are there on the shelf. We ought to have the Huntress high priestess burn them when she's here with her dragon-wearer; return them to the valley. But for now, they sit. Let's go."

He turns and leaves without waiting on my response, leaving the door open behind him. He drops his outer cloak and golden mask immediately outside, where they lie in a pile for me to gather up from frost-gilded grass. As his assistant, I'm to clean and care for them, then return them to him after the ceremonies are complete.

He could just hand them to me, but that's not Bartholomew's way.

I should follow him. Call the day done. While it's not expressly forbidden, it's frowned upon to be in the matching hut alone. It can be dangerous, especially so close to a matching.

And besides, it's creepy.

Even now, the skulls whisper through me, their wants pulling me toward them. Not the phoenixes, but the others. They want me to stay. To pull down the phoenixes. To rub oils and herbs into their ancient bones.

"Do you not hear them?" I call after Bartholomew. "The skulls want us to stay."

He actually considers. "Of course they do. They are beasts of want." He shrugs. "In another decade or so, you will learn to ignore their clamoring."

He turns and marches back to his quarters, no doubt eager to get back to the two illicit dragons he keeps as pets. It breaks the keeper's code. Creatures are beings of magical, sacred purpose and are not to be coddled—or trusted. But Bartholomew is not the only one who lives with them in their home, though most choose an adorable, fuzzy jackalope, not two full-grown dragons.

I look longingly toward the village in the far distance, across the meadows. I want to get out of the hut, to breathe the cold evening air and get home to soak in hot, fragrance-free bathwater until I pickle. But the phoenix skulls are like an itch I can't quite scratch. I can't walk through the door.

He notices I still haven't followed. He stops marching across the half-frozen ground and turns. His thick white eyebrows are severe across his ivory brow. "Well? Come on."

I make a flimsy excuse. And yet, I cannot help myself. "The new rosemary and lavender oils will be done infusing soon. I'll get those decanted and be along shortly."

He studies me as a herd of jackalopes dances around him, hopping in a chaotic circle. In the sky above, the shadowy figures of two pegasi fly in figure eights, with Bartholomew in the center of one loop and the matching hut in the center of the other.

Since they still have their flesh and their breath, I can't hear their wants, but their playful exuberance speaks volumes. The living creatures like matching ceremonies, too, and they especially like Bartholomew and me just after we've worked with the bones of their dead ancestors. Cecelia claims they're drawn to the magic of their brethren. I think they're just macabre little beasts.

"Suit yourself," Bartholomew says with another shrug, and walks away. "Don't do anything impulsive."

"I would never," I lie.

I lug down first one phoenix and then the other, plopping them onto the workbench and gathering up my supplies. Up on the shelf, they looked plain, old. The bone paler and their beaks duller compared with the sharp, serrated edges of a gryphon's. Up close, they are breathtaking.

They speak to something deep inside me in a way that makes me wonder, for just a moment, if maybe I am exactly where I'm supposed to be, doing exactly what I was meant to do. Exactly as I imagine all the other keepers feel when they're given their calling. Dad as a head carer, Cecelia as a valley historian, even Bartholomew as a matcher. For the three of them, who they are and what they do seems to align so perfectly. As if the goddesses created them specially to fulfill their roles.

But I've never felt that.

I've only ever felt awkward, inadequate, and vaguely disturbed preparing the bones for matching. All I have are ill-conceived impulses that I follow too often; like polishing the skulls of two phoenixes after being instructed very clearly not to.

And yet.

This feels right. Standing before these phoenix skulls, I feel something subtle, but powerful, shift inside me. For perhaps the first time in my life, everything within me feels aligned.

"You're magnificent," I whisper.

The skulls of the phoenixes have a broad, angled brow and distinctly curved beak. One pierces my thumb as I move it into my lap. It's sharper than it looks. Instinctively, I bring my thumb to my mouth to suck away the blood, but my mask is in the way. I wipe it on my tunic instead—I don't want to stain the bone.

I turn the one I hold this way and that, examining its unfamiliar shape. There are no living phoenixes, so I struggle to match the arc of the solid skull upon my lap to the graceful, feathered creatures depicted on the tapestries in the great hall or in my childhood storybooks.

Someone long ago had rubbed a thick layer of golden mica across both the exterior and interior of the bone, a costly addition for so much surface area, and no doubt what caused the sun to shine off it so strongly that it caught my eye after seventeen years of being hidden from me in shadow.

Somewhere in our history, a matcher had clearly expected these two phoenix skulls to choose someone important, maybe even future high priestesses.

But now . . . I hold first one skull, then the next in my bare hands, closing my eyes.

They're silent.

I try one sample after another on one skull and then the other, to no avail. There is no hint of a hum vibrating across my palms, no preference for saffron or vanilla, safflower oil or beeswax. I could spend the rest of the night preparing them, but it would make no difference.

They are utterly still. "Are you gone? Or just resting?"

I stare down at the beautiful twin skulls and imagine their living calls. Would they have been high and bright like the prairie warbler on springtime mornings or low and forlorn like the yellow-billed cuckoo? I want to awaken them, to hear the echo of their voices in their hum beneath my hands.

The want surprises me. The voices of the dead creatures are the hardest part of my role, the element that most makes me ill at ease. I turn this desire to hear them over and over in my mind and realize, it's deeper than want. It's a persistent, urgent need.

When I was first assigned to my role as Bartholomew's apprentice, I had gobbled up absolutely everything Cecelia could find me on the matchers. There was one whose journal was full of scandalous, bordering on dangerous, methods. But her matches were legendary.

Bartholomew hated her, scoffing when he found me reading her journal with interest and awe at her boldness. Which, honestly, might be all the more reason to try.

I lift my hand to my mask.

Showing your face to the skulls is the most sacred part of the upcoming ceremony, the final determination of a match, and not a risk any keeper, let alone a matcher, would ever take. Magic is reserved for the orders, those who directly serve the Huntress, the Pupil, or the Spinner.

I have my back to all but these two, but still I'm careful to push up the edge of my mask barely enough.

I shouldn't do this. And yet, once again, I run headlong into foolishness.

Cradling one phoenix skull in the crook of my elbow, I rest my bare cheek against the cool bone. I had hoped to feel the faintest whisper of a hum, but what happens instead is more of a scream or an explosion. Or both.

Sound, light, emotion, heat, all thrust at me with the force of a storm and ripple through the small building like a the force of a pegasus storm. Nothing moves, and yet it is as if the walls themselves begin to shake. I think I hear the rattle of the windows, and I hurriedly set the phoenix skull down beside its partner. I slide my mask firmly back into place when I turn to check the wall of other skulls behind me. They are exactly as I had left them, pristine and still in the lantern light. And yet.

And yet.

I cover my ears against the cacophony. I've never heard their voices so loud, so distinct. They cheer and shriek, swear and celebrate. But their attention is not on me. It is as if every single empty socket looks past me to the two phoenix skulls on the bench.

They wait with vicious anticipation.

Out of the corner of my eye, I catch a glow of light that is a different hue than the lantern's, and I turn slowly back around to face the phoenix skulls. They sit side by side on the bench, just as they had moments ago. But whereas before they looked pale and listless despite their expensive dusting of mica, now they glow from within, as bright and menacing as a dragon's fiery breath. The golden mica practically dances across their surface, and I understand now why some matcher long ago had bestowed them with so much. It suits them perfectly, highlighting the shifting red and coral, orange and yellow of their molten surfaces.

I take an involuntary step back, overwhelmed by their beauty and the worry that I just opened a door to somewhere I have never been, that I cannot close again.

I will clean up, store the supplies, pick up Bartholomew's discarded things that are no doubt frost-covered by now, and go home. It feels like fleeing, and it is. Something has changed. Something I don't understand.

Before I can move, I hear a roar outside that freezes me in place. That is the call of a creature hunting, a creature about to kill, to win. The skulls go silent for one long second, and then match the victory screech.

I don't know what they hunt or what they have caught, but I'm worried it might be me.

Chapter Two

ADELA

I open the matching hut's door a crack, removing my mask to look up, but all I can see is the quiet, starry sky. I hope whatever creature roared is now far away.

I leave behind the lantern so I can move unnoticed through the snow-dusted meadow toward the warm glow of village. The light of the large, pale moon is enough to navigate through the jackalope warrens.

I creep out quietly and quickly, firmly closing the door on the softly glowing phoenix skulls and cursing my own impulsivity. Why can't I just ignore the horrible ideas that pop into my head, rather than run headlong at them?

But I push away the thought, scooping up Bartholomew's abandoned mask and cloak. I shove them beneath my arm with my own mask, moving swiftly across the meadow.

A jackalope hops out of a nearby buttonbush, and I pause. They're adorable—rather sweet and loppy bunny-like creatures with round faces and soft fur. But their antlers are as sharp as razors, and they can be aggressive, especially when strangers get too near.

I am no stranger. I've been traveling back and forth between the village and the matching hut for seventeen years. They tend to be shy around me because they don't feel the need to protect themselves.

Not tonight.

I am barely twenty steps away from the matching hut's safety when I hear the muted thud of many soft paws on the frozen ground behind me. I look over my shoulder to find a pack of twenty or so. They are close on my heels, with their velvety noses pointed toward the ground, aiming their sharply spiked heads at my legs.

I walk faster.

So do they, hopping quickly to match pace. I hear a familiar weeping from one, and then another farther away. The call is hypnotic and disorienting. I want to stop, to look for the woman making the sound. But I know she is long gone. This is a distraction method of jackalopes and a bad sign.

I speed up. One dashes forward, catching my skirts. I jump away and hear fabric tear but don't look down. It's a warning strike. If they really wanted to catch me, they could. I cannot outrun the jackalopes, or any of the valley's creatures, but for the moment they seem more interested in herding me back toward the village than nibbling away at my flesh, thank the Spinner.

Above me, I imagine I hear the faintest rush of wings. I flinch and glance up, but see no movement in the bright night sky. Surely there is nothing dark and dangerous hunting me from above.

I am practically jogging now, clutching the masks and Bartholomew's cloak to my chest and gulping down the frigid air. I silently curse myself for not joining Cecelia on her morning runs more regularly. But I am round, with a tummy and breasts that bounce and jiggle and thighs that rub. When I push too hard, as I always do, running hurts. Unfortunately, at the moment, breathing hurts, too.

I slow down, and this time I am certain I hear the telltale whoosh of very large wings above me. I look up to see a section of stars blotted out, but whether it is a gryphon, a dragon, or a pegasus in the air above my head, I can't tell.

Not that it matters. They are all predators, and all delight in a chase.

I stop hurrying. Or at least, I try to stop looking like I am hurrying. Instead, I walk in an exaggerated, quick-paced stroll. I am terrified, but I begin to sing a drinking song my cousin Melinda once taught me. I am big. I am unafraid. I am not prey.

The jackalopes swarm around me, biting at my hems and rubbing rough antlers on my legs. It hurts, but my cloak and skirts offer protection. The small creatures aren't doing any lasting damage, and I am safer with a herd of angry jackalopes poking at me than meeting a flying beast. I let them chomp away, pulling at me as I get closer and closer to the edge of the village, which is eerily quiet. But it is late. I stayed in the matching hut much longer than I had planned.

When I cross the invisible threshold into the village, the jackalopes stop and gnash their pointy teeth at me in a show of dominance. They were gentle with me, considering the size of those teeth and their sheer numbers. They could have done much more damage.

I check the air over the meadow I just traversed, but whatever was following me is gone. I am safe.

"Dad?" I call out, even though I can see the hook at the back door that should be holding his cloak is empty. I set my mask and Bartholomew's things on a small table. I'll clean and return them to him after all of the ceremonies this week are complete.

Before I can take another step into the quiet house, the back door slams open, and Dad walks in, soaked in green-black blood. In his arms is a small kelpie—half-horse, half-fish–like creature—with a tangled seaweed mane. Her mouth, lined with rows of knife-sharp teeth, gulps for a breath she can't find out of water.

I spring forward to help, but he gestures me away, grunting.

There are only two kelpies left in the entire valley, and they're not easy to differentiate, especially if the light isn't shining directly on them and illuminating the subtle color differences of their scales.

"What's happened? Who is she? Why is she bleeding? Why is she *here*?"

"Duschwa. Fill the tub. Quickly, love."

I do as he asks, bolting down the hallway and throwing open the spigots into our wide copper tub. The water is cold, of course, with no time to light the fires to warm it, but kelpies live in rivers. She doesn't need warmth; she just needs water.

Water barely covers the bottom of the tub when he is there, straining to gently place the kelpie mare inside. Much smaller than the horse that her head, neck, and shoulders resemble, she still barely fits in a tub that I can luxuriate in. He splashes water over her, particularly on the gills at her neck, and gestures for me to do the same.

I do, soaking the tattered cloak I still wear. He notices the tears—Dad always notices everything—but just gives me a look that promises he'll ask later, and continues to focus on his patient.

When it looks like she is breathing again, he says, "Found her on my way back from the barns. Bleeding out in the middle of John's backyard."

"And then you *carried* her here?"

He shrugs, as if carrying a full-grown kelpie is not an impossible feat of strength, even for a man who is strong from his work. As head carer, he is in charge of the physical health and well-being of the community's equine population—the horses, donkeys, and mules that we use for transport and as beasts of burden and, more important, the unicorns, pegasi, and last pair of kelpies left in existence.

"It was closer than the river," he says, so matter-of-fact. As if it isn't bizarre that a kelpie was inside the village, so far from the river, in the first place. "Now help me turn her so we can get to her wounds. This is too much blood to lose."

The tub is nearly black with blood. I reach in where he indicates and push when he tells me to. The kelpie snaps her sharp teeth at me. If she weren't half-gone already, she could take my arm with one quick chomp, but this snap is more from fear than any malice. Her eyes are wide and white like any other equine's would be, and her gills open and close far too quickly.

Dad and I flip her over to find the cause of all the blood. Three deep gouges run the length of her torso.

"Get the sewing kit," Dad says. His voice is tired, despairing.

"Dad—" I begin, and lose the words. There is no saving Duschwa from this. The wounds are deep enough that I can see rib through one gash. But he hears the rest of what I'd say in the tone of that single word.

Through gritted teeth, he replies, "I cannot lose two in one day."

My heart stutters at the ominous words. Who else has he lost? But I get the kit.

I am holding the sides of Duschwa's flesh together as he sews when I find the strength to say, "Not Etana?" I can barely whisper her name. I search his front, but if there's any silver unicorn blood on his clothes, it's hidden beneath Duschwa's.

I pray to the Pupil for wisdom, to the Spinner for healing, but most of my silent prayers go to the Huntress, begging her to protect Etana and her unborn foal from death. Not that the Huntress is swayed by mere prayers. Still, I silently plead and promise a sacrifice once the matching is over.

While I would never think to contain or tame her, Etana is almost as special to me as Bartholomew's dragons are to him. She and I were born at the same moment, under the same falling star. It's an inauspicious birth date, especially for mothers. I nearly lost mine in the birthing room. Etana had had to be pulled from the carcass of hers. And so, we were raised together, fed bottles of goat's milk by the man standing before me, covered in blood and attending to Duschwa with the same strong, steady hands he's used to help countless others.

All keepers have seen tragedy, and my father more than most. For reasons unknown, creatures' birthrates have been declining for a century, and the unicorns, kelpies, and pegasi seem especially impacted. They hardly ever breed, and when they do, at least a third end up losing the foal before or during the birth.

I think of the now-glowing phoenix skulls high up on the shelf in the matching hut and wonder if their decline was as profound.

After closing up the first wound, Dad finally shakes his head. "Not Etana. Just an ordinary mare. Donna. Heart failure from some sort of infection."

None of Dad's charges are *just* anything to him. He cares for the magical and mundane creatures of the valley with the same depth of feeling, and I know he'll feel the mare's death just as profoundly as he'll feel Duschwa's once the rush of these moments has faded.

I pull my hands away. She has stopped thrashing. Or breathing. Her wounds were too deep.

He places his forehead against Duschwa's, holding tight to her seaweed-strand mane. His voice is thick with pain when he says, "I suppose we'll have another skull for the holies to choose from at the matching."

It's a bleak bright side.

I step out to give him some semblance of privacy to grieve another lost charge. Two in one day. My poor father.

Silently, I say a prayer of thanks to the Spinner for protecting my Etana for now, and hope Duschwa will sate the Huntress's endless hunger for death. So she will not come for yet another creature.

I am at the sink, scrubbing Duschwa's blood from under my nails, when a high, piercing bell interrupts the quiet night. Dad's out of the bathroom and putting his cloak on before I can rinse the suds off my hands.

"What is it?" I ask, not recognizing the alarm's meaning.

"The fire bell."

I follow him out, pulling my hood up against the cold. It doesn't help. It's still soaked. On the heels of the cold seeping through, I think of the jackalopes and whatever roaring creature followed me silently through the night, the cacophonous skulls, Duschwa's strange wounds. It all began with the pulse of energy when I touched my cheek to the phoenix skull.

But surely that is coincidence. I am not responsible.

Right?

We hurry down the gravel path toward the center of the village. Across the square, the skeletal remains of a house are smoldering, but it's impossible to tell which one in the smoky darkness. All the houses look alike until you can see the plants in the front window boxes or the color of the painted front door.

This house has none of that. It doesn't even have most of its roof. Or walls.

A figure runs toward us, silver hair gleaming in the starlight. When she gets closer, I recognize Petra, one of the elders who serves on the council with Dad. She meets us and doubles over, her hands on her knees as she gulps big breaths of air. It's so cold and dry, it must hurt her lungs, and she is not a young woman to be running through a late-February night.

"Where is the fire? How can we help?" Dad asks. Identify the problem; discover potential solutions; work toward them. The same as always, despite the heaviness of his own losses today.

"The fire. Is. Out," she manages to say, which is both obvious and impossible. The bell just rang. Surely no one missed it for so long that it would be able to destroy an entire house in the time we crossed a small village?

I think of the roar I heard.

Unless the fire was not a natural sort but created instead by a creature whose fiery blasts burn so hot that they instantly annihilate whatever they touch, leaving behind nothing but smoldering ash.

When she catches her breath, Petra blurts, "Bartholomew is dead! The dragons attacked him and then fought each other. Only one dragon survived. Come quickly, Oscar. We're meeting."

"What? No. What?" I cannot wrap my head around her words. My mentor cannot be dead. I just saw him. I have his robe and his mask to clean at my house. I was going to return them after the week's ceremonies.

And a dragon gone as well? Gilcriss and Enkidus are only fifty or sixty years old. Basically young adults amongst dragons, which live for centuries.

Neither Dad nor Petra replies as we hurry, half walking, half running toward Bartholomew's house. Or what's left of it. Half the structure is gone, wood and glass and plaster scattered across the grass nearby as if it all exploded outward, another quarter charred and still smoking. A ruin.

But that is all nothing compared with the blackened remains of Bartholomew himself or those of his beloved pet Gilcriss. The dragon lies beside him, red-black blood continuing to leak from a gaping wound at her neck. Bartholomew's body lies in what used to be his kitchen, now nothing but splintered wooden floor. Or what's left of it.

I gag.

I have seen violence; you can't live amongst the creatures and not. Kelpies who've drowned unsuspecting cows and eaten their bloated faces, gryphon talons rending flesh to the bone, fat and muscle visible beneath the gushing blood of keepers' forearms or shoulders, and of course the traumas of everyday life in the valley for creatures, animals, and keepers—birth, disease, the abundant indignities of old age. Hell, moments ago I was holding together Duschwa's sides as she bled out beneath my hands.

But Bartholomew is worse than all the others combined and magnified by ten.

Somewhere to my right, someone is retching. I hear curses and prayers flying to the heavens. But the Huntress has already been here, and there's nothing the other goddesses can do even if they deigned to hear us.

One leg is gone, his body no longer holding snug most of his organs, some of which seem missing as well. The other leg is bent unnaturally beneath him, his whole body crumpled as if he had been dropped from a great height, landing in a heap.

A great height.

A fire.

A kelpie with deep gashes, far away from the river where she lived.

The roar I heard in the matching hut.

With soul-crushing certainty, I know then that the pulse of magic I felt when I awoke the phoenix went through the entire valley. It affected Bartholomew's dragons to the point that one killed its nest mate, a kelpie, and ate half of Bartholomew.

And it's all my fault.

I walk into the great hall in a haze, following along behind Dad and Petra like a duckling. The moment we're inside, there's a blur, and someone practically tackles me, covering my face in kisses and squeezing. I inhale the familiar scents of vanilla and almond in my best friend's silky hair. "I'm glad you're okay, too."

"I was so scared when they said it was Bartholo—" Cecelia sobs through the end of his name. "I thought maybe they attacked the matching hut while you were preparing."

"I'm okay." I hug her again. "I'm okay."

"Thank the Spinner."

"Why are you here?" I ask. While she's cleverer and wiser than the vast majority of keepers, elders included, at merely thirty-three years old, Cecelia's far too young to serve on the council.

She holds up some paper and a thin sliver of charcoal. "Honorary scribe for the night. Petra wanted all the elders to focus on the conversation instead of worrying about recording everything."

We turn to the group of elders, standing in the empty great hall, Petra at the center. Even in her nightshirt, stained with ash, her white hair hanging down one shoulder in a messy braid, she somehow looks regal. Her back straight, her shoulders squared, ready to tackle the heartbreaking burden of leading through disaster. She is the kind of woman I'd love to grow into; the kind of keeper I could never hope to be.

Around the perimeter of the room, there are tables and chairs, stacked up and ready to be laid for the impending feast, but no one moves to grab them, to sit. They're already talking. Half are still in their nightclothes, like Petra, with robes or coats held tight against the cold and horror of the night.

Niclas, the oldest member of the council by a dozen years or more, wears a blanket wrapped around his frail, curved shoulders like a shawl. He keeps shivering, his sparse white beard quivering.

Cecelia hurries closer to the group and plops down, folding herself forward to use the floor as her table for note-taking.

"I just don't understand what happened. They were always so docile," Ziba says, staring hauntedly into the dark recessed corners of the large gathering space. They are dressed, at least, but their large jowls and puffy undereye bags seem to hang more than ever. "Poor Bartholomew."

"May the Huntress guide his soul to the after," Niclas adds in a shaking voice, and the rest of us make the sign of the three at the blessing.

John, a slight, balding man with a quick temper and a tendency toward drama, says, "If you ask me, I think we should go out and hunt that dragon for what it did. Time for them both to do what they were made for. Become skulls."

The other elders gasp. Redonna might actually faint, her wrinkled, dark-brown cheeks go so suddenly ashen. Ziba finds a chair and has her sit before mumbling something about tea and heading off toward the kitchens.

I realize once they've left that I should've been the one to go. Like Cecelia, I'm too young to serve the elders, but unlike Cecelia, I have no real purpose here. I just followed Dad and no one had the heart to kick me out.

And then I realize. Bartholomew, our matcher, is dead. I am his apprentice.

Of course they need me here.

Petra stomps her foot, the hard heel of her boot echoes on the marble floor and throughout the large, empty room. The others quiet. Softly, but with steel in her voice, she admonishes John. "You forget your place. We are in this valley for the care and keeping of our charges, not to hasten their demise. If I ever, ever hear you mention intentionally harming another creature, you will be expelled from the valley immediately, I don't care how long your keeper lineage stretches back. We do not *hunt*."

Niclas wipes away a tear from his cheek before it soaks into his beard. "I just don't understand why Gilcriss and Enkidus would do this to Barty."

A low murmur of voices breaks out as the elders talk amongst themselves, giving potential suggestions for the why of it all. Ziba returns with the tea, but no one moves to take any. They all just talk around and around in circles about how and why the dragons snapped, unable to settle on anything reasonable.

They must not have felt the pulse of magic that the phoenix threw out. I wonder if Bartholomew did, before he died. I wonder, too, what I should tell them. The wisest, most experienced minds of our community need to know so they can work through solutions. A bright spot of hope flares as I realize there may be a chance this giant misstep means I would be punished and not be allowed to step into my role as matcher.

Instantly, I flush, a hot storm cloud of shame rolling through my body. Not only did my actions lead to death, but now I'm silently hoping to avoid my destiny? My embarrassment keeps me quiet for longer than it ought.

"We can discuss this more in depth later, once we've had a chance to rest and discover more facts." Dad's voice is low and soft like Petra's, and the others quiet to hear him. "Let's focus on the immediate for now. The Huntress's high priestess, entourage, and novitiates will be here by midday tomorrow."

"And we have no matcher for the upcoming ceremony," John points out, a bit sulkily.

Cecelia turns to me, fidgeting with her quill, watching me closely for a reaction, but I am as still as stone.

"Yes, thank you, John," Petra says with a nearly silent sigh. "First order of business: we need to ensure the order's safety on their trek through the forest. Niclas and Redonna, please gather a dozen careful, levelheaded keepers to patrol their path in the morning. We don't know what's gotten into Enkidus, but we know better what signs to look for than blindfolded outsiders will.

"Stay out of sight as much as possible, but do not hesitate to raise an alarm if necessary. The last thing we need is their blood being shed. They're already talking of tightening their belts and reducing support because of their dissatisfaction with the diminishing magic.

"I'll join you as soon as I'm able."

Niclas and Redonna both agree and move to leave the meeting. The night is encroaching on morning, and if the order arrives when they ought, then they'll be hitting the far edge of the valley's forest in a couple of hours at most.

I am thinking about their journey, about the danger the creatures pose and what they might do to a band of blindfolded, white-clad strangers traipsing through their territories.

I'm just hoping no one else will get eaten when Petra stops them. "A moment please. Before we disband, we need to discuss the issue John rightfully raised. We need to formally install Adela as matcher for the ceremony. And choose a new assistant."

All eyes turn to me. When I don't speak, or even move, Petra prompts, "Adela, you're going to have to lead the ceremony. Are you prepared?"

"Yes?" I reply, more a question than a confident statement of assent.

"She doesn't sound very certain," John says. No one replies. Everyone can see I am about to bolt or puke or just start sobbing and never stop.

I glance at Dad, who looks stricken. Is it because he knows, deep down, that I should not be given this sort of power in our community? That I will only cause further ruin?

Ziba hands me a mug of tea from the tray, and I wrap my hands around the warm porcelain, breathing in the earthy steam. I take a sip. It's sweet and tangy with lemon and honey and tastes like liquid comfort.

I still cannot find my voice.

I had planned on spending decades still as an assistant. Matchers should have gray hair and wrinkles, soft bellies, and hard-earned wisdom. They need time to learn the skulls, how to match their whims and magic to the personalities and needs of the religious novitiates and their superiors. As rude as Bartholomew was to me, he was expert at navigating the tetchy temperaments, demands, and politics of the three orders and their high priestesses.

I have none of that knowledge. Or the finesse.

Ever practical, Petra brings me out of my stupor by digging deep into the details. "Of course, we will need to get you outfitted. I assume Bartholomew's robes went up in dragon fire. I will talk to the tailors, see if they can work quickly to make you a suitable robe for the ceremony. We cannot send you before the skulls and goddesses in assistant lavender. The mask is another matter, however."

"I can search for Bartholomew's mask in the ashes," Ziba offers. "Perhaps I'll find some of his ceremonial jewelry, too."

I think of the charred husk of a house, of a body. What gold-crusted bone or aspen would survive those temperatures? But Petra nods. "Let me know by noon at the latest so we can figure out an alternative if we must."

"Maybe some paint," John offers with a chortle.

No one laughs.

I think of the neat pile of Bartholomew's things beside our back door. The robes would never work; they're too plain. But the mask sitting on top could. "I have a suitable mask."

The elders turn to me, waiting.

"From our prep work today. Bartholomew left it behind with his robe, for me to clean. I was going to return it after the cerem—" My voice cracks.

"It's gold and aspen," Dad points out the most important details for me, a heavy hand on my shoulder. I lean in to the comforting weight of it, the way it grounds me.

"That'll do then." Petra nods, her tone firm, leaving no space for argument. Not that any sane keeper would argue about this. We know dead skulls don't care how fancy the mask or robes or jewelry the matcher wears is. The precious metals set the matcher and assistant apart. All the rest of the pomp is for the orders.

She turns to me, and says gently, "You will need an assistant immediately. Have you thought of who you'd like to replace you?"

The instant she poses the question, my mind goes blank of anyone and everyone I know. Danni, our torchbearer, would be the next in line traditionally, but she's far too young at only twelve. And though torchbearer to assistant to matcher is the common progression, it's not the only path.

I've never thought about who would succeed me. Typically, keepers are tested with the skulls as children and a list is kept. Many of us can hear the skulls, but some have more affinity than others. Then, when a matcher grows old and tired, they have lengthy discussions with the elders to choose the next assistant.

I began as assistant matcher when I was sixteen, and I know Dad's role as a respected elder had more to do with my appointment than my own unique talents, despite my affinity to the skulls. I wouldn't want to choose someone too close to me in age, as they'd end up stifled in an assistant role that lasts longer than typical, but neither could I choose a child.

The role is physically and mentally grueling, and I'll need someone strong, intuitive, and responsible to assist me.

I have no idea whom to name, and take another gulp of tea. I cannot get this wrong. They expect leadership and confidence from their matcher, not a breakdown. But I am frozen with both rage and shame.

"Beadda might be a good choice?" Cecelia offers softly.

Her voice startles me. But of course her younger sister is a great choice, and I'm mad for not thinking of her immediately. She's just sixteen, so neither a child nor too close to me in age. She's steadfast, hardworking, and clever without being overly ambitious.

Plus, she hates her current position in the kitchen. Being suddenly promoted to assistant matcher would be a welcome status change for her. And not having to listen to her whine about how long it takes bread to rise would make Cecelia happy.

I hardly have to give it a thought when I agree. "Beadda is perfect."

John gives me a look that clearly says I have no idea what I'm doing. I agree with him, for once. But I can't show fear. I must be strong. That is what they expect of a matcher.

Petra says the words to make it official, and they all assent—even John in the end—and she dismisses us to our tasks.

And so I walk out of the hall and into the deep blue of a midnight sky, officially a matcher.

Dad leads us home, his steps heavy. Beside me, Cecelia follows, talking nervously through the preparation I will need to do, and where she can find the scrolls that discuss the herbs and oils I'll need to bathe in and apply, and the ones that demonstrate how a matcher must braid their hair and also when I'll be able to squeeze in at least one fitting with her mother, the valley's best seamstress.

Now that I'm no longer in front of the elders, something inside me crumples. I follow along, numbly agreeing, letting her lead as she chatters about how much impact I will have on our community and the wider world in my new role.

One touch of a cheek to a long-dead creature skull led to three deaths in the span of one night. If that's the path of my impact, no one deserves it.

Chapter Three

KIAN

Guarding the body of a recently deceased priest as part of asinine Huntress death rituals is as ridiculous as it is dull, especially when you have the overnight shift. There aren't even any histrionic mourners to hustle through as they gawk at his flaccid body, already stinking beneath its jewel-encrusted vestments.

But of course, that's why I volunteered for this shift. Fewer potential witnesses. Unfortunately, there's a snag I hadn't anticipated.

I sit on the shined-up parquet floor of the apse with a sigh that echoes down the cavernous nave. Abundant candlelight, placed for maximum effect rather than efficient lighting, glints off the gilded ceiling and leaded windows, throwing the majority of the main sanctuary into dramatic shadow.

When I first joined the order as a scrawny fifteen-year-old, raw from the pain of my parents' recent murders and bent on unclear but resolute vengeance, the Huntress's temple terrified me at night, with its brutal and beautiful decor and haunting echoes. Fifteen years later,

I just find it dull. I lean back against Brother Victor's black-and-gold marble dais.

"Novitiate Kian," my snag hisses, appalled by me as usual. A rule follower, ass kisser, and my ex, Ulric loves to try to bring me in line. Unfortunately for him, nothing brings me more pleasure than watching him squirm. Maybe that's why we didn't work out? "Get. Up."

"No thanks," I say with a wry smirk I know he'll hate. I fake a yawn that turns real halfway through and stretch. "Thought I'd just take a small catnap here. You don't mind guarding solo, do you?"

While I'm never one to pass up a nap, sitting with my eyes closed is a ruse like most of what I do as a novitiate in the Order of the Huntress.

The skull and robes that Brother Victor wears are encrusted with the rubies, diamonds, sapphires, emeralds, and pearls he's earned through a lifetime of serving various high priestesses. Even the gold filigree decorating the gaps between gems would fetch enough coin to feed a neighborhood of Insborough for an entire winter. And it is all about to be torched in a funeral pyre.

I've got to get rid of Ulric so I can pop some of those precious jewels off Brother Victor's decaying body. Stealing from the order is dangerous. If I'm caught, it will derail the goals I've spent a lifetime chasing, and just as I'm about to achieve them.

But I've been stealing the occasional gem or six from the skulls for a decade. I haven't been caught yet. And the good my family can do with extra resources is worth the risk.

"You will give Brother Victor the honor and respect he deserves and do your duty as his guard," Ulric growls, looming over me.

Too bad his growls don't work on me anymore. "He's dead. He's not going to care if I watch him rot from my feet or my ass."

Ulric splutters, then tries to force me up by looping his arms under mine. Not many people can manhandle me, but Ulric has size to his advantage, being easily as broad as I am but significantly taller. He leverages me to my feet and begins a tirade of admonishment. "What if we were attacked? What if we were robbed? What if someone came in to deface the temple? You cannot defend Brother Victor from your bottom."

I raise an eyebrow and lower my voice barely above a whisper. "You of all people know I can accomplish quite a lot from my *bottom*."

Instantly, a violet-red flush spreads up his neck and onto his cheeks, visible despite his dark complexion and the low, flickering candlelight. He's just so, so easy to rile. I lean in to say something more, but then I see movement behind him. Or think I do. I stiffen, trying to squint past him into the dark, shadowy recesses of the sanctuary.

He begins to turn, but I put a hand on his chest. He freezes instantly. "Relax, Ulric."

He shoves away from me, glaring.

What I want to say is that I can guard him from the floor or my feet because who would risk the Huntress's ire to steal from the decaying corpse of an ancient, mid-level holy?

No one besides me.

But I have a part to play. While some irreverence is tolerated in a Huntress novitiate of my standing, outright derision for the order would not be. So instead, I just say, "Have faith. The Huntress will protect us from thieves and vandals."

Or at least, the threat of her retaliation will.

As soon as I think the words, a figure steps out of the shadows. She wears a dark tunic tucked into dark breeches and a black coat with a flared skirt and black embroidery. A waistcoat or something fitted and short for warmth might suit her tasks better, but my aunt has always loved drama. At least her waist-length hair is braided tightly to her head, the salt-and-pepper strands shining in the candlelight.

Aunt Ujvala's smirk matches my own as she steps fully into the light.

I suppress my smile, hiding any reaction from Ulric, who has not seen or heard her. He's pacing across the marble floor of the apse, the echoes from his hard-soled boots ringing through the vaulted ceiling.

He lectures me on the importance of guarding the dead priest; how High Priestess Sarai would be so disappointed in me; how I can't mess up our positions in the order now, after over a dozen years of grunt work and servitude, just days away from the matching ceremony where we will finally pair with skulls of our own and be inducted as full-fledged priests; how I probably got my white novitiate robes dirty on the floor and they will be a pain to wash.

But I hear little of it. It's boringly familiar.

"Ulric, will you get me some ale?"

He gapes.

I don't blame him. It's a ridiculous request. He is not a servant to fetch my things, nor do I even like the bitter, bubbly alcohol, but I can think of nothing else to get him to leave the sanctuary, and Ulric is a natural caregiver. There's a small chance he'll agree.

"You fetch the best ale," I say honestly. He always chooses the best options for my palate, somehow knowing better than me what I might actually like.

"I . . . choose good ale?" he splutters. "You want me to leave my holy post guarding our brother, to get you *ale*?"

Rolling her eyes at me, Aunt Ujvala takes a step, her black cane softly clicking on the stone floor.

Ulric hears the step and startles. Before he can turn, Aunt Ujvala quickly closes the gap between them and wallops him over the head with her cane. He collapses, his face hitting the floor with a moist smack. The sound echoes through the cavernous room, and I wince on his behalf.

"So much for subtlety, Aunt."

Aunt Ujvala steps over Ulric's prone body, moving straight to the high dais where Brother Victor is displayed. She takes in his deep-red vestments—the color of blood, the color of death—but her focus is on his jackalope mask.

"When I was a girl, the dragon-wearers used to burn the priests in public. Right in the center of the city." She makes the sign of the triune goddess over the priest's body. "People would come and watch, sing songs of praise to the Spinner, petition the Pupil, offer sacrifices to the Huntress."

Her tone is strange, almost wistful. She sighs and turns back to face me. Gone is the mischievous smirk of earlier. The worry on her face makes my blood run cold. She looks old. Or perhaps just her age. I still think of her as she was twenty years ago, when she took me in after my parents died.

She hands me a small pouch, and I open it, finding the small red stones my family uses to mark paths. I try not to think about how similar in color they are to Brother Victor's death robes.

"Will you come home?" she asks. "After?"

Home. I've spent fifteen years here in the order, fifteen years of plotting and planning, figuring out how to infiltrate and then ruin the most powerful religious order in the world. It started as revenge for my parents' deaths at their hands, but it's grown into so much more than that. A fight for change, for equality.

And while I have every confidence in my impending success, not once have I thought about the after.

Going home had never crossed my mind.

"Or perhaps you want to stay?" She looks down at Ulric. She has never met him, of course, but she knows who he is. She's heard me talk of him, and no doubt she has informers of her own as well, keeping tabs on me and those close to me. You don't lead the largest smuggling ring in Camphor without having eyes and ears everywhere.

I clench my fists and grind my teeth. "Stay?" I let loose a harsh laugh. "In the order? Amongst the hypocrites and power-thirsty priests?"

She holds up her hands, as if I'm a wounded animal who might attack her without provocation. She's the closest thing to a mother I have left. "You know they're not all bad, my love. They do good in the community. Defend the downtrodden, feed the hungry. Take in the orphans and give them a life full of hope and meaning." She glances down at Ulric's unconscious form, and the softness in her eyes sends anger shooting down my spine, hot and tingling.

Ulric isn't the orphan she's speaking of, but it is not the order who's provided me with hope or meaning. I've done that myself by continuously honing my plans and striving toward my goals.

"They charge for healing, for hope." I gesture around the sanctuary—at the golden candelabras, the marble floors, the beeswax candles burning for no one, the statues carved of rare rock and studded with gems, even the silk of a dead man's robe. All flagrant displays of wealth, and for whom? "They hoard resources and power."

"Who doesn't?" She steps forward to put a warm hand on my shoulder. "If you joined them in truth, you could embrace the good and continue your work. Change the bad from within."

I shrug off her kindness and pity. I need neither.

She continues. "The life you'd lead here would be an easy one. You'd always know your role, where you'll lay your head every night, that your next meal is guaranteed. Vengeance makes no promises for a future."

I don't understand my aunt's intention here. She is nothing if not complex, but she's generally steadfast. I need her to follow through on our agreement.

The plan was I'd mark the path we novitiates take to the valley, and she and a couple of the others would follow and hide out during the matching ceremony. Then, once everyone is drunkenly celebrating the matches, my family will help me destroy the remaining skulls.

It's essential they're on board before I leave with the rest of the novitiates tomorrow, or I will have to do it on my own. Panic builds. My breath comes sharp and quick.

My life has been lived alone, away from the warm community of my aunts, uncles, and cousins. Instead I've been surrounded by priestesses, priests, and novitiates who could never know who I truly am.

I step around Ulric.

Even those closest to me.

Now, I am almost at the pinnacle of my goals, and I find I don't want to do this last part by myself. If I'm going to destroy the valley's creature skulls and ensure the orders a generation of future priests and priestesses *serve* their communities instead of profiting off their magic, I need my family's help.

And Aunt Ujvala needs me.

As the leader of a vast network of smugglers and thieves, she wants access the resources that can be found only in the valley. The priceless agate that gryphons lay alongside their eggs, the kelpie manes that can be used to heal wounds.

My parents were the only ones who knew the way in. Their knowledge, and my family's ability to trade for these rare goods, was lost when they died. Aunt Ujvala has sought to find path often through the years, but she's tired of sending out scouts who come back maimed or worse, never come back at all, because the intelligence they received about the valley's magical border was incomplete or just plain wrong.

Aunt Ujvala sees my panic. She widens her stance and picks up her cane, smacking it in the palm of her hand.

"Let's spar, my love."

I shake my head. This is what we used to do when I was a teenager, had just joined the order, and was miserably scared. It was a kind of comfort, to practice like I did at home, just in case I needed to fight. It still is.

But it's been years since I fought my aunt. I'm much larger than she is. A man in my prime. And she's aging.

I shake my head, not wanting to hurt her.

"Come on." She pokes at me with her cane. "You won't win, but you'll feel better. Get into your body and out of your head."

Adrenaline surges through me with the panic that they might not come with me. That I'll have to do all this alone. That I'll fuck up. That a decade and a half of work will be for nothing.

I want to fight.

I attack, a flurry of movement. I get a single solid hit to her side before she's bending away. I don't hold back. As she said, I've never won against her.

I kick out at her feet. If I can get her on the ground, it'll be over before we've begun. She launches her own attack.

Despite the fact that I'm on guard duty, no one actually expects anyone to come after a dead priest in his highest temple. I have no weapon stuck up the ridiculous sleeves of my novitiate robe to defend myself with. I put up my forearm, and the cane comes down with a hard crack on my left wrist. I gasp and shove her back, but the pain that shoots up my arm when I use my left hand is too sharp.

She sighs and gives me some space. I'm not sure what makes me angrier, her going easy on me or her gentle tone when she says, "Once you come home, you can follow in your parents' footsteps, smuggling to the valley. Or just stay here in the order and continue what you're doing, funneling us resources and information while you make the world a better place."

My lip curls into my own sneer as I circle, trying to get close to her. She moves to the other side of Ulric's prone form. I quickly reach over Ulric and hit her in the shoulder. She moves so the blow glances off her, but she's still surprised I've landed a second hit.

"You've been practicing." She looks down at Ulric. "With him?"

"He's fun to fight," I say with a shrug. Or he was, before I made him hate me.

She bobs forward, hitting me in the ribs three times in quick succession. I retreat to the other side of Brother Victor's dais. She stalks slowly after me, rounding my side of the dais now.

I lunge forward. I will simply tackle her. As long as she hits the floor before me, I'll win. She'll respect that.

But she sidesteps and swings her cane again, connecting with the back of my knee. I snatch it with my right hand on my way down, trying to wrench it from her grasp and maintain my footing. She grabs tight with both hands, hovering over me and pulling with all her might. I have a hold of it with only my one hand, the other still throbbing too strongly to be used, and I feel my grip slipping.

She must see it, too, because instead of fighting for her cane, she lets go with a shove. I land on the cold marble floor flat on my back. My breath whooshes out of me.

I stare up at the domed ceiling above us, with its mosaic of scenes—various personifications of the Huntress stalking and capturing her prey. I try to remember how to breathe. The candlelight glints off the golden accents. The art emphasizes the goddess's stealth, boldness, and strength. It's beautiful.

I want to tear it all down until it's dust.

Ujvala leans close, taking her cane back, and the sympathy I see there makes me want to scream. "It won't bring them back. No matter how successful you are, how badly you hurt the order. Your parents are gone forever."

"And?" I say when I can speak again. "You won't help me? Or what's the point of all of this?"

"Oh, Kian." She reaches out a hand, and I take it, letting her haul me up. She steps in to me, hugging me tight, then steps back and brushes my hair out of my face, just like my mom used to. I look away, hating that I want to lean into that nurturing touch. "I will always help you, my love. Always. I came to give you the stones. And some vital information."

"Cryptic." I open the pouch, taking out a single red stone, polished smooth again. I rub it between my fingers.

"The valley has had an . . . incident. Two of their dragons attacked their matcher. The matcher is dead, as is one of the dragons. There's also a newly dead kelpie."

I imagine High Priestess Sarai's glee at hearing the news. A new dragon skull is a rare and priceless opportunity. Not only are dragons the most powerful creatures to match with, but the closer a skull is to its death when it matches, the closer its bond to its priest or priestess, and more of its magic can be harnessed.

With magic dwindling, I cannot think of a better gift to lay at the high priestess's feet than a dragon dead two days before the matching ceremony.

Or at mine.

Matching with a dragon would be perfect. It would mean I wouldn't have to steal or seduce my way into getting some of Brother Thad's fire. If only we had a way to ensure what skulls we matched with.

At our feet, Ulric stirs. Aunt Ujvala notices. With a quick, fierce kiss to my forehead, she turns to leave.

"Wait! Take the skull."

"Think I'll avoid a hangable offense." Using the blade strapped to the inside of her wrist, she pops out a dozen of the largest, most prominent diamonds and rubies. "But an excellent excuse for his attack, and a lovely contribution to our efforts."

Then with one more kiss to my forehead, she strides out, the clicking of her cane a soft and steady sound on the marble. She's melted fully back into the shadows when I hear the clicking pause. But I know she's still here. "Do not abandon me, Aunt," I say to the darkness. "I am so close."

"Never, my dear," she replies. "We will be there."

And then she is gone.

As expected, Ulric and I are hauled before a collection of high holies. Our fellow novitiates line the perimeter of the room, instructed to watch our punishment and learn from our mistakes. Like us, they are barefaced and in various shades of gray, from the charcoal of the still-pimply faced newbies to the near-white of us nearly matched.

Some look nearly gleeful in anticipation. Assholes.

Peppered throughout are the black robes of the fully initiated priests and priestesses who attend to High Priestess Sarai, including her two favorites—Brother Thad and Sister Roberta. Their emotions are mostly obscured by their various creature-skull masks, as always.

Brother Thad steps forward. He watches me closely for a reaction as he reads a list of our sins aloud: failure to secure the sanctuary, disruption of a senior priest's most sacred rest, and the most grievous failure of them all—letting the thief get away after desecrating his skull mask.

I give none. Saying mean things to me is just a typical Tuesday; it's not going to hurt my heart. But I still can't stop myself from mumbling, "We are unarmed priests, not guards."

High Priestess Sarai steps forward, her unicorn skull shimmering with diamonds and opals, a stark and glittering contrast to her flowing black robes.

"You are novitiates, not priests," she replies, her words clipped and precise. "You wear no skulls. Your robes are gray. It would only be through my grace that you would be allowed to continue in the order at all, and I'm not feeling particularly gracious today."

I go absolutely still. I knew we would be punished. Humiliated, beaten, disgraced. But easily replaced gems shouldn't be enough to derail my entire mission. What an absurd thing to throw me off course, and so close to my matching.

Beside me, Ulric prostrates himself, landing on his knees with a hard thunk, then leaning forward until his forehead touches the floor. "Mercy, High Priestess."

I don't follow suit. I know it's the sort of groveling Sarai relishes. But in the long run, I need to become a peer, not a supplicant. So instead of kneeling beside Ulric, I step forward, standing very close to her. Around the room I hear sharp intakes of breath at my insolence.

"On your knees, Kian." Brother Thad tries to step between me and Sarai, but I don't give ground, so he's nearly pressed up against me.

"Maybe one day," I reply softly, with a quick glance up and down his body. He stiffens; then a smarmy grin peaks out beneath his creature skull. I barely withhold my grimace. I don't enjoy flirting with Brother Thad, but I may need him—or rather, the dragon magic he wields—and so I play coy to keep the option open.

I turn my full attention back to Sarai.

Begging is expected. I need something surer. And while I can't trust Sarai to be merciful, I can trust her greed.

I drop my voice so only she can hear. "Would you eliminate your two best chances to match with a newly dead dragon?" I'm not sure why I'm including Ulric in my preservation efforts; life would be easier if he weren't always around, watching me, caring for me.

She leans back slightly, to make space to look at me closely without impaling me with her unicorn's horn. I can see her ice-blue eyes gauging my face; no doubt trying to determine how much I truly know, or if I'm guessing on the details based on a half-overheard rumor.

"We are your two strongest novitiates. We work harder than the others. We're more devoted." I glance down at our feet, where Ulric still kneels, face to the floor. "Who else will have the strength to match and wield a dragon, and remain yours to command?"

She bristles, her always-straight posture becoming impossibly stiffer. "I am the high priestess of the Order of the Huntress, the fiercest and most powerful of the three orders. You. Are. All. Mine. To. Command."

I dip my head in supplication and take a half step back. "High Holiness."

There is nothing but silence in the room. No rustle of robes, no breathy gasps. I wait, head bowed.

This will work. Skulls know strength. They match, like to like. If she wants that dragon, her best chance is through the two novitiates before her, and we both know it. She cannot kick us out of the order.

Finally, she speaks, her words thick with anticipation. "You will earn my mercy through the lash. Remove your robes. Then we will leave for the matching. Let's hope they go as well as we'd like."

Thank the goddess.

Ulric stands, and we begin to undress as Sister Roberta brings High Priestess Sarai a nine-strand scourge, the tooth of a magical creature tied to each thong of leather. Novitiate Jasmyn takes our outer robes with a smirk, flinging them over her shoulder. Novitiate Svena whispers, "Huntress give you strength," as she gently takes our tunics and folds them carefully over her arm.

If there is uncorrupted good in the order, as Aunt Ujvala insists, kindhearted Svena would be a shining example of it. I'm surprised she's even here, instead of serving soup and yeasty rolls to the orphans of Tolepi, as she typically does at midday.

When Ulric and I are down to only our breeches, the intricate inked Huntress marks across our chests, backs, and arms bare to all, Brother Thad directs us to drape ourselves over the stone altar. It is typically used by priestesses for prayer and supplication, though it's not unfamiliar with the kind of ritual punishment we are about to receive, as the dark stains trailing down its sides attest.

None of the goddesses are squeamish, but the Huntress in particular likes violence.

Beside me, Ulric's eyes are wide with terror, and I wonder at his early life that he's so afraid of a few lashes. Not that I'm gladly anticipating what's about to occur, but it's better than being kicked out of the order entirely.

I try to breathe in through my nose and out through my mouth and take my mind far away. Fear will not lessen or prevent the pain I am about to withstand.

All around us, the others begin a chant.

"Your holy siblings pray for the Huntress's clemency," Sarai says, and her voluminous robes brush against my calves. "And I will dole out her retribution. Next time she assigns you a sacred duty through your betters, you will not fail her."

When retribution comes, it is hot and angry. Sarai does not believe in holding back her power. The scourge shreds my flesh badly enough that many of those standing around to witness turn away.

Ulric chants with the others, but every time the whip descends, he screams the words and loses the rhythm. I don't bother. I know that's what Sarai likes, so I stay absolutely silent in my prayers—or lack thereof. She hits me harder to try to make me vocalize, but the only words I speak to the Huntress and her ilk are silent curses.

I receive more blows for my soundless insolence, but eventually the pain spikes hot enough that it blurs and blends, the individual blows no worse than every other moment. Long after Ulric has collapsed onto the black-marble floor, Sarai finishes with me. She flings the bloodied lash down in front of me and leaves the inner sanctuary, the others following.

Only Svena pauses, to place our folded tunics beside us on the ground. Not that either of us can move to put them on. Instead, we lie there, side by side, punished but still novitiates.

I do not suppress my smile.

One step closer to destroying them all.

Chapter Four

KIAN

Whoever tied my blindfold never played Dupe the Dud with cut-throat cousins who enjoyed your cries of surprised pain as they whacked your shins instead of the ball. But what can I expect from the Huntress's holy and chosen few? Sister Roberta and Brother Thad obviously have little experience in playing dirty.

Unlike me.

One quick, casual rub of an "itchy" ear with my shoulder and I've knocked the cloth askew enough to see the ground flash beneath my hems. Swishing, voluminous white silk hems. Because what else would you wear when traipsing through an unknown forest? But like all the acts of the holies, it was chosen for symbolism, not practicality. White is the color of bone, of magic.

At least the robe has large pockets. Yet accessing the stones I've hidden there does me no good if I cannot drop them. I'm currently wedged in the center of the group and dare not risk it.

Each step I take reveals the same expected scene below my feet—a winding path covered in pine needles with the occasional twig, cone, or patch of frozen mud to break up the monotony. After five minutes of trudging, I finally discover an opening.

I trip on a thick root, flinging myself forward and catching my fall on Ulric's broad back before me. I try to hit the side—I know how raw our wounds are. But still, he hisses in pain and shoves me away, out of line. I pretend to stumble, as if I'm just barely able to right myself before biting it on the forest floor.

"Spinner's tits!" I cry.

Someone inhales sharply, and I know I've disturbed at least one of my fellow novitiates' rigid sensibilities with my swearing. I mumble an apology to them and the goddess; then feigning a limp, I drop back. Finally at the very end of our stupid procession, I reach my hand inside my robe's large pocket, take one of the two dozen red glass stones, and drop it on the path behind me.

Aunt Ujvala and whoever she brings with her will find it, then the next and the next, following my path to the valley along the careful route that few members of the three orders know. A wrong turn and they will hit the wards protecting the valley. What happens then depends on how deeply through the forest they've made it. They could simply be wounded and spend the rest of their lives with disfiguring scars, or they could be killed outright.

We continue our winding journey for another half hour before I realize they're leading us in circuitous loops. Of course they are further obscuring the path to the valley. Paranoid bastards. But if we loop back on our previous steps, my stones will easily be spotted and I will be discovered.

Brother Thad commands a halt. "What is that?" he mumbles.

Panic rushes through me, and I push forward through the other novitiates. If he's spotted a stone, maybe I can hide it under my hems or kick it under some half-decayed leaves before he recognizes it for the marker it is.

"Novitiate Kian!" High Priestess Sarai commands. "When you are told to stop, you stop."

I curse silently. What happens if it is a stone? What do I do if he finds others? I am about to risk moving again to be closer to Jasmyn. Maybe I can drop the rest of the red stones at her feet and hope they blame her.

Just before I move, a sharp, hot wind brushes past, hard enough to rustle our robes. I shiver.

"What was—" I begin, the words masking my footfalls as I take steps toward Jasmyn.

"Hush."

The unmistakable tremble of fear in Brother Thad's voice chills me. I have known him to be many things—arrogant, aggressive, libidinous—but I have never heard him afraid.

Then I notice the entire rest of the forest has fallen silent. There are no sounds of animal calls, no owls hooting, no skittering of small creatures through underbrush. Not even the wind dares to shake the pine boughs. It is as if everything has paused on an inhale.

Then a savage roar, louder and more animalistic than anything I've ever heard, rips apart the silent sky.

Instantly, I drop to the frosty forest floor and crawl toward the trunk of a large tree, yanking off my blindfold. Above us, I see the sky wink in and out of existence.

The creature shrieks again.

A dragon. Aunt Ujvala said there were two that killed the matcher, but there is only one skull, which means there is a second dragon in this valley. One with a taste for human flesh.

At least I'm not totally out in the open, in the center of a wide path, like the other novitiates. Markus and Jasmyn have lifted their hands toward their faces, as if to remove their blindfolds, but stand with them hovering above the knots because above everything else—even their own sense of self-preservation—they are a bunch of righteous rule followers.

"Move your asses, idiots!" I hiss, hopefully not drawing the dragon's attention.

Finally, they begin to move.

Jasmyn and Markus finish ripping off their blindfolds and hide near trees like I have. Ulric and Svena bumble forward simultaneously. Without being able to see, they collide and trip, landing with a large thud, one on top of the other. At least they're lower now. Illia and Marsi help each other remove their blindfolds, then run around High Priestess Sarai, staying on the path, and moving deeper into the forest.

It's not a bad strategy, as long as they are moving away from the dragon instead of closer. And stay away from the wards. Though if there is a dragon hunting us, we're fully in the valley.

Another roar echoes through the night, so loud it makes my ears ring.

High Priestess Sarai, Brother Thad, and Sister Roberta stand their ground like the noble imbeciles they are. At least Sarai is practical, holding up her lantern so she can see what's happening beneath the trees' dark canopy. Brother Thad holds a decorative dagger, its jewel-encrusted hilt winking in the moonlight as if to say, *I am utterly useless in a fight! But so pretty!* Just like him.

His other hand is clenched tight, holding something small. A stone?

Fuck. I am fucked.

As I hunch below a tree, trying my best to be small and insignificant, the dragon drops out of the sky between the three order members. It is stunning and terrifying, with a large reptilian body, a long neck, and gigantic leathery wings, all covered in scales.

Jasmyn screams dramatically as Sarai spins to meet the dragon straight on. Her unicorn skull's horn glints. The dragon roars, spitting fire and lighting up the forest around us. Svena cries out, her robes ablaze. She starts to stand.

"Roll," I yell. If she bolts, she'll feed the fire as she runs. I dart from my relative safety of the tree and half tackle her, pushing her back into the dirt and smothering the flames with our overly full robes. The impact makes the wounds on my back scream, and she curls onto her side, whimpering. Her side and back—visible through burned-away silk—are raw, covered by red blisters.

Sister Roberta hurries over to help as I whisper calming nonsense to Svena and watch the rest of the chaos continue to unfold.

The dragon roars again.

I have spent the last fifteen years surrounded by priests wearing the skulls of magical creatures—skulls that they use to wield magic, to build power and wealth and, at times, hurt people in their quest for both. And before that, I grew up in a family of smugglers who also used their skills to build power and wealth, though they never intentionally hurt anyone for, either.

Which is to say, I have seen some serious shit, but nothing—nothing—is as terrifying as an angry full-grown dragon hunting. It is massive, muscular but nimble in flight as it dodges through the trees. Its scales is a deep-purple color that shines, iridescent in the moonlight.

It lands, lowering its head and opening its mouth slightly. Its teeth are the size of my fingers. Its tongue flicks the air like a snake, tasting our fear. It makes a noise of approval deep in its serpentine throat and takes a step forward. Despite its long back legs and short front legs, it moves much more gracefully on the ground than I would have suspected, which bodes ill for us all.

It lowers its spiked head as if to charge. With a whimper I feel deep in my own bones, Brother Thad turns and runs.

High Priestess Sarai again stands her ground. Making herself as large as possible and swinging the lantern toward the beast's face, she screams back.

I'm not certain it's the recommended method for fending off a dragon, but it seems to work, because the creature turns away from her, takes two great steps, and in one fluid motion, bites Brother Thad across the shoulder and chest. Its massive, curved incisors must puncture something vital, because the priest instantly collapses on the path. Dead.

A cold, piercing panic runs through my body. Without a dragon-wearer, all of this is over. Only a dragon's fire can destroy the creature skulls, and Brother Thad was the last of them. Now he's dead. His now-useless dragon skull stares up at the silent, uncaring trees.

Sarai cries out. Brother Thad is her second in command and her friend. But the high priestess does not move closer to the dragon and its kill.

The dragon crouches over Brother Thad's limp body and opens its mouth wide, as if it'll unhinge its jaw. In horror, I realize we are about to watch a feeding.

Before the grotesquery can begin, new people come running through the underbrush and onto the path. They carry no lanterns to guide them through the thick forest or traditional weapons, but long, smooth sticks. Three of the four go immediately to the dragon and surround it. By their simple, practical dress, their confidence in approaching a dragon about to eat a dead man, and their presence in the valley at all, I assume they are keepers.

A man with more bravery than sense gets right up in the dragon's face, his stick pointed at one slitted silver eye. He pulls it back and takes aim until an older woman in furs and coarse fabrics the color of paprika runs out of the trees right beside me and Svena. She's breathing hard, but manages to bark, "John! Do *not* stab that dragon!"

She is petite, with fiery red hair that's gone gray at the temples and deep lines beside her eyes that reveal she is more used to laughing than fighting. But right now, her lips are pressed tight together and her expression is fierce.

The man scowls but does as she says, swinging his stick around so the sharp end is pointed away from the dragon.

I shift on the frozen ground, trying to ease the stabbing pains of the wounds on my back. It's a mistake. I barely stifle a groan. I don't want to make any noise or draw any attention.

The dragon bends his head and opens his jaw. The keeper, John, lifts the long pole and waps the dragon over the head before quickly flipping it around again.

The dragon doesn't attack John. Instead, it dodges forward, snatching half of Brother Thad in a quick, vicious chomp that reminds me of one of the starving street dogs in Insborough snatching a stick of satay from a heedless tourist. It shakes its head like a wet dog, the entire top half of Brother Thad in its maw, and launches itself into the air.

Nearby, Markus sobs and Svena vomits, whether from her burns or the sight of Brother Thad's body torn in half by a giant flying beast, I'm not certain. Probably both.

I laugh. I manage to keep it silent, barely, but my shoulders shake and my eyes water with the effort. A dragon has just eaten my only hope of destroying the skulls and the order's sinuous hold on society. I should not be laughing. It's shock, surely. Not an indication of how inherently twisted I am.

Not trusting my legs to hold me, I crawl around my fellow novitiates and over to Brother Thad's remaining hand. I bend low as if praying or crying and pry open his clenched fingers.

In the middle of his palm is a red glass stone.

Ulric puts a warm but shaking hand on my shoulder, carefully avoiding my ruined back. I flinch even as I palm the stone slowly, so his eye won't be drawn to any suspicious movement. In a soft voice I haven't heard from him in months, he says, "Need help up?"

I allow him to pull me to my feet, and then we both go over to Svena. Two of the keepers are there, fussing over her, while the other two watch the skies. From farther in the forest, Illia and Marsi slowly trudge back. It's obviously the last thing they want to do, and yet, they don't know another way out of the trees. Plus together seems better than alone tonight.

The keeper who seems to be in charge turns to Sarai. "High Priestess," she says, her voice warm and comforting in its surety. "This way."

She steps off the wider path and onto a much narrower opening between the undergrowth. I take it for a rabbit or deer trail, maybe.

"We will continue on." When no one moves, Sarai's voice becomes as sharp and cold as her eyes. "Retie the novitiates' blindfolds. We will remain on the traditional path."

We all turn to her as one, goggling at the instruction. We've all just watched a man be *eaten*.

Even Sister Roberta presses back against Sarai's declaration. "We're past the wards, High Holiness," she says softly. "Let's take a more direct route."

She is not swayed. "I will not repeat myself."

Sister Roberta gives a slight bow and takes a step toward Markus. He looks like he's about to cry, but he obeys, replacing his blindfold himself. Ulric and Jasmyn follow suit, Ulric flinching as he raises his arms. When he turns, I can see his wounds have reopened and the blood has seeped through the heavy fabric of his robes. No doubt mine look the same.

Illia and Marsi help each other with their blindfolds, weeping softly as they tie the knots. Only Svena and I remain unblindfolded, though Svena's disobedience is not willful. She appears to have passed out.

The lead keeper woman tries once again, her voice is steady and sure, comforting. "Let's get your novitiates back to the valley and to their lodging. Our healers can care for the injured." She glances at Ulric and the telltale stripes of crimson on his robe, and then Svena, still unconscious beside me. "And we can send food to their rooms. You can all eat, clean up, and rest. Tomorrow we can figure out our path forward toward the matching. In the meantime, you've had a terrible shock. You all need rest, and to recover."

Sarai pulls herself up to her full height and turns her masked face to the keeper. Standing there, tall and unreadable in diaphanous black robes, with half of a man's body at her feet and a bejeweled unicorn skull covering her face, she is terrifying in her silence.

But her visage is not nearly as terrible as her voice. "We will not diverge. We will continue on to the meeting. Your new matcher and their assistant will welcome us. And when that is complete, your community will fete us. Tomorrow, we will match our novitiates to the awaiting skulls. All. As. Planned."

The keeper woman stares at Sarai in undisguised horror just long enough that I think she might argue more. Then she simply bows her head. "As you wish, Your Holiness."

Sarai turns.

"But at least let us take this one." The woman gestures to Svena. "The skulls prioritize strength and wholeness. The sooner we can get her attention, the better her chances in the matching hut will be tomorrow."

The air grows somehow colder in Sarai's silence, as she observes the disaster surrounding her. Svena is unconscious, Illia and Marsi are terrified, Ulric and I are bleeding from the wounds she inflicted. None of us are as strong or whole as we should be. Especially Thad. But if she's wondering at her decision to beat us and trudge us through the forest, she does not show it.

"Do what you will with that one," she says to the keeper. To the rest of us, she just says, "Come."

She turns and steps over the leftover half of Brother Thad's body.

We do as she commands.

Chapter Five

ADELA

I meet Beadda in the horseshoe curve of grass in front of all the keepers' houses. There are fifty houses in total, with a new one under construction for newly engaged Ezequiel and Mathew, who are standing together cuddled tight, flush with excitement. Everyone loves the arrival ceremony and the day of feasting that follows.

Or typically they do.

This morning, very few keepers stand with us. Cecelia's large family is there along with Dad, the elders who didn't trek to the forest to find and protect the order, and a handful of others. Nearly no one with children, and none of the oldest amongst us have come. The arrival greeting isn't optional, but it appears as if my fellow keepers are willing to risk the elders' ire to stay safe in their houses today.

Not that Bartholomew's house kept him safe.

"Will the others join us for the feast at least?" Beadda asks quietly, her breath fogging in the morning air.

I look her over, and find her smile strained. I know that nervous expression; it looks just like Cecelia's. She's scared, but whether it's of her new role or the rogue dragon roaring through the valley, I'm not sure.

"Of course," I assure her, though I'm not certain of anything of the sort.

At least we are sartorially prepared for the meeting. Beneath Beadda's inky cloak, she wears a recently refashioned gown of deep lavender, embroidered with silvered bone beads. Her mask—also once mine—is silver-covered aspen carved to look like seedlings, stretching up as if in worship of the hot summer sun. While she wears her hood up to protect herself from the cold, I know her silky hair has been twisted into three braids of three strands, secured in a bun at the back of her head—the style I wore every arrival and matching night for a decade.

My own styling tonight is much more elaborate—six braids of six strands secured with a jackalope femur carved into the shape of a piece of wheat. In addition to the hair stick, I wear hematite-and-dragon-bone earrings, and a collar that once was wyvern ribs. Even the beads embroidered into a starburst pattern on my now-aubergine gown are made of bone, dipped in gold. On my hands, I wear four rings, each carved from a different creature's bones, each set with a different gem.

I steal a glance at Beadda's hands, warm and protected in their gloves. Until tonight, I also always wore gloves. Only the matcher and the paired novitiates will touch the skulls with their skin.

My cold hands twitch, unable to remain still, and a ring snags on a bit of the top layer of my skirts. I curse silently and smooth the chiffon. I have participated in this night for years. I know what I need to do, and still, I cannot shake my dread that something will go horribly, irrevocably wrong.

Beadda clears her throat. "Everything alright?"

I startle, the golden mask slipping slightly on my face. It is not the elaborate open-work mask as it ought to be, a golden twin to Beadda's, but that one is now nothing but ash and smoke, thanks to the dragons. Thanks to me.

This mask is still carved from a blessed aspen, like all matchers' masks, and gilded. All keepers wear masks around the creature skulls, out of reverence and tradition. Keepers must never show our faces to the skulls; we are not permitted to match with them.

The most welcome aspect of my mask tonight is it hides any truths Beadda and the others may see in the subtle expressions of my face.

"Everything is great," I lie again, and step into place. The others move to stand behind us without me saying a word. Before us, twelve-year-old Danni wears a bronze mask—carved slightly less elaborately than Beadda's—and holds her torch, a symbol of how the Great Goddess will always guide us. Together, the three of us represent the three aspects of the triune goddess.

As one, our procession steps forward and begins to sing, but before we can move out of the circle of houses and into the surrounding meadow, the sound of galloping hooves on gravel makes my voice falter. With shaking hands, Danni holds up her torch. Not that it'll help us see through the fog any better. Behind us the song stops, the notes turning into a murmur of concerned voices.

A prickle of worry tickles at my hairline, and I peer across the meadows.

My mind flashes to Bartholomew's body, lying crumpled in the burned-out shell of his house last night, but I force myself back into the present. These are hooves, not wings, which means it is most likely just a normal horse.

Pegasi would not bother running when they could get to where they're going quicker in the sky, and kelpies would not stray so far from their streams. Besides, I realize with a pang, there's now only one left in the world, and she is no doubt grieving the loss of her mate, whose body Dad returned to the river this morning. And while they might be gentler than the others, unicorns are also the most reclusive. With thousands of acres to roam and clear preferences for their own territories, they almost never venture near the village.

Unless something's wrong.

Half a moment later, I hear the flapping of large wings. The whole group of us practically flinches in unison, but I look up. I relax to find Lathai looping above us.

Now I know who the galloping sounds belong to. Sure enough, a half a breath later, Etana arrives out of the mist. Lathai's unlikely mate and my star sister. She's panting and snorting hard, no doubt annoyed that he made the journey faster. Though she has an excuse. Her belly is heavy with a miraculous pregnancy—a unicorn-and-pegasus hybrid, the first of its kind as far as we know and a bright symbol of hope as the valley struggles.

"Hello, sweeties," I say, and put my hand out to Etana. She nuzzles my palm, looking for a treat, and I scratch around her horn instead. "I don't have anything for you tonight, my darling girl. No pockets."

Lathai lands with a heavy thud behind Beadda, causing her to jump. He's loud and dramatic in the way of all pegasi, which obviously makes my new assistant nervous. He nudges her back with his nose, and she scoots away, which causes him to press more aggressively, rubbing his horsey head against her cloak and marking her with silver-tipped black hairs.

She groans, brushing them off unsuccessfully.

He nickers and flicks his wingtips as if laughing. A crack of lightning splits the air.

"Lathai, stop that," I scold, but he is only playing. It is nothing like the storm he could cause if he truly wished to.

"Is Etana alright?" a woman's voice calls from the crowd. Everyone is worried for her. I see Dad pushing forward. He knows these two better than anyone.

He checks them over quickly, running his palms along their bodies and legs, lifting their feet to check their hooves—calm and thorough, even as everyone grows restless around us. It's unusual to stop a procession, and if their thoughts head in the same direction as mine, they're worried it's an ill omen.

Also, no one wants to stand around in the open, mere hours after a dragon attack.

Dad turns to me and shrugs. "Nothing's wrong that I can find. Just being odd and dramatic."

I release an unsteady breath, and nod. That isn't so unusual for these two, a cross-species mated pair prone to hijinks. Typically, that involves stealing freshly gathered apples or tripping their keepers while we attempt to clean or shoe their hooves.

"I suppose let's press on then?" I ask Dad. Technically, I am in charge of this night, with Beadda as my second, but seeking Dad's approval is as habitual as morning chores.

He nods his agreement, stepping back, but there's a certain tension in his jaw that I recognize. He doesn't return to his old place near the middle of the group, but joins Cecelia in the front.

He's worried.

We turn, and I indicate to Danni we should start again. A bit shakily, she lifts her torch and opens her mouth, but before she can sing a single line, Etana whinnies, a sound somewhere between a traditional horse's voice and the sound of breaking glass.

I wince while Beadda covers her ears and Danni falters. Instinctively, I reach out to Etana, but this time she doesn't let me scratch her horn's base or rub her cheek. Instead she drops down to her knees, as if bowing.

Beside Beadda, Lathai does the same. Beadda takes a hasty step back.

From her kneeling position, Etana tosses her head as if impatient. I turn back to Dad, and he gestures to Etana. "Looks like you get a ride to the meeting."

It's impossible. We have horses to ride if we must travel farther than a few miles, a few oxen to pull wagons and planting equipment, donkeys, and dogs to carry supplies when we need them to. We never, ever ride the creatures we care for and keep. Not that it's forbidden. It's just not done.

As a sign of respect, I suppose, or just because. I honestly don't know why. But if I were going to choose a creature to ride, it would never be a unicorn. They're proud, temperamental, and fabled to eat people who annoy them.

Besides, Etana might be large for her kind, but she is pregnant, and I'm not a small person to carry for a creature unused to carrying humans at all.

Etana whinnies again, Lathai matching her with his own shrieking call.

Deep inside me, I feel the pull. The wanting. The one that I try to repress, to stifle, to drown. The one that never leads me anywhere good. I do not trust that pull. And yet, despite my most sincere efforts, I cannot ignore it.

I am already moving toward Etana when I hear Dad urge me. "Go on."

With shaking legs and hands, I step forward, curling my fingers in her mane. She bends lower still, and I hike my layered skirts and cloak with my free hand. The gown's high slit opens as I throw my bare white leg over her back.

Etana stands almost instantly, my additional weight seemingly insignificant.

"Adela." My name is a plea from Beadda, and rightfully so. I would whimper, too, in her place. Lathai is stalking her—getting close, then bending, standing to stomp his foot when she backs up rather than stepping nearer, then repeating the dance again. A few refrains of this move, and he traps her between the others and himself. His head is lowered as if in a challenge.

"He's going to put his head beneath you and flip you onto his back if you don't climb on willingly," Dad warns. "Then you'll fly through the valley backward on your belly. Looping your knees over his wings and holding on to his mane will be easier than holding on to his hindquarters."

I see the jaw of her mask shift downward as if she's opened her mouth to argue, but no intelligible words come out as Lathai lowers his head and stomps toward her. Instead, she throws her hands up and shrieks, "Fiiiiiine," which makes the pegasus pause.

She awkwardly climbs on, sitting half atop his neck to avoid his wings. "Just, no flying. Deal? Lathai? Lathai?" I swear he smiles a horsey smile before he extends his wings and launches into the sky. "Laaaathaaaaaiiii," Beadda cries.

At least he's headed in the direction of the matching hut, I have the clarity to think before Etana jumps forward, galloping with unnatural speed.

"See you there?!" I call over my shoulder, unsure if I am already too far away to be heard. I cannot risk turning around to look, for fear I'll lose my grip on her mane and be dumped in an unceremonious heap on the frozen ground.

As we get farther away from the others, I push my hands deeper into Etana's mane, enjoying the feel of her muscles working beneath my clenched knees. I can almost feel her joy, a pleasant hum much like the skulls I oiled yesterday. But it must be my imagination. We don't hear the living creatures, not like the skulls. They express their emotions the same way animals do, with physical tells and rare vocalizations.

Somewhere far off above us, I hear the call of Lathai, and Etana's ears prick forward. She bellows back, the sound ear-shattering and fierce, and then her horn begins to glow.

I've only ever seen a unicorn's horn glow a handful of times, and not since I was a child.

Once was when a new unicorn was born. I was six. Her parents' horns had glowed for a week. I remember my mother's wistful explanation that it was the unicorn's sign of ultimate contentment, of bliss; that everything was right in their world.

Before the filly's death, I remember taking my mom's larger hand in mine and asking, "Like ours, Mama? If I had a horn, it'd glow when I'm with you. And yours would glow when you were with me." But even at six, I knew it wasn't actually true. It was just the relentless hope of a little girl. My mother was horribly unhappy here in the valley, her misery leaking out of her between every good moment until she followed her own deep, irrepressible wants. And left.

The unicorn filly died of some common illness Dad hadn't even known they could catch. Her parents followed soon after. Dead, I think, from grief.

If I had a horn, would it glow like Etana's, as I had hoped for when I was kid? I think of Dad, back with the others. I think of Cecelia. I think of Bartholomew, before, and push away bleaker images of him. Instead, I think of my new role as matcher. My friends and community. The creatures I serve.

I think of the phoenix skulls and how I was able to bring them back with the mere touch of my cheek to their cool bone.

I think of Etana beneath me, carrying her joy within her, racing her mate toward a bright and beautiful future.

There is joy and pain, all tangled together within me. And all through it, want.

I try to suppress the want, which has things I can't face wrapped around it, something around letting go of my worries and sorrows and pain. It is the real reason I try to ignore the impulses, to repress my reckless desires. And yet, it is somehow still undefinable. But now, in this moment, I don't worry about the details of who I am or want to be. I simply let the pure, hungry, wild pleasure finally bubble up beneath my skin and flow.

If I were a unicorn, I might not glow, but maybe I could flicker.

This time when Etana calls out, I open my mouth and join her.

Chapter Six

KIAN

We don't exactly run through the forest—after all, we still wear blindfolds—but our pace is much quicker than when we began. Unfortunately, I feel like I can't risk dropping more of the red stones to lead Aunt Ujvala out of the forest, but at least they'll already be past the wards. They can figure out the rest of the way.

Despite the blindfold, I can tell when we step out of the forest and into a meadow. The light seeping through the edges of my blindfold brightens, the sounds change, a strong breeze ruffles our robes and hair.

I can feel an invisible release of tension from the entire group. Someone beside me sighs with relief. We are nearly there. At last.

We remain jumpy at every rattle of leaves by the wind, at the soft hush of long grasses as our robes sweep behind us, but nothing else attacks, or even approaches, and after a few more long minutes of walking, we stop and wait.

And wait.

And wait.

Beside me, I sense the others fidgeting and shifting, too. When my feet go numb, I begin to jog in place, which I assume will get my shoulders rapped, but the priestesses ignore me.

"Your fellow keepers are late," Sarai hisses to those who wait with us. Whatever response they mumble in reply, my ears don't catch.

What they catch instead is the faint screaming of a woman. It starts out sounding far away but gets quickly closer until everyone in our group is shifting uncomfortably, unsure of where the sound is coming from. It sounds like it's above us, and I briefly imagine the horror of a dragon with an entire, still-living person trapped in its teeth.

But there is something distinctly ecstatic laced in with the fear of the scream. Suddenly there's a loud thud that reverberates through my feet and the screaming stops. Then there's another lesser thud as something much smaller hits the ground. I hear Sarai's sharp inhale as I tear off my blindfold.

Sister Roberta scowls at me. "Put that back on."

I ignore her. Before me a woman with dark shining hair and the silver mask of an assistant matcher lies flat on her back with a massive black-and-silver pegasus hovering above her.

I hurry over alongside the keepers bending down and notice as I get close that she's crying and laughing and gripping two handfuls of long grasses in her gloved hands as if the ground itself might run away and desert her. The keepers and Sarai are staring dumbstruck.

The pegasus snorts and paws the ground but doesn't seem to mind my presence by his . . . rider? Captive?

She begins to shake and laugh uncontrollably, until the keeper John gently pulls her into a sitting position, rubbing her arm and back briskly. She slowly starts to calm.

"What is this?" John asks her. "Why were you *riding* Lathai?" He says "riding" like it is something shameful, and I take it joyrides on pegasi are not part of growing up a keeper.

"Where's Adela?" she replies, looking around. She still seems a bit . . . frantic.

"Who's Adela?" I ask.

Before she can answer, the quiet breaks with another woman's raised voice. But whereas the scream from the assistant matcher sounded mostly like terror, this new noise is pure exhilaration. I twist toward the sound, my heart jumping at what I see.

A large, well-curved woman, one white leg totally bare, with large swaths of rich, dark fabrics and disheveled braids streaming out behind her, bounces upon the back of a glowing unicorn. She looks like something out of a storybook, and I want to rip the gold mask off her face to see the bold ecstasy that's so clear in her call.

"Adela," the assistant matcher says, her voice even and strong again. She scoots away slightly from John, and though she doesn't immediately push up to stand, I know she's finding her way back to herself.

I want to ask her to tell me more about this Adela, but Sister Roberta grabs my arm, muscles me back into line, and ties my blindfold on so tight I may soon lose feeling in my ears from lack of blood flow. I almost expect her to give my shins a good kick like my cousins used to during our games, but instead she simply moves away with an annoyed scoff.

If a holy's opinion has ever mattered before; it certainly never will now. For the first time since I joined the order, I finally understand their burning fervor to bow, scrape, and worship. But whereas their divine is the Huntress, mine is all thick white thighs, bouncing flesh, and primal joy.

I have at last seen the true visage of the goddess, and her name, apparently, is Adela.

Chapter Seven

ADELA

E tana deposits me in front of the matching hut and a small crowd of people—the order and the keepers who went to ensure their safe passage through the forest.

I ignore them, focusing on catching my breath. I'm not sure who is breathing harder, me or Etana. We both gulp air, her swollen belly heaving, me trying to breathe through the solid mask. But she is tossing her head in playful delight, and I can't stop laughing.

I take a few steps and collapse on the ground beside Beadda, who is clutching the long grass like she will never part with it. I think she might be crying. Or laughing. Or both?

Etana and Lathai greet, rubbing their faces together briefly before turning to gallop off toward the cliffs they call home. As quickly gone as they'd come.

Worry slithers down my spine, chilling me as much as the frozen ground. I sit up and look back at the hut. Something inside calls to me.

Behind me, I hear a throat clear.

Right. I cannot ignore them all forever. I turn to find Petra, John, and Redonna, along with the order they've safely ushered here.

Or mostly safely.

They seem to be missing a priest and at least one novitiate from what we expected. The others look disheveled—their white robes wrinkled and dirty, with bits of dried foliage stuck amongst the heavily embroidered designs. Still, they stand in a row with their blindfolds firmly in place.

All except one—a man with dark hair and broad shoulders who is hovering protectively behind Beadda. He doesn't wear his blindfold like he ought, and he watches me with dark, hungry eyes. His robes are filthy and a little bit singed in spots, as if he's rolled across the forest floor and into a few embers. I can't help but notice the way he's built more like a keeper than most priests, who tend toward lanky grace or general softness.

"Novitiate Kian," a priestess says, pulling him back into line with his peers. She ties a blindfold on him so tightly it flattens his nose.

"Matcher Adela," Petra says formally with a raised brow.

I scramble up to my feet and brush my skirts back into place.

"Sorry, Petra," I mumble to her, and then turn to the high priestess. "Greetings, Your High Holiness. I apologize for our . . . unconventional entrance. I am Adela, your matcher. And this is Beadda, my assistant."

Beadda does not move to stand. I nudge her with my foot, but she just moans slightly.

"We will commence with the greeting ceremony as soon as my fellow keepers join us." We can hear them in the near distance.

The high priestess—a stiff, severe woman wearing an elaborately bejeweled unicorn skull—nods once.

We wait for a bit until the rest of the keepers join us. Beadda finds her feet. The welcome ceremony goes without a hitch. When everything is complete, the novitiates remove their blindfolds. Usually this is where cheering and more informal greetings happen, but their eyes are haunted, and I listen to the story of the dragon and their fallen priest on the way back across the meadow.

After my trip on Etana, my head is pounding, my vision blurry, and my hands won't stop shaking. All I want is to go curl up in bed, but the welcome feast for the Huntress is the best food of the year by far, and I need to eat. The last twenty-four hours have been too long, too odd. Consuming abundant varieties of smoked cheeses, sweet rolls, and pudding will most certainly help quiet the uproar in my head and heart.

I return home first to change. Slowly, I remove my unicorn-hair-covered matcher's garments and change into a deep-sapphire silk gown that Cecelia chose for me. The neckline is lower than I would dare on my own, tight across my shoulders and breasts, and then flowy everywhere else.

The Spinner priests and priestesses would hate this dress, at once both revealing and ethereal, but it's perfect for followers of the Huntress. They're very corporeal, enjoying food, and sex, and dancing, and games. They love bodies, both their own and others'. And so even though I squirm a bit at its drama, I say a quick prayer of thanks for Cecelia's forethought and skill in choosing me something that will meet their expectations of my role as matcher.

The fabric skims across my body as I move here and there, preparing myself.

My braids are fine if a bit frizzed around my hairline, but I leave them in rather than deal with the knotted mess I would create by removing them myself. I'll have to get help with them later. Tomorrow, perhaps.

In deference to my aching head, I skip the heavy jewelry Cecelia laid out, as well as the elaborate leather-laced boots. The boots would look nice, crisscrossed and tied up the length of my legs, showing through the skirts' slits when I walk or dance, but they're too much to bother with. I slip on thin slippers instead. I make a small effort with my face, dabbing a shimmering powder on my lids, some beet-stained oils on my lips and cheeks.

Finished, I stand before the mirror and really look at myself. Cecelia's work is stunning, and all I can see is the fiercest, boldest version of myself.

Is this who I am?

I followed my whims and awakened the phoenix, sending a pulse of magic through the valley that has hurt us but also potentially strengthened us beyond our understanding. Imagine if I could match a phoenix to one of the novitiates. The creatures are wild and wonderous; the skulls are loud and eager; the keepers and order are keen with anticipation of influential matches despite the day's losses.

I did that.

Before the door to the great hall, I pause, inhale, prepare myself for whatever's about to come. I step through the doors and brace myself for any whispers, stares, or judgments that might be directed my way.

Instead, nothing happens.

People wave in distracted greeting or nod hello as I thread my way through dancing, feasting, imbibing bodies. I must have taken longer than I thought to prepare, for everyone is already well into the day's merriment. I find my spot beside Dad, and our guests' leaders at the head table. He is in deep discussion with the high priestess, and when he sees me, he bends closer to her and lowers his voice.

Apparently, I am not welcome to participate in their conversation. Which is fine; I cannot hear him over the rowdy tune of the musicians anyhow.

They are in fine form today, with cherry-red cheeks and quick hands. And loud. No doubt they feed off the energy of the room, which is raucous, but strange. We've all lost someone recently—the order lost one of their priests; we've lost Bartholomew, Gilcriss, Duschwa, and Donna—and it's as if by drowning and dancing away our sorrows, we could bring them back to us. Or at least forget the pain of their absence for a day.

Tomorrow, we will continue to mourn and move forward. Today, we will forget.

I watch as novitiates and keepers alike hunt each other, staking claims. No one's bed will be cold tonight for lack of company unless they prefer it that way.

The sour tang of ale and cider permeates the air and mixes with the rich, peppery scents of various veggie dishes and sweet-smelling pastries. My mouth waters, but before I can move to find my way to the food, Cecelia walks up carrying two heaping plates. We sit, and she places both before me. One has savory foods, one sweet.

"You're an angel," I say as I dig into marinated mushrooms and cornmeal pudding and egg pasta with béchamel and purple cabbage and honey-glazed carrots. Thank the goddess for feasts. And Cecelia for knowing me so well.

She snatches a stuffed quail egg off my plate and asks through a full mouth, "So . . . how was it riding Etana?"

"Oh my goddess. Toe-curling, life-changing bliss."

Dad must have finally finished conspiring with the priestess or heard Cecelia's question, for he shifts on my other side and attends to me for the first time since I arrived. He gives me a half hug and steals a chunk of roasted sweet potato.

"Take another and I'll stab you with my fork," I warn him.

He chuckles and leans back, resting his rough hands on his belly. "The priestess is pleased we have a new kelpie and a new dragon skull as options. She's prepared to provide us a generous offering of thanks if they match."

I frown.

"She wants the novitiate Kian in particular for Gilcriss."

Kian. The one with the dark hair, delicious shoulders, and ravenous eyes. I scan the hall and am surprised to find him looking back at me with an intensity I can practically feel. Between us, bodies writhe and sway to the music. But it's as if the rest of the room falls away. Deep in my belly, I find my want awaken.

I glance away and take a large gulp of mead. I swallow wrong.

"It doesn't work that way," Cecelia says for me as I splutter and cough. She's always concerned with clarity and rules. But she's right. The skulls talk to me, not the other way around. Maybe Bartholomew could sway the skulls' choices, but if it was a developed skill, it's not one he'd trained me in yet.

"Why Kian?" I ask. I would guess him a poor match for a dragon skull. Despite their love for indulgence, they're persnickety and lawful. Based on the way he stood separate and unblindfolded from the other novitiates, I imagine he defies rules when he feels he must.

Dad shrugs with his whole body and snatches a pistachio baklava from my plate of sweets.

"What are they offering?" Cecelia asks. So practical. So thorough.

"Increasing their contributions. It's enough to bring in four new keepers and cover the expenses for the additional buildings we'll need to house them. Plus, an additional annual sum for discretionary use."

Cecelia whistles low beside me. While we match skulls with novitiates for all three orders, the Order of the Huntress has more ceremonies and people than the Pupil and Spinner orders, and so they control our funds. And they've become stingy.

They obviously have some sort of agenda to make such a generous offer. Extra hands, extra lodging, and extra funds will make life easier for all of us. Especially now that we have a rogue dragon with a taste for people to worry about. I wonder what strings come with the money, or what their plans are for Kian.

"Will you try?" Cecelia's tone clearly says she thinks I ought to.

I stare at her, shocked that rule-abiding Cecelia is the one to encourage this. Not that there's any sort of official rule against trying to sway the skulls. It just feels like an exercise in futility.

"If you do this, just be careful," Dad says, always ready to protect me.

These two are cut from the same cloth. They want to protect me—and our whole community. But that means being aware of the present and looking toward the future. Something strange is happening, but also, the valley is in decline. The extra resources would be a lifeline.

I make my decision.

"I'll try and I'll be careful," I say. "Not that I have any idea at all how to pull it off. But that's a dilemma for tomorrow's Adela."

For now, all I want is to put aside my worries and enjoy the feast. Still sitting, I move slightly to the music while focusing on my food and, specifically, my mead. Which is why my face is basically still in my goblet after my last large gulp when I ask Cecelia, "Want to dance?"

Before she can agree or not, someone takes the goblet from me and gently places it near my plate. The sleeve of his robe falls back, revealing Huntress markings trailing up a muscular forearm. His voice is husky and laughing when he says, "I'd love to."

Typically, I'm not much of a dancer, I have little sense of rhythm and worry too much about stomping on toes or looking awkward. With

Kian, I am even more atrocious than usual. Something buzzes in my head and hands, distracting me. Him? His nearness? The mead I was just gulping down like water?

But no. I know what it is.

My wanting.

He's not a lot taller than me, but he is broad and distractingly firm. Our bodies fit together well.

"How are you?" I ask, trying for gentle, but my voice is a bit squeaky even to my own ears.

He's in new white robes now, clean and smelling like the lemongrass soap we make specifically for the orders. I want to lean in closer and inhale. Instead, I lift my hand slightly from his shoulder, realizing he may be sore or wounded. He'd been very dirty and his back had a little blood on it earlier from the trek through the valley.

"Not breakable. You can touch me," he replies gruffly. He pauses briefly, and the corners of his lips quirk up. "In fact, I'd like it if you'd touch me."

I relax my hand, resting it again on his shoulder, which is firm and warm. Involuntarily, I flex my fingers, gripping him slightly. His smirk deepens. "Good girl."

Something deep in my belly—or lower—clenches. An involuntary, but not unwelcome, flush blooms across my skin.

"Ooh," he says, noticing the reaction. He traces the flush across my face, down my cheek and neck, with his eyes. "You liked that, eh?"

I give a small nod. I wonder again at what the high priestess wants from this smirking, irreverent man who wears the robes and tattoos of a proper Huntress novitiate but somehow feels as wild as a newborn gryphon. I cannot imagine Kian leading Huntress rituals as he'd do as a high-standing priest wearing a dragon's skull.

He moves me around the dance floor. The song is long and exuberant, chosen by our musicians specifically for the Huntress's order. Like all the goddesses' religious houses, they are a confusing mix of standards and priorities. On the one hand, the Order of the Huntress is the most hierarchical of the three orders. It demands the most obedience from its novitiates and junior priests. On the other hand, they enjoy pleasure more than most.

Dancing is one of those pleasures.

They like to move. In this, Kian fits his order perfectly. He is so . . . solid. Present. Physical. I do my best to keep up as we twirl until I find I'm not trying at all. I'm just following, feeling the music.

The longer we dance, the more my mind lets go. It's exhilarating. I am laughing and sweating and out of breath when one song, then another, and then a third ends, and he finally releases me.

He is smiling and breathing hard, too, his broad chest rising and falling quickly. There is a sheen of sweat on his forehead that matches my own.

We step apart, and I move to bow, the traditional departure for a dancing pair. Behind him, I see three of my fellow keepers milling about not quite casually, obviously eager for him to notice them next.

But he does not let go of my hand.

"Thank you for the dances," I say, pulling gently to escape his grasp. The want is flaring; another moment of his touch and I will be past the point of intentional thought and into pure, impulsive need.

His grip tightens further, but it's no longer flirtatious. He's holding me too tightly. So tightly his knuckles are turning white.

"Kian?"

I look up at his face, expecting a smirk, the indication this is a game of some sort, but his expression is slack, his lips slightly parted. More disconcerting, his eyes are rolled back in his head so all I can see are the whites.

"Kian?" I repeat. Then I realize he must be having a vision. It happens sometimes, just before the matches. Not with the jackalopes and more typical creatures, but with the rarer, more powerful ones.

Maybe we will be able to fulfill the high priestess's request to match him with the dragon after all.

I try to move him to the edge of the dance floor, but he wobbles and half-collapses in my arms. It's a good thing I am not petite like Cecelia, or I'd collapse beneath him and we'd both be on the floor. But I wrap his arm around my shoulder and place my hand at his waist, managing to keep my feet beneath me. He remains conscious enough to grip me and follow my firm instructions as I navigate us out of the great hall and into the much quieter kitchen and then beyond into a small pantry. It's cooler here, which I sense he needs. His skin is on fire.

I get only a couple of slightly jealous glances as we go.

When we're free of the stifling laughter and warmth, I plop him down on a low bench before closing the pantry door to protect him from any prying eyes. If I were out of my body, unaware to the world around me in the midst of a vision, I wouldn't want busybodies observing me.

He grips my waist tightly, his fingers rough but not pinching.

His eyes focus for a moment, taking me in. Devouring me. They look feral, and I see the strength he'd need to wield a dragon.

"You are fucking perfection," he says. His words are thick like honey, and he's obviously still being affected by whatever vision he sees. But still, they go straight to my core and light a fire there.

Perfection.

Me.

Who has messed up so much in the last two days; who has the blood of creatures and people on her hands. I am foolish. I am impulsive. I am not anything close to perfection.

And yet, I believe him. And it makes my wanting flare.

His hands flex on my waist. He moves his legs farther apart so that when he tugs me closer, there is space for me to stand between them. My breasts are practically in his face, and a wicked, reckless part of me wants to arch my back to close the small gap. I want feel to his lips and tongue and teeth on my skin. But he is still not himself. His eyes are unfocused again, his breath comes hard.

I shiver in the cool air.

"Kian?" He still grips me, but he doesn't respond. This vision is lasting too long. Or perhaps it's something more. Trying to get through to him, I lift my hand. When my thumb grazes his cheek, his eyes snap into focus.

On my breasts.

There's a moment of surprise that jolts through him. I can feel it in his hands at my waist, see it in the slight widening of his eyes as he looks up into my face briefly. And then, it's gone, replaced instantly by a smug sort of satisfaction. His eyes go heavy-lidded, and those lips twist up once again. Wherever the vision took him, he is back to himself, fully.

His face a hair's breadth from my breasts, he whispers, "Hello, beauties," against my skin. It pebbles instantly, covered in gooseflesh, which makes him chuckle.

He pulls me slightly closer, and I lose my balance, falling forward. He inhales sharply as he leans back into the pantry shelves. He adjusts quickly, sitting forward and half-lifting me. Suddenly, I am not between his knees, but straddling him. The slits on either side of my dress part, exposing my legs. He sees and growls, finally letting go of my waist in order to grip a thigh in each hand.

"Goddess," he whispers again before he dips his head forward and kisses me.

For once, I don't even want to do what I ought to. I want to just be. Reckless. Wild. Present.

His kiss is sweeter and more intoxicating than the mead. Wet and hot and wanting. There is no hesitation, no coyness. There is none of the awkwardness of many first kisses, where two new partners are unsure what each other likes.

Not that we're partners. At least, not the long-term sort. This is a casual, one-time fling.

Beneath me, I can feel him hard and ready for more. But he does not grind against me or hurry his exploration of my mouth, rushing toward what feels like the inevitable conclusion of these kisses. Instead, he takes his time. It seems he knows exactly what he likes and demands it with his lips and tongue and teeth.

And what he likes sets me aflame.

Taking my butt in his hands and pulling me impossibly closer, he nips at my bottom lip, and I feel the small bite between my legs. I gasp and writhe on his lap, and he chuckles again, the deep laughter reverberating through his chest into me, which makes me wiggle more.

He kisses down my neck and across my chest, his hands trailing up my back.

"Do you like what I do to you?" he asks. I mumble my affirmation, and he stops kissing me and pulls back to look directly in my eyes. "Tell me."

"I like it," I say, a little surprised at the shy tone accompanying my words. I am not typically demure or embarrassed by this sort of wanting.

And yet.

Something about this confident, appealing novitiate has me feeling unsure of myself, of my ability to curb myself and my most reckless desires.

"What do you like?" he asks.

"I like your lips on me," I reply, surprised at how breathy I sound. As I speak, I move on his lap, relishing the way his body moves beneath me. Finding a touch of confidence at his reactions to me, I smirk and lower my voice, teasing as I lift my hips up slowly so our bodies don't quite touch. "I like your firm grip, your firm . . . other things."

I lower my hips, grinding down against him with intention.

He groans deep in his throat and resumes his kisses down my neck. I tilt my head back to allow him more access, and he licks along the neckline of my dress. Low and demanding, he says, "Take what you want from me."

A chill shoots up my spine at the command.

I do.

I want his mouth on me, on my body. I tell him so. He obliges with a delightfully wicked smile as he deposits me on the bench in his place and then kneels in front of me, moving my skirts out of his way.

He kisses up my left leg, and then my right, until I am squirming with want, practically thrusting myself into his face.

He connects, and I lose all ability to move.

His mouth is hot and insistent, teasing and obliging. When he pulls back, I let out a whimper. Horrifyingly needy, but he makes a sound of amused approval. "That's it. Move for me."

I arch into him, now matching the movements of his tongue, meeting his rhythm. Or perhaps he matches mine. Whoever is leading is brilliant and sets a quick, delicious pace that does not hurry me toward climax, but luxuriates in the pleasure of the moment.

As he works me with his mouth, his hands move across my body, pushing apart my knees to lean in closer, brushing over my nipples, gripping my waist and holding me tight.

Until finally, it is too much.

"I want you," I murmur, too quietly for him to hear. I clear my throat, find my voice, and say again, "I want you."

He sits up, his mouth wet with me, and smiles, his dark eyes crinkling slightly in the corners. Those little lines somehow turn me even more molten. How can a man be this beautiful?

On shaking legs, I stand and switch places with him so he is once again sitting on the bench, and I crawl onto his lap. He rests his hands, large and frustratingly patient, on my thighs and waits.

"Take what you want from me, beauty," he says again.

I do.

I reach between us, fumbling at his robes and pants. He is ready. I am ready. But just as I am about to sink myself onto him, he pulls back a bit. "Do we need a sleeve? I have one in my room. I can go fetch it."

"Spinner's tits, no," I exclaim. "I take herbs. No unwanted pregnancies here."

"Thank the goddess for brilliant, well-prepared women." He inhales sharply as I sink down on him in one slow, steady movement.

We move together, forehead to forehead. My hands grip his shoulders; his hands hold my thighs so tightly that I suspect I'll wear bruises beneath my matcher's robes tomorrow.

The thought spurs me on. As do his words. For as we move, he talks.

"I love the way you take me." He thrusts up into me and moves his hand to the base of my neck, weaving his fingers into the gaps of my braids. He pulls my face toward him, kissing me as I continue to ride him. I adjust my angle slightly, so he hits me just right. I moan. Nothing has ever felt this good.

"That's it," he says into my mouth, his eyes watching my own. "Just there."

I close my eyes briefly against the intensity of him, and he loosens his grip slightly on my neck as he stills beneath me.

"Need a break?"

My eyes flash open, and I grip his shoulders still tighter. I have lost most power of speech, but I manage to half croak, "No break."

He grins, his hand tightening. "Excellent. Then look at me."

I do. He hisses as I begin to move again, a sound somewhere between pleasure and pain. I still, but he does not have any tolerance for slowing. "Don't stop," he demands, moving with me. "Take me."

I match him, burying my face in his neck, unable to withstand his gaze even as it urges me on.

Sex with Kian is like dancing with him. At first, it's as if I'm barely keeping up. But then it continues until I find I'm not trying at all. I'm just moving, feeling his words and his body as my mind lets go of its worries, its obligations, even its wanting. I am not a poor keeper or a reticent matcher. I am just a woman, existing.

It's exhilarating.

My body moves closer and closer to climax, tightening around him, my legs shaking, my breath coming harder. He urges me on, rubbing me in just the right spot, at just the right speed, whispering how good I feel, how well I'm doing, how spectacular I look, until I am just at the edge.

"Now come for me, Goddess," he demands.

I do, breaking apart atop him. Half a moment later, he joins me.

Chapter Eight

KIAN

The next morning wakes with me with a slap, harsh and unyielding. I squint against the brilliant sunlight streaming in through the small window of a small, unfamiliar room and try to orient myself.

Right.

I am in the valley. Today is the matching. Yesterday was the most brilliant sex of my life, and my body wants more. But of course, that's impossible. Not that I wouldn't eagerly sink into Adela's warmth again—my cock twitches at the thought—but I have revenge to enact.

Even though pursuing her once again would be much more fun.

I roll over, groaning at the way the sheets stick to my destroyed back. Between the trip through the forest, the dancing, and the vigorous exertion with Adela after, some of the wounds that had started to scab over have reopened. I eye the bottle of whiskey I had snatched from the pantry, but as much as dulling the sharp stabs of pain would be welcome, it's a bit early, even for me.

A knock sounds on my door, and I sit up with a wince. I make sure my blankets are covering the important bits and grunt, "Come."

I don't know who I was expecting, but nothing could surprise me more than Ulric.

"I wanted to check on you," he says simply, and I stare at him, blinking for too long. He sounds more hesitant when he adds, "Your back. Can I come in?"

I nod and he does, closing the door softly behind him. My heart pangs a bit at his beauty. A deep piece of me misses him, and these gentle kindnesses that were part of us. But there is no room in my schemes for any kind of real relationship, and Ulric requires no less than full realness.

He sits on the only chair in the small room, perching on its edge.

"How are you?" he asks softly.

I blink at him.

"You and Thad . . . It seemed like you might have had some hopes there."

Ah. He's checking on my heart, not my back. Or not just my back. "No hopes." Besides wanting to use him for his skull. "His death was upsetting, but I think that had more to do with watching him be eaten."

If he judges me for the callousness of my words, he doesn't indicate it in any way. He simply touches my shoulder. "Turn so I can see."

I twist around. He gasps, jumping up from the bed and going to the pitcher, pouring water into the basin.

"Looks as bad as it feels, eh?"

"Let me clean it."

I pause. The gentleness he'll approach me with. The kindness. Can I handle this intimacy?

I nod.

He arranges the small table, pitcher, basin, and all the towels that are in the room and sits beside me on the bed. Carefully, so very carefully, he begins to clean my back. He dips a corner of a towel in, pats it on my skin, then dips again. I watch the water turn pink as he continues, over and over.

The silence morphs from comfortable to heavy. I recognize it. He has a question he wants to ask but doesn't know how.

"Do you have a question for me?" I say softly.

He pauses his ministrations, and I think for a while that he won't respond. Then he dips a new towel and says, "What happened to you on the dance floor? Before you left with the matcher?"

Thad. The matcher. I hear the faint edge of hurt in his voice, but I focus on the question he asked and not the implied one that I suspect he doesn't really want the answer to.

"I . . ." What did happen? I pick the words carefully. "I saw something in my head. I was soaring over a lush valley, teeming with wild creatures. I was responsible for it. For its growth and prosperity." A shiver runs through me, remembering how heavy it felt.

He grows absolutely still. His voice is small and purposefully light when he says, "Visions happen before big matches. Was it the dragon?"

It didn't feel like a dragon. It felt both smaller and somehow more powerful. But how the hell would I actually know what it feels like to see through the eyes of a dragon? Or any of the creatures. I shrug as if I couldn't care less who I match with—as if a lifetime of plans wasn't tied up in me matching with the right skull. He rubs the cloth across a wound, and I inhale sharply at the pain.

"Would you want that?" His voice is full of a sort of wistfulness that makes me know he would.

I'd guess a gryphon was a better match. After all, he's tending to me now before he has any magical gifts to help with. But I know the Huntress is important to him, and she values strength.

Matching with the newly dead dragon would be Sarai's wet dream. It'd mean instant access to the order's inner circle. Power and prestige. And since dragon fire is the only way to destroy the skulls, I have to want that.

And yet, I find myself thinking, *No. Please, Goddess, no.*

"Of course," I reply. "Which of the Huntress's faithful wouldn't?"

The sun is high in the sky when we gather together with the keepers in the meadow and start the long walk to the matching hut. It's a whole thing, the procession. There's a torchbearer despite the bright day, and Adela and her assistant lead the way, followed by Sarai and Sister Roberta. Behind us novitiates, the keepers follow, chanting. They call for the Spinner's guidance, the Pupil's wisdom, the Huntress's mercy. My back aches with every step, but I am electric.

And not just because I get to watch Adela's supple hips sway beneath her matcher's robes as she takes long strides across the still-brown grasses. My hands clench, remembering the soft fullness of her thighs in my grip.

When we get to the matching hut, the keepers stop in a semicircle behind us. There are more of them here, in the bright sun of the afternoon, than there were last night at the meeting ceremony. But they look wary, glancing over their shoulders at the forest, flinching when a cloud moves over the sun and causes a shadow.

We stand in our own line between them, facing Adela, who looks like a goddess in her flowing, deep-purple robes, gold-encrusted bone jewelry, and simple golden mask. On either side of her are her assistants—the young torchbearer, who holds a stack of simple aspen-carved masks for us novitiates to wear as we first enter the matching hut, and her assistant, the young woman who rode the pegasus.

It is strange to see Sarai beside us in line, her head half-bowed in supplication. But today the matcher reigns supreme.

Adela speaks, her voice deep and confident. Somehow, the sound of her taking charge is even sexier than the thighs hidden beneath her voluminous robes.

"Today we join together to represent the triune goddess—keepers, creatures, and order.

"Keepers, have you done your duty for these creatures? Ushering them through life and into the glory of death, preparing them with care and keeping until they meet their natural ends and begin their journey of service to the goddess?"

"We have," the community of keepers behind me replies.

"Novitiates, have you done your duty to prepare for these creatures? Have you studied the ways of your goddess, served her with your mind and your hands, done her good work on this earth in order to prepare your soul for the pairing that is holy and eternal?"

"We have," we reply.

She turns her back to us and faces the matching hut. She raises her arms, and I swear I can feel the excitement of the waiting skulls, even though that's impossible. Order members only ever feel the emotions and wants of their paired skull, and even that sort of bond is rare. As I understand it, the flow is simply single skull to priest.

"Creatures, we have fulfilled our duties in preparation for your blessings. We beseech you now to meet us in our mundane humanity, see the imperfection of our souls, and aid us in our potential for good."

The next few hours start slow, but gain a fervency I suspect no one is prepared for. Rare match after rare match occurs. Two-thirds of a gytrash triad pair with Ylysia and Molvi, who happen to be two-thirds of a romantic triad. Linden, their third, stands at the end of our row, beaming at his partners in their dog-like skulls and practically bouncing on his toes with anticipation of his own match. Gytrash always match in threes.

Personally, I wouldn't be as pleased by the match. Those paired with gytrash are responsible for the death rites of the orders, cleaning and preparing bodies for burial or burning. It's valuable work—the order charges citizens significant sums for a gytrash-assisted death ceremony—but, Goddess, how depressing.

The blur of muffled, chanting voices of the keepers behind me seems to grow faster, louder, more dynamic as Ulric steps forward and prepares to face the skulls. My heartbeat syncs with their rhythm, speeding up as he enters with the matcher. I'd hoped to go before him, to let that new dragon skull meet me first, but assure myself it'll be fine. Like calls to like, and Ulric is too gentle for a dragon. Too kind.

In mere moments, he emerges, his smile wide, the dragon on his face.

Fuck.

Sarai practically dances, unable to keep her feigned humility in place.

I panic. Not Ulric. Anyone else except Ulric. I cannot use him without destroying him. But I'll have no other option.

Adela steps close to me and I nearly step forward, the desire to touch her overwhelming. But she's not coming for me. "Are you ready to meet your soul's fate, Svena?"

Svena sways beside me, exhausted from her injuries. She had a long night, according to the keeper healer who had protested her joining us at all. But High Priestess Sarai won out in the end, and so here she stands—barely.

I hear Svena murmur but don't catch her words.

Adela replies, "That depends on what your past contains. Before this week I was a matcher's assistant for seven years, and a light bearer for ten before that. I've known only two who went unmatched. One from the Order of the Spinner, one from the Pupil."

Unmatched. I knew it was a possibility, of course, but hearing the matcher say it aloud makes fire shoot across my back. I was convinced the worst possible outcome of tonight's ceremony might be getting paired with a jackalope.

"Both of those failures were within the last year," Sarai says coolly. "Your magic is waning."

Adela turns away from Sarai and pointedly toward the gytrash, the pegasus, the unicorn, and the dragon she matched. "Is it?"

Oh, I like her bite.

I lean slightly forward, even as I wonder at this strange draw she holds over me. She is the opposite of what I should want. A member of the system I'm here to topple, a farmer of creatures. She uses their bones to provide society's most powerful, and most corrupt, with even more power. And yet . . . I think of her on the unicorn yesterday. Surely no livestock would carry their captor and eventual slaughterer so willingly?

Whatever the cause of her pull, surely it's meaningless, physical, base. My goals are higher than a woman who rides unicorns as if they're mere war horses and she's leading a charge to battle. She cannot distract me from my task.

No one can.

As if she senses my longing, she steps closer to me, and I feel her skirts practically engulf my legs. "You seem eager, novitiate Kian."

"Who isn't eager to meet their future?" I reply in a voice huskier than intended.

She makes a sound deep in the back of her throat. "Perhaps we give Svena a bit more time to rest." She steps back, and I shiver as she says formally, "Novitiate Kian, are you ready to meet your soul's fate?"

"Absolutely," I reply. The next words have been practiced so much they're rote. "Lead me, Matcher, and prepare me to show my face to the goddess's helpers. May one see my worth and mark me as their own, so we can be joined forever. First in this world, then beyond."

I reach out my hand, and she turns. The assistant matcher takes a mask from the torchbearer, placing it on my face. It's solid, without holes to see or speak through. She positions my right hand on Adela's shoulder and she leads me to the hut and the grotesque bones of the creatures inside.

Behind us, the chanting grows steadily louder.

We step onto the porch and I pause, gripping Adela's shoulder to avoid tripping over the unevenly hewn boards. I hear the door open and we step inside. The matching hut smells earthy, like once-green things now dried, and there's a zing in the air that is like inhaling dried, ground peppers.

It makes me itchy, and I remove my hand from Adela's shoulder to scratch a spot on my neck.

It's a mistake.

She keeps moving. I try to follow her soft steps across the uneven wooden planks of the floor, but without her warm shoulder to guide me, I instantly run into something low and unmoving.

"Water cistern," she says and I can hear the slight smile in her voice.

I curse under my breath, move to my left, and hit my hip.

"Workbench."

I move forward, and something dry and fragrant bounces off my mask.

"Sage. We hang it to dry."

I take a much more tentative step, shuffling, and trip on the edge of a floorboard. I throw my hands up in disgust. "Help me."

She chuckles, and the soreness of my shin, hip, and toe fly away at the allure of her amusement. "Come here," she says.

She guides me to an open area. She slides her hands under my robe's neckline, removing it from my shoulders. It collapses in a heap at my ankles, and I shiver in my plain white linen shirt and matching pants.

Her voice envelopes me. "How do you come before your soul's match?"

"Bare of wealth or warmth," I intone.

I hear the faint clink of glass against glass, smell oil and herbs, then hear the slick slide of her palms rubbing together. I reach my hands out, and she rubs hers on mine.

"How do you come before your soul's match?"

"With empty hands, prepared to toil for goodness."

I hear her open a jar and smell the sharp tang of pine. She moves close, and I bend my head so her fingertips can push beneath the mask's edge and rub ointment into my temples.

"How do you come before your soul's match?" she asks for the third and final time.

"Clearheaded, with eyes that search for truth and a tongue that speaks of both justice and mercy."

"Then kneel and prepare yourself."

I pause then, suddenly nervous. I know my next step, and my broader path, but I hadn't thought through exactly how I would feel just before I'm bonded with the bones of some creature.

Or what happens if I'm not matched.

Adela takes my hands and helps me kneel. I lift my face, and she removes the mask. The inside of the matching hut is both everything

I expected and surprising. It's small and practical. Workbenches line one wall, dried and drying herbs hang from the ceiling. The wall toward the forest is made entirely of windows, which let in the silvery moonlight.

And then the fourth wall is skulls. Dozens of skulls. I should be taking it all in, noting it all for my later plans, but mostly I can't stop staring at Adela.

Her hair is pale blond with a few copper strands shining in the tapers' light, tied back in braids ten times as elaborate as mine. The little skin I can see of her hands and around the edges of her golden mask is ivory and freckled. The mask doesn't fit her well. Perhaps it belonged to her recently deceased mentor.

Adela's body is lush, curved, thick. My hands clench involuntarily, wanting to touch her abundant softness again, to grip those curves and pull her close to me.

Standing above me, Adela traces a finger along my jaw before giving herself a little shake. I smirk. Apparently, I am not the only one affected.

She sets the aspen mask I just wore gently on a workbench with a pile of others and gestures to the wall behind her. "Look to your future, Kian. What does it hold?"

Bile rises in my throat at the juxtaposition of her warm beauty before a wall of death, of loss, of twisted magics. One of those will become part of me. Forever.

I force myself to look pleased, eager. While I cannot see her face, I must remember mine is on full display. I want to ask her how to choose, but then my eyes skim the skulls of long-dead jackalopes, unicorns, gryphons, and even another dragon. I did not realize there was another. But it doesn't matter.

I never had a choice at all.

At the top of the shelves, half-hidden beneath a cloth, is a beak. It calls to me. Not in words or thoughts, but with a deep, aching need.

I stand and move toward it, but I can't reach the shelf. I look around for a stool or chair to stand on, and my eyes meet Adela's. Instantly, I know something is wrong.

She's standing perfectly still, frozen, except for her long fingers, which are twisting, untwisting, twisting together. She sees me staring and gives a small shake of her head. I swear she whispers, "Not that one." But I'm not certain with her mask covering her mouth.

"Is there a problem?" I ask.

She startles, as if just noticing me, though she's been looking right at me. She says ominously, "Not with them."

I laugh, but she does not join me. She shakes her head, and her ill-fitting mask continues shaking for a moment after she's stopped moving. I look at the shelf and skull that sits waiting beneath the cloth. The wall is macabre, a shrine of death. Whatever's under there must be awful and precious if they've covered it. I move close, reaching up, and she reaches out as if to stop me. I pause, step away, then pretend to trip over my discarded robe still bunched up in the middle of the floor. If it worked in the forest, it can work here.

I catch myself hard on the shelves beside her.

Adela cries out, twisting away to straighten a wobbling jackalope, looking away just long enough that my hand can snake out and capture a corner of the cloth. I jerk it, and it slides to the floor.

She turns at the sound of fabric hitting the floor.

"No." Her objection is a whimper of pain, but there is pleasure laced through the word as well. Or perhaps longing. She says again, "No."

I want to turn, to explore what I can see of her face, but I cannot stop myself from staring at the shelf and what the cloth has revealed.

There, on the top shelf, are two perfectly identical skulls. From the way the beaks curve to the breadth of the brow bones to the shape of the empty eye sockets, they are an exact replica of each other. I would assume they were made from a mold.

Except they are not molded of plaster. They're bone, and both glowing from within, emitting a golden light.

There is no sound, no movement, no anything besides a feeling deep inside me. Like a fish who has swallowed the hook, I have been caught. I have no choice in my destination. I am being called. I have been chosen.

I know, somehow, that these two skulls are phoenixes, and one is mine. He is the creature I was in the vision, and he will not stop pulling at me until I accept him.

"What—" I begin, but Adela hushes me. Moving as if resigned to a fate worse than death, she fetches a stool to climb up on, lifting the skull that calls to me. She cradles him to herself as she steps down, grimacing, as if touching it is unpleasant.

She gestures for me to kneel again, then pauses, exploring my face, then neck and shoulders. Her eyes trace down my chest, and it is as if her gaze is a finger I can feel trailing down my body.

My body responds, of course. I'm human, and she's beautiful, but whether she appreciates or even notices the effect she has me, I don't know, because she turns back to the glowing phoenix on the shelf. She seems to compare the two, and I wonder what she sees or hears or feels that I cannot.

Whatever it is, she shakes it off, and begins to fit the skull to my face. The moment the bone touches my skin, my body shudders in pleasure, flush with energy. Even the wounds on my back stop aching.

I can't enjoy the rush. The main ritual is over; I've been matched with a creature from the storybooks. But something is most definitely wrong with Adela. I want to reach for her, gather her up, and care for her. The feeling is not lust, and somehow it seems not to be entirely my own.

I clench my fists.

Based on our training for the night, she ought to be speaking, finishing the ritual. The prayers from her fellow keepers can still be heard beyond the thick walls of the building, but she's gone completely silent. Her brow is furrowed, but I don't know if its annoyance or pain or something else entirely. I cannot see her jaw beneath the solid facade of her mask's lower half, but I suspect her teeth are clenched tight. Is that why she doesn't speak? Or perhaps because she cannot catch her breath, which is beginning to sound wheezy and a bit beleaguered.

Her hands tremble as she pads the interior of the skull so it will fit me comfortably and then adjusts leather bands around and beneath my braid. The bone is cool where it connects with my cheekbones and forehead, but I suspect it continues to interact somehow with her touch. I notice after she removes her bare, shaking hands that she wipes them on her skirts and shivers, despite the warmth of the building.

Suddenly, mid-ministration, she steps away and bends in half as if to catch her breath, as the chants outside grow louder.

I move to stand and help her but freeze when a vision of a quick-moving forest below me overtakes me.

I twist my long, feathered neck and spiral toward the sun, flapping my expansive wings as I climb higher and higher in the midday sky.

Back in reality, I lurch forward, dizzy. I collapse onto my hands and knees, trying not to be sick.

"What just happened?" I ask.

"Another vision. They're rare, but a good indication of a strong bond. It seems that you've just made a powerful match." Her voice comes out strained, her words squeezed between clenched teeth. She is definitely in pain of some sort.

Again, I want to go to her, and this time I don't stop myself. I stand and move toward her. As I do, I look out the windows, just in time to see my sixteen-year-old cousin Ivo step out of the forest.

Shit.

I'm supposed to meet Aunt Ujvala and whoever she's brought with her after the ceremony so I can provide details about the matching hut and my plans for how to burn it. Plans that no longer work with Thad dead. And details I haven't even taken a moment to notice, I've been so caught up with the matcher.

What in the name of the great goddess is he doing out in the open?

Thankfully the matching hut must be between them and the rest of the keepers—there's no cry of alarm or pause in the fevered pitch of the chanting. But if she turns even slightly, Adela will see him easily. As if my very thought inspired her to do so, she begins to turn.

I reach toward her, pulling her close.

Her eyes widen as I press my body into hers. If she didn't notice her effect on me earlier, she has now. She wiggles slightly against me, pressing her body into mine, and I groan at the contact. Whatever discomfort she experienced earlier seems to have eased.

The skull likes this, which is slightly disturbing, but since I also like this, I don't examine the feeling too closely. She wraps her arms around my neck, pressing into me.

I bend to kiss her neck, angling my head so I don't mark her skin with the beak of the phoenix.

The noise she makes, a low, hungry moan, transforms this from a pleasant way to distract her into something dangerous. Last night was supposed to be a one-time thing. An itch I hadn't scratched in too long. A fling with no long-term effects. But now the taste of her is in my mouth, and I want more.

I can't get to her like I want to, so I remove the skull, setting him on a workbench behind her. I can still feel the phoenix. His joy at my kissing Adela, and at being matched to me. *No visions*, I think at him, unsure if he will hear me, or if I even have any influence.

"Don't—" she begins, but I press her back into the bench, putting my hand between her and the hard edge. My tongue and lips insistent, pressing.

She tilts her head for me, and I kiss up her neck. It isn't enough. I want her. All of her. Her jaw and her mouth, and to see her face. In one quick move, without a thought for consequences, I remove her ill-fitting mask.

Yes! I hear in my head at the exact same moment she cries out, "No!"

It's too late. I have a mere moment to enjoy her beauty—her full mouth with a slight scar in one corner, wide cheekbones, and a tiny upturned nose studded with a small blue stone before a scream pierces the air.

A second later, the world flashes gold, then goes dark.

Chapter Nine

ADELA

I wake up on the floor of the main room of my own house to the worried faces of the two people who love me most in the world.

"Who died?" I grumble.

"Spinner's tits," Dad swears, and hugs me so tightly I feel my ribs creak.

"We were worried you had!" Cecelia pushes flyaway hairs off my forehead.

I moan and sit up, stiffly. My head hurts, and I reach up to find my hair still tightly bound in the ceremonial matching braids. I'm also still wearing the bone jewelry and the first layer of the matching robes.

"What happened?"

Dad begins to bluster, turning an alarming shade of red.

Cecelia, calm as ever, turns to him. "Oscar, would you make Adela some tea?"

A helper to his core, he stands up reluctantly. "Of course. Good idea. Tea." He gives me a kiss on the forehead and goes to the kitchen. There is a long, silent pause where Cecelia and I glance warily at each other, and then he begins to bang around.

I open my mouth to ask again, but Cecelia holds up a hand. "Let me say this quickly before he returns."

"Quickly" is an anathema to Cecelia. She's a detail-obsessed historian and a natural storyteller. If she's allowed, she can stretch a tale out from ten minutes of actual activity to an hour-long laugh-out-loud, emotional, heartfelt epic. But I stay silent.

"We were going through the ceremony. It was obviously fantastic. *You* were fantastic. The matches you made! I swear their high priestess was going to shit her robes with joy. And then you went in with Kian. Something happened while you were in there, like a pulse of vitality flowed over us and into the rest of the valley. We all felt it. I assume that was him matching with the phoenix?"

I nod. It must have been. She pauses, and I know she has a million questions. But she sets her jaw and continues.

"After that, things got strange. There was sort of a hush that followed, and then an explosion."

"An explosion?" I move to get up. I need to get to the matching hut. See what's left of it.

She holds up her hands. "No, not literal. It was another pulse, I guess. Like the other, except massive. And with this strange golden light. Honestly, it was beautiful and terrifying. But the creatures got strange after that. They sort of swarmed the matching hut and started posturing as if to attack, especially the jackalopes. You know how territorial they are around there, with all their warrens. Then Enkidus came out of the forest and snatched a gryphon right out of the sky. We're not sure which one."

Another dragon attack. Another dead creature.

"Thankfully she took off for the farthest mountains after. Hopefully the feast will keep her away for a while." Cecelia looks off in the direction of the mountains, a haunted look in her eyes.

She sort of shakes away whatever memory is plaguing her and continues. "The rest of the creatures scattered and Kian came out, wearing the phoenix skull and carrying you in his arms."

A primitive, dirty-minded part of me is turned on by that. Goddess, he must be strong.

We hear the kettle whistle. Dad is still banging around the kitchen, but now we have mere minutes until it's finished steeping.

"Your turn," Cecelia says. "Quickly."

"I..." The details are hazy. "The night was hard. The skulls were loud."

Cecelia grimaces. She knows how much I hate the creatures' voices in my head.

"And exuberant in their matching. It was like they had been waiting and were all cheering on the most powerful. And then Kian came in, and I thought I'd never be able to hear another one of my own thoughts ever again. They... We—" I search for the word, wanting to be precise for Cecelia even as I wince at the memory. "It was a riot of noise. Painful. And then he saw the edge of the phoenix skull. They paired."

"But that's good?" Cecelia says, making it a question. She can tell *I'm* not sure it's good.

"It is. I think," I agree with a shrug. "Maybe. We'll find out, I suppose."

I pause. Do I tell Cecelia? How *I* felt nauseous and aflame and called? Even now, I can feel two pulls, insistent. One is the direction of the matching hut. The other across the courtyard where the order is staying.

But no.

She'll just give me the look that they all give me. The one where I know I've done something wrong, said something wrong, been somehow wrong. And yet, the desire to tell bubbles up inside me until I can't hold it back. I tell her.

Her eyes, brown and kind and curious, grow wider as she takes it all in.

"And then he kissed me."

"On the mouth?!" She squeaks, half delighted, half appalled. The clanging in the kitchen pauses. She yells to Dad. "Could Adela also get some cheese? And maybe olives? And salami if you have any? She's peckish."

"Of course," he hollers back, and resumes moving around.

"So he removed your mask?"

I nod.

I've never seen her more horrified.

"And that's it. I don't remember anything more."

She doesn't speak. She doesn't say anything at all. She simply gives my hand a squeeze and stands up as if to leave. "I need to do some research. We will figure this out."

I am just about to ask her to stay, to continue to hold my hand and maybe tell me everything will be fine and surely nothing will come of it, when the vision takes me.

We spiral and spin, our feathers brushing together and drifting apart as we dance beneath the evening rain. The air is heavy; we ought to huddle together beneath the canopy, nestled on a thick branch.

But our joy is too immense to fit below even the biggest tree's branches. After decades of searching—through lifetimes—we have found each other at last. Neither of us will continue to suffer the endless loneliness of death.

And so, we fly, twisting together, then apart, splattered by cold droplets of an angry sky. Far off in the distance, thunder rolls and lightning blooms. The storm's heart is moving toward us, but we have time before we must take shelter. We continue our celebrations.

I come to moments later. Or at least, I assume it's mere moments. Cecelia is still standing over me, and I can hear Dad in the kitchen.

"Did you . . . ," Cecelia starts, her voice shaky. "Did you just have a vision?"

I nod almost imperceptibly. But she sees it. She sees everything where I'm concerned.

"You're pai—" she begins, a whisper.

Dad comes in with a tray. He pauses in the doorway, looking between us quickly, and I wonder if my face holds the same amount of shock and horror as Cecelia's or if my guilt overrides those feelings.

"All well, girls?" The same thing he's asked since we were six and simultaneously fell out of the tree we were climbing. We both came home howling with bruised knees and bruised egos.

"Yep!" I reach for the tray. "This is perfect!"

It's a little too perky of a response considering I'm still lying on the floor. He looks between us and, with a nearly invisible shrug, brings the tray over and settles it in my lap. Cecelia remains standing, staring until he turns and asks what she'd like to eat.

"No, nothing, thank you," she replies. "I have some research to do. I'll check back in later."

"Okay," I say with a mouth full of crusty bread. I give her a big, fake grin that I can tell she sees through completely. But she nods and leaves.

"You're sure you're okay, goosey?" Dad asks.

"Perfect," I reply, ignoring the twin pulls in my sternum and pushing away the worries of what they could mean, of what the vision could mean. I am here. With Dad. Eating snacks and being a keeper, and if there's something wrong with me, well, what else is new? There has always been something deeply, fundamentally wrong with me.

I ignore it and take a bite of cheese.

A few days later, I'm asked to head out to the pegasus cliffs to fix a fence. Maxia's grown clumsy in her old age, and no one wants her to stumble over the edge of the crumbling rock. She may end up flinging herself into the abyss before her ancient wings fully unfurl.

I've just left the barns when Etana finds me. She's been following me around for days, watching me closely, but shying away anytime I approach too directly.

Yesterday, I found her in the town square, eating Petra's holly bush and waiting for me to finish my turn cooking the order's breakfast. She followed me all through chores to midday meditations, then stood outside the house, moving from room to room to room as I cleaned.

The children love it, to have a typically elusive unicorn so close. They toss her apples and carrots and handfuls of grass and dare each other to climb upon her back or stroke her silky nose.

She's been tolerant, but thankfully none of them has gotten too close. They run away squealing whenever she turns her curious, but intimidating, horned head in their direction.

I went to bed last night with her peering up at my window, then woke to find her gone at last. Relieved, I collected my tools, hitched up a mule, and loaded up a wagon with the necessary lumber for my repairs, blissfully unencumbered by a pregnant unicorn with a newly developed attachment disorder.

We head out to the cliffs, skirting the edge of the small creek that winds through the valley and the hills where the jackalopes most often play. I keep an eye on the sky for Enkidus, but no one has seen her since she ate the gryphon.

As we approach the matching hut, Etana gets aggravated and begins to circle, pacing before me and the trudging mule.

"Stop that," I say sternly as the mule tries to sidestep and the wagon dips into a rut, then slides a bit toward the creek. The mule's ears are flattened agains his head, and his teeth are showing slightly as he champs on his bit. "You're making him anxious."

Etana snorts.

I can see the pegasus cliffs in the far-off distance in one direction, the forest to my right, and the matching hut and its meadow in the nearer distance to my left. For a moment, I feel as if the valley inhales, waiting for me to choose a course between three life-changing paths, which is silly. The big life change just happened. I became the matcher.

My life is determined.

I click my tongue at the mule, a signal to start going again. There is a fence to fix. Etana moves in front of us and lowers her head, her horn pointed right at him. He throws his head back, taking a step backward and then another, bumping into the wagon and pushing it off the path.

I hurry forward to stand between them and clap at Etana. "Stop. We do not threaten our friends. Especially not while they're working."

Etana stomps and tosses her head at me. The mule tries to move sideways, to get away from this strange, threatening creature in his path. If he pushes the heavy wagon any farther into the field, we'll all be stuck in the soft, lumpy earth. I step close to Etana, and she bows low like she did before the matching ceremony.

"Not again. You're pregnant. And creatures aren't for riding." She snorts at me, and I rest my hand on her back, sighing. She is even more stubborn than the mule. "But I'll follow, if you insist."

After a long moment, she moves forward into the firmer, untilled meadow and out of the mule's path, which he takes instant advantage of. He maneuvers the heavy cart around then stomps toward home at the quickest clop I've ever seen any mule achieve. He does not need me to lead the way.

Before he is even fifty yards away, Etana begins moving quickly across the uneven ground, and I have to half walk, half jog to keep up. I know where we are headed, and the closer we get, the more my stomach roils.

She stops before the hut, practically on top of the narrow porch. I hear a thumping, low and steady, but I'm uncertain whether it is coming from inside the hut or my own anticipatory heart.

I want to run.

Thud-thud. *Go away.* Thud-thud. *Run away.* Thud-thud. *Get far, far away.*

But I do not run. I creep up to the door, creaking across the porch to whatever waits, impatient and hungry, in the dark.

I should be wearing a mask or should at least cover my face in some way. I know this. And yet, a deep part of me also knows it doesn't matter. The worst has already happened.

She is waiting to welcome me back.

I open the door and scan the dim room. There on the top shelf sits the phoenix. I swear I hear it singing. A song of relief, of joy, of satisfaction.

Mesmerized, I step closer and reach up. My fingers barely brush the beak. I look around, find the step stool just to my left, and tug it over, climbing closer until I can gently lift the skull.

On, on, on, it sings to me through my palms. *Yes, yes, yes.*

I should not do this.

And yet, I do. I rest the phoenix on my brow. The fit isn't perfect. I need to adjust the leather bands, hollow out a bit at the brow to better suit my face, and pad the bone to sit snugger on my cheeks, but that would all come later.

Right now, I sway as the phoenix's feelings rush through me.

I experience the joy of flying, the grief of losing an egg out of a precariously high perch, the contentment of nesting with my soul's mate. Interspersed with her living memories are her current feelings. Elation at being awake after a long sleep. Her fondness for me. Satisfaction from seeing her mate match with Kian.

I wonder at that, and the phoenix responds, sending a visual image of Kian and me, naked, together in a nest of blankets, enjoying the intimacies of our featherless bodies pressed and moving together. Paired. Forever.

"No!"

I pull at the mask to remove it, my face hot. But now that the phoenix has put the image in my mind, and feelings in my heart, I can't seem to shake them. The broad expanse of his shoulders, the definition of his arms, the perfect expanse of his stomach. The softness of the fine, dark hair on his legs, tangled with mine.

I know what he would feel like, his body on my body, and I want that again with a fierceness that terrifies me.

But he was temporary. Not forever.

I tug the mask again. It does not budge. I feel around in my hair for the leather ties, my fingers scrambling, but they hang loose. Nothing holds the skull to my face but the phoenix herself.

She will not release me.

I pull again, digging along the edges of the skull, scratching the skin on my nose and forehead as I tried to leverage better purchase. I begin to panic. I pour on oils, massaging them into my hairline, and then when that doesn't help, I dump the old, leftover water from the pitcher onto my face. I splutter, wet and oily, bleeding.

"Phoenix," I say aloud, "let me go. Please."

If a long-dead bird could laugh, she does. She floods me with feelings and images. There aren't specific words from her, but it feels like, *There is no letting go. Our souls are joined. And until you acknowledge that joining, I will not release you.*

Impossible.

It's impossible.

A keeper, matching with a skull. It is an abomination.

Magnificent, flows from the phoenix.

I whimper, feeling sorry for myself for one long moment; then I get to work. I spend the afternoon doing everything I can think of to pry the mask from my face. I use tools. Cajoling. Empty and then very sincere promises. Threats. My own fingernails, trying to dig under the edge of the skull, until they are broken and my face is bleeding.

Nothing works. Finally, exhausted, with eyes puffy from crying and fingers sore from trying and failing to pry the bone from my face, I exit the matching hut.

Etana waits.

This time, I climb upon her proffered back, too exhausted and desolate to protest. She takes me to the village square, to the steps of the great hall. I try to climb down. I want to go home. Preferably before anyone sees me and I have to explain why I'm wearing a fucking skull. But before I can slide off, Etana trots up the steps of the hall, and pushes open the larger double doors with her head. With a great shiver, she throws me off her back into a heap, right into the middle of the meeting of elders and order.

I stand in my dirty woolen shirt and trousers, covered in oil and dirt and water, and look into the face of my father. He's sitting at a large, round table, the eight keeper elders surrounding him, along with High Priestess Sarai, her assistant, and the newly matched, and unmatched, novitiates.

I feel Kian start forward before I see him. Apparently the bond between our matching phoenix skulls comes with a disturbingly precise knowledge of where that too-beautiful man is at all times. I shove away the numerous implications of that; one crisis at a time.

I turn to the shocked, despairing face of my father and feel as if I am three again, instead of thirty-three.

"Dad." My voice cracks. "Help me."

Chapter Ten

ADELA

"I can't remove her," I admit.

For a brief moment, it is so quiet that I can hear Etana's breath echoing in the painted, domed ceiling of the great hall, and then the room erupts. Keepers, priestesses, and novitiates step forward, talking and yelling. I stand frozen with a unicorn pressed against me like a dog seeking comfort.

Or perhaps I am pressed against her.

How stupid I am to have followed the call back to the matching hut. To have raised my face to the phoenix and allowed her to capture me. To have ever put my cheek against her bone in the first place.

I do not want this.

I wonder if any of the novitiates ever felt this way. If they ever wanted to escape the fate of wearing the skull of a dead creature for the rest of their life. But of course not. The goal of being in an order to begin with is the opportunity to pair with a creature, to obtain magic, and, with it, power, influence, the ability to help their communities.

But I am not a novitiate; I am the matcher. The order and people of Insborough are not my community; the valley is.

I plead with the phoenix again. *Let me go. You are not meant for me.*

If anything, she grips harder.

A bubble of hysterical laughter escapes me, and I reach across Etana's swayed back, burying my fingers into the coarseness of her hairs. The touch solidifies me somehow. I try to look past everyone at the walls of the great hall, covered in familiar tapestries and sculptures, paintings and sketches and carvings. There is even an ancient, hand-hewn boat hanging from a corner of the ceiling. The stories and records of a millennia of keepers.

Cecelia and I used to spend hours here as kids, staring at the pieces, finding our favorite little scenes and arguing about which stories were true and which were legend. Not that it matters. Truth exists in both history and fiction.

If one of our artists portrays this moment, there will be no need to embellish the impulsive matcher who accidentally paired herself with a phoenix. The barest of facts will be scintillating all on their own.

People rush us, surrounding me and Etana, peppering me with accusations.

"What is the meaning of this? What have you done?"

"Is that a phoenix? It looks just like his."

"What were you thinking, girl?"

"Of all of the stupid—" someone begins, a raw, building violence in their voice. I don't turn to see if it's someone I know, or someone from the order.

I turn my face into Etana's side, nauseous. This is not who I'm meant to be. A matcher should be revered by the order and respected by their fellow keepers. I am a disgrace.

Dad finally maneuvers through the others and reaches me. The moment he touches my arm, the chaos of the room softens. He pulls me away from Etana, turning me toward him and takes my jaw in his hands, moving my head this way and that, assessing. He grimaces when he finds my self-inflicted wounds, the places where I've tried and failed to remove the skull.

My lower lip wobbles uncontrollably. "I messed up."

"Looks like it." His thick, calloused fingers are gentle as they trace the edges of the skull. He pulls on it so, so carefully, his healer hands both strong and tender.

The skull doesn't budge.

High Priestess Sarai steps forward. She wears her typical flowing black gown and a sheer black floor-length veil over her bejeweled unicorn skull.

Etana lowers her head, taking a threatening stance against the priestess. I place a gentling hand on her back, but she does not relax. She stomps the marble floor, hard enough that I feel the reverberation through my own feet.

The high priestess stops but does not cower or retreat. She ought to be more afraid, but she probably has never seen someone impaled by an overprotective unicorn.

Dad watches Etana carefully.

He has.

If only I could climb back on Etana and we could both run away. But she brought me here to seek everyone's help—or perhaps to face their judgment. Creatures' motives are their own.

"I'm glad you've joined us." The high priestess steps forward again and loops her arm through mine. Etana allows it, but watches closely.

High Priestess Sarai leads me to the large meeting table and now-empty chairs. She sits and pulls me down beside her. "We were just discussing timelines for Brother Thad's funeral and completing the matching ceremony, and we could use your input."

"The-the matching ceremony?" I stammer. Surely she can see the phoenix skull on my face. How I've failed. "I can't complete further matches."

She tilts her head, a kind smile on her face, and reaches for my hand. "Can't you?" She squeezes my hand like Mom used to, as if to give me courage. "I think it's worth trying. Especially since the high priestesses of the Pupil, the Spinner, and I have recently been discussing our contributions to the valley. I don't want to give them an excuse to follow through on their threats of reducing donations."

There is some grumbling amongst the elders, though this is nothing new. The orders are constantly insinuating that they will withdraw their financial supports if the magic and matches don't improve soon. But I always thought it was the Order of the Huntress who wanted to reduce their funds. High Priestess Sarai implies otherwise, which is comforting.

John points at me. "The rest of us shouldn't have to suffer for *her* failures." I barely hold back, sticking my tongue out like a child. He's rude, but unfortunately, also right.

"Failures?" A small voice pops up. The crowd parts, and I see Cecelia. She must be taking notes for the elders again. Her ears are bright red with embarrassment. She hates confrontation. "She made unprecedented matches at the first ceremony she led. A dragon. A phoenix. Gytrash."

"What use will two-thirds of a gytrash trio be to them?" John scoffs, and I hear the unmatched novitiate of the gytrash triad mumble in agreement.

Petra steps forward. Her back is straight, her lined face thoughtful, and her tone as gentle but firm as always. Just like Dad's. "We will find out what the gytrash can do when we prepare Brother Thad for rest. In the meantime, blame does not get us to solutions."

Still red-eared, Cecelia clears her throat. Despite her unease, her words are steady. "I'd like to check the records more—the art, journals, the older books. I started looking into the pulses we felt, but hadn't gotten far. I'll also try to find information on phoenix skulls. Maybe there's some sort of ceremony or magic that could—"

John interrupts. "Undo this mess?"

Petra gives John a look that silences him, then takes the notes from Cecelia. "Thank you. We can manage the rest here if you'd like to get to work immediately." As Cecelia hurries out of the room, Petra asks the rest of us, "Any other suggestions?"

"Burn it off," says the male novitiate whose partners wear the gytrash. He's not mumbling now. His voice is ice. "We have a dragon-wielder again."

The room grows heavy with silence. All I can think of is Bartholomew, the ashes of his home, his body. There was so little left of him. Are they all actually considering this for me and by an untrained novitiate? There's no way I'd survive.

Dad wraps his thick arms around me, pulling me close as if to shield me. I lean my head forward, to rest it on his shoulder as I've done since I was teenager. Only my head doesn't fit where it should.

When I lean forward, the beak of the phoenix skull connects with his bare neck. He flinches, and I see a line of blood form. I've cut him. After a brief hesitation, he pulls me in again, positioning my head, but the damage is done. For the first time in my entire life, my father has flinched away from me. I have harmed him. I am unsafe.

Now I do crumple. I sink onto the ground, wrapping my arms around my knees and burying my masked face between them. Etana stands over me, but she is not enough to block out the sound, the anger, the disappointment of everyone.

And through it all, the phoenix shoves feelings through me. I cannot tune her out. I cannot tune any of them out. I am sinking, drowning in the noise, in the pain. And then there is another figure above me.

"Stop this!" He demands it with enough confidence that the others hush. "No one is trusting Ulric to control a newly dead dragon's magic with such precision. He would likely destroy the skull and the matcher in one go. And then where would you be? You'd have no matcher and no phoenix."

I look up, unsurprised to find Kian beside me. I wish I could see his beautiful face. But of course he is wearing his phoenix skull, the mirror image to mine. Members of the order who have been paired to creature skulls wear them in public forever. Even after death.

A pang of disappointment ripples through me, but it's not as if I'm entitled to miss his face. He was a brief fling, a distraction, and ultimately, the impulse that got me here.

"You wear a phoenix, so we would have one. What do we need with two?" snaps the man without the gytrash. His resentment is palpable. "Besides, we don't even know what good the phoenix is. So what loss is that?"

"The phoenixes are a matched set," Kian replies, softly. "The visions have been clear."

Everyone falls utterly silent. I can hear Etana's soft breaths. Even the phoenix's feelings stop bombarding me. I could kiss him.

No. Kissing him is dangerous. Kissing him is what got me in this mess from the start.

"There is no rush to unpair Adela," High Priestess Sarai says. "We will move forward with our plans for Brother Thad and completing the matching. If she cannot perform her duties, then we will worry about unpairing—" Her red lips twist into a smile that sends chills down me. "Or not. And she'll join the order."

Everything shifts. *That* is not an option. I might not have wanted to be a matcher, but just the thought of leaving my community to go join the Order of the Huntress is agonizing.

Kian places fingertips beneath the edge of the skull just like Dad did. The phoenix basically purrs, a feeling so deep that it resonates through me as a sound.

His fingers are warm and soft against my temples.

I lean in to his comforting touch.

He whispers unintelligible words in a sweet tone, and I can feel the phoenix relax ever so slightly. He is able to get fingers underneath the skull, up to his second knuckle. For a brief moment, I have hope that this time will work. That I will be free.

The moment I think it, the phoenix clamps down, pinching his fingers and scraping me raw. I feel something warm and wet trickle down my cheek.

Dad steps forward and wipes it away. His thumb is bright red with my blood.

"We have to get this off of you," he says.

Before I can agree, the world goes hazy.

I am flying across a clouded sky alongside my love. Below us is a field of corn that should be golden and rustling, healthy. The humans should be harvesting the ears as jackalopes and ordinary hares and birds hop around, munching on spilled kernels.

But the keepers are hidden away in their building. The creatures' and animals' bellies rumble with hunger. The cornstalks do not rustle. They are black and wilted.

Rotten.

With a gasp, I return to the present just in time to see a golden pulse of light.

Etana rears up, coming down hard beside Kian, who is sitting next to me on the ground, holding his head. He doesn't react. My phoenix is distressed at his distress, but before I can move forward to check on him, I hear the screams of children.

No. Not again.

As I scramble up, I pray to the great goddess. The first time Enkidus attacked was just after I had recklessly put my cheek against the skull. The last time just after I matched with the phoenix. Let this not be another.

I cannot be responsible for this much death, this much destruction.

Etana rears again, snorting and throwing her head. I ignore her, too busy rushing out of the hall, hoping that the dragon will stay far away, satiated with her gryphon meal. Though he's wobbly on his feet, Kian joins us. The phoenix is glad for his presence. Or perhaps I am. It's hard to tell what is the two phoenixes drawing us together and what is our own, very obvious, chemistry.

We burst out of the hall and down the steps. The screaming of small voices continues, growing louder as we near the open field next to the school. There, I pause and take in the scene before me.

Half a dozen children huddle tight together on the ground while three spotted cath palugs circle them.

Cath palugs are disturbing. They're like large house cats, with their round eyes and sweet faces, and unnaturally fast, aggressive when they feel threatened. They're also typically reclusive, living in the mountainous caves at the far outer edges of the valley, and not coming anywhere near the village except when they are about to die.

I have seen only a glimpse of a single cath palug in my entire life as a keeper. Never within the boundary of the village, which is protected by magic from any ill-intentioned creatures.

And now here are three, who've invaded just after the golden light pulsed through the valley, at the heels of my vision. A chill goes through me. This is most certainly a result of my actions.

At least it's not Enkidus. Though cath palugs are plenty capable of bodily harm. As they've already demonstrated.

The large feline creatures stalk back and forth. A handful of other keepers have arrived, including some parents of the children. One, Marcella, steps forward out of the gathering crowd. She tries to get to her daughter, Aya. The little girl wails as blood drips from a seemingly shallow cut on her cheek.

A cath palug hisses and swipes sharp, hooked claws at Marcella when she gets too close. The swipe connects, cutting open her shin so deeply that I can see the shine of white bone beneath. She falls too far to help her daughter and struggles to get up again.

The cath palug crouches, preparing to pounce.

On the other side of the bloody scene, I yell, catching the attention of the creature. She paces away, allowing Frederic and Taylor to pull Marcella back and start to help her staunch the bleeding.

Some of the keepers grab sticks and small rocks and wave or toss them at the cath palug. No one wants to risk throwing things with any heft in case they hit a child. The cath palugs hiss and growl.

The order arrives, but do nothing but watch, concerned but useless. Not that they could do much, despite the skulls they wear. They're mostly novitiates. Untested and untrained.

"Why are you just staring?" Marcella screams at them in pain and panic. "You have magic! Use it! Help them."

High Priestess Sarai and Sister Roberta are the only competent magic-wielders, and they wear a unicorn and a pegasus. Depending on the strength of their magic and will, they can set magical barriers and affect moods, or influence the weather. Not exactly useful for an offense against large, magical felines.

Marcella knows this. But she's desperate with her child in danger. Who wouldn't be?

Cecelia arrives from the library. She cries out as the largest of the three creatures stalks forward, predator eyes very clearly focused on Cordelia, her littlest sister. The small girl is at the edge of the group of children, curled into a ball, her back to a cath palug. She whimpers softly, already covered in blood from a large, jagged cut down one arm.

A slightly older boy tries to pull her into the center of the group, but he doesn't have the strength to move her on his own, and the other children are concerned with the other two cath palugs, who keep lunging at them.

I yell and rush forward, Etana on my heels. I have nothing with which to defend or attack, but I can't just stand and watch Cordelia be killed.

The phoenix is noisy in my head, trying to communicate something to me that I can't understand. An unfamiliar pressure builds up inside of me, but I push it down deep. She wants to help, but I don't understand how she could—no living person has any idea what magic a phoenix contains, and even if I did, I would not know how to wield it with any certainty. I'm not going to risk wild, uncontrolled magic around children.

The two cath palugs nearest me turn their attention my way when I get close, including the one stalking Cordelia. If they are intimidated by my noise, or the massive unicorn at my side, they do not show it.

Nearly in sync, they crouch down, then spring in one fluid motion of attack. Etana stomps and throws her head, getting between us. The cath palugs retreat momentarily but circle back. They're pacing, watching, waiting for the right moment to attack again.

I need to defend us. I scan the ground for something, anything, to use and spot a large fieldstone half out of the ground. I drop to my knees and dig frantically, using my fingers to leverage it out.

It's substantial. Using both hands, I heft it up over my head. My arms wobble with the effort, but when a cath palug gets near, I fling it as hard as I can.

It connects, but barely, glancing off the side of one of the creatures. It's enough to scare her, and she jumps away, toward Etana, who kicks and makes contact. The cath palug flies through the air, landing in a limp, unmoving pile. That one will never be worn by a priestess or priest. Even amidst the chaos of keepers rushing to it, I can see its skull has been crushed.

The other two continue their stalking and attacking.

Pip, Mathew, and Esme arrive with actual bo staffs. They swing the long poles much more effectively than those with small, randomly found sticks and branches. The cath palugs still easily dodge the sturdy poles. At last they're distracted from the children, but they remain aggressive.

One turns to the small group of novitiates. When it focuses on Svena, the unmatched woman, the novitiate wielding Gilcriss steps out of their huddle. He inhales and raises his hands. I want to stop him. I want to encourage him. He has no training. But what else is there to do?

In the air, a pressure that feels like an oncoming storm begins to build. The hairs on the back of my neck raise with the growing magic. The cath palugs and Etana stop moving.

"No!" Cecelia and Dad call out simultaneously. But it is too late. The dragon-wearer drops his hands suddenly and dramatically.

His gestures mean nothing. It is his will that releases the wild, explosive magic. A torrent of fire flares up from the ground in a perfect circle around the children. The cath palugs scream, an awful, panicked sound that cuts through my soul.

Nearly instantly, they are gone. Nothing but two piles of ash. The fire dissipates almost immediately.

Parents rush forward to their children, scooping them up and attending to their wounds. Cecelia picks up her sister, who is still bleeding profusely, but her breathing is steady.

"Hi, Lia," Cordelia says in a small voice, using their family's nickname for Cecelia. "Those were mean kitties."

Cecelia doesn't bother correcting her sister on calling the creatures "kitties," just carries her alongside the other wounded children into the squat stone school for caregiving. Dad follows, his healer's nature irrepressible.

The children who aren't hurt are bundled up by their parents and taken home, their little faces streaked with tears or frozen with terror.

No one is going to sleep well tonight.

I step back from them all, being neither a healer nor a parent, and bump into something firm. I turn to find Kian hovering.

He must see something around my eyes or in my posture. "You okay?" he asks.

"Of course." The quiver in my voice betrays the lie. The muscles in my legs tremble. People and creatures keep dying; now children are hurt.

And all of it began after I had woken the phoenixes. If I had just done what I needed to do with a keeper's willingness to serve, without impulsively chasing my disastrous curiosity, no one would be dead. No one would be hurt. I wouldn't have a phoenix skull permanently attached to my face.

I hate that I cry. The skin around the skull feels bruised and broken, slick from the various fats I used trying to remove it, and stinging from the salt of my tears.

The phoenix tries to communicate with me in images and feelings, but I shove her to a tiny corner of my mind as well as I can and plop down on the mostly frozen ground.

Kian sits beside me. "How can I help, beauty?" His voice is as dangerous as the rest of him. He puts a hand on my shoulder, and a warmth flows through me, soothing me. Even the pain of my wounds eases slightly.

It gives me clarity. I have to sever this bond.

But not tonight.

I stare up at the sky. I wonder what the spring skies will bring to the valley. Likely another disappointing season, with too-frozen ground preventing a timely planting and then too much rain drowning the slow-growing seedlings.

It's the same sky I have looked at my entire life. The sky that I have cried beneath, had sex beneath, dreamed beneath. When I was little, those dreams were silly. I wanted purple hair and a kitten.

Now I'm uncertain of what my dreams even are, and the sky feels wholly unfamiliar.

I turn my face to Kian, pressing the forehead of the skull against his forearm. I am borrowing worries from the future when I have one attached to my face to fret over now.

I am not particularly faithful. Faith has always been something that's just a given. The Spinner, the Pupil, and the Huntress are a given—three aspects of the great goddess. As keepers, we serve her alongside the orders. But she hasn't meant much more to me, either as a force to fret about, or as one to lean in to for comfort or guidance.

I think about one of the last conversations I had with my mom, about how outside the valley, people do not speak to the great goddess. They go to the orders and ask, or pay, for intercession. But here in the valley, we are closer to her. We care for her creatures, and in thanks, she hears us directly and answers us.

If only we are brave enough to hear her voice.

Mom said the goddess is complex, and her answers are hard to find, but answers to supplication come in three varieties.

Yes.

No.

Wait.

Silently, I speak directly to her.

Goddess of all, lightness and dark, the complex and the simple, growth and death, I beseech you. Guide my heart and my feet. Show me what paths I have available and provide me with clarity as I make my choices.

And please, get this skull unstuck from my face.

The clouds part. I see the wink of a star in the darkening evening sky. This is my answer. The star disappears behind a cloud. Wait, it seems to say. Wait and see what will be revealed, or hidden.

Whatever the future holds, I will figure it out. As long as I am brave enough to try.

Chapter Eleven

KIAN

Adela asks me to take her home, and I do not hesitate. She looks so fragile, so defeated, so different from the confident, bold woman who joyously rode a unicorn across unseasonably wintery fields, took her pleasure from me, and then the very next day led the most successful matching ceremony in recent history.

I put my shoulder under her arm and hold her tight, making her lean on me. We cross the village in the direction she points out.

I breathe in Adela's soft floral scent and murmur calming nothingness into her hair. The phoenix skull wants to nurture her, to protect and comfort her. And while I am no sort of caregiver, I find myself wanting the same.

There is a sort of buzzing sensation where her body connects to mine, and I can't tell where my own pull to her stops and where the phoenix's begins. I wish I disliked it more than I do.

But she is fiery and vigorous and more enticing than anyone ought to be. I have no space for depth or constancy, but part of me wants to keep her close. Forever.

Surely *that* compulsion is the phoenix.

I shiver and scour my mind for something, anything, else to think about.

In the distance, there are snow-dusted fields waiting for spring thaw. And beyond them, the forest where my aunt, Ivo, and whoever is with them, wait.

Right.

Perhaps that's where I should be focused—on the whole reason I'm in this valley to begin with. I need to make my way to my aunt. It's been two days, and she's surely growing impatient, but there hasn't been a chance yet.

The phoenix throws images of Adela and me fucking in the pantry.

Okay, there's been a chance or two and I let myself be distracted. But I'll make my way to my family. Later tonight. I'll get back on track.

We crunch across the frozen grass, and I consider how unjust it is that the valley has all of the magical creatures and none of the advantages of magic.

"In Insborough, there are gardens that grow fruit and vegetables all year round, regardless of the weather. There are lemon trees and blueberry bushes thriving while snow accumulates along the gardens' fences."

"Oh." It's a simple sound, but full of awe, with a touch of sadness. "How lovely it sounds. I wish I could see it."

Of course she can't. Keepers are kept inside their magical, dying valley just like the rest of us are kept out. They don't know the path through the wards, and trying to leave would mean death or dismemberment, just like it does for those trying to enter.

The phoenix sends a certainty that he will stay with his mate. Perhaps he's right. Now that she wears a phoenix skull, her future might be different. Moments like the one in the pantry could happen again, and again, and again.

The phoenix flares with joy, but I shove the sensations away sharply. Whether she stays in the valley or leaves, whether she stays matcher or pursues some other future now that she wears a creature skull, she is not mine to want.

Nor would she consent to be, if she knew who I truly am. How I desire to destroy the valley's skulls and rob her friends and family of their security. She would loathe me.

After just a few minutes, we're at her door. I release her. I should go. I think of my aunt and whoever she has with her, waiting in the cold forest.

She sways. I cannot leave. "May I help you into bed?"

She gives a small, exhausted nod.

Inside, I help her remove her cloak, hanging it on the hook beside the door, and have her lean on me up the steep, narrow stairs.

"Bath or bed?" I ask. She's clearly exhausted, but she's also filthy, covered in dirt and oil and blood.

She hesitates.

"I can help or give you space," I offer. "With either."

"Help. Bath," she says softly, and points down the hall.

A large copper tub with running water and supplies to heat it sits in the middle of a bathroom. She leans against the wall while I lather soap under the running water to create bubbles. Once it's finished heating, I gesture to it.

In one quick movement, too fast for me to even turn away and provide her a modicum of privacy, she reaches down, grabs the hem of her shirt, and strips it off.

I'm a lecher for wishing she were fully naked, but a thin chemise still covers her. Not that I need to see her skin to marvel at her beauty.

"Help," she says, her voice small and pathetic, and I snap my eyes away from ogling the poor, exhausted woman's tits to find her stuck with her shirt around her head. Or, more specifically, around the phoenix skull.

I half cough, half guffaw in surprise, then spring to action, trying to unhook her newly attached beak and ease it and the rest of her head through the shirt's neckline. It's too big, and after a few minutes of trying it this way and that, I finally rip the shirt down the back seam and get her free. Then I help her with the rest.

I manage to ignore my loud, base instincts to soak in the lushness of her body and focus on assisting as she climbs into the bath.

I kneel behind her on the floor and begin to gently undo her braids. I should hurry. Go to the forest. But I move slowly, enjoying the way her silken hair feels in my fingers.

"Do you have cousins?" I ask, thinking of Ivo.

"No. My parents were both only children." Her voice is a little wistful when she says, "I always wanted a big family."

"I have twenty-seven cousins on my mom's side."

She gasps. "I didn't think families came that big. Were you close?"

"Still are." I find a comb and brush through her wavy strands, finding any snarls. "They live in Insborough, so I'm able to see them frequently."

More frequently than is smart sometimes, sneaking away to provide information on where the order leaders will be and when, or targets for stealing precious objects.

She sinks a little deeper into the water.

"I'll wash your hair for you." I take the soap, lathering it in my hands and scrub her scalp, especially along the edge of the phoenix skull, then rinse. I repeat the steps twice to get the blood and dirt out.

"What do you do together?" she asks in a sleepy voice as I help her rinse the second time. She says it as if she's asked me to tell her a bedtime story, and so I do. Half to distract myself from the intimacy of it all. And how much I like it.

"One of our favorite things to do as a family is play games. A family favorite is Dupe the Dud. Do you know it?"

She shakes her head.

"It's a vicious game. Most of the players are on the same team and blindfolded. The others are working to put a ball in a goal. The blindfolded players aren't allowed to move from their designated spots, but they have sticks that they can use to hit the ball."

"Sounds fairly straightforward. What makes it vicious?"

"My family." I laugh. "Especially when the littlest ones play. They don't have any regard for how much power they're capable of yet, so they don't hold back when they swing their sticks, even if they're more likely to connect with your shins than the ball."

"Sounds treacherous." Her tone is teasing.

"I have actual scars from this game. It's brutal." I stand and move around the tub, lifting my robes. I like the way her eyes, even while clearly exhausted, take in my legs. I flex my calves as I bend down and point to a couple of white scars.

She inhales deeply, clearly enjoying my obvious display. I like the way she watches. The way I clearly affect her. As she affects me.

Even her freckled shoulders sticking out of the sudsy water turn me on.

I focus on the scars.

"This one is from Cousin Ava, and this one from another cousin, Jaxa. She was only six when she did that. I swear it bled for a week."

"If it did, you needed sutures."

"I had them!"

Her smile is like a shooting star, a brilliant, delightful brightness, and I move back to my place behind her so I don't stand gaping at the beauty of her.

"The tenderhearted girl cried for about a week," I say as I lightly oil the ends of her hair, to prevent future snarls. "Because she hurt me."

"It sounds perfect." Her voice is thick with sleepiness, so I don't respond with words. I take a cloth and wash her face, trying to be gentle with the self-inflicted wounds.

I think of how gently Ulric washed my back, which oddly doesn't hurt at the moment. But I push Ulric from my mind. I cannot face thoughts of him right now. Of how I failed to reciprocate his kindness when we were together, of the ways I might have to use him in order to obtain the dragon fire I need to destroy the skulls.

Or perhaps he won't come into play at all, if I can figure out the magic of the phoenix in time. If it is anywhere near as powerful as I suspect it might be.

When Adela's fully clean and fairly prune-like from soaking in the water, I stand her up and dry her off, wrapping her in a large towel. The intimacy of it all leaves me feeling raw, exposed, but she needs help and I'm not a monster. I comb through her hair once again and then put it in a simple braid so it's out of her way as she sleeps.

She directs me to her room, which is tiny, with a simple, narrow bed. There's a trunk at its foot covered in various pieces of gilded bone jewelry and a small table with a pitcher, basin, and wavy mirror. In the corner sits an armoire so old and rickety that it looks as if it's barely able to hold up Adela as she leans against it, her eyes closed, either in pain or exhaustion.

"Why's your room so sad?" I tease. All I can focus on is her narrow bed. All I want is to climb in with her and hold her. Teasing is safer. "My guest space is bigger and nicer than this, and I thought that was rather pathetic when I first arrived."

"We live simpler lives than those in the Huntress's service." A wry smile curves her lips below the phoenix skull's edge. "And have fewer bed partners to entertain than your lot typically does during your visits."

I like seeing her smile, the way it erases a tiny bit of the pain from her eyes. I plop down on the bed and bounce. It releases a loud squeak, then another when I jump again. "How do you entertain any bed partners with that racket?"

"I do alright."

"Of course you do." My voice is huskier than I expect, thick with want. I look her up and down. She's beautiful and kind and powerful. Who wouldn't want her attentions? "With a bit of lubrication, you might eliminate the wrong squeaks and increase the right kind."

She blushes, as if she can read my carnal thoughts. I can see the flush roll down her neck and onto her chest. I've embarrassed her with my interest, but she doesn't turn away. She's considering. But then she gives her head a little shake. Her voice is playful but distant when she says, "Lubricant. Got it. Tip top of my priority list. As soon as I sleep."

With an unbothered shrug, I get her dressed in warm clothes and rub an ointment that smells of lemon verbena into the tender skin of her face around the edge of the phoenix skull. She flinches and sucks her teeth, and I feel a sharp pang of worry from my phoenix.

When she is rested and feeling up to it, we'll have to discuss all of this. Our matching skulls. The emotions they send through us. The draw to each other. What it means, and most important, how we get rid of it. I cannot mortally wound a religious order if I get a jolt of concern every time Adela stubs her toe.

But that's a conversation for another day.

She crawls up to the head of her bed, where she collapses on the pillow and does not move. I wrestle the covers from under her, then pull them up to her chin, like I used to wish my parents could do for me after they died.

I was too old to be tucked in, but I still wanted the comfort of being put to bed.

"Thank you," she mumbles.

If only I could do more. I hate that she has to sleep with the hard shell of the phoenix's skull attached to her face. It can't be comfortable. Mine is currently resting too hard on the bridge of my nose, and a handful of hairs have gotten caught in the tie, pulling whenever I turn my head.

"Stay."

There's no question at the end of that one, simple word and yet it is not a command. It's a request. And I find myself longing to meet it. Maybe because the phoenix is elated to be so close to his mate. He wants to touch her, to reassure himself that they are both here after their long, silent sleep.

Maybe for my own reasons that I can't quite define.

Either way, I can't. Of course I can't. I need to go traipse through the dragon-infested woods to find my family. Make sure everyone is safe. Figure out a new plan to destroy the skulls that avoids harming Ulric.

But she reaches out a hand from under the covers and takes hold of me. Her eyes are still closed, in the twilight between wakefulness and sleep. I wait a moment then try to disentangle myself, causing her to whimper.

With something between resignation and elation, I carefully remove the skull and shift to push it up atop the small table, propped against the pitcher and basin.

I lie down beside her, on top of the covers, my ass half-hanging off the narrow bed, and hold absolutely still so I don't disturb her. I intend to stay only long enough to see her firmly cross the threshold of sleep and then leave. Her breathing grows heavy and steady. Before I know what's happening, I follow her into sweet oblivion.

Chapter Twelve

KIAN

I wake with a large, warm, perfect ass pressed against me. The pink and golden glow of sunrise shines in through the single window of her room, illuminating her thoroughly disheveled and curved form. Spinner's tits. I've slept here the whole night.

Who knows what Aunt Ujvala will do after another night of camping in the valley forests. Probably follow the path back out of the valley and home. Her philanthropy toward the endeavors of her favorite, and most obnoxious, nephew only extends so far.

I hop up out of the bed, shaking myself to divert blood flow back to my brain. I hurry to straighten my clothes and rub the sleep out of my eyes, grabbing my phoenix skull as I rush down the stairs as quickly and quietly as I can. The day is cold but beautiful, with fluffy white clouds in the still-vibrant sunrise sky.

I don't return to my rooms. One of the advantages of robes is that they look the same one day to the next, so no one will know that I slept in them—except perhaps for the wrinkles. I head immediately to the forest to find my family. But I stumble across Sister Roberta in the village square. I curse silently under my breath for forgetting we were supposed to meet here by the fountain for morning prayers, and to begin our work accessing the magic of our creature skulls. Her eyes narrow slightly in suspicion. "Unlike you, Kian, to be the first to arrive."

"Just eager to find out what this thing can do," I reply, tapping on the beak of the phoenix. While I do want to connect with Aunt Ujvala, it's not an exaggeration. I'm eager to learn what magic I might be able to exploit in my quest to disrupt the order.

"So say we all," she replies earnestly.

When the others arrive, we make a semicircle as instructed, and I brace myself for yet another absurd ceremony or song or prayer to perform. Can't take a step forward to full priesthood without performing some ludicrously complex ritual.

Sister Roberta begins, "You are fated to pair with whatever skull has chosen you. The power you are able to yield is directly proportional to how highly the Huntress values you."

Right.

Fate is not something I believe in on the best of days, and blessings even less. Why would the triune goddess give a single fuck about whether I wear a common jackalope or a rare extinct phoenix when there are people in this world dying from hunger or disease? Surely she has other things to take up her time and attention.

But if she does give a shit—or even exists—I hope her attention is on those being taken advantage of by the orders and she'll find my quest worthy enough to bless. Or at least not thwart.

Sister Roberta continues, gesturing to the hard ground. "The bulk of your training and practice will happen back in the temple, but here, where the magic originates, is where we begin. Kneel, pressing the foreheads of your skulls to the ground."

I groan as I drop to my knees and lean forward. Beside me, Ulric hisses in pain and shifts his robes so they aren't so tight across his back. I roll my shoulders. I'm a little stiff, but there's no sensation of skin about to rip away from scabs like there ought to be. Just yesterday I woke with pus dried to my sheets.

"Say your thanksgiving to the great goddess and to the valley and the creatures who serve her through you."

It's odd to hear a priestess talk about the great goddess. Usually they are all about just the individual goddess they serve, especially those who serve the Huntress. But I suppose here in the valley, at this moment, the scope is wider.

With my head pressed to the cold ground and the smell of half-thawing grasses in my nose, I find myself drifting through the visions I've seen and the feelings the phoenix has sent my way. I thought being matched would be awful. I dreaded it, but there are moments I've actually found it rather comforting. There's a strange sense of camaraderie that I haven't felt since I decided to join the order and live with my feet in two different worlds, never allowing either to fully know me.

I whisper my gratitude to the earth beneath me and to the creature whose skull I wear, surprised at my own sincerity. After a few moments of quiet contemplation, Sister Roberta leads us through the typical prayers. Then we're each instructed in where to go and who to meet with. Except me.

"What do I do?" I ask.

"Ah, yes, Kian. To be honest, I'm not entirely sure how to help you access your magic. I thought High Priestess Sarai was planning to work with you personally, but perhaps she's changed her mind or been delayed, now that we have the additional complication of the matcher."

She bites her lip, watching the others go in their various directions. Her hands twitch. If she directs me wrong, Sarai will be angry. An ass-kisser like Sister Roberta can't stand the thought of her precious high priestess being cross with her. "I suppose we should have you work with the others. Experiment. See what sparks. You may begin wherever you'd like."

Perfect. I'll briefly see what the others do and if I can mimic them, ending with Ulric, who is out in the fields, closest to the forest. Once I've found at least a sense of my own magic, I'll hurry off to finally meet my family. Surely it won't take long for the phoenix to reveal its power. Before the day is over, I'll know exactly what my next steps are.

Deciding to go in order of most unpleasant to least, I make my way to the chapel where the bodies of the dead are being prayed over for the requisite three days. The chapel is small and old, built with field stones and crumbling mortar. Like many of the smaller places of worship, it consists of six sides with large, leaded windows on each to let in the light. Inside is a marble altar where the bodies lie.

On well-worn aspen benches sit keepers in their bright woolen clothing, continuing the death rites for their former matcher and Thad. I suppose they must ensure their rituals are completed, in case two-thirds of the gytrash can't access their death magic.

Molvi, Ylysia, and Linden are hovering over the bodies. One of the keeper elders, Niclas, explains the differences between the magic of the living gytrash and the abilities wearers can access. He pauses when they see me.

"Why are you here?" Linden asks, chest practically puffing up. He steps between me and his partners. "Trying to steal my place?"

I hold my hands up in mock surrender. "Sister Roberta sent me." While Ylysia and Molvi are perfectly fine humans compared to many order members, there is no world in which I want any part of Linden's life. I'm not certain I even believe in an after, and I have no desire to pretend I'm able to hurry souls there.

Niclas walks forward with the aid of a cane as gnarled as his liver-spotted hands. "Welcome, novitiate Kian," he says. "Join us and we'll see what that phoenix can do, hmm?"

At least he understands.

My stomach rolls as I step closer. Herbs and incense line the space, but it is not enough to cover the scent of rot and char.

"Now," Niclas instructs. "I want you to close your eyes and access your higher self. You ought to be able to sense the souls of the dead."

"I can feel them!" Molvi reaches a hand forward, hovering over the ragged edge of flesh where Thad's right shoulder should be. "It's almost like a little heartbeat, but . . . opposite?"

"Excellent," Niclas encourages, his white beard bobbing as he nods. He turns to Ylysia. "What do you feel?"

Ylysia opens her eyes and just blinks at the keeper, her attention flicking to Linden.

He glowers at us all. "This is ridiculous! We should be making that matcher go back to the hut and finish what she started. What good are we like this?" He gestures to his partners with their gytrash skulls and then at himself, barefaced.

I roll my eyes at his little outburst. A small, petty part of me hopes Linden doesn't receive the match that he's so certain he's entitled to.

"In time, young Linden," Niclas replies and turns his attention again to Ylysia.

"Focus on you, novitiate Ylysia. On the deepest, hidden parts of you. Where you keep your secret hopes and fears. What does that part of yourself tell you about the souls of the beings in front of you?"

Ylysia shifts on her feet, as if she wants to run. Her eyes well with tears. "I–I don't know! I don't have secret parts. And I don't want to do this without Linden." She doesn't look at the bodies before her. "I've never even done the normal death rites. No one I've known has died. Why would the Huntress curse me with a gytrash? I should have matched with a pegasus and been responsible for growing flowers or something."

"The Huntress does not choose your matches," Niclas corrects. "And neither the skulls nor the great goddess make mistakes."

"Just close your eyes, Lys," Molvi replies a little tersely. I've never heard the three of them argue, and a twisted part of me sort of hopes they will. But instead she reaches out a hand and takes her partner's. Her voice softens. "You won't know unless you try. But I'm sure you'll be able to. You're great at everything."

The frown eases from Ylysia's face at the encouragement. I close my eyes along with her, seeing if I, too, can feel the souls of the dead men, but all I get is their stench.

Ew. Enough of that.

Grateful that I have no affinity for the dead, I make a hasty retreat, on to my next attempt.

I find Markus, who is in Svena's room, which looks exactly like my own, except her quilt is composed of soft pinks, purples, and greens. Markus works with soft-spoken Ziba, the youngest of the keeper elders as far as I can tell. They hover over Svena, Ziba observing as Markus rewraps her bandages. He and Ziba half nod to me in greeting, but continue with their work.

Svena waves feebly.

While not totally healed, her side looks significantly better than it did just after she was attacked, much more so than it would on a natural healing timeline. Markus obviously has quite an affinity for healing.

"Looking better, Svena," I say. Her typically light-brown skin is sallow and deep-purple circles sit beneath her eyes. Her breathing deepens and I realize she's fallen asleep. I hope Markus's efforts will return her to herself soon.

When he's done and has cleaned up his supplies, Markus turns to me, his face alight. I grow leery. While Markus and I aren't mortal enemies or anything, we're also not what I'd call friends. "Let me see your back."

Now I realize why he's so keen to see me. He moves behind me, motioning to Ziba to follow. They do.

Except I can't feel the wounds. I pull at my robes and the tunic beneath, and the fabric moves freely. It isn't stuck to any pus or blood that oozed and dried in the night like it has been since the lashing.

Ziba helps, gently pulling the neckline away from my body. "Why would you need to see his back?" they ask Markus.

Markus makes a noise of surprise, tugging my clothing down so far that the front chokes me. "That's strange."

I try to see over my shoulder, but I can't twist far enough around, especially with the phoenix half blocking my peripheral vision.

"Did you have someone heal you already?" Markus asks.

"Who could?" I point out.

Sarai wears a unicorn, and Roberta a pegasus. Neither can heal a scratch. Nor would they, since one is responsible for the wounds and the other an accomplice to their creation.

"Maybe the phoenix imbues healing," Ziba offers. "It'd be an unexpected trait of a creature called a firebird, but in my experience, the goddess has her own sense of humor when it comes to these things."

"What are you talking about?" I ask, a little impatient. They're not being rude per se, but they're being awfully cryptic. "Will you just tell me what you see?"

Markus slaps my back, and I wince, but it's out of instinct, not pain. "Your back is smooth. Except for the scars, but they match the old ones well." Scars I also earned from Sarai's lash over my years as a novitiate. "Funny," I reply.

They're moving on to help some of the keeper children who were attacked by the cath palug. I say my goodbyes. While my back has been my first indication of what my powers may be, if healing is a part of it, it's entirely unconscious and I'm hoping there's significantly more.

My next stop ought to be Jasmyn, working on creating illustrated manuscripts in the library; or Illia, whom I see working with Redonna at the edges of the village. They're focused on the border that supposedly keeps creatures out of the village, but apparently isn't working, given that the cath palugs got in easily enough.

Time is getting away from me, so I move directly to Ulric in the fields. Here is where I truly want my power to unleash its full potential.

I find Ulric with the head of the keeper elders, Petra. She is watching him closely, and I don't blame her. His power was a bit . . . overabundant when dealing with the cath palug.

At least we know he's strong.

When I join them with a nod of greeting, I see that his fire is coming in starts and stops. He waves his hands around, and tiny sparks form on the end of some dried weeds.

He looks to Petra like a kitten presenting her first kill. And like anyone who has found a dead mouse on their pillow at bedtime, she's unimpressed.

"What are you trying to accomplish?" I ask. Maybe aiming small is the goal here.

Petra gestures to the large field around us, full of dead grasses and other plant matter. "We want to clear this, to prep it for planting."

He tries again and he gets even more lackluster results. But at least there's still a spark. A whiff of smoke. Ulric pouts. "It's going poorly, as you can see."

I try to mimic him, waving my hands around. I think about fire. Starting fire. Just a little spark of fire. Nothing happens.

"Just feel it," Petra encourages. "You've done this already. You can do it again."

Ulric stands up tall and raises his arms and then drops them dramatically as if he's the Spinner's choral director, performing for the masses on a feast day. More dead weeds light.

"Pretty," I say honestly. He does a little dance of joy. Then a breeze trickles by and smothers them.

I raise my arms and then drop them quickly. Nothing.

"Tell me what it feels like for you," I say. "When it works."

"You know what it's like when you pop a pimple?"

I stare, thinking he's fucking with me, but of course he's not. It's Ulric.

"It's like that. There's a buildup of pressure and then a little burst when the magic goes out. And if there's a bigger buildup, there's a bigger burst."

He makes an explosion gesture with his hand and I think of another bodily function where there is a buildup of pressure and then an eruption. And how sometimes, the moment of climax is better when you hold back for longer.

"Have you tried intentionally holding back and letting the pressure build?" I can't help myself. I have to torment him a little bit. I smirk. "Like edging."

Petra laughs and a high-pitched, anxious giggle bubbles out of him then quickly subsides as he turns his attention back to the field. He concentrates, and I can see a new sort of flush rise, darkening his ears and neck.

I can feel his power building. Hairs stand up on the back of my neck, and my skin tingles. I wonder if some of the pressure is my own magic starting to respond. I begin to try to focus it when Ulric unleashes a torrent of magic with a moan. The weeds in front of us incinerate, as does the field surrounding us. And then the next, and the next.

The fire spreads quickly. If only it were traveling in the direction of the matching hut, he would take care of my problem for me.

"It's too much!" Petra says as the fire gets closer to the village. If it catches the houses, who knows what kind of destruction it will do, or how quickly. "You control the flames. Draw them back."

He's frozen in some sort of daze, not processing. I try to do it myself. I imagine the pressure building in me and try to call the fire.

Nothing happens.

There is no tingle, no movement. He has to do it. I get up close in his face, putting my hands on either side of his head and bring his face close to mine as if to kiss him. It wouldn't be easy to accomplish with the creature skulls, but kissing is not my intention. He always said he liked my voice, especially when I praised him. I make myself calm. I drop my tenor. "Ulric," I say. "You're brilliant. You've done such a good job. You can do this."

His eyes lock on mine instead of into the middle distance. They are panicked, but present. It's not magic, just connection. One human to another.

"Ulric, call the fire back to yourself." I lean even closer until I can feel his breath mingle with mine. "Do it now."

Ulric closes his eyes and, with a shudder, does. The fire goes out in the fields, and the tiny flame of hope inside of me is also snuffed out. If I have control over fire, it is buried deep, but I suspect whatever my magic happens to be, it's nothing that will help me burn creature bones.

I'll have to find another path to vengence. Until I can find that path, I can't face Aunt Ujvala. Instead of heading out to the forest, I cross the burnt fields on my way back to the village. Time to visit Adela's friend, and see if her research has revealed any secrets to the power of the phoenixes.

Chapter Thirteen

ADELA

I love the brightness of the little library off the great hall. Windows above the shelves let in brilliant streams of light, and the darker corners have lanterns for yet more. It smells of oranges and some herb I can't quite place, and if there is a speck of dust to be found, it is hiding well.

In the center of the room, at a table so large that you can barely scoot around it to access the shelves, sits Cecelia.

Despite her small size, Cecelia takes up space, especially here. Maybe it is the fact that she appears utterly in her element, surrounded by half-unrolled scrolls, piles of books, and almost as many piles of scribbled-on parchment and papers. Her own chaotic notes.

She's currently flipping back and forth in a massive illustrated manuscript. It must be very old, because the colors swirl on the page—something jackalope-wearers used to do, but haven't been able to access in a hundred years or so.

She looks up from the giant tome in front of her, her large brown eyes unfocused as she thinks through whatever she's been reading.

"Morning." I set down the overloaded breakfast tray on a small side table, using its corner to gently shove aside dirty plates and mugs without toppling them over. I plop into a chair beside her. Partly I'm here to learn how to sever the bond between me and the phoenix, but I also just miss my best friend. "When was the last time you left this room?"

Her attention finally shifts to me. "I've been in the hall looking at tapestries, too." She grins, knowing that doesn't count. "What's the word from the outside world?"

We chatter as if everything is normal; she hasn't been locked away researching for two days, and I don't have a phoenix skull permanently attached to my face—and possibly my soul. She doesn't touch anything I've brought, even though it's all of her favorites.

After a few minutes, she stands to retrieve another book, but I lift a pot of hot chocolate off the tray. If she's not going to eat anything, she should at least have a bit of sweetness to get her through the morning. "A researcher cannot survive on tea alone."

She shoots the teapot and multiple half-drunk mugs scattered around the table a dirty look, as if their very existence has betrayed her, and sits down. Her foot taps. She wants to dig into her research and hide from her own overwhelming feelings, but she'll suppress that for a bit. For me.

I pour us each a cup of the thick, almost pudding-like liquid, and we hold the steaming chocolate to our faces and inhale. We sigh simultaneously, just like we've done since we were children.

Kian comes in just as I've taken a big swig of chocolate. I splutter, I'm so surprised. I didn't take him for the type to spend any time in a library.

"Quite the welcome." He steps close, bending low, and I tilt my head up, as if expecting a kiss. He simply takes his thumb and rubs it across the top of my lip.

It comes away with a smear of chocolate on it. My breath catches on an inhale, and I'm surprised the tension in the air isn't enough to curl the corners of Cecelia's papers. Then he licks it off. An electrified shiver rolls down my spine.

"Damn." Cecelia clears her throat and arches a brow at me when I look her way. I'd momentarily forgotten my best friend, along with the rest of the known world. It all rushes back, along with a violent heat that no doubt reveals itself as a blush.

I bury my nose in whatever book is in front of me, pretending to read it closely, though my eyes can't focus. Still, I keep up the pretense, even turning pages, until Cecelia makes a soft tsking sound and turns it right side up for me.

Looking for anything to draw their attention away from my horrifyingly intense reactions to a simple touch of my lip, I ask Cecelia if she's come across anything on the phoenix yet.

"Yes!" Cecelia hurries to a particular shelf far in the back of the small library, squeezing past Kian.

She lugs over a book nearly as big as her torso. The cover is a deep burgundy, with no title, author, or illustration on it. The way her mind keeps track of these books amazes me.

She flips through the massive pages quickly and carefully. When she gets to the passage she's looking for, she reads it aloud to us. "The firebirds of lore are the most magical and mystical of all of the nineteen mythical creatures that are currently known."

"Nineteen?" There are only ten species of creatures currently in the valley. I had no idea there were so many extinct varieties. "How'd we lose so many?"

"It wasn't necessarily *we*," Cecelia replies. "Some of them never migrated to the valley. And like all living species, things happen. Some creatures were lost to disease, some because they were a threat—or delicacy—to other creatures. The keepers were partly responsible though. Our ancestors killed off at least five species with poor caregiving."

"That sounds ominous," Kian says.

"It was pretty awful." Cecelia grabs another book from one of her piles and flips through it. This one is tiny, and looks to be handwritten, more like a journal than a reference book. She points to the page that's covered in script so full of flourishes I can barely read it. "There was a time when magic was so strong and wild that it had started to leak beyond the valley, affecting folks in the villages in the surrounding countryside. That's when one of the large creature migrations began. Everyone was afraid of what would happen with so many creatures in the valley, even as large as it is."

I sit up straighter, listening closely.

"They captured and caged some of the newest arrivals, which were mating pairs. Wyverns, vargs, spirit moths, basilisks, and chimeras—" She looks up at us, wearing our matching skulls. "And phoenixes."

Feelings of anger and despair from the phoenix flood through me so violently that I wonder if she herself was one of the caged phoenixes.

I've never heard anything about any of this. The creatures' influence extending beyond the valley, efforts to contain creatures. This is part of our story as keepers, yet it's not taught to us like the rest of our traditions and history. Purposefully?

Possibly. It doesn't sound like a time to be particularly proud of if it resulted in the extinction of five species of creatures.

Cecelia continues. "In a year's time, not one of them reproduced, and within three years, they were all dead."

"Three years?" My voice cracks with sorrow for some unknown

creatures hundreds of years before. Three years is nothing in the span of a creature's life.

Cecelia nods. "Except for the phoenixes. I haven't found what happened to them yet." She continues to share with us what she reads, taking momentary pauses here and there when she forgets we're in the room. At some point she changes books, and stops sharing altogether. When it's clear she's so engrossed with her own research that she's forgotten we exist, Kian and I pick up our own books.

He grabs *Death Rites of the Blessed: A Primer*. It's a pretty little book with a soft black leather cover, embossed with a gold-foil bird skull. It's a stylized design, so I can't be certain, but I suspect it is a phoenix. I'm surprised Cecelia isn't hoarding it in her growing stack like a dragon with their preys' bones.

In mere moments, he's deeply engrossed in his reading, but I'm a bit too affected to make much headway.

He's sitting near enough that I can smell him when he moves, some combination of lemongrass soap and his own natural scent, which makes me want to bury my face in his neck and inhale his deliciousness. And he keeps licking his finger to turn pages. I'm afraid he's going to make either Cecelia or me combust. Her from anger if she surfaces from her research long enough to notice he's transferring saliva onto her precious book, me from desire.

I can't stop thinking about the way his lips looked when he licked the chocolate from my mouth off his finger. The way his tongue feels against my neck and lips, and . . .

I fan the pages of my book to cool myself.

Goddess, he's hot.

Cecelia gasps, and I think she's caught him until she swings around the table, sliding between us. She points to a page with illustrated birds winding together in the margins. They're beautiful, all orange and red and yellow. Like fire.

She begins reading, her voice growing higher as she gets more excited. "'While their powers frequently mimic those of their charges, they are wholly unique. A harmonic pair, they must exist together. Two halves for a whole. One does not exist without the other.'"

Kian and I share a look. Two halves of a whole.

Surely that is just the living creatures.

"'Living, they are as wild as the original magic itself, and cannot be caught or contained. Dead, they awaken only in tandem.'"

My mind whirls. Fated pairs. Wild magic.

"But what does that tell us about what we can do? It has to be done together?" Kian asks. "How do we harness it?"

"Or escape it?" I ask.

Cecelia doesn't answer either of us. She's far away in her own mind, flipping through the book and then various pieces of parchment and papers she's been scribbling on all afternoon. Finally she says, "In the stories, a single phoenix dies and then comes back from the ashes of itself, right? But in my readings here, there are two and their magic represents a balance, yeah? Death. Life." She closes the book with a thunk. Kian and I both jump. "My theory is that it's a combination of the stories and these writings. Two halves of a whole. One is destruction, and the other is rebirth."

She continues, but I can't process what she's saying now. I'm stuck in the horror of what she's just said. She's confirmed everything I've been afraid of over the past couple of days. That I am responsible for all the recent deaths, that my impulses have destroyed lives. I had to go and stick my cheek against a phoenix and then my lips against a novitiate and upend everything.

If one half of the phoenix is destruction and the other is rebirth, my new fate is clear, and it's what I've always feared. I am destruction, and there's no escaping my ruin.

I tune back in when Cecelia says, "—and they're romantically entwined. The phoenix. I think the best way to explore the magical connection is to explore your own romantic connection. Or at least, the physical aspects of it. I'm not sure your actual hearts need to be involved." A wild smile crosses her face. She's delighted at her cleverness of piecing it all together and absolutely certain she's gotten it right.

"So you think we should fuck to unlock our magic?" Kian asks. I've never heard a man laugh so loud or so long. "Done and done."

"I do, yes," she says.

I want to slink between the stacks of books and never come out. Not because I don't want to explore my physical connection with Kian. I do. Too much. That eager, desperate wanting has never resulted in anything good.

Without another word, Cecelia gets up and leaves. Surely she doesn't expect us to start going at it here, in the library.

I look at Kian, about to make a joke, but the way he is looking at me steals the words. His brown eyes are somehow impossibly darker. With desire? He sits up on the table, pushing books and papers aside, and slides over until he's directly in front of me.

I move back, making space for him and his knees bracket my body. I could lean just slightly forward and kiss his stomach or his chest. I look down his body, at his legs on either side of me. At other parts of him that begin to show interest in our positioning.

Sitting in front of me, he removes his phoenix skull and carefully sets it beside him on the table. He's moving slowly, carefully, and I get the sense that he's giving me time to bolt if I want to.

And I do.

But I also want to stay. To see what happens next.

He wraps his hand around the side of my neck, gently pushing on the edge of my jaw with his thumb until I tilt my head up to look into his face. His eyes never leaving mine, he leans down, so close that our breath mingles. His smells of mint and tea and I self-consciously hope mine is as pleasant. He's going to kiss me. I want him to kiss me.

I turn my head slightly in anticipation, giving him space to duck under the edge of the phoenix. He's taking his time, and I squirm with impatience. I'm tempted to push him back on the table, to climb on top of him like it I did in the pantry, to show him what I want, how eager I am to touch him again. To be touched by him again.

He chuckles knowingly, as if he can see every one of my wants in every move of my body. But if he can, he does not give them to me.

Instead, he kisses the beak of the phoenix. "Oh, we are going to have fun, beauty." Then with a smirk, he leaves.

Chapter Fourteen

KIAN

I run away. I want to dive into Adela's bed immediately, explore this connection that Cecelia insists is the way forward, but I can't let myself get distracted again. As soon as it's dark, I'm heading to the forest. To my future.

In my stark guest room, I remove the phoenix skull and flop onto the bed to stare at the whitewashed ceiling. My mind spirals with everything that I just learned. I'm going to be attached to the matcher for the foreseeable future through these paired skulls—which is both fortunate for my lasciviousness and devastating for pulling off my plans.

I pop up from the bed and start pacing, looping through questions.

Is sex really going to help us unlock the phoenix magic?

Do we both have the capacity for both destruction and rebirth?

Do we have to do magic literally at the same time?

But no. That would be far too complicated. The gytrash are always matched as a triad, and they don't have to do their magic simultaneously.

And it's just as unlikely that we would each contain both magics.

I have to be the destruction side of things. I have to. Like calls to like, after all. And Adela isn't destructive. She is consumed with serving her community and being seen as good. I am consumed with good, too—people's lives will improve in the absence of the Huntress order having quite so much power—but my means are destructive.

Sure, I somehow healed my own back, but maybe that was Markus. Maybe he did it unintentionally, like how Ulric torched the cath palugs almost accidentally.

I bounce back and forth from pacing between my bed and the hard chair, back to pacing, then to my bed, ad nauseam until finally darkness descends and I'm able to head to the forest. I hate to go without a clear plan of what's next, but I can't put it off a moment longer.

I barely step within the tree line when Aunt Ujvala and Ivo find me.

Ivo gives me a quick hug, then glances at Aunt Ujvala like he might've done something wrong. Her face is very intentionally expressionless, which terrifies me. A quiet Ujvala is a dangerous Ujvala.

They both look disheveled, but of course, they've been camping in the woods for two nights. They're not going to look fresh-faced and well rested. Hoping a bit of humor might break the tension, I throw out my hands as if in greeting. "Welcome to the valley. Hope you've enjoyed your stay."

It's the wrong tactic.

"Where in the fuck have you been?" Aunt Ujvala swings her cane wildly. I step back to avoid a thwack. "You had another hour and I was going to leave you here on your own."

I put my hands up as if she's a riled horse. "Woah."

Again, wrong tactic. Her eyes grow wider in the moonlight, and I swear I can hear her thoughts, and they're all about my impending death and dismemberment at her hands.

"I've been trying to—" I was going to say, "Get to you," but she rips the phoenix skull off my face. I flinch, thinking she's going to clobber me with it, but she just throws it in the dirt. Before I can respond, she starts in.

"Oh, we know you've been trying. Trying to get into the pants of that matcher. Trying to practice magic with your little novitiate friends. While we steal food scraps for nourishment and sleep on rocks, exposed to rain and bugs and cold, under the same trees as a man-eating dragon."

"I believe the dragon's lair is actually in the cliffs, if that's comforting at all."

"It is not." Her teeth grind.

"Why didn't you start with your plans while you waited? You know—trade stuff."

"Under the nose of the most vindictive high priestess in Insborough? And what? Risk everyone?" My aunt levels me a look like I am the stupidest man in the world. "Kian."

I sigh. She's right and I know it. I've taken her support for granted. Getting them home or making them comfortable should have been my first thought. I'm not used to prioritizing anyone besides myself. "I'm sorry."

"I don't need you to be sorry. I need to leave this valley until the order is gone and I can come back and establish contacts. I have endeavors to oversee, runs to organize, people who are counting on me. And instead, I'm stuck in a magical valley, sleeping with owl pellets next to my face because I don't want to abandon my favorite nephew—"

"Ouch," Ivo says, then hunches into himself when she almost whaps him with her cane. He pouts.

"We're leaving." Aunt Ujvala places the end of her cane onto the hard earth, finally using it as an assistive device instead of just as a makeshift weapon. "Tonight."

I want to argue. I don't have fire, and I don't know how to get it. I had been planning on stealing Thad's fire when he was showing off for some keeper, or seducing him and then stealing it, but Ulric is too humble for the former and the latter would kill him.

My mind whirls, thinking through the possibilities. There are no good options, especially without my magic manifesting yet.

I need time. More time.

And then I realize the answer's been camping in the woods the whole time. My aunt is an expert smuggler.

"We'll steal the skulls."

Aunt Ujvala starts shaking her head. "I am not taking a hundred magical creature skulls to Insborough and stashing them in my cellar."

"Of course not! Just help me get them out of the matching hut and into the forest to buy me some time. Then go home. Take a bath. Sleep in your beds. Once they're hidden somewhere, I'll figure out the rest."

Somehow.

Aunt Ujvala is quiet for a long moment, then shakes her head sadly. She steps forward and puts a gentle hand on my shoulder. I shrug to dislodge it, but she doesn't move. Unless I'm going to physically push her away, I am going to have to accept her comfort.

But I don't want it, because I know it's going to come with her abandoning me.

"You are asking too much, Kian." Her voice is still soft, and the gentleness she is handling me with enrages me. I hate that it's comforting. I hate that I want to be soothed.

And I hate that she's right. I've been so selfish. They are tired, hungry, cold. If they had been discovered in the valley, the entire family would be at risk of exposure and retribution. Unless we are strong like my parents, who kept their secrets until the end.

No one else is that strong.

"Aunt, please. Don't do this." I hate how pleading my voice is.

She takes my face in her hands, rubbing the pads of her thumbs across my cheeks like my mom used to. "Kian, I love you. If you want to come back to us, to be a part of *our* efforts, you are always welcome. But I'm not risking everything we've built for an already-dead sister and your twisted-up quest for equality and vengeance."

I open my mouth to argue, but she speaks first.

"I loved her, too. And I know Lesa would want me to help you." I flinch at the mention of Mom. "This is my offer. We'll go with you to collect intelligence on the matching hut, and I'll help create a plan for moving forward."

I can't help but push. "That's it?"

"That's it. After, we're going home, love."

I still think to argue, but I can see by the set of her shoulders that I'd get nowhere. "Thank you."

We immediately set out across the meadow for the matching hut, moving quickly and quietly. Not that it matters much. There's little chance of running into anyone this late at night in this little agrarian community where everyone seems to go to bed with the sun.

I wish the moon were a little less full, the stars slightly less bright, but at least it's not raining or snowing. We cross the field, ascending a small rolling hill and crest the top.

Beside me, Ivo is practically bouncing on his toes; he's so excited to be participating in our little quest. Honestly, I'm probably just as excited. I haven't participated in a run since I was a child and brought on some of the smallest, most straightforward operations with my parents.

We pause to catch our breath. We're about halfway there, but now that we're over the largest hill, the matching hut is within sight. Full of skulls and drying herbs and jars of ointments and tonics and all the magic that the order would be able to control over the next decade or so. A cloud passes in front of the moon, making the night darker at just the right time. If I believed in the Huntress, I'd thank her.

We've just begun to move again when Ivo suddenly drops to the ground beside me.

"Spinner's tits!" The exclamation is soft, but pain laces his voice.

I lean over and help him to stand up. "What happened?"

"Something stabbed me in the ankle."

"A stick?" Aunt Ujvala suggests from his other side. She sweeps the ground with her cane, but doesn't connect with anything. He stands and takes a step, grimacing.

I bend and pat down his leg. There is a dark wetness on his pants, and I hold my hand up to my nose. Blood. If he hit a stick, it was a fairly large one, possibly with a vendetta.

"Going to make it?"

The boy grunts out something in the affirmative and begins to limp forward, down the hill. Aunt Ujvala and I follow half a step behind. We're moving slower, worried about running into bushes or branches that we can't see.

We also have to be careful of just tripping on the ground, which is significantly more uneven than I remember it being the last two times I was here. But we came at it from other angles then. Tiny mounds keep slightly tripping us, but we manage.

The hut is growing closer, and we're all eager to get to it. Aunt Ujvala begins to move a little quicker. Not least, Ivo, whose limp has become more pronounced.

Suddenly, Ivo swears again and sort of half hops, half falls sideways. This time he doesn't fall to the ground, but his breathing is ragged and his voice shakes when he says, "Can I please light my lantern?"

I am about to say no, when Aunt Ujvala also cries out. "Ow! What the . . . ?"

Ivo doesn't wait. He pulls out the lantern and tries to get the flint to catch. It doesn't work.

He cries out again.

Then I also feel something sharp dig into my calf, puncturing the skin and sliding down the muscle. It feels like a small knife. What is happening? Does the matching hut have some sort of strange border around it that attacks intruders' legs?

I can hear the swish of Aunt Ujvala's cane. It collides with something. There's a high-pitched squeal and shuffling. "We need that light!"

If only I had Ulric's magic. I close my eyes and concentrate, willing the wick to catch with Ivo's next attempt. It does. We gasp in unison as a small pool of light illuminates what's been attacking us.

Amongst a landscape of little hills, there are approximately fifty jackalopes shuffling back and forth in front of us, their noses pointed toward the earth so their antlers are aimed at us. A couple of them drip blood from the sharp tips.

Compared to Ivo, whose leg is bleeding profusely from multiple wounds, Aunt Ujvala and I have minor scratches.

"I don't think you were tripped by a stick," I point out.

"Thank you for that brilliant observation," Aunt Ujvala says.

Ivo swings the lantern back and forth, as if it's a weapon to keep the jackalopes away. And honestly, it kind of is. They seem to dislike the light, hopping away when it gets too near.

I move toward the matching hut. It's so close now, only thirty or so feet away. But the moment I start to step out of the light, the jackalopes begin to scratch the earth and chatter their teeth, like excited cats watching birds and dreaming of murder.

"They dislike the lantern. When we get to the matching hut, we'll tend our cuts. There are all sorts of herbs and supplies. Then we can figure out . . ." I trail off. Aunt Ujvala has already half turned around and started back toward the forest. She stops. Hope blooms. She'll agree. She won't just leave me here to figure it all out on my own. "We're so close."

Then Ivo wobbles on his feet. The little light bobs and sways. He's pale, either from blood loss or distress. I see the moment Aunt Ujvala makes her final decision. She moves over to him and puts her shoulder under Ivo's armpit, and they begin hobbling away. Away from the matching hut, away from me.

I'm frozen. I want to continue on with my ill-formed plan. I want to see them to safety. I can't seem to get my feet to move.

Aunt Ujvala and Ivo don't have the same issue. They ascend the small crest of a hill. The moment the light swings away from me, the jackalopes swarm. One tries to bite me, and I kick it, hard, flinging it across the grasses. This doesn't dissuade the others, who still try to attack.

My body decides for me. I run toward the light.

We reach a small rolling hill, which would be nothing physically strenuous normally, but Ivo is flagging and Aunt Ujvala is not a young woman. I go over and scoot under his other arm. He's nearly limp.

The moment we're at the top, the jackalopes stop following.

Relieved, we slow our pace, and manage to get back to the forest. The sky has cleared, and above the nearby treetops of the forest, stars glisten. Somewhere far off, we hear a dragon's call, but it is soft, a safe distance away.

At the tree line, Aunt Ujvala pauses. "I'm sorry," she says softly.

"Me, too."

"You should go back in case you're missed by your matcher or your friend." She places a warm hand on my cheek. "Be safe, my love. Come home when you can."

I nod, but can't find any words to respond as she turns and disappears with Ivo into the trees.

I am all alone, but I will not give up. I will still get to the matching hut. I will still destroy the skulls.

But first, I will sleep.

I don't sleep. Instead of heading down the hallway where the novitiates' guest rooms are, I turn toward the library again. If I'm going to get to the matching hut, I'm going to need to get past the jackalopes. And if I'm going to get past the territorial little fuckers, I'm going to need to know more about the little beasts than what magic their skulls are capable of imbuing after death.

Easier now, when Cecelia is no doubt in bed.

Unfortunately, the library is locked and I don't have any tools with me to pick it. At least, not with any kind of subtly. With a sigh, I start back to bed.

I'm crossing through the main room when I hear voices coming from the direction of the kitchens. I creep closer. It's too late for the keepers who clean up after dinner and too early yet for the bakers. I stick to the shadows and lean around the corner. There sits Cecelia and Adela, sitting in front of a fire in some sort of nook off the kitchens. They're deep in conversation; a serious one by the look of it.

I hear Cecelia blurt, "Will you go with them?" She mashes the question all together, as if it's one singular word instead of a whole sentence.

"I'm scared it's inevitable," Adela replies. She faces away from me and speaks softly. She's hard to hear. "I can't be a matcher with a skull on my face."

"Have you been back to the matching hut?" Cecelia quirks her head, her curiosity plain even from a distance.

I'm also curious. I listen closely to her response, wondering if there's some way I could convince Adela to take me with her when she returns. Then I scoff at myself. As if that would work. I'd have to, what, steal the skulls from under her nose? And still have no way to destroy them.

She either doesn't respond, or I don't hear what she says.

"Until you try to commune with the skulls, you won't know your capabilities. If you could still match, I think the elders would insist you stay. But are you sure you don't *want* to go?" Cecelia sits forward and the firelight illuminates her, bringing out the auburn strands of her deep-brown hair and the faint lines of worry in her brow. "You never wanted to be a matcher, and this could be your out. Plus, your chemistry with Kian is exceptional."

Indeed it is.

"I wouldn't leave the valley for a man I had sex with once."

Thank the Huntress.

Cecelia waves away the comment. "Of course not, it's just a perk. You've always been intrigued by Insborough. Don't you remember when you were a little girl, how excited you were when goods from the outside came in? Until . . ." She trails off, and I wish she would finish the thought. What changed for Adela that she stopped loving the outside world? Instead, she says, "I think there's a part of you that wants to go, and you're allowed to want a different life than what was chosen for you."

I barely hear Adela's reply. "I'm afraid." Adela pulls her legs up onto her chair, shrinking her shoulders down, making herself as small as possible. "I don't trust that part of myself. That is curious about what life would be like, outside the valley. In the order. With—"

I should step forward, interrupt. I shouldn't be eavesdropping on this. It's obviously difficult for both of them, and honestly, I'm terrified, too. Of what comes after that "with."

"You should trust all of yourself." Cecelia takes Adela's hands, and squeezes. "Sure, sometimes you get snippy or flaky or make mistakes, but who doesn't? You are fundamentally good."

"Am I? Sometimes I just want to break shit." She looks so uncomfortable, admitting that she's human.

Cecelia laughs so hard she snorts. Adela's shoulders and head come up. She playfully swats at her friend. Between gulps of air, breathless from her laughter, Cecelia says, "And?"

"And that makes me a horrible person!" But Adela's voice has grown more confident with her friends' amusement. Her smile can be heard in her tone.

"It absolutely does not! It just makes you a person. Everyone wants to just break shit sometimes. You're still allowed to have a life that you love. Even if it's not the one everyone else says you should want."

From there, they change to more mundane topics—worries about the late spring, a bit of gossip about one of the keeper couples who's expecting a new little one, some back-and-forth with how Beadda is doing with all of the sudden changes.

I should go to bed. Go sleep off my disappointment and abandonment and just plain old weariness. If I can't learn more about the jackalopes and how to get to the matching hut tonight, I should just sink into the cozy keeper quilts and say goodbye to the day.

Instead, I silently back up a dozen paces and then practically stomp forward, so they'll hear my footfalls and not suspect me for the eavesdropper I am. I come around the corner and feign surprise at finding them.

"Oh, hello," I say, hoping to hit just the right note of delight.

Their surprise is genuine. They talk over one another greeting me.

"What are you—"

"Oh, Kian—"

"You should be—"

Adela gestures to Cecelia to go first.

"You're not wearing your phoenix," Cecelia points out.

I look at it hooked to my belt. "So I'm not." I leave it there, and she doesn't press.

I turn to Adela. "Uh . . . hi. Hi," she says.

"Hi," I reply, loving the color that spreads up her neck, the same shade she flushed when she orgasmed on me in the pantry. I imagine turning her whole body that shade of pink from pleasure. The last time we saw each other, Cecelia told us we needed to do more of that—bring each other pleasure.

And I want to. Oh, I want to.

But I can't. Not yet. I have to focus on my whole reason for being in the order to begin with.

They don't ask me to join them, but I've never needed an invitation to insert myself where I'm not exactly wanted. I pull a stool over, practically wedging myself between them. "I hate to interrupt, but I couldn't sleep. I went to the library but it was locked up for the night."

"Oh, I can let you in." Cecelia stands up and begins to move toward the library. Up close, she looks rough. Clumps of hair stick out from her bun, her eyes are red, and her clothing is rumpled as if she hasn't left the great hall for days. She probably hasn't.

"No, no, sit back down," I reply, smile firmly in place. She does, almost instantly. "I'd like to learn more about the different creatures in the valley and what they're like. No need for books, when I have two experts who can just tell me."

Adela rolls her eyes, and she's not wrong. I went a bit heavy on the charm, there. But the sentiment is genuine. I'd much rather them summarize what I need to know about the jackalope than spend hours pouring over books. I'd just as likely come away with none of the information I need.

Cecelia gives me a look I don't quite recognize. "So you're not looking for ways to send skulls to their rest any longer? Because the only way I know to do that is dragon fire."

The valley researcher is too smart by half. Or I am too dumb. Of course she would notice what books and scrolls I had picked up previously and connect what I was trying to do. But she doesn't seem suspicious, only mildly intrigued. I find myself really enjoying my time with her. Something about her calm curiosity reminds me of my mom, I think. But she's difficult to read. Polite to a fault and kind, but ever so slightly angry.

Probably because I screwed up her friend's future.

"I assume you wanted to help Adela rid herself of the skull. I've been looking for the same."

"You do?" Adela asks and sits forward slightly, leaning toward me. There's a gentle note of hope in her voice, and something inside my chest tightens in reply.

I stumble over my words. "Right. I do. Did." I don't know the right answer, and I'm unsure of how to navigate these women. My usual tactics, to be confident and beguiling, don't seem terribly effective on either of them, and I don't have a whole lot of other talents to pull from. "If that's what you want, I want to help."

The women share a look and I realize I've just made a major misstep in gaining their trust. This is what they were just talking about. What Adela wants. But if they suspect me of listening in, they don't say so. Instead, Adela sits back, as if relieved.

"I'll tell you about whatever creatures you'd like," Cecelia replies. "On one simple condition."

Warning tingles shoot through me. Favors are rarely simple, but I push aside the reaction. She's not going to ask me to fight a dragon. Whatever it is, I can navigate it. "What's the condition?"

She looks at Adela with a raised chin and crosses her arms. Whatever she's about to say, she believes her friend is going to hate it.

"Take care of her. If she goes with you, and I think she will." She speaks quickly, not giving any space to Adela to speak up herself.

Not that Adela could. She's too busy gaping.

"If she is threatened or if she needs help to escape, help get her out. Bring her home."

"Cecelia!" Adela objects.

"Agreed," I say with absolutely no hesitation, and push aside the feelings of protectiveness and nurture that pop up when I think of her. I want to care for Adela. I shiver at the realization.

With a nod, Cecelia sits back, her relief palpable. "Perfect. Thank you. Now which creatures would you like to know about specifically?"

"All of them," I reply as if I'm just so interested about magic and the valley that I want to soak it all up. I pretend to think carefully. "Let's start with jackalopes."

Chapter Fifteen

ADELA

It's been four days since the deaths. Three full days of preparation. Three full days of mourning. And now, on the fourth, the souls of the priest and Bartholomew are ready to cross into the after. We will also say goodbye to the creatures, Duschwa, Gilcriss, and the cath palug that Etana killed. The gryphon's remains were never found. As matcher, I have no specific role in funerals, and yet, I am expected to be present.

But I cannot manage to get myself out of bed.

All my expectations around what my life is and will be have shifted. I can't find my balance.

The reckless part of me just wants to jump. Into Kian's bed. Into his arms. Like Cecelia said we should, to unlock the magic. But I've spent a lifetime trying to repress those reckless parts. Embracing them could mean disaster.

I hear Dad's footsteps moving around the house, preparing. I have to get up. Instead, I bury my face in a pillow and pull the quilts over my head.

My nose is instantly full of the scent of Kian. He's lingered in my bed long after he left it.

I think of the way he touched me in the library, his hand wrapped around the back of my neck so his thumb could gently push on the edge of my jaw and tilt my face ever so slightly up.

I wish he would have kissed my neck and jaw, dipped below my phoenix skull to reach my eager lips. Or maybe taken his kisses even lower.

There is a knock at my door.

I groan and throw back the covers. "Go without me. I'll be there."

"Planning on it," Dad replies through the closed door. "In the meantime, you have a visitor. Novitiate Kian is—"

I hurry out of bed and across the room, flinging open the door. "Here? Now?" Did I somehow beckon him with my longing for that almost-kiss? Did the phoenix?

"That got you going quick." Dad's eyes crinkle in amusement. "He's downstairs."

In many ways, keeper funerals are the opposite of the matching ceremonies. There are no special garments, no elaborate hairstyles or jewelry, no specific words to say. Our final goodbyes are as simple as our everyday goodbyes.

Especially for the creatures, who don't quite leave us. Their skulls are set aside for immediate cleaning and preparing. Their bodies are prepared in the usual ways, with herbs and prayers of thanks to the great goddess. And then we bury them, returning their energies, and magic, back to the earth. Usually. But only out of necessity. Since there is a dragon-matched novitiate present and dragon fire is the only thing that can burn creature bones, today's funerals will involve burning. Fire will return them more quickly to the valley than burial.

I dress just as I normally would and try not to spiral into despair at the thought of how many we've lost since I released the magic of the phoenixes.

"Hello!" Kian says when I enter the kitchen. He is wearing bright red, the funeral color of the orders. As the valley's tailor, Cecelia's mom has been working on their robes since they arrived, roping in her daughters to help. As usual, she's done an excellent job, even embroidering the cuffs, which sparkle in the kitchen window's streaming light as he reaches for a mug of tea from Dad.

"What brings you here?" I ask. He takes up so much of my small kitchen. Not with his size—it's his presence that overwhelms me.

Before Kian replies, Dad says he'll see us shortly and bustles off.

It's just me and Kian, alone. I avoid staring at him by grabbing an apple from a wooden bowl on the counter and take a big bite.

"I know we need to . . . explore." Kian's voice is low and full of promise.

"We do," I agree, not liking the way my voice is thin and reedy with desire. There is a tug toward him, a distraction of knowing where he is and wanting to be there with him. I need to explore that. To quench it or embrace it. At the moment, with the almost-kiss of the library still echoing through me, embracing it sounds best.

Surely he feels this, too.

He gestures to me to sit and takes the hand that isn't holding the apple in his. He traces his fingers along mine. "But today is for saying goodbyes and I don't want to rush our mourning."

Oh. I sit back, pulling my hand away, and take another bite. Or perhaps he feels nothing for me. Around the apple I say, "Were you and the priest close then?"

"Brother Thad was . . ." Kian searches for the word, but apparently never finds it. He shrugs, not finishing the thought.

"Well. Then I can see why you would want time to say goodbye. Funny, I thought that was what the three days of preparation and grieving were for, but maybe you do things differently in Insborough than we do here in the valley?" I take three large bites of the apple in quick succession and throw the rest into the compost crock on the counter.

"I think we do a great many things differently," he says.

Whatever that means.

"But we can still tell when we've hurt someone. I'm sorry for the delay. I can't wait to have your body on mine again. I think about it constantly. Incessantly. Our first time was rushed. I want this next time to be . . . luxurious."

His words have more of an effect on me than I would like. When he says it like that, sweetening the disappointment, like honey on Brie, I can hardly begrudge him a bit more time.

I nod slightly, and a smile lights up his beautiful face.

"Tomorrow then?" he asks.

"Tomorrow," I agree. Then, because I am slightly petty and don't want to be the only one questioning where they stand, I say, "No need to rush."

Except that he and the order will hopefully be leaving soon, and I will be staying. As long as I can get this skull off my face and sever the bond with the phoenix. Which is definitely what I want.

He gives me a look and I imagine that beneath his phoenix skull, he has raised a skeptical eyebrow at me. But he just smirks and stands. "Ready to go to say some goodbyes?"

There is not a speck of grief in this man's voice, but we all have our own ways.

We walk across the village to an open field where there are four pyres. It's farther out than we typically do our funerals, but I suppose the newly matched dragon-wearer did destroy two cath palugs and burn a couple of fields with his overexuberance.

As befits his personality and station, Dad moves to the front. I follow, understanding what's expected of me as matcher, even as my feet feel as if they are tied to fence posts firmly planted in a winter ground.

I do not want to see this. I do not want to be here.

Just as I drag myself into position beside Dad and Petra, the novitiate wearing the dragon skull lights the pyres for Gilcriss, Duschwa, and the cath palug. I wonder if the dragon skull has any feelings about burning its own body.

The heat is immense, but I barely register it. There's something buzzing under my skin—unsettled and rising. Complex feelings flow from the phoenix into me, but I don't understand them. There's tension, like a string stretched too tight.

Beneath my buzzing is a heaviness, almost a yearning. Grief?

I'm not sure which feelings belong to whom.

"From the valley," the keepers say as we watch the pyres burn. There is a faint briny smell on the breeze, there and gone, replaced with smoke and ash. Before we finish the words, the bodies of the creatures are gone. "To the valley."

The phoenix pulses with a note of relief and a deeper contentment. This, at least, is right.

We turn to the next pyre, taller than the creatures.

Bartholomew.

My mentor for seventeen years, and a good one, I suppose. Not kind or patient or pleasant, but he took his role as my teacher seriously and he was thorough. My failures were my own. He made sure of that.

No family steps forward to share final goodbyes. He always said his dragons were his only family. But one killed him and is hiding in the forest. The other is about to be used to burn his body.

Part of me hopes that the skull mourns, that the bonds we form with those closest to us continue into the after.

I think of the phoenix I am wearing and the bond I cannot break with her. And of Etana, who is standing a far distance away. As soon as I matched with the phoenix, she stopped following me around the valley. But today many of the creatures are nearby, watching closely.

A lock of my hair blows in the wind and gets caught on the beak of the phoenix, so it's covering one eye. I brush it away, back behind the skull. It's a small movement, but it steadies me for a beat.

The elders didn't ask me to speak. Of course they didn't. They don't want me standing in front of everyone, wearing a skull, reminding everyone of my failures. Of their deaths.

I'm too strange. Too wrong.

I can feel eyes on me, watching to see what I'll do next. Or maybe they're waiting for me to realize what they already believe. I do not belong here anymore.

Petra steps forward. She lights a torch from the embers of Gilcriss's pyre and moves to Bartholomew's.

"Thank you for your care and keeping," we say as his pyre is lit. The fire explodes upward. That heat, that force—but this time it feels more personal. Like it's burning away part of me, too. My past. My future.

I stare into the flames, feeling them lick at the edges of my shame.

It is so fast. I barely blink and what's left of my mentor is gone. He will serve the valley in his death as he did in life.

But me? How will I serve the valley now?

The rest of the day we pass along to the high priestess. The order funerals are much more elaborate than ours. There are songs and prayers, places where we kneel and stand, and many, many calls and responses.

I'm not there. I am in the wind, swaying in the trees, in the sun as the day lengthens.

Toward the end I want to snatch a torch and set the priest ablaze myself. I cannot stand another moment of ritual; another moment chanting about goodbyes. But I don't have to.

Finally, High Priestess Sarai lights the pyre. Finally, it is done.

Everyone meanders away except me. I stand frozen in my own self-loathing as piles of soft gray ash begin to dissipate in the wind. Everything that was left of these five lives—gone.

Because of me.

Chapter Sixteen

KIAN

Adela stands watching the pyres burn, half-crumpled into herself. I ache to go to her, wrap her up in my arms and smooth back her hair around the phoenix skull and give her kisses. It's the sort of caregiving and emotional support I didn't think I was capable of wanting.

And I'm sure I'm not capable of successfully providing.

Honestly, I wouldn't mind some soothing myself.

The funerals were gruesome.

I'm not surprised they stopped the dragon-fire burnings in the temple square if this was what they were like. The scent of rancid meat cooking mingles with the warm, pleasant aromas of the herbs and oils used to prepare the bodies.

Only this was surely worse. At least the order funerals involve whole bodies. Today not a single body that we burned was whole. Bile rises, remembering how they all looked up on their pyres. Partial bodies prepared to burn. The creatures had no heads. The former matcher and Brother Thad were both missing significant chunks of themselves to the dragon.

The only thing I've experienced that felt more violent was my parents' executions.

The phoenix throws feelings at me, urging me to go to Adela. I know she blames herself for it all. But I can't. Because there's only the tiniest bit of dragon fire right there in front of me and my destiny waits just past the jackalope warrens. Which I now know how to get past, thanks to Cecelia.

I take a small stick and shove it deep into the embers, waiting to see if it will light and hold a flame. It does.

Thank the Goddess.

It's a small enough flame that I think it'll go unnoticed in the midafternoon light. I'm sure I can smuggle it into my room and keep it burning. I have the candles already, so I just have to wait. Apparently jackalopes only mate during storms, and when they do it is . . . fervent. So the moment lightning strikes or thunder rolls, they are too busy with their amorous pursuits to pay attention to strangers in their territories. I'll be able to get past them and to the hut.

And then, poof.

The skulls will be gone.

I think of Adela as I traipse back to my room. She really could use a friend. But of course, she has Cecelia. She doesn't need me. They're so close, and I imagine what that would be like. To have someone who actually sees all of you, knows all of you, and still loves you.

I haven't had that since my parents died, and I don't need it now.

Just after the midday meal the next day, I take Adela back to my room. I offer her a bit of the whiskey that I snagged from the kitchens my first night in the valley. She takes it with a small smile and downs it in one gulp, holding the glass out for a refill. I oblige, nervous about how much she might drink.

"Thirsty?" I say as I pour her another glass, slightly less full than the first.

"Nervous," she admits, and sets the small amber glass down on the bedside table beside the burning dragon-fire candle. "I've never been ordered to perform before."

"Lucky you," I reply, not thinking.

She looks at me with such an expression of horror that I can see it even past the skull covering most of her face. "That's so hard."

Her compassion, the easy way she seems to see me, makes me squirm. I shrug. "It's not as bad as it sounds."

Or probably as direct as she was thinking. It's not as if I'd been coerced by someone in particular into sex. I've never been assaulted or had any of the tragedies that regularly happen to people happen to me. But I have a goal I've been chasing at any cost since my teens. And if using my body to ingratiate myself was required, well then, I did what I needed to.

Like with Thad.

"If you'd like to talk about it, I'd be happy to listen," she says softly.

"Absolutely not." I can think of nothing worse. If I open up even a little bit, she'll ask more questions, and the last thing I need is the matcher to find out my ultimate goal is to destroy all of her precious skulls.

Or worse, to know me.

Adela's beautifully rounded shoulders slump at my harsh tone, and I feel guilty at the cruelty of my response to her kindness. I enjoy her. I enjoy our connection.

I have a ping of worry about this community after the disappearance of the skulls is discovered. They subsist largely through the offerings of the orders, which will surely stop the moment they can no longer provide skulls for matching.

Deaths happen in the valley all the time, so it's not as if they will permanently go away, but it will take a generation or more for them to ramp up production of skull matching to its current levels. My actions will have a broad, and devastating, impact.

I have a moment of wondering if I should follow Aunt Ujvala's advice and abandon this path of revenge. For Adela and her community.

But no.

This is the right step to disrupt the entire system, and it can't be a simple blip and still be effective. The old ways have to crumble for new, better ways. Instead of hoarded resources that prioritize the wealthy and withhold from the poor or disadvantaged, the community gardens and fresh foods could be open for all. Education and art could have more space to exist without common laborers having to work so hard just to make their tithes. And a more decentralized leadership could have space to form, where each of the orders had an equal voice and the ability to influence society in ways that feel good to their various missions, instead of the Huntress always having final say because they are the largest and wealthiest order.

If only Adela's community didn't have to suffer for the greater good.

I reach out and stroke a finger along one of those beautiful shoulders, enjoying the way she leans into my touch, like I am something comforting instead of destructive. Part of me wishes this connection we share could be real and lasting. "But thank you for the offer. It's just . . . not something I like to talk about."

She places a hand on my knee. "I'm here if you change your mind." It's an innocent enough touch. No doubt meant to comfort, but still, it enflames me. I move closer, hovering over her.

"There are more fun things we could talk about." I wrap an arm around her back, moving slowly, unsure how she feels at this moment. Obviously she'd been eager to have her way with me just days ago, and it's not as if we were forced into the room at knife point. She walked here willingly.

But I want to make sure she's as interested as I am.

And I am interested.

My body instantly wants her. I love the softness of her. The smell of her. The noises she makes deep in her throat, involuntarily, as she arches into me, pressing her breasts against my arm and chest as she twists toward me.

"Hey, beauty," I say as I lean forward to access her mouth.

She pulls back.

Instantly, I loosen my grip. I'm still touching her, but she can scoot away easily if she wants to.

"Problem?" I ask. My voice is deep and soft with desire.

"I don't want the beak to scratch you," she admits. Then she chuckles. "And the stubborn part of me doesn't want to do this. Just because we're supposed to."

Her eyes flash with mischief. I think of the way she took me in the pantry, the way she rode me, how she came. I think Adela may like playing with power.

"Rebelling can be very fun," I agree. "Let's not have sex."

Instantly, she deflates, which makes my body even more excited. She wants me, too. "Okay, sure. Let's not." I can hear the forced chipperness.

"Or at least, not the kind they expect." I lean close, nearly pressing my lips to her ear. I lick at the lobe, and then say, "There are lots of other ways to find and bring pleasure."

She exhales a shuddering breath and arches close to me again. I nip at her ear, and she gasps. "Yes."

I reach to strip her of her clothes. Her thighs have been haunting me for days, and I cannot wait to see her body naked before me, but she wiggles away. "Yours first."

It's not shyness that wants me unrobed before her. I can see it in her eyes; it's pure, naked lust. She wants to see me. And I want her to see me. I take off my outer robe. As it falls to the floor, I say, "I want to taste you. I want the skin of your neck, of your shoulders, salty with sweat from our bodies moving together, on my tongue."

She licks her lips, listening, watching. She leans back on her elbows on the bed, and it takes everything in me not to jump on top of her. "Where else would you like to taste me?"

"Your nipples." I think of the milkiness of her breasts, with their large pink nipples and how responsive they were to my touch. "I want to make them hard with my tongue, with my teeth."

"I want to make you hard with my tongue, with my teeth," she replies, looking up and down my body. I am very obviously already hard. "Or harder, I suppose."

My hand slips as I try to remove my inner robe and tunic in one motion. I get them half-twisted around my head, trip over the discarded outer robe, and nearly fall to the floor.

She chuckles, and then stops as I discard the clothes. I am now bare except for thin linen breeches. Her eyes trace the tattoos that cover my torso and arms, symbols of the Huntress that will always be with me. "Oh, you are beautiful."

She reaches out, and though we are just supposed to be talking, I immediately go to her. I cannot resist her touch. She traces fingertips up and down my shoulders, chest, arms, and belly. Her touch is so light it's nearly painful. I feel as if she is touching my soul itself, and a part of me wants to run, far and fast.

Not from her, but from the part of myself that wants this, desperately.

"Now these," she commands, hooking a single finger at the waistband of my breeches.

I focus on the physical and push aside any feelings.

It's just lust.

She's beautiful, and my body remembers vividly how good she felt on top of me, taking me, riding me. That's all.

I scoot out of my pants. Awkwardly, but still, I manage it. I am totally bare. The hungry way she looks at me makes me twitch.

"May I?" she asks, her hand hovering over me. I nod, and she wraps her fingers around me. Gone are the gentle caresses. She grips me with a firmness that makes me moan. She leans her face close to mine, very carefully, not getting the sharp edge of the phoenix's beak anywhere near my skin. "Now tell me."

"Tell you what, beauty?" I ask. My mind is not working. I literally cannot think of a single thing beyond this moment.

She smiles as if she can read my mind. "Tell me what you want to do to me."

I do. I tell her how I want her body around me, on top of me. I tell her about the filthy things I want to do to her. The way I want to make her scream with my hands and mouth and cock. As I do, she moves her hand up and down on me and makes encouraging sounds. She is still fully clothed, wearing a skull of a creature, a symbol of power that I abhor. And she's about to make me climax.

I should stop. I should reciprocate. The things I am telling her are true. I know I suggested no sex, but I regret that choice in this moment. I want my mouth on her, my cock in her.

I need her.

"I will tell you what I want," she says when I lose my words. I am so, so close to losing all control. I have not even touched her. "I want you to come."

"No," I say, holding back with every ounce of my will. "Not yet."

She pauses, instantly. Her voice is earnest, serious, when she says, "Do you want me to stop?"

I thrust up into her hand, loving the feel of her on me. I don't want her to stop, I just don't want to come. Yet. A good lover brings their partner pleasure first. And here I am, naked and about to lose myself all over her hand without even having touched her.

I'm incapable of words, but Adela sees to the heart of me.

"I want to watch you." Her voice is low, thick with desire. "I want to watch you take your pleasure. But only if you want that, too."

Again I move my hips, grinding against her. "Yes." I moan. She licks her lips and instantly begins to move her hand on me again.

"Come for me," she demands. "Now."

I do, an explosion of want that makes a mess of us both. After a few moments so the world can right itself again and I can breathe, I move to kiss her, but she pulls away again. I hold her jaw and tilt her head. I know she worries about scratching me. "That was amazing. You are amazing."

She smiles and scoots to the edge of the bed as if she is going to get up and leave. "That was very fun."

"Oh, we are not done, beauty." I go down on my knees before her. She still has her clothes on, which is suboptimal—I really am desperate to see her—but I can't wait another moment to taste her want.

I push up the hems of her robe and bury my face in her without preamble. She is as delicious as I expect, already wet and swollen with want. I lap her up, loving the way she moves and moans against my face and fingers.

I grip one perfect thigh and press it away so I can get deeper into her. I press hard against her, licking. She clenches and throbs around my fingers, and I gently hook them in a "come hither" motion.

And she does. Suddenly climaxing hard, spasming beautifully. I tease her with little licks that make her twitch and when she whimpers for mercy, I give her a kiss on each thigh.

Afterward, I lie down in bed and hold my arms open to her. She crawls up next to me, tucking the beak of the phoenix down and into my chest. I put my chin on top of her head. I both love and hate how well we fit. Some part of me I don't understand wants more of her. Not sexually—I'm satiated there, at least for the moment—but to know her more.

I think about her life in the valley, what might matter to her. There's been one thing that I've been curious about since I realized her family is just her and her dad.

"Tell me about your family," I say. "When did your mother die?"

"Die?"

"Surely she's dead," I reply. "I haven't met her, and it's not as if keepers leave the valley."

She tenses in my arms, and I wish I could see her face.

"She did leave, actually. When I was twelve. She left a note saying she'd be back by the time the spring trees had bloomed. I haven't seen her since. I honestly don't know if she is dead or alive. But she did leave."

I get the sense she doesn't want to talk about this anymore, and something deep inside of me that I don't understand compels me to share something as well. "I lost my parents almost twenty years ago as well. But they are most assuredly dead."

I think of that morning. It was crisp, and the sky was a brilliant, beautiful blue, thick with fluffy clouds. Against Aunt Ujvala's direct instructions, I went to the courtyard of the Temple of the Huntress and stood on the steps so I could see. Mom spotted me first, and then Dad. They were too far away to hear, but I watched them each say, "I love you."

I was so full of anger and despair. I was still so young, but I knew with certainty I would never be okay without them. So instead of saying the thing I always said in response—"I've loved you for more of my life"—through tears and snot, my fingernails digging into my palms, I replied to the air, "I hate you."

And I did. I hated them for getting caught. For leaving me.

My only comfort was that they never saw. Their executioners completed their tasks before "hate" left my lips.

"I watched them die."

She doesn't reply, just nestles in closer until we fall asleep. When I wake from the short nap, she is gone. I tell myself not to miss her. She is not mine.

Even if my body and my heart want her to be.

Chapter Seventeen

ADELA

I walk home, but it is not far enough away from the gorgeous, distracting novitiate. I can still feel him, and all I want is to go to him. To fling myself into his arms and beg him to take me again.

I need to do something with my hands, and my mind. Beside the back door is Bartholomew's golden mask. Four days since he's been gone, and it feels like a lifetime.

I suppose it's my mask now. I should put it away with the rest of my matcher items upstairs or give it to Beadda. But a small part of me wants to keep it. To keep both—the phoenix and the matcher position. My conversation with Cecelia about accepting what I want and who I am, even when I'm ashamed, circles through me.

If I cannot rid myself of the phoenix, but I could match, I would have so many more options. I could stay in the valley, or—there was a time when people moved in and out of the valley easily. It's in the old matcher journals. Perhaps I could do that. I could serve both the Huntress and my community. I could have Kian. I could have Dad, and Cecelia, and Etana.

Everyone I love.

And then I catch the thought that slid its way in without me noticing. No. I do not love Kian. I enjoy the way his body feels, and the way he makes me laugh, and looking at his gorgeous face when it's not covered by a phoenix skull, but surely I don't love him. Not yet. It's still so new.

Maybe in time, if we have more of it. If I go to Insborough with the order.

To decide what future I will embrace, I need to know what my options are. I snatch my cloak, throwing it on my shoulders, and grab a carrot in case Etana is nearby, then march out to face my fate head-on.

The sky is bright blue with wisps of clouds peeking out over the mountains. I inhale deeply. No matter how impulsive I am, how much I do things I never mean to, at least the late afternoon sky does not judge me.

I'm supposed to be heading to the matching hut, but there's something pulling me toward the forest. A compulsion I don't understand. I let it guide me, assuring myself it's not just to avoid the skulls and what I may or may not still be capable of.

I step into the forest, and the moment my feet hit the squishy floor, littered with pine needles and decaying leaves, waves of emotion overwhelm me. Some of them are my own. I haven't spent much time in the forest since I was young, but in the year after Mom left, I spent almost every waking hour here. Walking. Thinking. Crying next to trillium and wondering what was so wrong with me that she would just . . . leave. Praying to the great goddess that she would come back to me. Bargaining everything and anything I could think of.

I would have traded the world for my mom. Mom, with her silvery-blond hair and eyes that were always either crinkled with laughter or streaming tears, and rarely anything in between. Mom, who gave the best, squishiest hugs and told me I was more rare, more powerful, and more beautiful than the long-extinct phoenix.

She's really one of the only keepers I know who even told stories of the phoenix, and I wonder if she somehow knew what my future held.

But no, of course not. How would she?

We didn't even know the skulls were up there. It was just one of the silly things she said to make her silly daughter feel special.

And it worked.

My tears soak into the bone of the phoenix skull, and a wave of hurt and overwhelm flows through me. The phoenix has feelings about the forest as well. Fear and anger, sorrow and pain.

She urges me deeper, into the heart of it. The trees become thicker the farther we go. In the summer, the undergrowth here would be sparse, starved of light by the thick canopy above. Today the leaves are still just buds, and eager shoots sprinkle the ground, stretching toward the thin early spring light straining through the heavy clouds.

I walk on, crushing as few of the little plants as possible until I find the narrow path we keep clear for the orders to use on their way into to the valley. As a symbol of the novitiates' ascension to full priesthood, it's intentionally winding. It'd be silly of me to follow the entire thing, but taking it for a while is easier than forging my own way.

And by now, I suspect where the pull is leading. In the center of the forest is a massive oak. As kids, we used to trek out and climb it between chores, daring each other to go higher and higher into its branches.

The phoenix flashes images of it at me. Not visions, precisely, but quick memories. It is smaller than I remember it, but also more vital. To me, it was always just a big old tree, beautiful but insignificant. To her it is something important. But I cannot figure out what. Was it her home? Where she died? There's a sense of loss and longing and . . . hope, perhaps.

I am nearly to the oak's base when my toe hits the edge of a root, and I go sprawling. I catch myself with my face, which is a very stupid way to catch oneself. The beak of the phoenix digs into the soft earth.

Beside me I see something little, red, and shining in the soft light. I pick it up, squinting at it, so out of place here in the forest.

There is nothing natural about this glass stone, and I wonder if the keeper children have been playing out here like we used to. With the dragon still roaming, still hurting creatures and animals and people, they've been instructed to stay in the village, where it's safer. Or at least, hypothetically. After the cath palug attack, many of the keeper parents are keeping their children at home as much as possible.

I push myself up from the ground as a slender beam of sunlight breaks through the clouds and illuminates a spot on the path a few steps ahead. In the spot of sunlight is another red stone. I scramble forward and snatch it, then begin to search for more.

Again, farther down the path is another.

And a bit farther, another.

Someone has marked the path. I begin to follow the stones through the woods. The phoenix urges me forward. Whether that's because they've caught her curiosity as well or just because we're still heading closer to her tree, I am uncertain.

I collect another half-dozen stones before I feel the world shift beneath me.

We catch an updraft, soaring over the pegasus cliffs and the dragon caves, the wyvern warrens, and the gryphon nests in the far-off trees, enjoying the summer bounty below.

The safe and verdant valley. The land provides us with sustenance. The people on it, protection.

The magic's growth is as swift as a lark trying to escape being my mate's breakfast. Or, no, something far more dangerous. The magic is wild, viscious, destroying.

The gryphons are dying in birth from having too many babies at a time. The kelpie are shedding chunks of mane at the edges of the riverbank. The jackalopes so aggravated that in their fights for territory, they are killing one another.

And we cannot tell what is wrong.

The vision might be the most powerful one I've had yet. It was the clearest. I was the phoenix, and the world was sharp, not the golden haze of the usual ones. I'm having a hard time shaking the worry in it.

And then I hear a shattering equine scream from the other side of the tree.

I rush to find Etana on the ground in a pool of blood and mucus, Lathai over her. She's giving birth. He paws the ground and flaps his wings, screaming again. He nudges her, and she moves, slightly, but is clearly exhausted. Her belly heaves, but no foal emerges.

I hurry to her, dropping the red stones on the earth beside me. I am no healer, not like Dad, but I hope instinct will be enough for me to help her, to save her.

Because like the gryphon in my vision, she is dying in childbirth.

Lathai screams again as I get to her, and the heavens open above us. Lightning and thunder and torrential rain.

"The timing isn't great, my friend," I say to the pegasus, who is obviously not doing this on purpose. It's like the pulses of magic that happen. I am the cause, but not intentionally. Same with him and the storm, though I have never seen one so large caused by a pegasus. They're usually more like a summer shower. This is full of rage and grief, just like Lathai. He snorts at me and bares his teeth, stomping the ground again.

I raise my hands, palms empty and up, and dip my head. "Friend," I say. "I'm her friend."

He knows this. He knows me. But he is a wild creature, and his mate appears to be dying. Cautiously, I approach her, afraid he will attack. He does not like it. He paces as the storm rages above us. But he allows it.

I check Etana. Her breathing is shallow, and she's covered in sweat. There should be a foal's nose and two feet sticking out of her, but there's nothing but a red, velvety membrane. This is bad. I reach forward to try to rupture the membrane, but Lathai snaps at me, not wanting me to touch her.

"Let me help," I plead, and try to reach forward again.

He rears and lands hard next to me, a clear warning.

I don't know what to do. I don't know how to help. I want to scream, but it's not Lathai's fault he's protective. And then it all gets worse. Lightning strikes the giant tree above us. Lathai protects Etana with his body and wings, but I am scraped raw by the flying bark.

Beside him, Etana rears, screaming a warning at the same moment that I feel a gust of too-warm wind at my back. I spin in time to see Enkidus descending quickly, her taloned feet stretched toward me. I remember the way Duschwa's insides spilled out of her, the way Bartholomew's body lay broken and half-devoured in his home.

I fling myself backward at the same moment Etana flings herself forward.

But no. She was just barely surviving birth. And now she is up, using hooves and her horn to kick and rend. To protect me. Lathai jumps in as well, nipping and kicking.

Enkidus was coming for me, but she defends herself from the attacks, like any living thing would. Lathai dodges the dragon, but Etana, who is closest, slowest, as weak as she is, cannot move fast enough.

Enkidus slashes at Etana. Deep-red blood gushes from a wound on her back, yet Etana fights. Somehow she manages to pin the dragon's wing to the ground and uses her horn again. It sinks deeply into Ekindus's eye. The dragon cries out and then lashes with her tail, catching Etana hard in the belly and throwing the unicorn off, then launches herself into the air. She hovers momentarily, pulling her neck back. She's going to spit fire.

"Etana, run!" I shout, but she can't. She can barely stand.

Enkidus hisses flame. The fire catches Etana on her back. She goes down, hard, skidding across the old leaves and pine needles. Enkidus flies away with Lathai chasing her, and I hurry forward. Etana's belly is heaving, her back is covered in blood, and along her neck are burns so bad it looks as if her flesh and hair have all melted. I gag at the smell of it, like burnt meat.

"Etana, my love. Stand up for me." We have to get back to the village. We have to get to Dad.

She struggles to do as I ask, but she cannot stand. She is making low, awful noises, and her breathing is shallow and raspy, a rattle I do not trust. I stand, considering my options. I can stay with her and watch her die, or I can risk the trek to Dad. She still might die, but she'd do it alone.

I scream into the night sky.

At the skull on my face.

At Etana, trying to protect me instead of running away and saving herself.

But mostly at myself.

This is my sin, my fault my star sister is dying at my feet. If I hadn't polished the phoenix, the first pulse would never have gone through the valley in the first place. Enkidus wouldn't have lost her mind.

I have to fix it. I have to save Etana.

I run back to the village. Or at least, I do my best. It's too far for me to sustain a straight sprint, but I move as fast as I can, ignoring the stitch in my side and the clamoring phoenix skull on my face, which wants me to return to the forest, to the tree. She seems to care nothing at all about the dying unicorn who just saved us both. But she does not have feet. I do.

"Stop!" I yell into the night, to her, frightening a rabbit from the underbrush. "Unless you can get me to move faster through your mysterious magic, I don't want to feel another thing from you."

Surprisingly, the phoenix listens, falling still.

In time, I make it to my house. Dad is not there. He could be anywhere in the village.

I go outside and practically run into him. Thank the goddess. He takes one look at my face and asks what's wrong.

"Etana," I manage between gulps of air. "Dying. Dragon. The foal."

We hurry back to the forest, as fast as we can. I fill him in on the way, and the more I share, the faster we move. But Dad is not a young man. We do not move as quickly as I'd like, and I half wish I'd taken the time to get one of the horses.

The whole way, I silently say prayers to the goddesses. The Spinner, for strength. The Pupil, for my father's wisdom in how to keep Etana alive. But most of my prayers go to the Huntress to stay her hand. To show mercy, though she is not known to do anything of the sort. I make promises I'm not sure I can keep. That if she will spare Etana and her baby, I will go to the order. I will serve her, gladly, for the rest of my life.

When we are close, I hear another scream. We get to the clearing and find Lathai back. His anger has waned, and the storm along with it. He is on his knees beside Etana, nudging her gently. She is already dead. I brought Dad too late. I was too slow.

I left her here, to die without me.

"I'm so sorry," I say to the night. "I'm so, so sorry."

Dad crouches down beside her, checking her vitals. He sits back, shaking his head.

"She's gone?" I ask.

He looks at me, tears in his eyes. "Not yet. But now is the time to say your goodbyes."

Chapter Eighteen

KIAN

I am lying in my bed, thinking of Adela and how much more pleasure I want to give her, when I hear the first rumble of thunder. I look out the window. There is a storm raging. Lightning, thunder, torrential rain.

This. This is my chance.

A sudden, intense flash of light makes its jagged path across the sky, and thunder crashes almost immediately after. The storm is close, and so sudden.

I grab the dragon-fire candle.

I hope that I don't run into anyone in the hallway. I'm not sure how I'll explain carrying a lit candle into a storm. Not even the truth would be very believable.

I hurry out of the great hall. I see a few keepers crossing the village square, but everyone is running to their homes, getting out of the rain. They pay me no mind.

Thank the Spinner.

I hurry across the meadows and get to the rolling hill at the edge of the jackalopes' territory. I can see the matching hut just sitting there, beckoning me, but I pause, remembering Ivo's leg. The way the blood gushed, how deep and long the last wound was, how quickly he went pale and weak.

This needs to work.

There is a tug deep inside me to somewhere else. The phoenix has been quiet recently; now he floods me with feelings and images, shoving them through me. He wants me deep in the forest, in a clearing with a large tree that's somehow important to him. He presses me to go, more insistent than he's ever been. Is it a ruse? Perhaps he does not want me destroying his kin. He shows me Adela, and I'm certain he thinks I'm about to make a mistake. To hurt her.

And he's not wrong.

This path is harder now than before I arrived in the valley. Now that I know the people I'm hurting. Not the order—every year amongst them has made me believe more firmly that this is necessary. But the keepers. Another community that is being controlled, just like the working poor in Insborough.

With no masks to match, keepers will likely be cut off from their current supports—the goods that keep them alive. They talk frequently about how harsh the winters are, how slow the spring thaw, how miserable the harvests. And it's not as if they can simply harvest some of their farm animals. They don't eat meat, and not even keepers can survive on cheese and eggs alone.

I will certainly harm them with this action. Adela's family. Her friends. Her. But I have to trust their ability to adjust, because there won't be another chance.

Magic is what gives the order their power, their influence. It is what allows them to offer forceful favors and monstrous threats. If I want to make space for the people of Insborough to better govern themselves, to break free of the inequitable tithes and unfair rule of the order, removing their access to as much magic as possible is the best way to do it. I have to move forward, and I have to do it now.

I climb over the hill to set it down just within the border of jackalope territory. Cecelia wasn't exaggerating. Everywhere, jackalopes are mating. Hundreds of them. So many more than I knew existed, and not one is concerned that I exist, let alone that I'm in their territory. The candle flickers in the rain as I maneuver through them, but holds. I'm careful not to step on any of the randy little beasts.

I stop before the porch of the matching hut. Like all the buildings in the valley, it's so unassuming. Just a simple wooden hut, but it holds so much history and power.

If only the magic inside were wielded well. How much good the orders could do in the world.

I lift my face up to the pouring rain and think of my parents in the temple square, how even in the end, they held their tongues. They didn't give away the rest of the family's operations. They didn't reveal whatever secrets they died for. They stayed loyal to their principles. They were so good. So much better than me.

"I've loved you for more of my life," I say to the weeping sky and toss the dragon-flame candle onto the wooden porch.

The flames rush up—virulent, an instant blistering heat unaffected by the rain. The dragon fire's crackling flame rips through the wooden-framed building. Within moments, there are pops of oil jars exploding and the groan of a beam giving way.

The ceiling collapses, smoke pouring out into the stormy sky.

It's all so fast.

The storm rages above, as violent and swift as the burning

matching hut. Thunder roars as a spear of lightning shoots from the thick black cloud hovering over the valley, directly into the center of the hut.

The forest watches silently, an uncaring witness to the devastation, while the jackalopes continue to copulate, simply moving their activities away from the scorching heat.

Window glass shatters outward, and the lightning's fire joins the dragon flame, a dance of hot colors mingling against the storm's gray skies. The walls of the matching hut creak and whine, then collapse, too. The workbenches and shelves and floor of the hut are already gone, burned to thick ash, but I can see a pile of skulls, still vibrant and white amidst the flames.

Terror they will not actually burn slides through me, overwhelming me, until the skulls begin to darken around their edges. Finally. My glee is almost immediately replaced with repulsion. I choke back bile. The smell is staggering, the scent of burning creature bone so much worse than the bodies at the funeral pyre. The wind of the storm howls, shifting the odors away from me and encouraging the hungry flame. It grows brighter and bigger.

This is what I've worked for, sacrificed a comfortable, familiar life with my family for. This is what I wanted. It should feel like victory. I've reached my first goal, crossed a line no one can ever recross.

There is no going back.

I expected to feel the shift deep within me, as if the world sat up and noted how much it had changed, but there's no great transformation. The late afternoon is wet and smells of smoke. With nothing more to burn, the fire begins to peter out, as if it's just an overly large campfire being allowed to die in the night.

Instead of any sort of delight or pride, I experience a slow, creeping ache that I don't understand. And then immediately on its heels, a piercing horror pours into me.

Adela is in trouble. Adela is in anguish. Adela needs me.

The phoenix sends me images of the large tree in a clearing in the forest again. I have no idea where that is, nor do I need to.

I follow the pull of Adela into the forest.

Chapter Nineteen

ADELA

The forest is dark, expectant. Harsh winds move through the trees, dropping thick beads of rain from broken leaves. Everything feels on edge. The air carries a heavy stillness that comes just before the world breaks apart. It's not silence, but waiting. I go to Etana, sitting down beside Lathai. He does not threaten me now. He's defeated. His love is dying. The ground is soft beneath us, churned by our fight with the dragon. Mud clings to the roots like old blood.

Or perhaps it *is* blood. The blood seeping out of Etana.

I want to collapse on top of her, somehow hold her together with my body. But I'm afraid my weight will only make it harder for her—her breath is already sharp and labored.

The forest around us seems to close in, like spectators at the scene of an accident, unsure of what to do but wanting to bear witness to the horror.

Kian bursts out of the forest and into the clearing. "What?" He cannot speak, he's breathing too hard. But relief obviously rushes through him at the sight of me. "The phoenix—"

He sits beside me in the dirt and tries to draw me close. I shove him away. His comfort is suffocating, and besides, I do not deserve his soothing. My chest is tight and my breath comes in short, sharp gasps, my hands trembling from the intensity of my emotion. Waves of helplessness, guilt, and anguish wash over me, threatening to drown me. I shift, trying to get closer to Etana, and it's as if the roots beneath me shift, like the forest itself is recoiling from the emotion spilling out of me, wild and raw.

I want to rip the bird skull off my face. What use is it, wearing one of the beastly skulls, if I don't even have the magic to go along with it? If I cannot help my friend.

My thoughts spiral, a vortex of anger, regret, and confusion, and I feel my vision narrow. Images, clear and cruel, flood my mind and confirm what I have suspected since Cecelia shared her theories in the library—the phoenix magic is two halves of a whole. Destruction and rebirth. And I am the destruction half of this pairing.

But to use destruction to save my friend would mean—A strangled laugh, bitter and hollow, escapes me, and the air buzzes with a charged anticipation. Is this who I am now? I was born a keeper, the daughter of a healer. If there is one thing you learn early in the valley, it is that life is cyclical, and there are worse things than death. Like futile suffering. If there is no chance that Etana could live, the kindest thing to do would be to end her agony.

But I am not strong enough for that.

Again, emotion and images flood through me. Strength. Grit. Duty. Stewardship.

"There is absolutely no hope?" I ask Dad.

He shakes his head. "I'm sorry, love. She's still here, but it's a matter of time. You should go home."

"Home?" I would never. I could never. It feels like the forest leans in, but I'm uncertain if it's an offer of shelter or a trap.

"This is going to be a long and drawn-out goodbye. Don't stay to watch her suffer and struggle. Remember her brave and strong. Not in agony." He gives my arm a squeeze. "I won't leave her."

"Neither will I." My voice is sharp, cutting through the howl of the storm's wind.

I place my hands on Etana's burnt skin. I do not want to do this. I hate this. I have always tried to be so careful.

When I slip, I fall hard.

I slipped with the phoenix, and my actions have led directly here. There is no going back to undo them. There is no future in which they're fixed. There are only two awful choices—to let Etana languish in pain or to stop being selfish and use the power the phoenix is promising to end her misery.

Though it feels as if my heart is shattering, I pull from the phoenix skull. There is no gentleness in me. There is no hesitation. I will not stop until I'm done. If this is all I am good for, all I can do to help my star sister, then so be it.

"Do this," I say aloud. "You will do this. Now."

The phoenix flows through me. There is no resistance, no hesitation. The magic bubbles up into me, flowing wild and ruinous.

I feel my magic flow into her. I kill Etana.

Chapter Twenty

KIAN

The moment the unicorn passes, Adela's phoenix mask finally releases. It falls off her face, onto the earth, right beside a pile of red stones.

My red stones.

The ones I used to mark the path into the valley.

But I can't think of the implications of Adela finding these right now. I'm too busy staring at her face. Her beauty, and her pain. She has gashes across her perfectly rounded cheekbones. The slightly upturned curve of her delicate nose is red and raw. The pale arches of her eyebrows are tinged slightly pink from where they've caught seeping blood from her scrapped forehead.

Lathai rages, the storm growing more violent as he stomps and snorts and flashes his wings. I expect him to attack us, to get us away from his love, but he must understand. There is nothing more we can do to hurt Etana now. She is gone.

I wrap Adela up in my arms, to protect her from the wind and rain. I use my sleeve to dab away what I can, and she buries her face in my chest.

I'm surprised her father isn't there beside me, instantly examining her cuts and scrapes, but he's hovering over the unicorn. He removes a small blade from his bag of tools and kneels beside Etana's corpse. After whispering some words to the dark forest, he slices down her belly.

There is a sickly sweet, coppery scent, and I involuntarily shift away from the violence of it. Blood, guts, and a small, unmoving foal still in its embryonic sack pour out on the forest floor.

This is the work of a healer. It is not all tender hands and tidy bandages. Her father gently releases the foal from its sack. "She would have been magnificent."

"Dad?" Adela's raw, terrified voice cuts through me, and I want to pull her back into my chest, shield her from it all until she no longer sounds as if she must either sob or perish. Or potentially both. Her sorrow is palpable.

Her dad shakes his head, a universal sign. There is no luck or blessing from the goddesses that would make this foal live. Adela's magic has killed it along with its mother. Or perhaps it died before Etana. I don't know enough about the process of unicorn births to tell.

Adela pulls farther away, putting a hand on the unicorn's back. I glance quickly at Lathai, concerned he'll object, but he is too busy nosing at Etana's face, as if trying to revive her. He isn't paying attention to Adela, or even his lost foal.

Adela strokes Etana, as if her touch will calm the dead creature. She needs calm herself, but I know that her night is just going to get worse. She is free of the phoenix at last, but by destroying the matching hut, I have stolen any hope of her returning to her old life.

Shortly, Etana will become a skull. The first and only skull in the valley for a time, but keepers do not need a matcher for a single skull. And High Priestess Sarai will never allow someone with Adela's newly revealed power to escape her machinations.

Adela's fate was fully sealed the moment I tossed the dragon-lit candle. I've burned any hope of her staying to the ground. And she doesn't even know it yet.

"Kian." Her voice trembles with hope and trepidation. It cuts through the oppressive silence, and my guilt.

"Save them."

Save them? The words, so simple and yet fully unfathomable, splash against me like the softening rain. They fly up into the forest canopy and then crash against me. I stare at Etana, then the small hybrid creature torn from her mother's womb. Save them. As if I am capable of such a thing. I am no keeper, no healer.

Adela takes my hands. She places them on Etana. Still red with despair, her eyes brighten with frantic possibility. "Use your magic. Save her. Save them."

My magic. Of course. The phoenixes work in tandem. Two parts of a whole. If Adela is destruction, I must become rebirth.

But how? To destroy is simple, straightforward. Break it. Smash it. Kill it. But to recreate life? I close my eyes and see the matching hut burning before me. I am made for destruction.

She whimpers. "Please."

For Adela, I have to try. I focus on Etana, but the moment I even begin to think about pouring magic into her, the phoenix sends a refusal through me so strongly that it hurts. Adela must feel it, too, because she cries out as if I have stabbed her. He either cannot or will not attempt to revive a creature killed by magic.

Images of the foal pan through instead. Running through a flower-filled meadow, bedding down beneath a bush, flying amongst the pegasi.

Adela scrabbles for my hands, placing them back on the small creature, pressing them tightly into her unmoving ribs. "Try to revive the foal. Please. Try the foal."

Adela's father is beside her, trying to pull her away. He tucks her head into his chest, protecting her from whatever comes next. But she doesn't want protection. She wants resurrection.

The foal's coat is white, like her mama's, and still sticky with amniotic fluids. She is so thin, spindlier than even a typical horse foal with long legs and a narrow, delicate face. On her forehead is a small bump, the beginnings of a horn. A gift from her mother. Lathai's gift, wings, protrude from her back, massive compared to the rest of her and majestic, even covered in goop.

As if my thoughts somehow broke through his grief, Lathai attends to us. He stomps a heavy hoof.

Now is my chance, if I'm going to do this.

I close my eyes. I imagine a building of pressure like Ulric discussed and let my will flow through me. What does it matter if I don't believe in myself? This beautiful, hurting woman who means more to me than I'm ready to admit believes in me.

I bend down over the foal, whispering in her overly large, wet ear, "If you do not revive, some smelly novitiate is going to wear your face for the rest of their days and you will have never known the taste of fresh summer grass or the warmth of a midday sun."

The pressure is building, but I cannot access it. The phoenix feels as if it is beating frantic wings inside me, chipping away at the wall I've put between us. I drop my defenses and release the impossible pressure. I imagine shoving the magic into the small body of the foal. She will breathe. She will stand. She will pop up and canter into the night, or whatever shit newborn unicorn-pegasus hybrids do in this valley.

The foal shudders.

"Spinner's tits," Adela's dad whispers, something like reverence lacing his words.

I scramble backward.

The foal's eyes open. They are solid black, lined with thick lashes. She springs up on wobbly, twig-like legs. We stare at the creature who looks more like some ancient illustration of a creature than the flesh and blood of her parents.

"Is-is that how it's supposed to look?" I ask.

Adela is too busy sobbing and trying to crawl across the forest floor to the foal to respond. Her tears mix with the rain, and her whole body lurches forward, undone by loss. Mud cakes her hands, her clothes are soaked through with rain and grief. The storm lashes through the forest, wind tearing at branches, scattering new leaf buds and pine needles.

Her father answers.

"There's no 'supposed to' here. But also . . . no. Not what I'd expect." He steps forward, reaching out with hands still covered by blood. His voice is steady, but his eyes flicker to Lathai, then to Adela, and back to Etana. He clearly wants to examine the foal, but he's wary of the grieving pegasus and no doubt aches to comfort his daughter.

He takes a step forward, but Lathai is there between them. He stomps hard enough to make divots in the forest floor, which instantly fill with rainwater. He bares his teeth in warning. No one will approach his little one. Not now. Not while his grief is still so raw.

The foal headbutts Etana's belly to release her milk, but all that happens is more of her insides seep out through the cut Adela's dad made.

Adela stands, soaked and shivering, and approaches Lathai. The trees stop whipping in the lessening wind. Rain still falls, but slower. Lathai drops his head, waiting for her. She has just killed his mate, and still he allows her near. She kneels by the foal, and reaches out a shaky hand. "Come here, little one. I'll tell you of your mama as we get you some milk."

The creatures of the valley trust her, but this one doesn't know her yet. The foal flinches, ears pinning back, and twists away from Adela, skittish as a barn cat. And then, without a look back, she runs into the forest.

"No!"

Lathai goes after the little creature.

Adela moves to follow, too, but I quickly put an arm around her waist. She struggles against me, but has no strength left to truly fight.

"You're not catching her tonight," her dad says. "Let her go. And hopefully she'll come back when she's hungry or tired. Or Lathai will bring her."

"Hopefully?"

Her father shrugs, but it's not dismissive. He simply doesn't know for certain what will happen. He's a healer. He knows the ways of creatures—their habits, yes, but also their unpredictability. He turns back toward the faint, flickering lights of the village. "Let's go home. We'll come back in the morning with a cart and take care of our Etana then. Nothing we can do for her now."

The storm sighs above us, not yet done, but easing. We turn and walk back to the village and to whatever fate awaits me and Adela.

Chapter Twenty-One

ADELA

I follow Dad and Kian through the rain-slicked fields, numb. My legs move, but only because they're supposed to. Kian holds my hand—warm, steady, tethering—but I can barely feel it. I don't look at the grass underfoot or the dark outline of trees and brush or the moody, post-storm sky. I can't.

Because if I let in the details of the surrounding world, I'll let in the feelings of what just happened in the forest. And then I will be crushed.

We crest the hill.

On the other side, amidst the small mounds of jackalope warrens and puddles of rainwater, a group of people stand huddled together in the fading silver stormlight. Keepers and order members have voices raised—tense, frantic.

I shake my head, trying to push past my haze to figure out what is happening.

Or rather, what is missing. Because where there should be a building that holds both my past and my future, there is nothing. The matching hut is gone. And not just the hut, but everything inside it. Even if I could hear the skulls while paired to the phoenix, it would be silent. The skulls are gone. Nothing but wet ash sits before me.

Memories wash through me, threatening to drown me. Bartholomew's insistent voice, the old wood smell of the workbenches, the skulls arranged on the shelves with care. And then Bartholomew's house, a smoking pile of rubble, and his body, torn apart by the dragons he loved so dearly, in the middle of it. And Etana's body, currently lying in the forest, burnt and cut.

I wail, a raw, unintentional sound torn from my chest.

Heads turn. Faces sharpen in alarm.

Jasmyn points. "Her skull is off!"

I reach up. My fingers find bare skin where the phoenix skull has been for days. I have a brief moment where I wish she were back. Protecting me from their gazes.

Kian's hand tightens around mine. "I have it," he murmurs.

I want to rip it from him. I want him to have left it behind in the forest. I want it to have been in the hut when it burned. I want to throw it in the river with the last kelpie left in the world. I want a hundred impossible things at once. Grief surges and only some of it is mine. The phoenix is crying out through me, and I'm unable to untangle her sorrow from my own.

Dad strides ahead, pushing through the stunned crowd toward the elders. "What happened here?" he demands.

Redonna's face is streaked with tears. John looks ready to break something with his bare hands.

"The storm," Petra says, calm as ever. "Lightning struck the fountain. Took out a wing of the great hall. We assume it hit here as well."

My voice is hoarse when I find it. All I've heard is lightning hit the great hall. "Cecelia? The library?"

"Safe. It hit the wing with the novitiates' guest rooms, but no one was present. Most were eating dinner." Petra takes in Kian, covered in mud and grime. "No one was harmed."

A tiny flicker of relief, barely enough to spark.

"Ordinary lightning didn't do this," John says. "Or there would still be skulls."

Right, of course.

The skulls should be amongst the smoking remains, untouched by fire, protected by their own magic. But of course, it wasn't ordinary lightning. It wasn't an ordinary storm. Grief tore open the sky. Rage and sorrow with wings.

"Lathai caused the storm," I say.

"Would lightning from a magical creature's storm be enough?" Sister Roberta asks.

Petra cocks her head. "I suppose it could be a possibility. But we've always understood that only dragon fire could destroy the skulls."

"Perhaps it's broader than that and you've lost your history," High Priestess Sarai offers.

"Unfortunately, that is a real possibility. I believe we've lost much more than we've retained. But isn't that true of all histories? That is a question for tomorrow, after we've rested and the sun comes up to illuminate what we can learn from the ashes, if anything." Petra turns her attention toward me. Her gaze scans my face, the gore on my clothes, the unworn phoenix skull in Kian's hands. "In the meantime, what happened here?"

Dad looks at me.

It should be my story to tell. I am the one who brought this storm down on us all. But the words turn to gravel in my throat. I shake my head. I can't.

So Dad tells them.

I watch it unfold in their faces: shock, sorrow, fury. But the worst is the heartbreak. The pity. They do not know all the details—Dad intentionally left a lot out. But they know the worst of it. Etana is dead, at my hand.

Petra steps forward and enfolds me in her arms. Like Cecelia, she is not an affectionate woman. Her hugs are rare and reverent, like prayer. I cling to her, soaked and shaking, grateful for the silence, for the lack of questions.

In the moment. I know they'll come later. They always do.

High Priestess Sarai steps from the back of the crowd, the hem of her black bedgown soaked and covered in mud, her unicorn skull crooked on her head as if she put it on in a rush. The veil she always wears is gone. What I can see of her face is pale in the lantern light.

She studies me for a long breath, then speaks. "The bond?" Her gaze shifts to the phoenix skull in Kian's hands.

"Still there," I admit, wishing I could lie and stay behind in the valley.

"Come," she says, and turns away from the matching hut's remains and toward the great hall. "Let's talk."

I don't want to. Talking will lead to decision-making, and decisions will lead to me leaving the valley, as there is nothing left for me here but ash and pain.

Kian shifts beside me, instinctively protective. But Dad is faster, stepping in front of me like a shield. My constant guardian.

But I don't need protection from the high priestess.

She is the Huntress's voice. And I need the goddess now—need her to speak to me, through her priestess, through anything at all. To tell me why the goddess chose me to bring death. To tell me how to survive it, how to bring good into this world with it.

"I will come with you." I step out from behind Dad and Kian.

Dad places a hand on my cheek. "Adela, come home. Rest."

I lean into it. For a breath, I let myself believe in the possibility of it.

But his hand is sticky with blood and placenta. And there is a deep certainty within me that home is no longer an option.

Not now. Maybe not ever again.

I drag my tired, dirty, bloody body to the great hall, following behind High Priestess Sarai like one of our newborn lambs.

Kian walks beside me, carrying my phoenix skull. I can still feel her—can still feel them both—but I push away whatever emotions the phoenix sends my way and ignore the feeling that desperately makes me want to curl up in Kian's arms.

Every few steps he reaches for me, but I cannot reach back. It would feel too good.

I do not deserve comfort or warmth. I've caused so many deaths in a single week, but until now, they were all indirect. Repercussions of naive actions. But today I crossed a line I will never be able to come back from. Etana.

I killed Etana.

I reached for her with my magic, and it responded. And with that magic, I ended her life. And that of her unborn foal. It's only because of Kian that the little one is alive. I walk past the paintings and tapestries and sculptures of my people, past the library. I say a prayer of thanksgiving to the great goddess for sparing this at least. I can smell the smoke from the other wing and grieve the destroyed art and history that hung on its walls. We've lost so much.

We walk through high priestess's door. On the other side of it, she eyes Kian. "Are you staying?"

"Yes."

I sigh. "I don't need a guardian, Kian."

"Perhaps I do," he replies, with his familiar smirk. "If no one is watching out for me, I think I could cause all sorts of havoc. Destroy entire systems and societies."

I ignore his quip. I have no energy for them. I barely have the energy to collapse into the overstuffed chair she gestured to. If the high priestess isn't going to argue with him, I'm not. Kian scoots a wooden chair just beside me. Close enough to touch me if he needs to, though he doesn't.

I've been in this room before, of course, but never while a high priestess is in residence. It smells of cinnamon and rose and is lavishly decorated. Thick rugs line the floors, and heavy draperies are pulled back from the windows. Lathai's storm is almost entirely over, and I can see a few glittering stars in the now deep-blue night.

"Tea first, some salves for those wounds, then we'll talk." The high priestess swings a kettle to warm over the coals in her fireplace and throws a log on top. The fire roars. I close my eyes, soaking up the warmth and the quiet.

I hear the sounds of the water boiling, of her steeping the tea and preparing a tray. She brings it over and pours. She hands me a cup that is wide-mouthed and delicate. I despair for a moment that I will not be able to drink from it without breaking it with the phoenix's beak. And then I realize I'm not wearing the phoenix skull.

Right.

I hold the porcelain cup up to my nose. I rest the rim of it on my chin. I inhale deeply. The steam is fragrant, smelling of turmeric and ginger, and eases the sharp pains on my face.

She pours tea for herself and Kian. Kian removes his skull to drink, setting it on a small side table with my own, but I watch the high priestess carefully as she maneuvers around her unicorn skull.

I will have to learn how to imitate her movements, no doubt.

When we have drunk the tea and eaten the small snacks of spiced black walnuts and sugared apricots, she stands up again and goes to her washroom. She comes out with a small tin of salve and steps close to me.

She holds it out, her finger hovering above it. "May I?"

I nod, and she scoops out a generous portion, gently layering it over the sorest spots of my face. Again, I close my eyes at the care. If I weren't so numb, I suspect this might break me.

While no one can fault Dad's nurturing spirit, I have wanted this sort of mothering since I was twelve and woke up one morning abandoned. High Priestess Sarai's touch is gentle, and she murmurs soft kindnesses to me. I don't hear the words themselves. I don't need to.

The most powerful unicorn-wearers can sometimes influence feelings, and I wonder if she's using magic to relax me, or if it is simply tenderness.

Whatever the reason, my tired, bruised, broken soul soaks it up.

"Adela, I want to speak with you about your future," the high priestess says gently. She sets down the jar of salve within my reach and takes a seat near me. She leans in, watching me closely.

My future.

With the matching hut gone, so is the only future I ever knew as a possibility. The skulls had been gathered over decades. Even if I am allowed to stay here in the valley, I wouldn't be needed until my old age. Not as a matcher. And what else would I do?

This is what I have trained for since I was practically a child. And sure, most days, I wished another had been chosen instead. I didn't feel worthy. I didn't feel eager, like I ought to have. The voices of the skulls haunted me, and sometimes I felt trapped even within the immense boundaries of the valley.

But at least that future was comfortable. Knowable.

Now, a vast unknown sits before me. Powers I never imagined wielding. A city I can hardly fathom living in. An order I don't know the rules of.

All because I could not resist a kiss.

I don't speak. I have no words, but High Priestess Sarai seems to understand.

"I assume there are no other skulls? No secret stash somewhere else in the valley?" Her voice is absolutely neutral, but the question is no idle inquiry. To admit we did would be treachery.

Kian watches me closely, an expression I don't understand on his face.

I answer immediately and absolutely honestly. "We would never hoard the creatures' skulls from the orders. We caretake for the creatures and keep the skulls safe until they can match. If the skulls grow quiet, as more and more have over the years, we give them back to the valley as we ought."

I glance at the phoenix skulls on the table next to Kian.

Or we typically do.

I don't know why Bartholomew left those to sit on the shelf in silence for so long. He's not here to ask. But he made the right decision, whatever his motives. The phoenixes weren't gone, only dormant.

I look at Kian, sitting beside me so steadfastly. How strange to think that a man I'd never laid eyes on before last week, and had chased pleasure with only for the thrill of it at a feast, is now bonded to me for life. If he regrets our explorations together, I cannot find the feeling in his face. There is worry and perhaps some small desire in the way he leans ever so slightly closer to me, like a tulip reaching toward the sun.

Part of me imagines that perhaps he's excited to explore this undeniable chemistry between us. Perhaps he might even want to explore beyond our physical relationship, to explore what caring for each other might feel like.

"Since there is no role for you here in the valley," High Priestess Sarai says, pulling my attention away from Kian, "I would like to formally invite you to join the order as a novitiate."

I knew this was coming, and there is not only a rush of relief at the words, but a burst of excitement at the possibilities. A surge of guilt follows, that I am eager to leave behind the only world I've ever known, but I push that to a corner of my heart. I don't suppress it entirely. It's allowed to live in me. Of course there's regret at what I've done and what I'm losing.

Cecelia said I'm allowed to live the life I want. I'm allowed to want. I lean into that idea, into the bubbling excitement.

A new future. A new fate.

And one, I realize, that might have been destined for me all along. From the moment the sun glinted off the phoenixes' beaks. After all, the great goddess guides us all. I am not immune from her blessings, even if I don't always see the way she works in and through me.

"Be sure this is what you want," Kian says. I think I hear a note of hope in his voice.

I realize that I am utterly certain.

I pick up the phoenix skull from the side table and move to stand in front of Sarai. I kneel down and place it in her lap, keeping my eyes low. "Would you perform the matching?"

The high priestess quickly agrees. She picks up the phoenix skull. I close my eyes.

"Are you ready now to face your fate?" the priestess asks, echoing the ceremonial words of the matcher.

I open my eyes, relief surging through me. I nod, and she begins.

"How do you come before your soul's match?" she asks.

I have no jewelry on. I remove my blood-stained cloak. I never imagined being on this side of the words, but they flow easily from me. "Bare of wealth or warmth."

There are no oils or herbs, but I think of the tea with its fragrant turmeric and ginger lingering on me when she asks, "How do you come before your soul's match?"

"With empty hands, prepared to toil for goodness," I answer, meaning it with my whole heart. I may not be serving the great goddess the way I thought I would, but I can still be a force for good in the world. Even with a destructive power.

I will figure out a way.

"How do you come before your soul's match?" she asks for the third and final time.

Again, there is no pine ointment, so I close my eyes and imagine the sharp tang of the needles that were crushed beneath me as I knelt beside Etana's body.

Here my certainty wavers. Etana should not have been a casualty of me finding a new future. But I cannot undo her death. I can only atone for it. And with the matching hut gone and her foal safe with Lathai, the best way to do that is to serve the Huntress.

"Clearheaded, with eyes that search for truth and a tongue that speaks of both justice and mercy."

She places the phoenix skull back on my face, gently fastening the leather strapping behind my head. Carefully, she leans forward and kisses my cheek. "Welcome, little bird, to your destiny."

I am given a mere hour to pack and say my goodbyes. With the novitiate wing and the matching hut both ash, the order has decided to return to Insborough immediately. There is nowhere comfortable to stay and no reason to do so. It will be a long night.

I walk from the great hall to my house, stepping around the rubble of the lightning-stuck fountain, and realize that this may very well be the last time I cross this square. It's likely the last time I'm in the valley at all. Only specially trained order members lead the novitiates, and the high priestess, of course.

I'm uncertain what my future holds or if the great goddess will guide my feet back home in time. It's unlikely. Only one person I know has left, and she never returned.

I wonder how she felt in the hour before she left. Was her heart racing as if she had jumped from the loft of the hay barn and landed incorrectly, losing all of her breath in one big whoosh?

I push away my anxieties and enter the only home I've ever known.

Dad is there, waiting for me. He looks like a broken man. Unable to face him in the moment, I turn to go upstairs. I will say goodbye after I gather my things. But he stops me, wrapping me up in a hug. I stiffen, afraid I'm going to scratch him with the skull I am now voluntarily wearing. He tucks my head into his collarbone. Once I realize he's safe, I sink into the comfort. This is how he's hugged me since Mom left, with a sort of quiet desperation.

And though it hurts, it also helps.

My mind begins to spin, spiraling up and up, like the phoenix and her mate in my visions. My contrary wishes war within me. I want to keep my past close and also spread my wings to explore this new future. I worry about him and Cecelia and everything I'm leaving behind. With no new magic, the orders may begin to lose their power in society. There will be fewer boons, fewer tithes, even less money given for the community of keepers hidden away, caring for magical creatures that are slowly dying out.

Inside Dad's arms, I realize there's nothing I can do about any of that.

Except.

As a member of the order with ties to the keepers, maybe I can be a bridge. Maybe I'll be able to advocate for my community from the outside, to remind the high priestesses of the three orders and their councils that although it might take a while for the valley to replenish the skulls, it will be worth their while to remain steadfast in their promises.

His grief envelops me. I have never felt more loved. He places a hand on my head, and I press my forehead into his neck. "The order is leaving tonight?"

"Yes. I'm so sorry."

"Shhhh. No need for that. You will be brilliant," he whispers into my hair. The words he's said to me my entire life. I believed them until I was twelve and the mom I had always admired, that I was so alike, left us.

I squeeze Dad one more time and pull away. My time is short, and I still need to find Cecelia and say goodbye to her as well. "Help me pack?"

He nods and joins me as I collect a handful of mementos. There will be no need for the raiments of a matcher, the beautiful bone jewelry and the like. I place it all in a pile and ask Dad to give it to Beadda for the future, when there will be new skulls and new matches again.

In the meantime, she can study the journals and learn the rituals I won't be able to teach her. Cecelia will help, no doubt.

Cecelia comes to say goodbye, and Dad steps away. Her eyes are puffy and her nose and cheeks have a telltale flush, but her head is high and her smile is genuine. She's been crying, but she's good now. For the moment, at least.

She plunks down on my bed, and it squeaks as always. I sit beside her.

"Have the grandest adventures, my friend." Her tone is fierce. "And write me about them all in detail."

We've never been much for notes, but I suppose, why would we be? We've lived mere houses away for our entire lives. Once again I am nearly shattered at all I am about to lose. And how unknown the world is that I'm about to face.

Despite her sorrow, Cecelia's excitement for me is genuine, and it gives me encouragement to embrace my own. She chatters about everything I'm about to experience—new foods and new fashions, new people. Mostly, though, she talks about the temple's library, wondering aloud how it's organized and how big it is, what books they might have in common with the valley and if it would ever be possible for them to lend her materials.

I promise to visit it as soon as everything settles down. I even offer to sketch a picture of it, but we both laugh about how futile that would be at actually conveying anything about it. I can't draw.

There's one big thing that we haven't mentioned about being in Insborough, skating carefully around the topic, though I know it's at the forefront of both our minds. After all, Dad and I weren't the only ones who lost her. Mom's disappearance was almost as painful for my best friend as it was for me.

Cecelia takes a deep breath and says the thing that gives me shivers just to think about. "Your mom?"

I flinch, but Dad isn't here to hurt at the mention of her.

"Will you try to find her?"

"No." It's immediate. But I'm fairly certain it's accurate. She left. Abandoned us. Why would I go after her? Cecelia doesn't argue, or even respond. Just looks at me. I can't tell if she agrees with my choice or not. "Do you think that's foolish?"

She shrugs, with a thoughtful uncertainty. "I think family is hard. And you don't have to make a forever decision. Take it day by day and trust yourself."

I wrap my arms around her, squeezing tight. She stiffens for a moment, but then hugs me back fiercely.

"I will never have another friend as amazing as you," I say.

She laughs. "Neither of us is dying, so you'll still have me."

And yet we likely will never see each other again. But I can't say it aloud. I don't need to. We both know. When I'm finished packing, Cecelia follows me downstairs.

Dad is there, stress cleaning. He looks up, eyes wet with tears. He puts down his broom. "Ready, love?"

The actual goodbye is a blur. One keeper after another comes up and gives me a hug, saying goodbyes as if they'd never see me again. A sharp, coiled thing in the pit of me begins to vibrate. With rage? With fear? With hope and excitement? I shove it all away and sink into the same blissful numbness that came when Etana's foal ran into the forest. I let it wash over and through me.

Kian comes close. He interlocks his fingers through mine and begins to walk toward the forest. Without looking back at all I'm about to lose, I walk with him.

Chapter Twenty-Two

KIAN

Stepping into the city with Adela by my side is like sinking into a bubble bath. A noisy, colorful, stinky-as-hell bubble bath, but the same level of comfort. Even in the wee hours of the morning, it's busy. Vendors are setting up carts, children are selling flowers, shop owners are arriving to begin their daily tasks. And of course, they're all gawking.

"The gutter trash is out in droves today," Linden mumbles. Molvi shushes him.

I prickle slightly. I would also be considered gutter trash by Linden and the elitist snobs like him since this is Poyhia, the neighborhood where I grew up.

Around us, the crowds border on frenetic as news of us travels through the teeming streets. They push and pull each other, trying to see us as we make our way toward the temple square.

At first, I think it is just because it's not very often they see a group of wet, dirty, exhausted order members trekking through their streets.

Especially in Poyhia, where beggars sit on every street corner and children sleep on stoops.

And then I realize they are specifically staring at me and Adela. No one in living memory has seen a phoenix skull, let alone a pair. Of course that is what has their attention. People of the city are used to seeing priestesses and priests. The main industry of Insborough is religion, and it surrounds us. In the crowds, I spot those wearing the red robes of the Spinner, the navy of the Pupil, trying to make their way through the morning. Even they turn to look.

We pass my family's street. They are out, watching, waving, calling out requests for blessings. The best way to go unnoticed is to fulfill expectations.

Aunt Ujvala's eyes skim over me as if I am a stranger, and a relief I don't expect floods through me. They made it. It takes every ounce of willpower I possess not to run over and check in on Ivo. I don't see him with the others, but it's early. No doubt he's still resting.

We walk past a bakery, and the scent of fresh-baked bread fills my nose. My stomach rumbles, and I think to pop over and buy a bun until I hear one flour-dusted woman whisper to another. "Look at her dress. Her freckled skin and rough hands. What's a keeper doing in Insborough?"

Adela stiffens besides me.

"A keeper? If she is, she's a terrible one. Wearing a skull." The second baker spits, a large glob of saliva landing near our feet.

Anger rises, and I can feel the phoenix's awareness awaken, but Adela presses close. She's quivering slightly and turning her head away. She needs my calm, not my ire.

Even without the cruelty of the women's judgment, this must be overwhelming. She's never been in a crowd this size, or even seen a city outside of paintings or books. She hasn't seen streets wet from human and horse piss, or felt the urgent press of rowdy crowds, trying to get a glimpse of the newly matched order members.

I put an arm around her shoulder and whisper nonsense words into her hair about how she is safe, here, with me.

She practically melts. Goddess, I love the way she responds to my care. She would hate me if she knew the truth of me. But she doesn't, and I do not let her go.

The closer we get to the temples, the nicer the neighborhoods become. The streets go from dirt-packed to wood to cobblestone and brick. And then we are there in the temple square, at the edge of the city.

The Temples of the Pupil and the Spinner are lovely. One made of stone, the other of whitewashed brick with stained-glass windows and gilt ornaments at the edges of their roofs and windows. Compared with the Temple of the Huntress, both resemble the valley's small chapel.

The Temple of the Huntress is monstrous. Its facade is a rare black marble, shot with gold and silver, glittering in the sun. A building decorated with such extravagance that selling a chunk of just one small corner could bring in enough coin to feed all the inhabitants of Poyhia for at least a month. I hate it.

Whether sensing my annoyance or simply being on firmer footing now that we're out of the crowds, Adela steps away. I miss the warmth of her body against mine, but I restrain myself from reaching out my hand to pull her back.

We follow High Priestess Sarai and Sister Roberta inside and are greeted by Sister Ihi, Sarai's secretary. The priestess is one of the few who has refused ornamentation on her jackalope skull so it remains bare of any jewels or gilding. I like her better for it despite her proximity to the high priestess.

"Welcome, matched," she says to us all.

Sarai and Roberta walk away without even greeting their compatriot, off to their typical duties. Or maybe just to take a nap. That's what I wish I were doing.

But no, of course there are more rituals and rules to discuss first. Ihi walks us through it all, reminding us that over the next few weeks we will be working in the community as a chance to hone our magic further and discover better where we might serve the Huntress. Then we will take our final oaths and settle into new roles as full priestesses and priests.

The more she talks, the more exhausted I grow. It's overwhelming, how much they want us to do. And I have no way out.

Or do I?

I have accomplished my goal of destroying the skulls, and thanks to Lathai's grief-fueled storm, I don't even have to dodge suspicion.

There's an emptiness, or maybe just a quiet that I haven't quite gotten used to, now that I've accomplished the main part of what I've been working toward for so long. I itch to fill it. But with what?

I'm not sure what I want anymore, or what my life could even be. I suppose I could leave it all behind and watch from afar as it begins to crumble. It will take years, and it's not something I need to actively participate in. I have done the work I set out to do.

I could do something outrageous, like join a traveling troupe or begin a new life across the sea. Or perhaps I could go back to my family. Oh, the comfort of that, to be surrounded by people who truly know and love me again.

But then I see Adela perk up as Sister Ihi goes on and on. She's so eager, so bright. She's excited by the opportunity to roll up her sleeves and cover the gray hems of her matched-novitiate robes with the filth of my city. This new world is just opening up to her, and I find I can't bring myself to walk away from her vitality quite yet.

I could stay in the order and continue to try to undermine them. Pass information to my family, disrupt their plans, just cause mischief. It's not a future I imagined, but I realize that is one area I failed to plan for entirely. What would happen after. Perhaps I don't have to know for sure.

There's no one insisting I decide right in this moment. It could be enough to give myself some time and space to explore whatever this thing is between Adela and me. And meanwhile, I can figure out what I want for myself, without striving toward any secret goals.

Suddenly Ihi is done with her instructions and dismissing us. "Meet back here at seven tomorrow morning. In the meantime, rest, eat some food, and, for the goddess's sake, get cleaned up."

She leaves. The other novitiates all go separate ways—some to eat, some to bathe, and some toward their rooms.

Adela lingers.

I turn to go to my own room, but she stops me. "I thought I could join you today? Maybe?" There is a note of hope in her voice that makes me squirm. Or maybe it's that I want to say yes.

When I gaze into her wide, hopeful eyes, I can't shake the images of the matching hut engulfed in the fire I set. The future of the valley, of everyone Adela loves, reduced to ash by my hand. Just moments ago I was admiring her excitement, and now I'm withdrawing from it.

But it's because today I need to disappear for a bit, to check on Ivo, and make sure Aunt Ujvala doesn't hold any permanent grudges. If I show Adela around the temple and then suddenly run off, she'll certainly notice my absence. And she'll ask questions.

"I need some space and time today, I think. It's my first day back..." I gesture to the temple and nearly choke on my next word. "Home."

Adela shrinks away from me slightly. Voice thick with hurt, she says, "If you change your mind..."

I want to reach out, to soothe. But she's not mine to have to care for.

Proprietary feelings flow from the phoenix, clear and unwelcome. I shove them aside.

"I won't change my mind." I don't look back. I leave her in the cold marble hallway and scuttle to my room to hide, like the coward I am.

A few hours later, after a restless nap, I sneak out a side door typically used by the lay kitchen helpers. I wear the neutral clothes of a working-class man and carry a lumpy pack that contains some stolen bread and cheese and mead. And the phoenix skull, because the last thing I need is for someone to find it left behind.

It's raining, again, and chilly, but I make the trek back across the city. I pass the neighborhoods with cobblestone streets and large homes with small yards and flower boxes at the windows. The spaces between the homes get tighter and tighter the farther I get from the temples until there is no green anywhere. There are, however, brightly painted facades and the occasional mural or mosaic.

Even we gutter trash enjoy beauty. We just don't have the time to devote attention to nurturing flowers within the stink of Insborough's filthy streets. We're too busy cobbling together an existence.

The rain mixes with the dirt and shit, both animal and human, but it doesn't have anywhere to go. The temples haven't bothered to improve the waste and runoff areas in the Poyhia neighborhood. But of course they haven't. The orders only care about who and what they can leverage for power, and the poor have none.

I turn onto the small side street where I grew up.

I step through the front door, kissing my fingers and placing them gently against the rosemary hanging from the frame as I pass. It's a silly tradition my dad used to do with me when I was little, lifting me up to poke at my mom's drying herbs in the kitchens.

After they were killed, Aunt Ujvala always kept dried rosemary in the kitchen doorway in their memory, even after I moved into the temple. It's an odd bit of sentimentality for a woman who typically has no space in her life for anything other than practicality and schemes.

I walk through the house, snatching a persimmon. I find my aunt in the center courtyard, training with Ivo and Ava in the rain. I take it my little cousin is feeling better. The way he limped into the forest, I thought it was a significantly larger injury. He was covered in blood and leaning heavily on Aunt Ujvala.

I watch, standing out of the drizzle beneath an overhang as they beat on each other. "Do you ever take a break?"

"The temple has made you soft if you think life is for leisure." My aunt sweeps Ivo's feet out from under him. He lands in a shallow puddle and stays there, groaning. Ava steps back, not wanting to join her twin on the ground. Aunt Ujvala beckons her forward. "The goddess demands perfection."

I roll my eyes and push off the doorframe.

She knocks Ava on her ass with one quick shove, chuckling as she puts away her sparring gear. The twins are old enough to know by now that until she's back in street clothes, they should watch their backs.

Just like in real life.

After toweling off a bit, Aunt Ujvala begins to lead me through the labyrinth of connected houses that make up my family's space. From the outside, they all look like independent houses, squished together to save space and heat in the coldest months. But inside, through passageways and barn-sized doors that can be left wide and open or closed up to look like walls, they are connected.

She leads me into the kitchen and points to the table I sat at while growing up. It is soft, worn from use.

"I take Ivo's going to live?" I ask the moment I'm settled.

She takes out the stolen cheese and bread and mead. "Indeed."

I wait for her to elaborate. Eventually she sighs and admits, "We went to one of the Spinner priests for healing."

"No!" Aunt Ujvala hates paying for the temple's blessings. Ivo must've been seriously hurt if she even considered it. "How much did that cost you?"

"Just a couple of the rubies I stole from your dead priest," she says with a smirk.

I laugh at her audacity, and think again about how nice it might be to come home. "I'm glad he's well."

"Me, too." She tries to repress a small shiver.

She toasts the bread over the fire, then slathers it with rich butter and a thick slice of cheese. She peels the wax seal off the mead and drinks it from the bottle. She holds out the bottle, and I take a swig, too.

"The temples make good mead," I admit.

"Even better when it's stolen." She pours us each a glass and toasts us. "To the power of resurrection, of rebirth."

I choke on a mouthful of mead. She knows. Of course she knows.

"I'm not surprised." She continues, "That you have the power of rebirth. After all, it's what you always wanted. The ability to restore the world to how it *should* be."

She makes me sound almost noble, and I duck my head, wishing for the first time that I were wearing the phoenix skull so I could hide within it.

We eat our bread and drink the mead in silence as I take in the kitchen that looks the same as it has my entire life, with its wide hearth and mismatched shelving, all stuffed to the brim with dry goods, flatware and cups and plates and pots and pans and strange-shaped cooking utensils from all over the world. "What else is new with everyone?"

Aunt Ujvala stands and heads to the cellar, gesturing for me to join her. I follow, wishing "rest" was a word my aunt knew. I'm tired from a night with no sleep followed by a wet trek from the valley. But I don't have the energy to argue with her about why I should stay in the warm, light-filled kitchen.

"Nothing really new that you don't already know about, apparently." In the dank cellar, Aunt Ujvala digs through the root vegetables, picking up a particularly large potato. "We've found buyers for the gryphon agate, and have been gathering supplies to offer in trade, so we've set a date to return to the valley to begin negotiations."

I'd totally forgotten about my aunt's goals to reestablish smuggling to the valley, I've been so caught up in my own shit. "Great idea to come in with offers."

"Yes, I know," she deadpans. "It's like I've been doing this for awhile."

I suppose I deserve that for telling the matriarch of a successful multigenerational smuggling operation that I approve of her business tactics. I change course. "When do you go back?"

"A week."

Now it's my turn to be surprised. A week is soon. But I'm not going to insinuate I know her job better than she does. Again.

She adds, "Check for correspondence about the valley for us, will you? If there are any updates on what the keepers might want or need, or if there are any spontaneous trips planned?"

"Of course."

It's been a while since she's asked me to snoop through the desks of the high priestess and her lackeys. I assumed she had another mole within the temple, feeding her information. But I hadn't asked for details. Better not to know, in case I'm caught.

Hopefully they know nothing of me, either.

Back in the kitchen, Aunt Ujvala cubes the potato and drops it in the pot of water hanging over the kitchen fire while I tell her about burning down the matching hut. She knew this as well, of course. There's a lull in conversation where she has the look of someone who has things to say. Since she's not someone who typically holds back her thoughts I turn to go, certain that whatever she's hesitating to share is something I don't want to hear.

"Stay."

"I don't want my absence missed." I sound like a petulant child.

"Missed by your pretty matcher?" She salts the potato and stirs. "I saw the way you held her through the streets. You care for her. She feels safe with you."

Shame floods me.

She shouldn't. I destroyed her future and community with a single stolen flame. I shove away the feelings. This had to be done. So many more are already hurting. My efforts will help. The ends are worth my means.

"Fine," Aunt Ujvala waves her spoon at me. "Go. We'll talk later."

I nod and run, just like I did earlier with Adela.

If only the phoenix could resurrect my courage.

Chapter Twenty-Three

ADELA

My first full day in the temple, Ulric sits down with me at breakfast. It's early—prayers begin at seven so we have time for whatever assigned tasks the day will bring as well as magic lessons—but I'm used to a keeper's schedule and so was up with the sun, already full with worries.

"How are you?" He takes a bite of a fruit I've never seen before and blinks away his sleep.

"I am . . ." I stab at whatever decadent egg soufflé thing I was served. I thought a life in the valley was the only future available to me, and now I'm wearing the gray robes of a novitiate, with a phoenix skull on the table before me in the Temple of the Huntress. And I got here by way of death and destruction.

I settle on a slightly less exposing truth. "Nervous. I want to do well."

"You will," Ulric says softly, kindly. "After all, you want to. And that's the first step toward goodness."

Kian plops down next to us, bumping me with his shoulder in greeting before he practically inhales a piece of toast with some tea.

"Ready to do some grunt work, Adela?" He huffs and points to a group of young people clearing away dirty dishes. "As the newest novitiate in the Order of the Huntress, it's time you learned the truth. Novitiates are the housekeepers and scullery maids and drudge workers of the priestesses."

"Serving has its own nobility," Ulric says.

I like that.

"Well, today, we're going to be nobly serving the dead." Kian rolls his eyes. He turns to me. "Will that be alright?"

"If I were home, I'd be preparing Etana's skull for matching. I don't think preparing the dead of Insborough is going to be a challenge."

Besides, at least if they're already dead, I won't be able to hurt them.

We make our way to the end of the temple to where the elaborate process of funeral preparation occurs. I expect a room of easily cleaned stone. Instead it is just more of the black marble, veined with gold. The only difference from the grander rooms is this one has large drains in the floor and more sconces on the walls so the room is awash in light.

It's actually quite beautiful, despite the piles of naked or shrouded bodies laid out on marble slabs through the room. There are already priestesses and priests at work, preparing the bodies. And the gytrash pair. Linden glares.

Kian steps in front of me. "Stop glowering at her."

"I can glower if I want," Linden counters. "She failed me. She failed the order."

I flinch at his bluntness, but understand his fury. I start to apologize, but Kian speaks over me. "The matcher does not serve the order. She serves the great goddess. She owed *you* nothing."

While I appreciate the defense, Linden's not wrong. I did fail my community, and Linden and Svena especially. If I had been more careful with the phoenix skulls, or had gone back to see if I could still commune with them after matching, before the hut burned down, then maybe things would be different.

I tell myself that the deep ache of failure is just feeling, not fact. The matching was interrupted, yes. Partly through my actions, yes. But it was not intentional. It was not malice.

"What do you want her to do?" Kian's fist clenches. A threat. "Go back to the valley and kill a trio of gytrash, unmatch Molvi and Ylysia, and let you all try the matching ceremony again?"

"Stop making it worse," I hiss at Kian. Startling slightly, he steps back and relaxes his clenched fist.

But it's too late. A ragged hope flares on Linden's face. Surely he knows this is impossible, but hope is a hard thing to quench. Linden steps closer to me. With a small voice, he asks, "Would that be possible?"

I answer the black-marble floor, unable to watch him as I reply. Not even the wildest of matchers left notes about unmatching a bonded pair. I would never even try. "No. The bond of creature and human is eternal. It continues in death, even after their ashes are returned to the earth."

Ylysia steps forward and wraps herself around Linden. "It will be alright, sweet."

"We will figure out a path forward. The three of us. Together, as always." Molvi joins them.

He tucks his face and lets out a sob of sorrow against Ylysia's skin.

I turn away to give them privacy, determined to at least help the dead, since I can offer no comfort to these three.

Brother Liarn, a young, handsome priest with a high, nasally voice, wearing a gytrash skull, instructs us on how to wash the bodies, then scent them with clove-imbued oils, and wrap them in their burial shrouds. It's not unlike the process of preparing a skull for matching, and I'm glad for the familiarity.

He explains, mostly for my benefit since I'm unfamiliar with the city's ways, that those whose families or friends can pay the death tithes receive the blessings of the gytrash. He gestures to his partners, Brother Keil and Brother Robin, who continue their work in another part of the room. Their efforts speed up the process of mourning and allow the soul of the deceased to cross to the after quicker.

No one knows yet how the rites will be affected with one of the triad missing. Sister Roberta could do only so much with them back in the valley. And so that is their primary focus today, to figure it out.

He leads Ulric, Kian, and me to a large pile of bodies, and crosses the room to work alongside the other gytrash-wearers.

Some of these people have waited far longer than it should take for the preparation of death rites.

"Why have these waited so long?" I ask.

Kian replies, "Their families didn't pay the required tithes for expediency."

It can't be that simple. Maybe there was a spate of illnesses that swept through the city, or some violence that caused an influx of deaths. After all, a main purpose of the Huntress order is to help the people cross into the after. If they're just sitting here, waiting, their souls are trapped.

The priestess walks away, to her own tasks.

I pin back my sleeves and tie up my hair. I want to remove the phoenix so I can see without having to tilt my head this way and that, but I'm sure I'm not allowed.

We begin to work.

Beneath his dragon skull, Ulric wrinkles his nose and groans low as he picks up the oil and begins working on the first body. He moves slowly, staying back as far from the dead as possible. His concentration seems to be on not heaving.

Kian teases his friend, but I understand Ulric's reluctance to touch something living that is now reduced to a slab of meaty nothing. Fortunately, I learned as a child how to shove down my repulsion to do the messier chores of a keeper. I find a rhythm in the work, cleaning, oiling, wrapping.

"Why would people refuse to pay the death tithes?" I ask Kian.

"It's not refusal; it's inability." His words are clipped with anger. "They can't afford the exorbitant fees."

My hands continue their tasks as my mind works. "The gytrash ought to be used to help the poor expedite their death rites, rather than the wealthy. They are the ones who need the blessings more urgently. Not those who can afford to take time away from their everyday toils."

Kian gives me a look as if I have said something compelling. But wasn't that what he was implying? The creatures stay behind after death to gift us with more ease and abundance. They serve alongside the orders to do good. That's the whole point.

From somewhere far away, I think I hear the murmur of voices. I pause my work and listen carefully. It's more like the impression of sound, like how the skulls felt prior to matching, but it's different—sad instead of excited, sharper somehow, and more abundant. Like something between the skulls, a normal human voice, and a quick-moving stream.

I shift to work on another body, and the sound grows fainter. Eventually I don't notice it at all. It's strange how quiet working with the dead is, compared with the creature skulls. I'm surprised at the small part of myself that misses feeling their wants inside me.

Well, it would be quiet.

Kian fills the silence, chattering about everything and nothing. I catch myself staring at his hands, which are large and appear strong, but do the work gently, almost reverently. As if whoever it is that lies before us is someone precious and it's an honor to assist them in their body's last physical moments in our world.

The day passes quickly, and I'm glad to have made a lot of progress on the waiting dead.

"You're well suited to this," Brother Liarn says to me as we wrap up our day. "If you'd like a permanent role here after this week, you would be welcome."

I'm tempted to agree, right then and there. I would rather use my strong back and stronger stomach than embrace the destruction that flows through me. But then I imagine how disappointed High Priestess Sarai would be if I chose a role that didn't utilize my magic. She's given me a tremendous gift. I don't want to disappoint her.

I thank him for the offer and go to the bathing chamber, where I scrub my skin nearly raw. I may be glad to aid the dead, but I do not want them to linger upon me.

At dinner, the only discussion is practicing magic. We have time after we eat, before the loosely enforced curfew. The others are excited, eager to go to the courtyard and see what they can do, but the thought of joining them makes my stomach clench. If I'm not able to access my magic, I will disappoint everyone's high expectations of what I'm bringing to the order as an outsider.

The phoenix sends excitement and enthusiasm through me. She's confident and eager to truly explore our bond and what we can do together.

Which feels even scarier. Her power is so volatile in my hands, so destructive. My success will result in danger and damage. I hate to admit even to myself that I question the great goddess, but tonight the phoenix magic doesn't feel like a blessing. It feels like a weapon I cannot wield safely.

Across from me, Ulric laughs just as he takes a sip of soup, half choking as Kian tells one of his ridiculous stories of childhood—something about trying to catch a miniature pig in a busy market.

I'm not listening closely, just letting my eyes and mind wander.

I watch them laughing together, and I admire the curve of Kian's neck, the way his eyes crinkle at the corners as he teases his friend. He's so beautiful. Sharp edges and polished, just like the rest of the order, with his dark, braided hair, gold earrings and rings, and a hint of his tattoo peeking out from beneath his robe's neckline.

But I admire more than his beauty. I admire the way he finds reasons to laugh, the reverence with which he met the dead, the way he tried to defend me against Linden, and how he stepped away when I told him to stop.

He's so alive. Such a contrast to our day.

I cannot stay in my head like this for another moment. I need to be fully present in my body. Kian can help. I stand up from my spot on the table. The moment I move, his eyes are on mine.

His dark lashes lower, and his full lips curve up. He recognizes my want. He stands, ready to meet me, and says a perfunctory goodbye to a chuckling Ulric.

We only make it a handful of steps before he pulls me down a short hall and into an alcove. He takes off our phoenix skulls, setting them aside on the floor. Then he kisses me roughly as his hands roam my body. His lips move to my neck, and he laces his fingers through my hair, tugging gently so I move my head aside for easier access. All of my difficult thoughts and feelings flee.

I rub my body against him, loving the way I make him hard, the sounds my movements pull from his lips. Our pleasure echoes, magnified by the slick marble surrounding us.

I close my eyes, enjoying the sensations, and he spins me around. He pulls me back by my hips, so my butt is pressed firmly against him as he bends over me. His belly and chest press into my back, and his hand twines in my hair, his lips and tongue and teeth tease me, trailing across my shoulder.

With his free hand, he reaches around my body to grab my breast, finding my hardening nipple with his thumb. I moan and open my eyes.

I gasp. Not with pleasure but in shock.

We're not in some nook, but in the balcony of the empty temple sanctuary. A thick marble railing is in front of me, but beyond that is nothing but the open eaves of the sacred space. No wonder our moans echo.

"Kian!" I whisper.

The sanctuary seems deserted, thank the Spinner, but it has numerous entrances. Other balconies on our level, as well as half a dozen doorways below. Anyone could walk into any part of it at any time. Part of me is horrified, the other aroused.

He finally pauses his kisses and notices he's lost some of my attention. He chuckles and nips at my shoulder. "As if we are the first to do this, in this space. It is practically the Huntress's favorite way to receive worship."

She is the goddess of bodies. Death. Violence. Dancing. Strength. Sex.

He continues to kiss and touch me, one hand pulling me impossibly closer as he grinds himself against my ass. The other trails down my leg in order to pull up my robes.

He reaches between my thighs and finds me naked and wet. I fail to hold back my moans; his fingers are too deft, and too insistent. His breath is hot in my ear as he dips a finger into me. "Put your hands on the railing, Goddess."

I do immediately. My palms have barely touched the black marble when he drives himself inside me. He stretches me, but I don't ask him to pause and let me adjust. I thrust my hips back into him, enjoying the fullness. He reaches around me, rubbing me as he moves.

I am bliss.

He laughs, and I love the way his voice, thick with desire for me, surrounds us. "Do you like that?"

"More" is all I manage. He gives me what I've demanded, rubbing at me while he pounds into me. The pressure inside me builds, coiling and sharpening until I shatter. My cry of ecstasy echoes through the sanctuary.

When my orgasm ebbs, I expect him to stop stroking me and focus on his own pleasure, but he does not remove his clever fingers from me. I feel the pressure building again, but surely I don't have another climax in me.

Kian obviously believes otherwise.

"Again," he demands into my hair.

I oblige, twitching and bucking, loving the way he strokes me inside and out. Again the orgasm slows. This time he removes his fingers and begins to slide out of me.

I push back into him, twisting to see him over my shoulder. "But you . . . I want . . ." Words are hard, but he knows what I want.

"We'll get to me." He drops to his knees and uses his hands to spread me. "But I am not done with you quite yet. Once more, Goddess."

He licks at me for a mere handful of moments before I'm once again at the peak. I come again, pressing my body onto his face and screaming his name into the sacred space before me.

When my spasms finally cease, he gives me a small kiss on each butt cheek and sits back on his heels, laughing. He's proud of himself, and he should be. He has done excellent work.

He stands and holds his hand out to me, half turning as if to go.

"Oh, no. I am not done," I say, echoing him, and drop down onto my knees. I push his robes up and the waistband of his pants down, releasing his cock. I take it in my mouth, tasting myself on him.

I hum with pleasure, moving my mouth up and down his deliciously shaped cock, then lick at the underside of his head. I work my hand up and down as well, stroking him in time with my mouth. He begins to thrust carefully, and I shove my head down harder on him until our combined motions are fast and messy with desire.

He comes, hard and fast, growling his pleasure and filling my mouth. I feel a rush of pride and swallow the proof of how good I've made him feel.

After we have finished straightening our robes and fetched the phoenix skulls, we hurry through the temple back to our rooms. I think we will say goodnight, but he passes his own door and joins me. He strips down the moment the door closes and pulls my robe off me.

"I don't have a round two in me. Yet." My legs still wobble slightly from the three amazing orgasms of round one. "But I'll do my best to rally."

He lies in my narrow bed, pulling with him. He traces his fingertips across my bare back. "No round two yet. Just this. This is lovely."

"I need a bigger bed." I am half on top of him and must be squishing him.

He scoffs. "Good luck with that. Only the most blessed holies are allowed suites with larger beds. The rest of us get the barracks."

"The most blessed holies?"

He freezes, like he's a child I caught stealing a honey cake from the kitchens before dinner. It's so quick I almost think I've misjudged the pause. "A silly name my family used to call members of the orders. Holies. Not very respectful."

I wave that away. I'm not worried what mildly derogatory name he calls the order members, especially when he's one himself. "But what does the most blessed mean? Who gets more or less blessings? Are these blessings bestowed by the Huntress?"

He snorts. "They're bestowed by Sarai to whomever she fancies at the moment."

Sometimes it seems as if he actively dislikes the order. But surely not. He's dedicated his entire life to it.

He continues, "Usually her favors go to those with powerful skull matches, or those with powerful families. But basically her favorites are whoever kisses her ass the best, like Roberta. And Thad before he got himself eaten. You can tell the favorites easily. The more gems, the more 'blessed' the holy."

He traces my shoulder blades, and I shiver, but I can't get past what he's just said. The Huntress's blessings should not be bestowed according to the whims of the high priestess. That isn't how it's supposed to work.

And it's not who High Priestess Sarai is. She's warm and caring and supportive. Surely she wouldn't bestow favors based on such shallow, self-centered reasons.

I turn my face toward him. "It doesn't sound fair."

He begins to kiss down my neck again. Between his kisses he says, "Adela, this is the Order of the Huntress. If someone promised you that anything about this place would be fair, they most certainly lied. Now lie back and let me taste you. Again."

I do as he asks.

Chapter Twenty-Four

KIAN

I can't sleep. The scent of Adela's pleasure has seeped into my skin and is stealing my slumber, and yet, my body is not capable of any more release. Especially by my own hand, when it still feels the echo of hers wrapped around me.

I get up, leaving Adela in bed.

There's no use tossing and turning, torturing myself with memories of the best sex of my life when there's nothing to do about it. I might as well make myself useful.

It's been ages since I've snuck through the halls of the temple to the offices where the high priestess and her assistants work during the day, but my feet know the way. It was a frequent path I trod when I was young and still directionless in my revenge for my parents. Now that I'm older and have accomplished the linchpin action of my grand plans, I find nothing terribly different. I am still waiting for new inspiration.

And for the fallout of the missing skulls. I thought it would be a much more drastic event with panic and chaos.

But other than the novitiates who are a couple of years behind us, no one seems terribly upset. Maybe because the full priestesses and priests already wear masks, and the lack of new skulls will only make their power more valuable? That would be typical of the egotistical worldview of most order members.

The quiet indifference from Sarai is the strangest. Sure, there ought to be some appeasement from the successful matches Adela made just before reawakening the phoenix, but I suspect there is something more, something I'm not seeing.

I'll keep an eye out for more insight there as I look for intelligence to protect Aunt Ujvala's next run to the valley.

My bare feet make no sound on the solid marble floors, and I make my way quickly. In front of Sarai's thick wooden door, carved with the various symbols of the Huntress, I pause. I check the crack beneath the door for any telltale glow of light, and when I see none, I knock softly.

The first time I opened the door to find High Priestess Sarai inside working startled us both, and I received an hour-long scolding for not respecting her privacy and entering without knocking. I was only seventeen. I haven't made the same mistake again.

When I see nothing but dark shadow around the edge of the door, I carefully turn the knob to the right, avoiding the squeak that always happens if I turn it left. Another hard-earned lesson when I once opened the door incorrectly and found her asleep at her desk in the middle of the night, drooling on a pile of papers. That time I was twenty, and it earned me light lashes since it was a repeat offense.

Thankfully both times she assumed it was eagerness to speak with her and not the more sinister truth—that I was there to steal her secrets.

This time, the office is empty. I slip inside and hurry over to the hidden panel in the wall, gently prying it open. The moment I glance inside, I know it's my lucky day. There is a pile of letters. I would consider it a gift from the goddess if I believed in such things.

I go through the letters, most of which are nothing. Boring notes about trade or the status of supplies for some upcoming ceremony they have planned. It's odd that that one is tucked away, but maybe it got tangled with the others. There's an interesting one about a meeting between the three high priestesses to go over what they plan to do about the missing skulls—as if they have many options.

But the only one that's super pertinent is one between the high priestess and the leader of the keeper elders. It's written with a bold hand on a thick, nubby paper that composed many of Cecelia's books in the valley library.

High Priestess—

We are glad to welcome your dragon-wearer and the ashes of the Pupil priest and his jackalope skull in a few days' time. He will be received with kindness and care.

As to your request, while we acknowledge your frustration with Adela being unable to access her power as quickly as you'd like, the solutions you propose as incentive are not ones we can—or will—ever sanction.

I understand our refusal to provide Ulric aid in his quest to find and capture the unicorn-pegasus hybrid will certainly result in the total withdrawal of financial support from all the orders. There, I would ask you to remember your sacred duties to maintain balance and share abundance. Your promises, after all, are not to us, but to the great goddess of us all.

Our sacred duty is to the care and keeping of creatures through their natural lives, from any and all threats. Including yours.

Creatures can never be caged.

—Petra

Cryptic. I wonder what the solution is that Sarai had proposed that would require Ulric to capture the foal, and to what end? It sounds like she wants to remove her from the valley, but that'd be impossible. Whatever the reason, it was obviously something that pissed Petra off. The keeper elder is blunt, but that was outright aggressive.

I wish I had seen Sarai's face when she read it.

I dig through Sarai's drawer and find paper and charcoal, quickly transferring the letter so I can share it with Aunt Ujvala. She needs to know that Ulric is traveling to and from the valley so no one runs into him on their way.

"Where do you go?" Adela asks the next evening when we're lying in bed together in her rooms. It's so sparse, without the years of built-up decoration that the rest of us have.

I freeze, but keep my voice light. "Go?"

"Mm-hmm." Her voice is low with satiation and sleepiness. "You're always heading somewhere. Into the city. Somewhere strange in the temple. Last night I saw you heading back to your rooms, barefoot, long past two."

Alarm erupts, but her voice is light and inquisitive, not judgmental or suspicious. I do my best to meet her energy and hurriedly try to find something that will intrigue her that's close enough to the truth that it'll hold up, but far enough away that she won't guess what I've actually been up to.

"I . . . explore."

Her face lights up. "The temple?" She sits up, the blankets falling down to her waist and revealing her perfect body. I reach out and skim my fingertips across her belly, unable to answer properly.

"Mm-hmm."

"Show me your favorite spot."

I start to point to a freckle high on the inside of her thigh, but she just playfully bats me away. She climbs over me awkwardly and throws on some clothes. When I don't immediately move, she hands me mine as well. I groan. I should have said I find places to nap and her bed is the best one, but I suspect that wouldn't have changed anything.

"Where's your sense of adventure?" she teases. "Get up and show me your secrets."

If only I could.

Taking her to the spot I think she will love the most, I lead her to a set of spiral stone stairs that spin away from us in both directions, up and down. Up will lead to the highest, largest bell tower in the city. I start up the stairs, and she begins to follow, practically bouncing on her toes.

Then she pauses and takes a few back. She peers down the twisting stone stairs, her head tilted sideways as if listening. She points. "What's that way?"

"Not up."

She gives me a soft smack on the shoulder, and I answer her earnestly, "Legend has it there are tunnels beneath us, connecting the three temples."

"Legend?"

"Well, there's a locked door at the bottom. But no one who's talking knows where it leads." And I've never found my way through, despite excellent lock-picking skills. I'm half-convinced it's sealed or the mechanism for getting through is blocked by magic, sort of like the path into the valley.

"If the legend is true, that'd be easy enough to tell with a simple visit to the other temples. Do they also have the same mysterious stairway and locked doors?"

She is too clever by half.

Because they absolutely do—matching locked doors, in fact—but

I am not about to tell her that I've gone poking around the other temples. As far as she knows, I'm an irreverent, but mostly obedient, matched novitiate on my way to full priesthood.

The phoenix sends a spike of amusement through me.

I ignore it and start up the stairs again, gently pulling her along with me. "You want to explore, beauty? Let's explore more than locked doors that probably just lead to a bunch of half-rotten vegetables or expired wine. I think you will like going up."

Up to the sky. Up to the stars.

She hops up a couple of steps until we're eye to eye, and she gives me a sweet kiss on the cheek. I squeeze her hand and lead. We climb and climb. The higher we get, the colder the air. Eventually we come to the top. The bell tower is open of course, so the city can hear the tolling of the giant brass bell at noon, on holidays, for order members' funeral rites, and a whole host of other things.

Thankfully it's currently still, just hanging in the eaves of the tower. Adela gives the thick woven rope an experimental tug and the whole thing swings slightly. She grins, and I'm convinced that she's going to fully go for it, ringing the bell madly. If she does, we'll have to run all the way back down the stairs before we're caught and reprimanded. Or outright punished. Thankfully, she stifles the impulse. Not that I wouldn't enjoy her doing a bit of mischief, but I don't want to risk her beautiful back being marred by Sarai's overeager lash.

I twist her around, away from the bell and toward what I actually want her to see.

Her breath catches as she looks out over the city, the uneven rooftops a mosaic of irregular shadows in the moonlight, small glimmers of warm-yellow lantern lights peeking out from windows and in the streetlamps.

"It's beautiful."

"Beautiful," I agree, though I'm not talking about the city. All I can focus on are her eyes twinkling in the starlight, bright enough to rival the valley's nighttime sky.

There is a small ledge on the outside of the belfry. We sit on it, and she leans against me, tucking her head between my shoulder and jaw. I give her a small kiss and sink into the moment.

"This is perfect," she whispers, her breath a gentle caress across my collarbone.

I take her hand and agree. It very nearly is.

The only thing stopping it from being entirely perfect is me and my deception. Because if she knew who I was and what I had done, she would hate me, surely. She wouldn't see my intentions to make room in the world for good. She'd just see an angry man, seeking vengeance for the parents who died twenty-one years ago. And who's to say that I'm not? After all, my grand plan isn't going great so far. Nothing has changed.

I take her hand. Her feet are swinging like she's a kid, joyful and carefree—unafraid of the ledge or the future. If only I were unafraid of the future, of her reaction. She's chaotic and impulsive, but she's also creative. She has great instincts. Maybe if I just told her the truth she'd see my heart and not only accept me but eagerly participate in my schemes. Maybe she would come alongside me to make Insborough a better place. Maybe I wouldn't have to be alone in this.

Or maybe she would hate me forever.

That final maybe is what prevents me from speaking. I do not want her to hate me. I want her to know me. I want her to love me.

As I love her.

Chapter Twenty-Five

ADELA

Our week finds its rhythm. Mornings are prayers and breakfast and then a day of work. I continue to work with the dead, where I feel safest. After dinner is magic practice in the courtyard, where I do not.

I continue to be too terrified of my power to even try to utilize it. I know I need to push through. I need to embrace my destruction. Huntress priestesses are not cowards. But I stand in the temple's private courtyard, with the bright-blue sky above me and the black-marble facade looming overhead, and I cannot act. All I can think about is what might happen if Kian and I have a simultaneous vision and a pulse goes through the city, or if I drain the life force out of one of the Huntress's chosen. It's bad enough that I have Etana's dead eyes haunting my nightmares.

Around the edges of the courtyard are small balconies for order members to sit outside and relax or watch any demonstrations that might be occurring below. High Priestess Sarai watches from one, a slight smile on her lips. She ought to be thrilled. The novitiates are all coming into their powers nicely. All except me.

"Kian, let's begin with the grass." Sister Roberta gestures to a large, manicured garden at the edge of the outdoor space. It is lovely, already lush and green despite the cool early spring temperatures.

I wish the grass in the valley were half so healthy.

Along the edges of the grass are small flowering trees whose petals float by in the slight breeze, along with their sweet fragrance.

Nothing is dead within the garden that I see. But Kian knows what she wants. With a slight nod, the grass lengthens and becomes an even deeper shade of green.

"Excellent. Now there." She points to a tree that is just barely budded. Spring leaves unfurl. Then small apple blossoms. She presses. "More."

He concentrates, and full apples begin to form. His success makes me feel even more like a failure. What I wouldn't give for such beneficial, productive power.

Kian turns and sees me watching closely. He smiles, wide and genuine. Not his typical protective smirk. "Gonna try that fearsome magic today?" he quips. "Destroy some shit?"

My eyes well at the barb, though I know he means nothing by it. Still, the last time I saw that smiling mouth, it was between my thighs, and I'd rather it there again, teasing me to climax rather than teasing me to tears.

He notices my wobbles and steps closer immediately, pressing his forehead to mine. I close my eyes and inhale. Perhaps it's my imagination, but he smells of late-summer grass and apples. "Okay, Goddess?"

I nod, but before I can reply, a vision takes me.

We fly out to the gryphon hills. There, adolescent gryphons, still with tufts of downy baby feathers, are being launched into the world. A bold one spots us and flings itself forward, trying to catch up. We slow and fly lazy circles with the little darling as it roars its joy into the bright-blue sky.

Below, younger ones gambol along the edge, tripping over tails and too-large feet, clumsy in their play.

In a nest, a mother gryphon is struggling with birth. She smells of blood and death. Her ninth gryphlette is stuck inside her. It is too many babies for one birth. Her body is too exhausted to push again.

When the two souls extinguish, we leave the pride to mourn their own. We'll return to restore them to the earth in three days' time.

We begin our rounds of the valley.

Out from the tree line, a figure all in black, wearing the bones of an ancestor, emerges.

Danger.

I come back to the courtyard in Kian's arms. He didn't share the vision, and his face is lined with worry. Before he can ask if I'm alright, the high priestess sweeps into the courtyard, clapping.

"Excellent work, all," she says. "Well done. Now go and enjoy some well-earned rest."

All the novitiates turn to go, including me and Kian. She stops the two of us.

She walks over to the grass and reaches down to brush a hand over the top of it. "The rebirth portion of your pairing is obviously functioning quite well." She stands back up and smiles sadly at me. "What is wrong with the destruction half?"

I can't tell her I'm too scared, so I say nothing at all.

"It's okay to struggle, but we need to find a path forward," she prompts.

"It's only been a week," Kian says, his tone edging a little too close to insubordinate. I want to tell him to shush. "She'll find her feet."

"I have no doubt that she will," High Priestess Sarai says patiently. "Because I will help her. Now come, Adela. I thought you might like to work on this with me directly, a bit outside of town, where you won't have to worry so much about . . . accidents."

My eyes well at the understanding and grace. She sees me, and will accommodate me so that I can explore my magic without pushing at all of my fears. "That would be lovely."

Kian joins us as we turn to go, but High Priestess Sarai holds up a hand to him. "Not you."

"But we're a pair," Kian insists. "Destruction. Rebirth."

I appreciate his eagerness to support me, but the more people who are with us, the more likely I am to hurt someone accidentally. I put a hand on his arm and shake my head. "I'll be back before you know it. Just gonna go destroy some shit." I wink, trying for jovial.

His eyes search my face carefully, and then he smiles in a way that feels forced. But he squeezes my hand and lets me go without saying another word.

I join High Priestess Sarai in her carriage, a large black behemoth of a vehicle with a golden symbol of the Huntress on the door, pulled by four horses as black as Lathai. We roll through the city, which is a much better way to experience it than the way I first arrived, trudging through it, damp and exhausted.

Insborough is nothing like I imagined. It's loud and full of color and movement. There is beauty, of a sort. The charming way one narrow, ruby-painted building meets its neighbor, which is a deep plum, which meets its neighbor, a bright teal green.

But it stinks. The stench is so much worse than any pasture or barn I've ever been in. Even in the carriage it seeps through. From my time as the matcher, choosing scents for skulls, I automatically try to categorize the smells. Waste. Decay. Disease. Death. All mixed together with the sweat of animals and the body odors of so, so many unwashed people.

The valley is not the idyllic paradise that outsiders expect—caring for creatures is work; it is often messy and violent and just plain hard. But it is not this . . . rotten chaos. I wonder, were they given the choice, how many would stay in Insborough instead of moving to the countryside or some of the smaller villages on the outskirts of the city. And then I realize, they have a choice. Of course they do. Only keepers are forced to stay in the community where they're born.

Everyone here *wants* to be here.

We arrive at a bend in the river that surrounds three-quarters of the city at an almost-empty lot. In the midst of the dried brown grass remains one lone rectangular building, listing sharply to the right.

We climb out of the carriage make our way toward it.

It's a tall building, about three stories, and was once lovely with a gabled roof, wrap-around porch, and intricate trim. The two windows that remain intact are thick, wavy glass. It looks like a stiff breeze could knock it over.

When we are nearly on the building's narrow porch, Sarai gestures up to it. "Tear that down." The opals and diamonds on her unicorn skull twinkle in the late-evening sunlight.

"'Tear it down?'" I repeat. But how? I have only taken a life, and that was done reflexively. But I do not want to fail her. I turn and face the building, and with no idea how to actively, intentionally access my magic. I simply will it to fall down. Nothing happens. I try again, imagining the building collapsing in front of us.

I reach for the phoenix for assistance, but she is strangely unresponsive, and I don't blame her. My fear is too big. While the risks don't feel as dire as they did in the middle of the temple courtyard inside the city, there are still people here to hurt.

I'm not able to manage moving even a nail out of place.

We try again and again, with the high priestess encouraging me, but nothing she suggests unlocks my block. Still, I try. Over and over and over again. Eventually, we lose all the light. The high priestess's servants come near with lanterns and lead us back to the carriage.

When we're settled, the high priestess reaches forward and places a single finger at the tip of the phoenix skull's beak. She lifts it up, sticking my chin into the air. I'm careful to move with her at the slightest pressure, not wanting to slice her with the sharp beak. She moves it up and down, then side to side, as if examining it.

"I had hoped my little surprise would be a celebration of our destructive achievements, but alas. It was a disappointing evening for us both." She removes her hand, and I drop my chin back to its natural angle. "I suppose it's just a gift."

"Thank you for your generosity and grace," I reply, confused.

She simply smiles at me. It's as warm as always, but shame floods me. Her time is precious—as the leader of the Huntress order, she has a hundred other more important things to do—and yet she spent hours trying to help me. Only for me to fail her.

We ride in difficult silence, each bump and rattle of the carriage adding to my worry that she's frustrated and discontent with my lack of performance.

When we finally pull up to the temple, I hurry out. But she stops me with her words, and kindness. "You will figure out the destruction half of the phoenix magic, I'm certain of it. You will not disappoint me."

If her encouragements were a fire, I'd lean close to warm my hands. Her benevolence makes her seem more like she'd be a Spinner priestess. The Huntress values cunning and strength and attracts followers who embody the same.

High Priestess Sarai closes the carriage door from the inside, and it rolls away. I turn to go into the temple and find Sister Ihi is waiting for me with her unadorned mask and quiet demeanor. Another that I wouldn't expect to serve the Huntress. I'm starting to wonder if maybe my view of the orders is too narrow. As a keeper, I have mostly only ever known novitiates.

"Good evening, Adela," Sister Ihi says. "With me."

She walks quickly, her black robes sweeping out behind her as we move through an unfamiliar hall. The priestesses and priests of the Huntress seem to be trained to move dramatically, and I wonder who teaches that lesson.

We stop in front of a door. She opens it to a large, well-appointed set of rooms. This floor is covered with overlapping rugs, and art hangs on every patterned wall. In the center of it sits a large bed with fluffy blankets and giant pillows. "What is this? Where are we?"

"Your new rooms," she says. "High Priestess Sarai arranged it."

"But—" I stumble for the right words. This is nicer than the rooms we have set aside for the high priestesses themselves in the valley. The room is huge and well appointed, so much grander than my previous space, with its bare walls and wooden floor. I want to enjoy it, but I don't understand how I could possibly deserve this. "I can't."

Sister Ihi gives me a look that makes me want to hide behind the long, thick curtains that frame the floor-to-ceiling windows, it's so thick with pity. "Your things have already been moved."

A door farther inside the room opens, and Kian steps out of a washroom. I see a glimpse of a tub large enough to fit both of us. But I barely take that in. Kian is bare-chested, wrapped only in a towel. He raises his arms and spins, showing off the room. "Welcome home, Goddess."

My eyes widen. "We're living together?"

Sister Ihi gives us each a key, then mumbles something about letting us have some time to get acquainted with the room and sweeps away. Kian closes the door and leans against the frame, his smile wide but frozen.

Oh. He's not happy. He's hiding. He enjoys privacy and isolation, and this shared space threatens both. A spike of fear that he doesn't want this, doesn't want me, flushes through me, but I push it away.

I am about to run down the hall after Sister Ihi and beg for my old rooms back when he steps toward me and wraps me in a giant hug. I love the feel of his still-damp skin under my hands and how it tamps down the fear and insecurity that still lingers from my awful magic session with High Priestess Sarai. Surely, I'm simply projecting. Kian's need for privacy doesn't mean he doesn't want to share these rooms with me. We can navigate this new reality together.

He squeezes me tight and picks me up. I'm laughing when he tosses me, sending overstuffed pillows and the goose-down blankets flying. He climbs up onto the bed. I love the way his arms bracket me, his tattooed biceps and forearms taut with the effort of holding himself over me. I am safe within his strength, and at his mercy.

I kiss his wrist, then nip at him a bit, loving the noise he makes deep in his throat.

"I want you."

I do not have to be told twice. I turn, meeting his mouth, kissing him deeply. This, at least, I can do with no hesitation.

Chapter Twenty-Six

KIAN

The day we're assigned to the community gardens at the edge of the Poyhia neighborhood, I practically bounce through the streets of Insborough.

The gardens of Insborough are one of the few efforts where the order actually does good, growing fresh produce for the neighboring communities. And this particular garden is my favorite.

"Why are you so peppy?" Adela asks, still blinking away sleep.

"Kian has a great love for strawberries, no doubt," Ulric teases.

"Strawberries?" Adela's sleepiness disappears almost instantly, replaced with wary curiosity. "This early, the most you could hope for is some wild garlic or maybe asparagus. Or your magic apples, in the courtyard."

She hasn't seen the gardens of Insborough yet. My step grows even lighter in anticipation. "You'll see."

She glances at me with suspicion when we come to the dilapidated tenements surrounding the garden. Like most places in the city, where fashions come and go quickly, this was a wealthy neighborhood at one point, and the buildings' bones still have the echoes of their former grandeur. But now their paint is peeling, their large windows are broken, boarded up, or missing, and their gabled roofs are caving in.

Adela looks around, open-mouthed. This is a different kind of desperation than what she's grown up experiencing. "What happened here?" she asks, her voice thick.

Her feelings live so close to the surface.

"Corruption. Greed. Abandonment." I try to box up the burgeoning hope that she also sees the truth of the orders, and could understand my actions.

Ulric joins the others already in the gardens, but Adela pauses in front of a crumbling stoop where children with matted hair and dirty faces sit huddled together. Their clothes are rags, and they shiver in the brisk air. She moves closer to the youngsters. I reach forward and put a hand on her arm, gently holding her back.

She pulls out of my grasp. "They need help."

"They'll pick your pockets if you get too near."

She scoffs. "And what would they possibly want from my pockets?"

I blink at her naivete. We grew up in two very different worlds.

"Whatever they can find. Money, ideally. If not that, things they can sell or use."

She frowns, but I turn and go through the garden gate, willing her to just follow. I want her to understand, but explaining the complexities of poverty and agency in the city without revealing who I truly am is too delicate a task for me to attempt at the moment. And revealing who I am—and what I've done—is not something I'm ready for. I cannot risk her hating me.

She follows, thank fuck. In an instant, she goes from concerned to awestruck. I love the way her flawless mouth drops open into a perfect pink O, the little noise of delight she makes. I look around the gardens, imagining seeing them for the first time. I consider how wonderful it must seem to Adela, someone has who has grown up with a dying valley that produces so little.

The air is warmer inside the fence than in the surrounding streets, the moisture levels consistently balanced, and the soil is rich with all the appropriate minerals, all thanks to the workings of Sibling Emi and their wife, Sister Evelyn. They're not bonded in the way the gytrash or phoenix are, but as a pegasus-wearer who influences the weather and a cath-palug-wearer who encourages growth, their powers work well in tandem.

The other part of the garden's charm is plain biological abundance, the scents and colors of the garden's produce. Much of it doesn't share seasons, or even continents, typically—tomatoes and corn and jicama grow alongside mangos and sugar beets and berries.

I'm so busy taking in the gardens myself that I don't notice the moment her mood shifts.

When I turn back, her teeth are clenched as tight as her fists. The hairs on the back of my neck raise as I anticipate a rising pressure.

But no. She's been so careful not to let even a sliver of magic through since Etana. She won't even pretend to practice with us most days, preferring to wander the halls of the temple, learning its layout instead. It's an act of defiance that shocks and impresses me, that she would risk the ire of the high priestess she admires so much.

But that's how deeply her fear of herself goes. Surely, she wouldn't let herself lose control now, over something as insignificant as a garden. The phoenix shoots a warning through me. This is not my imagination at work then. I truly can feel a buildup of pressure.

I have to calm her. Not only is the garden necessary to the community that uses it for sustenance, but she will hate herself if she loses herself here.

"Adela?" I reach out and take her hand. She turns to me, glowing with rage. I flinch at the anger blazing in her eyes. "Adela, beauty. Talk to me."

She lets loose a torrent of words. "You have access to this sort of magic, and keepers—" She stumbles on the word, and it comes out like a sob. But she is too angry for tears. "Keepers make do with bark tea and wrinkled root soup in the dead of winter and in the stretches between order visits. And now that the skulls are gone and there is no matcher, they will be even hungrier. And meanwhile, you have *this*."

She gestures at the heavy-laden fruit trees, at the vegetables that are so abundant some of them have gone to rot.

At least the pressure of her magic has ebbed with her outpouring of words.

I'm an idiot. Of course this would be enraging to her, a woman who grew up hungry and dependent. And it should. I grew up with so much compared with my neighbors and friends. My family had resources—many of them stolen, but still. We did not hunger. We did not have to grovel and pay for the "kindnesses" of corrupt religious orders. Or, at least, no more than most in the city, and significantly less than the keepers.

I should have known this would be painful for her to see. I try to say something—anything—but can't manage to squeeze even a word through the shame.

Her breathing grows ragged; the phoenix pressure builds again. She points to Ulric, working alongside barefaced Svena. They are pruning the large apple trees, making a pile of discarded branches beneath them, all with fully ripe apples still hanging amongst the leaves.

"Pruning should happen when they're done with their production for the season. You do not just throw them away." She flings an arm towards the fence, where the children reaching through the fence to snatch blackberries from snaking brambles. "Especially while children hunger."

I need to say something, but all I can think to say is how I intend to fix it. How I've taken drastic steps to lessen the order's power so that there isn't such disparity and waste, and how I take small ones as well. And while I don't know exactly how the valley fits into all of that, now that I've seen the keepers' circumstances—and have so drastically impacted them for the worst—it's something else I want to work on fixing.

Her anger sparks hope that I can share all that. In time. Maybe, just maybe, she would embrace me and thank me for my efforts instead of hating me for what I've taken. But I cannot risk it. Not yet.

I stay silent.

That silence breaks her. She closes her eyes, trying to contain the rising anger. I reach for her, but it's too late. The frenetic pressure releases in a quick, short burst. The entire length of blackberry brambles shrivels instantly, and there is a chorus of small, high-pitched screams. Her eyes pop open, horror clear.

The children run back to their stoops and stairs and watch, wide-eyed and a little bit shaken, but also intrigued at the display of a new magic. "They're safe," I say. "All safe."

Sister Evelyn hurries over and cuts into a thick part of a vine, checking the raw stem. It is totally brown; there is no green tinge of life left in it. Her lips press into a thin line. "You've killed the blackberries."

Adela trembles, no longer with rage. She doesn't hear Sister Evelyn; she doesn't care about a bush. Her eyes are on the children. Whether she's imagining Etana's death rattle or the keeper children's screams as they were attacked by the cath palug, she is not here with us.

"We'll have to dig this up," the priestess says matter-of-factly, pointing at the shriveled vines. "And take a start from another garden."

Her spouse leaves the work they were doing, picking thick worms off the potato plants, and joins the rest of us. Their voice is affected. "No wonder High Priestess Sarai adores you." They reach out and snap their fingers in front of Adela's face. Finally Adela's eyes focus on the here and now. "The gardens are an important source of nutrition for this community, so let's use our hands for the rest of the afternoon, yeah? No magic."

Adela turns as red as the tomatoes in Jasmyn's wicker basket. She nods meekly.

When we are alone, she asks me if I can bring the blackberries back. I try, but like Etana in the valley, I'm not able to. Maybe because her anger was too great, or my will too small.

Whatever the cause, I'm not able to do this thing she asks. Instead, I kneel beside her in the garden. We do not talk, but work in silence, pulling weeds and hacking away at overgrown vegetation. We collect coconuts and shuck corn.

At dusk, the rest of them leave, but Adela stays on her knees, toiling. I remain with her, digging in the dirt late into the night, atoning.

When it has grown too dark to see, Adela finally agrees to return to the temple. Rounded shoulders, arms wrapped around her soft middle, she stands hunched in front of our door waiting for me to unlock it. When I open it, she shuffles in without a word, her eyes staring into the middle distance, haunted.

I hate that her power has done this to her. If I could, I would take it from her in an instant and replace it with the one she should have—

healing. She wants so desperately to do good in this world, and my phoenix would help her do that.

"Can I make you tea?" I ask, and nearly sigh with relief when she agrees.

I add cinnamon and a large dollop of honey, debating whether a trip to the kitchens for a splash of milk is worth leaving her alone.

She removes her phoenix skull, setting her on a small table with quivering hands, and sits in one of the oversized chairs in front of the just-stoked fire, staring at the flames.

Nope, not leaving her. I give her the tea. She takes the cup in both hands and holds it up to her face, closing her eyes as the steam envelopes her. She's done this before, in moments of stress, and I hope that it brings her comfort.

She is like one of the many counterfeit books on my family's shelves. They look like their former selves, with strong, colorful spines, but they've been hollowed out.

And to think, just hours before, I wanted to unburden who I truly am to her. How much worse would this be, to know that the man she's been fucking and teasing and growing frighteningly close to is the same man who stole her community's future. When she discovers me—and she will, somehow, someday—she will hate me.

She sips her tea, continuing to stare at nothing. The silence is difficult.

After several minutes, I say, "Would you like to talk?" I keep my voice soft and even, hopefully hiding the desperation I feel to just make her better. "I'm a priest. I'm good at listening."

This gets her attention. "You are a matched novitiate, not a priest. And possibly the worst I've ever met. I'm not convinced you'll even make full priesthood." Her words are sharp, but she is teasing. There is even a small hint of a smile at the crinkles of her eyes.

Hope soars through me, and I rush to find the response that deepens that smile. "Would I have matched with a mighty phoenix if I wouldn't?"

My heart clenches as the hint of a smile disappears, replaced by that horrific blankness.

"The phoenixes apparently have poor judgment." She gestures at herself.

If the entire order was made up of people like Adela—who roll up their sleeves and work with the dead and in gardens with equal diligence, who are eager to learn and hesitant to use their magic because of a fear of harming others—I would not be here. There would be nothing to bring down. "Or they know better than the rest of them," I say.

"I feel like those." She points to a vase of husks between two of the large windows. One of the many infuriatingly charming additions of living with Adela is that there are often fresh flowers. These sad specimens used to be daffodils, but we apparently forgot to add new water, or they just lived out the course of their lives. Now they are little shriveled husks.

I concentrate briefly, and the daffodils come back to their former selves, bright and perky. Like Adela herself. It's meant to be a gift, something to brighten her dark mood. But I have misjudged, or perhaps nothing can help in this moment.

Her voice full of longing, she says, "What a gift you have been given."

I put my hand out. She takes it, and I trace my thumb across the soft skin of her knuckles.

"I destroy anything and everything I come across." She pulls her knees up to her chest and wraps her free arm around them.

"You don't destroy everything, Goddess."

"No? What about the foal? The blackberries? Etana?" She inhales, and it is ragged with despair. "I am a danger to everyone and everything. High Priestess Sarai will be so disappointed in my lack of control."

Anger flares. Sarai. She'd probably love that Adela has demonstrated her powers again. The woman is an exploiter, and manipulating Adela. Acting sweet and supportive, but undermining her confidence. And again, I cannot warn Adela without tipping my hand.

And I want to warn her. That Sarai is taking such an interest in her means nothing good. That the high priestess will certainly use Adela and her magic as a tool to hurt and harm, to intimidate ordinary people into tithing more than they have so she can grow her coffers by just one more coin. A coin that means little to her and would mean the difference between a week of coal for their hearth or milk for their children.

Adela is warm and soft and smells delicious. I want to pull her to the bed and heal this hurt with kisses, sink into the bliss of her body. Push away all her doubt and my excruciating hope and just be fully present with her. In her.

But I cannot.

I let go of her hand so I can move my chair to be right beside hers. I lean over so our shoulders can touch and take her hand back, tucking it firmly on my lap. I'm not sure if the touch is for her comfort or mine.

I do my best to find words that are both soothing and genuine. "You are a woman figuring things out. You have never done this before. You haven't trained for it. We don't even know what the phoenix is capable of." I lift her hand to my mouth and kiss the back of it, then turn it over and kiss her palm. I kiss each one of her fingertips. "We will figure this out. Together."

She looks at me with wide eyes full of a hope I want to live up to. "Promise?"

"Promise," I reply, terrified that I actually mean it.

Chapter Twenty-Seven

ADELA

When Kian and I returned to our rooms last night, we found a small ruby for each of us on the tables beside the bed, with notes of encouragment. A kind gift from High Priestess Sarai.

Kian forgoes adding his to the phoenix skull for unspoken reasons of his own, and I cannot bear adding mine. It makes me nauseous. So it sits on my bedside table, glittering at me. My reward for terrifying innocent children.

No longer able to continue sulking in bed, I get up.

The only thing that's felt good in the last few days has been my time with Kian and exploring. Since Kian is off doing his own thing, I wander through the labyrinth of the temple, which is both fascinating and infuriating. The amount of wealth just sitting in corners—golden candlesticks shaped like jackalope antlers; silken tapestries of creatures I do not recognize but Cecelia would surely know the names of; gem-encrusted frames with paintings of high priestesses through the centuries can be found in various nooks and crannies of the winding black-marble halls. All forgotten and collecting dust when they could be sold off and the proceeds used to help people.

High Priestess Sarai is generous with her time, gifts, and attention, so different from how stingy the orders are with the valley. I had always assumed it was a result of the dwindling magic and thus dwindling means. But if their resources have shrunk at all, their circumstances are still nowhere near dire.

The rooms I cross in my wanderings are just as compelling and strange as the art and accessories. Since I'm in common areas and not sleeping quarters, I open every door I come across—as long as I don't hear voices on the other side. There is one room that simply holds fibers in every shade of gray, black, and white and a large, gleaming loom in the center. In another, I find a large round table and six chairs, all carved of aspen. The table reminds me of home, as if it ought to be in the great hall, not here in the Huntress's temple.

I take a shaky breath, and on my exhale, I hear a strange and familiar sound. I pause and listen. It's so similar to the skulls before the matching ceremony. Murmuring, more like a vibration than an actual sound. But it's so faint I must be imagining it. My aching, homesick heart manifesting familiarity.

I return to our rooms and my bed and finally face the feelings I've been running from.

I miss home. I miss Dad and the valley's vibrant sunrises and crisp, clear air that smells of nothing and carries only sweet silence across the meadows. The city is so loud, so abrasive with its overwhelming scents and sounds and people.

I turn away from the judging rubies and let myself descend into the sadness.

An hour or so later, there is a shuffling at the door. I sigh, imaging

Kian, holding too many things in his hands and unable to use the key properly. I pad over, eyes puffy from sleep and crying, and open it to help.

Only it's not Kian struggling. It's Ulric in a low crouch on the other side. He looks up at me and blanches, as if I am the last person he wants to see.

"I, uh, was going to slip these under your door." He holds out a small packet of papers and a letter.

I open my mouth to ask why he wouldn't just knock, when I see the handwriting on the packet. It's Cecelia's.

"Have you been to the valley?" I do not give him time to answer. "Have you seen them? How are they? Why didn't you tell me you were going? I could've sent letters of my own, or at least a hug for Dad and Cecelia."

His eyes dart around the hallway, and he half turns, checking over his shoulder. He's acting so strangely. Probably he's exhausted, or maybe hungry, or cold. He's still wearing a traveling cloak, for love of the goddess. I've been rude, peppering him with questions instead of offering him a place to sit to warm up.

I tamp down my excited energy and step back, holding the door open wide. "Would you come in?"

He grimaces and shakes his head. He hands me the packet and the letter.

I can't help myself. I hold them up to my nose and inhale. They smell like normal paper, but I imagine the valley with its cliffs and meadows, simple village houses, and crotchety old creatures. I clutch them to my chest.

"Please," I say with my eyes closed. "Please come in and tell me about them. How they are."

"I'm sorry." Ulric looks like he's in physical pain and glances around the hallway furtively. I realize with a start that maybe he wasn't supposed to bring me anything back. Maybe that's why he didn't tell me he was going. Though I can't imagine who would have wanted to keep that from me.

Before I can ask any of the million questions swirling through me, Ulric turns and starts down the hall. "They're well, I promise. They're well. Please don't tell anyone that I brought you these."

I agree and turn to find a lantern to read by.

Sitting down at a small table, I pull out the thin stack of papers tied together with a yellow ribbon. Beneath the bow is a simple note from Cecelia.

Hope these will help you find your way. Come home when you can. —C.

I rifle through the handwritten pages, which she has neatly torn out of a very old journal based on the faded ink and color of the paper. I recognize the cramped and loopy cursive of the matcher who wrote about communing with the skulls through touch. The one whose writing convinced me that putting my cheek against a silent skull was a good idea.

But these are not her matcher's journals. They're more like field notes for experiments or some sort of research. I skim through them quickly. They speak on the importance of rest for renewal, and the bond of two. None of it makes a whole lot of sense. I wish Cecelia were here to help me understand the significance.

I move on quickly, carefully unfolding a piece of canvas, no longer stretched on its frame. I can't believe Cecelia's torn out journal pages and dismantled a piece of art. Especially given their ages. The art in particular is brittle. I might damage it just by touching it. But the canvas doesn't tear, and none of the paint flakes away. If it's going to suddenly dissolve into nothing, it won't be today at least.

Still, I move carefully.

When I finally get it fully unfolded, I gasp. Where did Cecelia find this? I've never seen it before. In it, a large group of keepers in an old-fashioned version of our colorful wools are portrayed alongside a much smaller group of novitiates in the same white robes they always wear. Half of the novitiates are already wearing creature skulls and the other half still stand in plain white aspen masks. Keepers and novitiates stand around a small building that is not exactly our matching hut, but similar enough in style that I can tell its function. It even has little mounds of jackalope warrens surrounding it.

None of that is remarkable.

What is astonishing are the two figures right in the center of it all.

The figures' roles are clear. It is the valley's matcher in purple and gold and a high priestess of the Pupil in their customary navy. Their faces are covered, but the matcher does not wear the aspen mask. Instead she wears a phoenix skull. Just like the high priestess beside her.

I set the painting aside with shaking hands, a feeling I don't want to look at too closely bubbling up inside me.

There is another small painting in the packet, and I unfold this one quickly. The style indicates it's from another painter from a different time period, but it, too, shows a pair of people wearing phoenix skulls. One is wearing the robes of a Spinner high priestess. The other wearing a set of wool trousers and tunic in a brilliant saffron—a keeper.

I drop the canvas beside the first.

This is impossible and glorious. It changes everything I've ever understood about the history of the orders and the keepers, between the valley and the outside world.

Relief floods me as the sense of my inherent wrongness, of impiety, washes away. I am not alone in this. I am not the first keeper to match with a skull. I look at the paintings, spread out before me, or specifically, to match with a phoenix.

I scoop it all up and hug it to my chest, then snag the lantern on my way out. I need to talk to High Priestess Sarai.

Chapter Twenty-Eight

ADELA

I immediately run face-first into Kian. He grabs my shoulders to keep me from flailing backward and pulls me close, giving me an easy kiss on the forehead.

I mumble a hello and try to step out of his gentle grip, focused on my task. I need to talk to the high priestess.

He lets me go but leans against the wall at a sharp angle, blocking me. I know if I step over his legs, he'll move in front of me. "Where are you off to so fast?"

I hold up the paintings and sort of wave them around. I sidestep, and he moves with me, just like I knew he would, an infuriating hallway dance. I speak quickly, panic building within me, threatening to overflow. "Cecelia sent some research. I think I can still match the skulls, and I need to speak to High Priestess Sarai. Maybe I can go home and double-check. Etana—" The panic bubbles over and steals my words. I squeeze out, "Maybe I can have my old life back."

He goes very still, and this time when I move, he allows me to go past him, but he joins me. "I'm coming along."

"Excellent." He can come with me all the way to the valley as far as I'm concerned.

The high priestess is leaving her rooms as we arrive. "Oh, Adela, how perfect," she says warmly. "I was just coming to fetch you. We're going to work on developing your magic again today. Follow me."

She does not wait for any sort of response but walks down the hall, her typical black robes and veil billowing out behind her. "I suppose you ought to come, too," she says to Kian over her shoulder.

I hesitate, unsettled for reasons I can't pinpoint. I quickly fold up the journal pages and art and tuck them in a pocket.

Kian notices. He turns me to face him. He leans in, pressing the forehead of his phoenix skull against my own. Softly he says, "Whatever she asks you to do today, you do not have to agree. You don't have to prove yourself. Especially not to her."

"She's the high priestess of the Huntress." And as long as I'm a novitiate, she's in control of my future. Maybe that will change if I can go back to being matcher, or some sort of hybrid between the two. Until then, of course I have to prove myself to her. But it's more than that.

"I want to try," I admit.

Kian is independent, strong-willed, bold. He fulfills his obligations, but ultimately doesn't care what others think of him.

I do.

I follow after her. When the carriage arrives, we climb in. High Priestess Sarai sits on one bench, we sit across from her. I tuck my feet back as far as they will go so she has plenty of room. Kian's thigh presses against me, a comforting weight against my own.

The feeling that something is off stays with me. I want to tell the high priestess about the art, but I can't. Not yet. Not until I can determine what's causing this writhing unease low in my gut. I scan the carriage and the priestess, trying to pinpoint what upsets me. And then I see it. She's added more gems to her unicorn skull.

Disappointment flares. It's one thing to have gardens that we don't have access to and expensive art and objects sitting dusty and unused in the corners of the temples, but the valley and the orders are supposed to be balanced and cooperative. My people are struggling, and the high priestess has added more opals and diamonds to her unicorn skull.

As if sensing my flash of anger, Kian presses his leg harder into me. It grounds me.

Maybe I just don't understand the ways of the holy city yet. Perhaps there's an expectation of the high priestess, for her to look a certain way, to display her power and the Huntress's favor with gems and grandeur. She wouldn't be able to effectively lead if citizens and priestesses thought her weak. Or perhaps the gems were gifts, offerings to her for her noble work, serving the Huntress.

I don't know, and I shouldn't be so quick to judge.

"Where are we headed?" Kian asks, watching the city roll by slowly.

"A place where Adela doesn't have to be afraid," High Priestess Sarai replies tersely.

If he notices her frostiness, he acts unperturbed, fidgeting with the curtains of the carriage, his robe, his nails, his skull.

"No safe place exists," I say. "Not when it comes to my magic."

"We will do what we must so you can push past that belief." High Priestess Sarai sits forward and takes my hands in hers. She squeezes tightly, rubbing her thumb across my knuckles just like my mom used to do when I was little and she wanted to reassure me. Just like Kian does. "And soon."

With her iciness toward Kian lingering in her tone, the promise sounds a bit like a threat.

Our trip through the city is slow. Eventually I find my courage and pull out the art that Cecelia sent.

She studies the paintings closely, tracing a finger over the central figures. "How did you get these?"

I open my mouth to reply, but I stumble. Ulric asked me not to tell and I agreed. I can't go against my word, but neither can I lie to the high priestess. I look to Kian, panicked.

"Carrier pigeon," he answers for me.

High Priestess Sarai is so engrossed in the paintings that she ignores his flippant, and very obviously false, reply. The valley does not utilize carrier pigeons, or keep any sorts of birds. The creatures would eat them in a heartbeat.

"This, little bird, is very interesting." She rolls the paintings up and tucks them away in her own robes. I want to ask for them back, but we roll to a stop before I gather my courage. "We'll set these aside so we can focus on your magic, hm?"

My hands practically aching with the loss of the paintings, I see past her that we're in the same field with the same crooked building we practiced magic on before. Only this time we are not alone.

There's a large cage with a young horse inside and a man in a novitiate robe beside it far across the field. I squint to see better what is going on. A flash of alarm flows through me from the phoenix, and I notice Kian startle beside me. He's felt it, too.

Then a sound like a high-pitched whistle echoes through the air.

That is not a horse. I fling off my phoenix skull, tossing it into the grass, and lift my robe's hems to my thighs. I bolt across the field, running as fast as I can. That is Etana's baby.

I get to the cage and throw myself onto my knees before it, trying to reach through the bars to her. She is crying out, throwing herself against the cage, trying to get free. There's not enough room for her to expand her wings, and her feathers get caught in the bars, bending. One rips out entirely and drifts to the grass beneath.

What is she doing outside the valley? And caged? Creatures are not caged. Not ever. I have to get her out. I pull at the door, but it's locked. I pull harder, rattling the bars. She cries out again. I'm scaring her. She's skinny and her coat and feathers are dull. From being captured, or had Lathai not been able to care for her properly?

I turn to the high priestess, who is watching from near the carriage. Too far to ask her why she would do this to a defenseless creature. Or to me.

Even though inside my heart, mind, and soul I am exploding, I turn back to the foal and force my voice to sound untroubled. I am the sun, quiet and warming.

"I know you don't know me, sweet girl," I say to her. She won't understand my words, but they help me find my center. "I knew your mama. We were born at the same time, under the same shooting star."

She stops trying to fly. I continue, voice even, hand outstretched. "Keepers aren't supposed to have favorites. But she was mine."

She stops stomping. She sticks her little nose closer, sniffing at me.

"I loved her so, so much, little one. And she loved me, too. She saved me. She fought a dragon to protect me. I wish she'd been selfish and run. But she didn't. Enkidus hurt her." The sorrow that has lingered in me since the first golden shockwave that I sent through the valley engulfs me. For the foal, I suppress a sob. "I killed her. I did not want to. But I did."

Kian kneels beside me. He traces a finger along my cheek, at the indent the phoenix skull always leaves. "You showed her mercy."

The foal nuzzles her velvety nose into my hand, as if to comfort herself. It consoles me, too. Once I have stopped being overwhelmed with panic and grief, I have room for other feelings. Like rage.

I turn to the figure standing beside the cage, livid. I expect to see some unknown monster. Or maybe Linden.

It's Ulric.

But no. Not Ulric. He's kind and gentle. He brought art out of the valley for me, which I'm fairly certain he was not supposed to do. He welcomed me to the temple. He's my friend.

"What is this?" My voice is rasping, my anger bleeding through my words.

His shoulders are hunched, and the knot of his jaw pulses as he clenches and unclenches his teeth. He will not meet my eyes. As if he's ashamed. He watches High Priestess Sarai closely, unresponsive.

I turn to her, confused. Surely the high priestess wouldn't do this monstrous thing. She cares about the creatures, about me.

I stand up and walk toward her. Kian joins me. I see his hand flex as if he wants to hold my hand, but he lets me stand before her on my own. I sound bolder than I feel when I say, "Did you do this?"

"I did." Her voice has an edge in it I haven't heard since the night I matched. She holds my phoenix skull out to me. "It isn't something I *like*. I don't want this little creature caged. I don't want her harmed. Listen to her cries. Only a monster would enjoy that."

"Then why?" I hate how whiney I sound, how desperate for reassurance.

"The problem is, Adela, you can only seem to access your magic when you're upset. And so I do what I have to in order to encourage you." She holds out the phoenix skull again. "Take down the building."

I don't move.

I stand there staring at her. At the cage. At the creature inside, shaking and stomping. Terrified. I am bolted to the ground. My hands curl into fists. I cannot—I will not—put the phoenix on and just do as I'm told.

The high priestess's voice sharpens. "This next part is your doing, little bird."

She nods at Ulric.

He flinches. It's subtle, but I see it. Still, he obeys. He raises a hand and twists it. A small ball of fire blossoms in his palm. He holds it closer to the creature.

A threat.

Kian takes my hand. "Adela. You don't have to do anything you don't want to."

I pull away.

But not because I agree with High Priestess Sarai. Not because I will just do as I'm told.

Because I am burning with anger. Livid that High Priestess Sarai believes threatening me with the life of a helpless creature—of Etana's baby—is an acceptable way to encourage me to access to my power.

Furious that Ulric goes along. That he burns when he's told to burn, with hardly a pause.

Irate that I have no other way to protect her.

"Don't let me kill anyone," I say to Kian. Not that he could stop me.

I turn away from the cage. My chest is tight and my breathing is shallow and too fast. My nails dig into my palms. I plant myself in front of the crooked old building with my shoulders back and my legs braced as if I'm about to start a fight.

Perhaps I am.

I stare at the rotten, moldy wood, the peeling paint, the torn-up porch, the half-fallen-in roof. But I don't see the building. I see the high priestess's cool, condescending expression. I see Ulric, obedient and dangerous. I see the creature, shaking in her cage.

I erupt.

Fire blooms, hot and bright. I thrust my palms away from my body, surprised but not afraid.

This fire is mine. It answers to me.

Etana's baby screams again. I don't blame her. How dangerous and unpredictable I must seem.

How dangerous and unpredictable I am.

I hear High Priestess Sarai begin to laugh—a delighted, frothy, full-throated joy. The flames snuff out as despair floods through me. This is what she wanted. Me to lose my temper to access my magic. And it worked.

"I told you that you only needed the right incentive, little bird." She loops her arm through mine, as if we are still friends. Her touch repulses me, but if she notices me grimace, she doesn't react. She guides me closer to the crooked building and points at it.

Practically bouncing on the balls of her feet, she says, "Now, no more fire. After all, we have a dragon for that. We're going explore what only you can do."

As if we're in a simple magic lesson. I am the pupil and she, my mentor. But she is not my mentor. I have had a mentor. A mentor who even when grouchy and mean, still taught me to the best of his ability, who guided me toward the best methods and pushed me toward excellence.

This woman wants to push me, but not because she cares about my ability to learn or wants the best for me. She hurt me, and the foal, and she enjoyed it.

"We'll start small." She points to a window of the building. "Break it."

Behind me the foal cries out, and I can hear her wings hitting the bars again in her panic. All I want is to let her out; to wrap her up in my arms and take her home. Not that she wants the comfort of my arms. She is a wild creature, not a human child or some domesticated lamb. Still, ignoring her cries physically hurts. I will attend to her soon.

This is almost over. Only I will not be starting small and breaking a window.

The high priestess of the Order of the Huntress wants me to be destruction?

I will be destruction.

Maybe Sarai is right. Maybe I am dangerous. But if I am, then she should be afraid. She has crossed a line.

I look at the crooked building, and I want it gone. I want this day, this moment, everything gone. The pressure inside me builds until I think I might explode.

"Now," Kian says, softly urging me. "Let it go."

I do.

The building vanishes. Not collapsed boards and shattered glass. Not bits of rubble. Not even piles of ash. Just a plain field with a patch of dirt where a building once stood.

Behind us, Ulric sighs in relief and I twist to see him absorb the flame. Etana's baby trembles in the corner of her cage.

Something a bit like fear flickers behind High Priestess Sarai's eyes. She's pleased, but also uneasy. Good.

"Wonderful," she says. "I knew you could do this. Prepare to do more soon. Now come. Let's go home."

I ignore her. I hate the self-satisfaction in her voice. She is proud of this monstrous act of hers. Of mine. With a shrug, she turns and walks away. I think I hear her laugh as she climbs inside, but I am too busy hurrying over to the foal to listen closely.

The carriage rolls away, leaving us. I do not care that we've been left. We can walk, or return with the foal and Ulric.

Ulric. Who threatened a defenseless creature. Who caught and caged her. This is why he returned to the valley.

"How dare you." I shove at Ulric's chest. "How *dare* you. I thought you were my friend."

"I am." His voice cracks, but I have no space inside me for his feelings. Sarai, and Ulric as her accomplice, woke this rage, and it will not quietly slip away. I want to argue. I want to fight. I want to destroy.

Kian moves to stand between me and Ulric. I scowl at him. I know he loves Ulric, in his way. They're important to each other. But surely Kian is not going to defend him to me now.

"He stole this creature. He caged her. He went to the valley and he—"

"Look at him, love," Kian interrupts.

His voice is too even. He's trying to calm me. I do not want to be calmed. Cautiously, he steps slightly to the side so I can see Ulric. Ulric has removed his dragon skull and he stands, swaying slightly. His eyes are empty, haunted. He looks like I feel deep down, below my simmering anger—defeated, utterly depleted.

"Am I wrong?" I demand.

Ulric shakes his head.

"Adela, that is not the look of a man who did something willingly, or with any kind of pleasure." Kian's voice is gentle, as if I am the terrified creature in the cage. "He's been harmed as well. For Sarai to get what she wants."

"I'm sorry I let her use me," Ulric says. "I hate that I did. I wish I were stronger, like you."

Stronger. I'm no stronger than Ulric. Someone stronger would have refused to do as she demanded. They would have fought back. They wouldn't have just capitulated.

All of us failed this creature today.

"Can you take her home now?" Kian asks, his hand on Ulric's shoulder. "Back to the valley?"

"The high priestess wants her close—" Ulric slides his eyes to me, then glances away guiltily. "Just in case."

In case I need a reminder. Of her power.

Kian is quiet for a long while, but I can tell he's thinking through something by the way he shifts. Finally he says, "I know some people. Who might be able to help get her home."

Who would Kian know who could get a foal back to the valley? Ulric is a recent addition to only a handful of people who know the path.

But before I can ask, Ulric says, "She has a place in the stables. If you need to find her. The little alicorn."

"Alicorn?"

"That's the type of creature she is." He's still tense, but he's starting to relax. I see the edges of my friend in his posture. "Cecelia told me. She'd been out by the remains of the matching hut and saw me creeping out of the forest. She brought me the packet to give to you, and made me promise to keep the alicorn safe. In exchange, she offered me a ten-minute head start before alerting the elders."

My anger at him seeps away. "And have you, kept her safe?"

"I have done my best. As safe and comfortable as possible. When she's not so scared, she is a menace. A tiny agent of ecstatic destruction." Ulric's voice is thick with affection. "There are a significant number of barn hands who would love to have her shipped back to the valley immediately."

"I hope she wears the mantle of destruction better than me," I say.

"She wears it with the confidence of a youth who's never been told she needs to make herself small to fit into this world." I can tell he wants to hug me, as does Kian. But I cannot handle any more feelings. Not Ulric's kindness, not Kian's sympathy.

I need action.

"Alright." I turn to Kian. "Take me to these people who can get her back to the valley."

Chapter Twenty-Nine

KIAN

We trudge through the city toward my family, slowly. Adela is not doing well. Now that her anger has seeped away, so has all her energy. She keeps stumbling over the cobblestones, and after about twenty minutes of walking, she begins to lean on me heavily.

I don't mind. I like the weight of her against my body, but her steps grow sluggish and her breathing shallower and faster. She shivers, and then her teeth begin to chatter. The air is cool, but not cold enough to cause these reactions.

She needs to rest, both her body and her mind. I hurry toward home, trying not to look too closely at how I feel about telling her the truth of who I am. Or at least part of it. My mind spins through what I can keep hidden and what I'll have to reveal. Obviously if she discovers I come from a family of smugglers, she'll have to know I'm not fully the servant of the Huntress I pretend to be, but she doesn't need to know anything beyond that. She doesn't have to know about my desire to destabilize the order. Or that I'm responsible for the destroyed skulls. Not now. Not ever.

"Come, Goddess." I kiss the top of her head and turn down the next alley. It is grubby and poorly lit, with debris in the corners of the street and missing cobblestones. Rats or mice or some sorts of small rodents skitter out from underfoot.

"We've turned the wrong way." She points to the temple square, now off to our right. The belfry of the Huntress peeks out over the Insborough rooftops.

"Shhh, Goddess." I wrap an arm around her and tuck her head into my shoulder. "We're almost there. Then you can rest, and we'll figure out the next steps."

She follows, meek and quiet. She's less terrifying when she's bringing down entire buildings with nothing but her will.

I am not sure what is more surprising for Aunt Ujvala to find on her doorstep, her nephew in his Huntress regalia and phoenix skull or the sniffling woman in matching garments on his arm.

"Hello, Kian," she says in her unflinching way. Because, of course, nothing ruffles my aunt. At least, nothing that she'll admit to. "Adela."

Adela blinks at her. "Have we met?"

"We have not. But it's my business to know things about people."

Unnecessarily cryptic. Aunt Ujvala ignores my look and welcomes us in. If Adela were feeling well, she'd instantly be suspicious of that statement. But she's too tired to take it in.

While Aunt Ujvala goes to the kitchens to fetch sustenance, I take Adela to the sitting room and get her in a chair next to the fire. I remove the phoenix skulls from our faces and set them on a small mahogany side table, then gather a pile of woven blankets from their stand in the corner and wrap her up. One around her shoulders, one over her head and around her neck, two around her legs and feet. I tuck them in tight until she looks like a giant, wool-wrapped caterpillar.

Slowly, she stops shivering. Pink blooms in her cheeks.

When Aunt Ujvala comes in with a white peony tea and sweets, I free Adela from some of my overexuberant tucking. Adela shoves a sesame shortbread into her mouth and holds the mug of tea up to her face, inhaling the steam like she always does to comfort herself. Though she still looks haunted, slivers of her personality begin to return.

Particularly her inquisitiveness. She looks around the room, soaking in the shelves of knickknacks. Aunt Ujvala is a collector. There is art in various styles, paintings and foreign-looking jewelry, dried flowers from far-off places, and jars of lotions made with ingredients even I've never heard of.

Her eyes snag on a small glass bowl tucked into a corner beside embossed, leather-covered books and a very old-looking phallic statue—a bowl holding more of the red stones Aunt Ujvala gave me to mark the path into the valley.

No.

She stands, shimmying out of the blankets still wrapped around her.

"Adela, would you like a scone?" I ask, trying to catch her attention. "I think they're chocolate and orange."

I'm not quite ready to tell her who we are. I wanted to tell her in the morning, after she got a night's sleep and ate a hearty breakfast. When she wasn't so raw, so emotional, so dangerous. Because the moment she connects these stones to the ones she found in the forest, she'll know. And I'm not sure what she'd do next.

She walks over to the shelves.

I look to Aunt Ujvala for help, but she's knitting, doggedly not meeting my glare.

Adela picks up a stone and rubs it between her thumb and finger. She opens her mouth to ask about then, but Ivo comes bounding in.

I close my eyes in relief. He'll distract her, surely. She's beautiful and he's a sixteen-year-old boy. He goes immediately to her and introduces himself. "I came to ask Kian to play dupe the dud with us. Would you like to join?"

"Ooh, I've heard of that game. Could be fun," she says earnestly. She holds up one of the stones to Ivo and says, "But first, what are these?"

I watch it all as if she were one of the furious little jackalopes bent on impaling me for daring to step into their territory. I try to catch his attention, to will him silent or, better yet, away. It's not that I don't want her to know. Just not yet. And not through Ivo.

"Ivo," I say when my silent, exaggerated looks go ignored.

He doesn't even see them. He's too busy smiling at Adela, whose full attention is on him. I've been a smitten sixteen-year-old boy, full of lust and hope. He's not listening to his tiresome older cousin. Ivo doesn't even know I exist. Or maybe he thinks she already knows who we are. After all, it's not like we invite random strangers into our home, which is grander than any house in this neighborhood should be.

"Oh, those are just glass markers we use to denote paths sometimes when we go on runs," he says. "Ready?"

She continues smiling at him, but it's a little too frozen, not meeting her eyes.

"Give me a few moments, and I'll do my best to join you."

It's not our link through the phoenix that lets me know her thoughts and feelings. I can see them on her face as she connects the small pile of red stones beside her in the forest, to these. And that I told her I knew people who could get us back into the valley. She's working through what it means, and it's only a matter of moments before she figures it out.

I'm not ready. To explain myself. And she's not ready to hear. We'll be lucky if she doesn't take down the whole house around us, like she did to the lopsided building.

"Come join when you can!" Ivo bops out of the room.

Adela turns around. She does not look at me, or Aunt Ujvala. Even I can see she's dropping stitches, waiting to see if Adela is as astute as suspected.

Unfortunately, she is all of that and more.

"Runs," she says to herself as she takes in the large connecting doors, the shelves full of unusual artifacts and books, my aunt in dark, close-fitting clothing. "These are the people who can help get the foal back home. You're smugglers."

"Clever girl." There is clear admiration in Aunt Ujvala's voice.

"And you"—she points at me and holds up a stone—"led them into the valley on your initiation night, marking the safe path in."

I hold my breath, waiting for the fallout, hoping she won't hate me for bringing outsiders into her precious valley and potentially jeopardizing the creatures her community is called to protect. But then she laughs and claps her hands, like a delighted child.

She turns to Aunt Ujvala. "You used to be the ones who brought us books and sweets when I was little! But why did you need Kian to give you the path back into the valley if you already had it?"

"Only two of us knew the path." Aunt Ujvala tucks away her knitting and begins to tidy up the mugs and plates. She looks at me. "And we lost it when we lost them."

"Your parents?" Adela looks at me with a pity I both hate and want to lean into. I don't want her pity. I want her admiration, her adoration. Her love.

I nod.

"We're actually going back to the valley tonight. If you'd like us to take anything with us?" Aunt Ujvala says.

Adela's eyes gleam. "There is something I'd like you to take back to the valley, actually. What do you know about smuggling creatures?"

Ivo's going to be crushed she won't be joining him for that game tonight.

If ever there was someone born to be a smuggler, apparently it is Adela.

She explains to us what she'd like to do and how almost immediately. She and I will return to the temple and steal the alicorn from the stables. Then Aunt Ujvala will lead her and the alicorn back to the valley.

"I'll come with you," I say.

She grunts a half-hearted agreement and turns back to planning with my aunt.

My aunt suggests she and my Uncle Jamie will meet us at the edge of the temple square with the wagon, and we'll hide her and the foal in the back just like we do any other illicit good.

I'm allowed follow behind on foot to protect them both and make any necessary distractions.

"Jamie won't go into the valley," Aunt Ujvala says. "None of the others will, after Ivo's stories about the dragon and his jackalope wounds."

Adela nods and gestures to our wet, dirty novitiate robes. "Do you have clothing I can change into that'll help me blend in a bit better?"

Happy to finally contribute something, I hop up. "I do!" I don't have a lot of options, but I have some nondescript pants and tunics that I keep here, just in case I need to run away quickly from the temple.

I return to them talking through the details of timing and paths through the city where either we'll be totally unnoticed or the inhabitants won't rat us out to any order members who come asking questions.

"What about our skulls?" I ask, pointing to where I've set the two phoenix skulls.

This makes them both pause.

Adela bites at her lips, considering. I can practically hear her thoughts, she's so open. On the one hand, she's finally figured out how to harness her magic, and it's a useful one in a heist, even if it is something that scares her.

On the other, there's no point in wearing nondescript clothing if we have giant magical bird skulls over our faces as we traipse through the city.

"We have to take them," she decides. "Just in case we need to pull on our magic."

When the two women are content that they've gone through all the contingencies they can think of, and I can't bear to sit still for one more moment, I grab a lantern and stand up. "Ready to steal a creature?"

"Steal?" Adela's tone is brittle. "I think you mean liberate. The order was the one to steal her."

I love her fire. "So they were."

Now that we have a purpose—and she's been fed and warmed—Adela seems to have significantly more energy, and we arrive at the temple quickly. She might actually make it through this long night. And it will be long with the theft of the foal and a trip to the valley ahead of us.

Hopefully after, I'll be able to apologize and explain better why I hid so much of myself from her.

When we get to the temple courtyards, we go between the Huntress and Pupil temples to the large stables in the back. The three temples share stable, which makes me wonder just how much the other two orders are involved in the theft of the alicorn.

But what would they have to gain from Sarai extorting Adela's magic?

The stables sit behind the three temples, on the very edge of the city, where Insborough looks out over the sea. Built of a sandblasted limestone and dark timber, they stand two stories tall, with one level for horses and mules and the second for the stable hands who care for them.

The doorways are arched and wide enough to fit a team through side by side. Between doorways are wrought-iron lanterns, currently dimmed to low glows.

It all is rather majestic, as if even the horses of the orders are ostentatious. But at least it's not a barn built out of ridiculously expensive marble.

We enter through a side door that dares to creak, grateful to find the stable empty.

No one is up and about doing late-night chores. We won't need to bother with excuses for why two novitiates would come to visit the horses in the middle of the night.

Though if we did, our plan was to abashedly admit to adventurous amorous pursuits.

Inside, the stable is like every other barn I've been in—which is admittedly few. It smells of hay and saddle soap and piss. We move quietly between the polished wooden stalls with their brass nameplates.

We know instantly when we find the stall we're looking for. Not only is Ulric sleeping, half-sitting, half-lying on a pile of feed sacks in front of it, but the stall is the only one that goes all the way up to the ceiling.

We hurry over. The foal is asleep in the corner, curled up with her head tucked under one wing. Adela steps around Ulric's sleeping form and tries the door.

It won't budge.

"I can go fetch my lock-picking set," I suggest quietly.

We don't think that Ulric will disrupt our plans, but it's better to not have to test him. The less he knows, the less Sarai can torture out of him.

Adela chuckles quietly. "Of course you have lock-picking sets." She gets a faraway look in her eyes, as if remembering. "That's why you knew the door beneath the temple was locked, and that it leads to other temples. You've explored it all."

I flinch even though there's no derision in her voice. If anything, I think there's a bit of admiration. But I'm not used to someone knowing who I really am. I keep expecting her to judge me harshly as a liar and a thief.

She wouldn't be wrong. I'm both.

And worse.

Hopefully she'll never find out about the skulls, and those will stay an accident of Lathai's grief in her mind. Burning down the matching hut is unforgiveable.

"We don't have time," Adela says, and it takes me a moment to realize she's talking about picking the lock. "Your aunt and uncle will be at the courtyard soon, and we don't want them to have to wait around for us or they'll draw suspicion."

From the ground, Ulric clears his throat. "It's not locked. There's a specific sequence to opening it." He remains in the same position with his eyes still closed. "Like the way to the valley, only on a much smaller scale. Sarai set it, and she's the only one who knows it."

Hearing our voices, the alicorn wakes up. She is instantly in the air, bobbing against the ceiling and the bars of the stall, hitting them hard.

"Well then. Let's get this little one out." Between one blink and the next, the front wall of the stall is gone. Goddess, she's hot when she leans into her power. Not just her magic, but who she truly is. The beating, fiery heart of herself.

Adela smirks. "Bet Sarai's going to be thrilled she pushed me to learn that."

Unfortunately, getting rid of the wall of the stall holding a terrified wild creature who can only kind of fly has less-than-ideal results. The alicorn dashes out of her stall, smashing into a wall of tack, knocking down finely kept bridles and a leather saddle oiled to a deep sheen. They crash to the ground, loud.

I grimace and look up at the ceiling, to where the stable hands' rooms sit just above us. I hear the faint squeak of a metal bedframe and hurry to dampen the lanterns at this end of the hall.

It's not fully dark. That would be too suspicious, but if someone does suddenly come down the stairs to investigate, maybe they'll assume the stall with its missing wall-and-door combo is just another nook for tack or straw. The stables have plenty of those.

Adela and Ulric hear the squeak, too, and stop trying to catch the alicorn. We all freeze, straining to listen. But there's no more sound of movement. Praise to the Spinner if it's just a light sleeper rolling over. If it's not, and they are also awake and listening carefully, we need to hurry. Silently.

Grabbing a handful of hay, I creep close to the foal, who has found her way to an open bag of oats and is happily munching away.

"That's straw," Adela whispers, "not hay."

I look at her blankly.

"It's for bedding, not eating."

"Huh." I toss the straw down and move quickly forward, hoping to snatch her, but her head whips up, and she startles away, kicking an empty silver pail. The pail flies and hits a trough, clanging.

"Shhh, shhh, shhh."

Adela steps forward and tries to calm the foal. For a moment, I think it'll work. The foal takes a tentative step closer, but then we hear footsteps above us. They cross overhead, moving swiftly in the direction of the staircase.

"Hide!" I say, and point Ulric to an empty stall. He dashes in, then carefully swings the door mostly shut.

I duck into one of the dark nooks between the wall of the barn and some stacked-up bales of hay, or maybe straw, pulling Adela with me. She's trying to reach the foal, who's hovering near the high ceilings. But where there's a chance the foal might not be seen high above a stable hand's gaze, there is no chance Adela would be missed.

I tug her down, until she's half-sitting on my lap, a slightly distracting and enjoyable weight in the midst of the chaos. I'm half-tempted to kiss her neck—just a peck—but I'll certainly get swatted.

At least if we're found, the amorous activities excuse would be an easy one to buy.

There's not much we can do about the foal, but the moment I see the stable hand pop out of the stairway, I worry less. He's just a kid, maybe thirteen or fourteen. I get the sense he got shoved out of bed to check on the noise, because he's wearing a nightshirt and his boots, shuffling down the aisle of the barn with half-shut eyes.

He looks around blearily, and I think he'll simply turn around and go back to bed when he pauses. He squints at the far end of the barn where the foal's stall is, trying to see in the darkness.

"Kian! The stall door!" Adela says.

I groan, not knowing how to put it back at the moment. Right now the stable hand looks confused, as if he doesn't quite know what's wrong, but if I suddenly pop a whole part of the wall with a door back into existence while he's looking, he will definitely suspect foul play.

I could throw something past him and make him turn in the opposite direction.

I look around, but there's nothing with enough heft within arm's length. Still, I'm scrabbling through ideas of what I could try when smoke starts pouring out of one of the lanterns on the other end of the barn.

The stable hand runs over to it and grabs a blanket, waving it at the fire, which only manages to stoke it higher.

"Fire!" He yells into the night, no doubt to rouse his fellows upstairs. "Fire!"

When no one comes immediately, he hurries to the stairs and starts clomping up them.

This is our chance.

I pop the door back into place while we climb out of the pile of hay. Ulric is in the aisle already, waiting.

"Thank you for the distraction," Adela says to him. Of course the fire was Ulric. And here I thought my prayers might have suddenly meant something to the goddesses.

"But how do we catch her?" Adela looks around, frantic for a solution.

"Oh!" Ulric pulls a peppermint out of his pocket.

"Hankering for a sweet?" I ask. Like now's the time.

He hands it to Adela. "The stable master gave it to me earlier when they saw me fighting to calm her. Said the horses often like them, but by the time we went through the nightmare of catching her in the valley and then the cage, she wouldn't come near enough to take it from me."

"Perfect." Adela hurries over to the alicorn with the candy in her outstretched palm. Curious in the way babies of all species are, the foal drops from the ceiling slightly, wanting to see what's being offered. She lands on wobbly legs.

Above us, we hear the scrambling of feet as others undoubtedly hurry to shake off sleep and put on clothes and boots.

The alicorn sniffs at Adela's hand, then takes the peppermint with her thick, sensitive lips. Adela scratches at the spot between the foal's wings with one hand and holds on to her mane with the other.

She nods to us. "Let's go."

Ulric takes a step forward, and the foal tries to bolt. Thankfully Adela holds firm, taking one of the little creature's wings in her hand and holding her mane tightly.

"I'll stay behind," he says. "She's too scared of me. I'll cover for your absence."

I think of the way Sarai lashed us when Aunt Ujvala stole some of Brother Victor's gems. I owe him an apology when all this is over.

"I don't want you to have to suffer for the alicorn being gone."

He points to the dragon skull on his face and then looks at the fire. The smoke is thick and stings our eyes. It flickers to almost nothing. "I'm too powerful to punish now."

I don't point out that Sarai had him threatening his closest friends and a defenseless creature just hours ago. But that's for Ulric to figure out.

"Be safe, friend," I say. "Protect yourself."

We hear hurried footsteps on the stairs, and with a whoosh, flame shoots up at the bottom of them. "Go."

We do. Adela guides the foal, and we slip through the door, closing it behind us.

I watch Ulric upend the bucket of oats and scoop up water from the trough. He hurries over to the stairs as if he's just discovered the fire. He douses the flames just as we close the door.

"Rope?" Adela asks me.

I hold some up that I grabbed when we ran by the wall of tack. The habits of a thief are hard to break. Especially when you don't want to.

"Thank the goddess."

Adela tells me where to place my hands, and I hold on to the alicorn as if my life—and hers—depends on it. Because they do.

If a baby alicorn suddenly shows up flying over Insborough, Sarai's going to have a whole lot of questions, and eventually someone will slip, or break. No one can survive torture and stay silent forever. Well, almost no one. My parents did. They never gave up the family, though it would have likely saved their own lives.

Thankfully, Adela is fast. She knots the rope into a harness that she slips over the alicorn's head almost instantly. We maneuver through the courtyard.

We arrive at the meeting spot to find Aunt Ujvala and Uncle Jamie waiting.

We work together to quickly unload the trade goods and the fake goods, and then Adela climbs up. She tugs on the rope-tied bridle, and the foal follows easily.

One peppermint and suddenly Adela is trustworthy. Who knew that's all it took?

Aunt Ujvala gapes. I don't know if I've ever seen her face so alight with joy. She looks like a little girl who's seen her first pony. But of course, she is in a way. Only my parents had ever entered the valley regularly. Aunt Ujvala was only there for a couple of days, hiding in the forest. Even if she'd been there for a month, it's rare to see a baby creature with the birth rates so low.

Let alone an alicorn.

"What's her name?" Aunt Ujvala asks as they get settled in the wagon.

"She doesn't have one yet." Adela strokes the alicorn's nose and considers. The foal blinks wide black eyes in contentment. "I think Tani. For her mama."

"It's a good name," I say.

Adela lies down in the back of the wagon and gently places an arm and leg over the foal. Partly for comfort and partly to contain her if she spooks.

When Tani doesn't seem to object, Adela nods, and I cover her with a heavy woolen blanket, then pack in bags of potatoes and crates of books and other mundane goods. It won't hold up to close inspection, but if there's one thing I've learned growing up in a smuggling family, it's that very few people look at things closely.

As Adela says, thank the goddess.

Chapter Thirty

ADELA

The trip home is uneventful. Despite my mounting anxieties, my exhaustion grows larger. Tani and I sleep in the back of the bumpy wagon, buried beneath the rough-spun blanket and pinned tightly by crates, barrels, and sacks, until we get to the edge of the forest that separates the countryside from the valley.

We roll to a stop, and after some muffled conversation, Kian lifts everything off us. "Still well?"

Tani pops her head up and snorts at him, and I move off her. I keep her lead wrapped around my wrist, just in case. While she seems comfortable enough with me now, it's safest not to trust creatures too thoroughly.

Kian reaches to help me out. All I want is to fling myself into those arms. Have them wrap around me and tell me everything is going to be okay and that he love—I stop the thought as I sit up, groaning.

My body hurts, having lain in one position against the wooden wagon bed. And my heart hurts, too. The thought pops back, unbidden. I want him to tell me he loves me. Because I love him.

But if he did, would he have hidden who he truly is from me? Surely, he should trust me to know and understand that his family are smugglers and he wanted to help them with their endeavors. I would also do anything for my family. It doesn't change anything between us.

"Can I help you down?" he asks, his hand still outstretched. Tani jumps out of the wagon, and I climb stiffly after her without his help. I grapple with my feelings.

A flash of something like hurt crosses his face, but he says nothing. I walk away, unable to face him.

Ujvala gives both Tani and me an apple, encouraging me to eat mine. "You're going to need the energy."

Then she hands me a skin. I take a large swallow, then splutter, not expecting a swig of brandy first thing in the morning. She grins, so like her nephew. "Woke you up, huh?"

I cough, thankful for the distraction from my looping thoughts. Love and reciprocity aren't things I can deal with now, and so I tuck the complexity of my feelings for Kian deep inside myself, getting out of my head and into my body.

We unload the wagon of as many goods as Kian, Ujvala, and I can carry in the packs she brought. Books and spices and decadent pastries, candied fruit and dried beans and even a bolt of fine lace—things we don't often have in the valley. Practicalities but also little luxuries to enjoy.

I wish we could bring in so much more.

But Ujvala assures me that if everything goes well with her talks with the elders—and I firmly believe it will—she will come back with more. And frequently.

We say goodbye to Jamie, and start the path into the valley. It's winding and strange, and I try to memorize it. I don't know how anyone could and suspect it's marked in some way, but I don't spot the markers and Ujvala doesn't share them with me.

The forest grows thicker and quieter the deeper we walk.

Tani grows restless. She pulls on the rope. She wants free; she wants to run.

"Have we crossed into the valley?" I ask.

"Not quite," Ujvala says. "But soon. I'll let you know when we get there. It's not something you can feel."

I trust her.

Tani does not. As we move deeper into the forest, she begins to get more agitated. The branches rustle with a slight breeze, and shadows start to grow as the sun begins to come up. She tries to shy away from every new sound and walks farther and farther from us, straining on her rope.

When a red-tailed hawk swoops low on the way to catch herself a chipmunk, Tani rears, and a small bolt of lightning blooms overhead. A rain shower starts.

"Well, that's annoying." Kian pulls his tunic over his head to protect himself from the rain.

I tilt my face up to the dark, angry sky, letting the rain wash over me. I laugh. This is not annoying. It's amazing. I check around us to confirm. Everywhere else is clear, pink morning sky. Outside of a small area we stand in, the trees and ground are dry.

This storm is Tani's creation. I've never known a baby creature to utilize their magic.

Ujvala is looking around, alert, holding the straps of her pack tightly as if she might need to run.

"It's Tani," I explain, hoping to ease her nerves. "She's afraid."

I turn to the alicorn. "You're okay, little one. We're taking you home. We're almost there."

And then I feel something else marvelous. A response of sorts. It's not the voices of the skull, but something subtler. As if the want is my own. I find myself wanting to let her go now. To release the lead so that she can run, be free.

I spent my childhood alongside Cecelia, reading about unicorns, asking elders for stories, studying the paintings in the great hall, wanting to know anything and everything about Etana. Which is how I know that influencing emotions is a magic they used to possess. It can still be accessed in tiny amounts through skulls by the most powerful priestesses, but a living creature hasn't manifested it in generations.

"Is she—" Kian stares at Tani, then at me. "Is she making me feel this way? Like there'd be no better thing in the world than to convince you to take her off her lead and let her run."

"She is."

"Well then," Ujvala says, "let's get her all the way into the valley and let her have her way, shall we?"

We walk quickly through the rest of the path until there is a small opening in the trees. There are splotches of dark color splashed up on some of their trunks, and the ground is disturbed. I suspect that this is where the priest was eaten by Enkidus.

Tani calls out. The call is less aggressive than her terrified scream when she was caged, but still sounds like nails against glass.

Nearly instantly there is an echoed response and the rush of wings above us.

Ujvala flinches, but I turn my face up to the sky again. There, skirting between the trees, moving quickly, is the dark outline of Lathai. The storm lightens up and then stops as Tani spots him, but the rush of her will through me intensifies until it is almost painful.

Let go. Let go. Let go.

Lathai lands heavily and stomps at the ground, lowering his head and snorting at me. Ujvala moves halfway behind a tree. I don't blame her. Lathai is large and angry, and he doesn't know her.

But he quickly sees there's no need for his threats. I slip the bridle off of his little one.

As I suspected, the moment I let Tani go, they run to each other, nuzzling their faces into each other's necks. Without even a backward glance, they disappear into the morning together.

Something deep inside me relaxes. She is well, and with Lathai. Safe. She will be safe.

Now, to get me to *my* family.

The trip across the meadows and fields feels like I've moved through time, as if I've crossed into a world that is somehow both familiar and foreign. It's unsettling, the dissonance between what I left and what I see now, in such a short period of time.

The meadows look like they do in my springtime childhood memories. The air has lost it chill. The grasses are growing. The sky is a bright, cheerful blue with fluffy clouds dotted across it. Wildflowers in the meadows have buds and small blooms, and the wheat is poking up through the tilled fields. I'd almost thought I misremembered these perfect spring days until now.

And the creatures are active. Pegasi and gryphons fly overhead, going from their hunting grounds back to the cliffs where they nest, and jackalopes are farther from their territories than I ever remember seeing them. There's even a gytrash trio loping over the hills far off in the distance.

Ujvala gives the jackalopes in particular a wide berth, but they ignore us, stockpiling food for their impending herds of babies.

When we get to the village, I see tulips and the first sprouts of eager vegetables beginning to poke up from garden beds. I blink hard, trying to make sense of it all. Everything feels so right and so wrong at the same time. The valley is brimming with life, where it was struggling so recently. A flicker of hope in my chest whispers her dangerous song that the valley can return to itself, despite its struggle and loss.

Maybe I can, too.

I hear my name being called and see no more of the suddenly verdant landscape surrounding me. Cecelia is running toward me across the square. I drop the pack of Ujvala's trade goods so it doesn't weigh me down and take off at a run myself. We collide in a giant hug, her arms around my neck and mine around her waist. She squeezes me so tight I momentarily lose my breath, but neither of us let go. I have missed her desperately. And here she is.

I inhale deeply, enjoying the scent of her hair, which smells like peonies and home. I tuck my face into her neck.

I am happy to hug her as long as she'll let me. Finally, we release our grips on each other and step back slightly.

Her palms are gentle on my cheeks as she cradles my face, her eyes scanning me from hairline to chin. "I missed this face," she says, her voice thick. "But where's your phoenix?" I point to my pack, which Kian now holds. "Stashed in there. It's more comfortable without."

"No doubt," she replies.

I am laughing or crying or possibly both. "How did you—"

She answers before I finish asking the question. "I saw Lathai with the foal fly overhead. And I just knew—"

Her voice cracks. I've never seen her so emotional. Not that she doesn't feel. She's sensitive and empathetic; she's not demonstrative. If my feelings sit on the surface like lilypads, hers are nestled amongst the base of the seaweed in the lake floor.

I wipe the wetness from under her eyes.

"I never thought I'd see you again," she says in a small voice.

I huff a laugh. "You sent a message to come back!"

"But I didn't think you really could." She sniffles. "And you returned the foal. I was so worried for her. Is she well? What did they want with—"

Her question is cut off. "Adela?" I do not even turn before Dad is there, wrapping thick arms around us both. Cecelia pulls away, and he squeezes me tight, kissing the top of my head. I'm transported to a time when I always felt safe and loved. Before Mom left.

"The goddess be praised. You came home. I . . . I thought I'd lost you forever. But why are you here?" He pushes back some of the pale strands of hair that have fallen out of my braids during the long night. He does not stop looking at me when he says, "And who have you brought with you?"

"Someone had to bring Tani home." I lean my cheek into his hand. "Ujvala and Kian helped."

"Tani?"

"The foal. Etana's baby girl."

The lines beside his eyes crinkle. "Tani suits her."

I stand up straighter, and open up so I can properly introduce him to Ujvala. She steps forward, and I gesture to her with a flourish. "Ujvala knew the path through the boundary. She's part of the family that used to bring us goods. Kian is her nephew."

"The family that used to bring us goods," Dad says with a knowing look, and puts out his hand. He and Ujvala grip forearms in greeting. But he continues talking to me. "Being part of a smuggling family makes a lot more sense than the boy being a priest."

I glance at Kian, who just shrugs in acknowledgment. Sometimes it's good to be seen.

"Come on, let's get some breakfast, and you can tell us the details of why they took the foal, how you brought her home, and what you need." Dad leads the way home.

On the windowsill above the kitchen sink sits a solitary candle, gently flickering in the soft morning sunlight. An ache of recognition flows through me. We'd lit a candle for mom for years after she'd disappeared. A tiny symbol of hope that she would find her way back to us in time. Only she never did and eventually we put away the candle and let go of that hope.

Dad makes tea and coffee while I scramble eggs and toast bread. There are conversations that need to happen, soon, before Kian and I are missed, but for this one brief moment we spread butter and fresh raspberry jam over thick slices of toast and savor every bite.

After we eat, Cecelia runs to fetch Petra, who will need to be a part of the negotiations and next steps with Ujvala. Probably all the elders ought to be called, but the more unnoticed our presence is, the better, until we can figure out what's next.

Because whatever our futures hold, they are not going to look the same. I cannot simply go back to trying to fit in as a Huntress novitiate, not now that I know the truth about the lengths Sarai will go to. But I also don't know there is a place for me any longer here in the valley. Besides Etana, there are no skulls to match, and even if there were, I don't know that I'd match them to the orders. At least, not to the Huntress while Sarai is high priestess. If she's willing to use a defenseless creature on her path to access my magic, what else is she capable of?

"The fields of wheat and flowers are far more mature than they ought to be at this time of year. And the creatures seem . . . lively." I say, as we wait for Petra.

"The valley is coming back to us," Dad says, cleaning up. "The creatures are stirring. 'Lively' is a word for it. They're wilder than they've ever been in my lifetime, and more active. Hunting more. Breeding more. We have a bunch of new pregnancies."

Petra comes into the house with Cecelia on her heels and picks up on the conversation without even a pause, as unflappable as ever. Cecelia must have filled her in on the short walk over. "Foliage is growing at tremendous rates. Much earlier and faster than it has in decades." She pours herself a mug of tea, adding honey, and sits down at the table.

"What's changed?" I ask.

"The skulls, we think," Cecelia answers. "When the matching hut burned, all of the magic of those skulls returned to the land. That's the only thing we can tell that's different."

Beside me, Kian shifts oddly in his seat. His face is tight, his eyes dart to the floor before quickly meeting mine and then skirting away again. But there's something in the set of his jaw—something guarded—that makes my stomach tighten. Maybe he's eager to get back to Insborough.

While Dad, Ujvala, and Petra begin to talk through what trade would look like, Cecelia silently gestures outside. I stand to go with her, also wanting a few moments away from everyone. I'm not sure how much she's shared with whom about what she found in the paintings, but this is the other reason I needed to come to the valley. To find out if I can still be a matcher.

Which means facing Etana's skull.

Kian stands to come with us, but I wave him off. Seeing Etana again, discovering whether or not I can hear her, is . . . I don't know.

Too hard with a witness who doesn't fully understand the bond we shared.

He sulks a little bit, but sits back down with the others.

Cecelia and I step outside and sit on the railing of the small front porch like we used to when we were kids. It's a bit more difficult to balance on as adults, but worth the effort. I love watching the valley wake up, especially in springtime. We sit in silence for a few long moments, just absorbing the day.

But mere moments are all we have. I stand. "Would you take me to Etana? I want to see how much truth there is in those paintings you sent."

"I thought you'd never ask."

I adore Cecelia. She's methodical. She thinks through things slowly. She makes sure she understands everything. And then she's all in, headfirst. Just like me.

She leads me through the great hall and to the library. I don't understand for a moment why we're here, but then I notice a small shelf of plain aspen masks just outside the library door. She picks one up and puts it on.

"Is this where you're keeping the skulls?"

"Skull," she corrects, making sure her mask is tight. Until I matched, I don't think anyone actually believed a keeper would match with one of the skulls. I proved the centuries of caution worthwhile.

"They're working on rebuilding the matching hut, but lumber is scarce at the moment, as are laborers. Everyone who's free is busy planting."

And it's not as if the voice of one skull would be terribly disturbing even to those who hear them most loudly. I stand outside the library door, waiting for Cecelia to go first. I'm afraid.

She's also hesitating, with her hand on the doorknob. "So . . . before we find out what you can do or not, I wanted to explain one more thing. About the matching hut." She finds her words carefully. "Lathai didn't destroy it."

"What do you mean? Of course he did. The storm. The lightning. How else would it burn?"

She shakes her head. "It took some time, but I found records where keepers and the orders worked together to document the scope of magic, both in living creatures and their skulls. It really is only dragon fire that can destroy them. Like we always believed."

This doesn't make any sense. Ulric is the only dragon-wearer, and he would never intentionally destroy the matching hut. But then again, he stole Tani and threatened her under Sarai's direction. Could someone else have manipulated him? Or is there some reason Sarai would want the hut destroyed?

I shake my head. Whatever the cause, it doesn't truly matter at the moment. The hut being gone ultimately helped the valley, returning magic to the land. And while it might hurt the orders, that doesn't feel so dire, now that the living creatures and the valley are prospering. The orders can figure out their own paths to the future.

Right now, I don't have a lot of time, and I need to know if I can hear the skulls.

Starting with Etana.

My palms begin to sweat, and I wipe them on my borrowed clothes. I don't know why I'm anxious. Etana is dead. I will never scratch her head or place my hand on her ribs to sync our breathing. I cannot harm her further.

Cecelia turns the knob and begins to open the library door, but I catch her shoulder.

"Does Beadda hear her?" I ask before I go in. "Or anyone else?"

"Even I hear her." Cecelia isn't terribly attuned to skulls, so this is a good sign. She reaches up and squeezes my hand. "Whatever faces you, you will handle. Just like you do everything."

"Would we say *handle*? Survive it, maybe."

"So? You're authentic. You have big feelings. And you also have great instincts." Cecelia drops the doorknob and faces me. I can't see her expression past her mask, but I can clearly hear the sincerity in her voice. And besides, Cecelia doesn't lie. "You're clever. You see the world as it is. And yeah, sometimes you're angry. But suppressing anger doesn't make us good. Horrible, horrible things happen. We should be angry about them."

She flings open the door and holds out her arm. An invitation. "Trust yourself."

I'm not brave enough to step through, but I also can't walk away. I have to move forward. I can manage whatever awaits me. Maybe not calmly. Maybe not with grace. But chaotic progress is better than inaction.

I take a deep breath and step inside.

There, in the middle of a tall shelf, is my Etana. Warmth, welcome, and glee flow to me. I hurry to the shelf and lift her to my chest, practically bursting. I can hear her.

I sit at the table, and position the skull in my lap, silently thanking the great goddess. "I wish I had ointments or oils," I say aloud, more to myself than Cecelia. Polishing the bones is the best way to commune with them.

"Oh! I do!" She fetches a couple of vials from a tucked-away shelf and brings them over. I open one, and a horrible smell that is both vaguely sweet and rancid, like fruit that's been left in the sun too long, fills my nose. I stopper it quickly.

"What is that?"

"Erm . . . overripe comfrey. Beadda and I wanted to experiment a bit. Since we don't have any of the recent matcher notes. We've been using recipes I found in that one matcher's journal; she's got some unusual recipes."

"If by 'unusual' you mean 'gross,'" I reply.

We both laugh.

Goddess, I missed her.

In life, Etana loved rolling around in the poppy fields or sleeping under the lilac bushes. I go through the rest of the vials and jars until I find something light and floral. I polish the bone, rubbing in the ointment while whispering to her. Contentment flows through me. Hers, and my own. I'm so grateful for the sound of her. It's different from what it was, but perfect.

Emotion flows through me. Gratitude for the care. Delight at the scent I've chosen. And then, forgiveness.

She knows me. I place my cheek against her brow, just beneath her horn, and wish, for only a moment, that I could match with her. If all of this had to happen, why not with my star sister?

Etana and I sit with each other, feelings flowing back and forth between us. I do my best to tell her about Tani, and am shocked when she seems to understand. The resonance of communicating with Etana is so much different than it was with the other skulls. A lower sort of murmur. Quieter but clearer, as if before, the skulls had to shout at me to be understood and she can simply chatter to me.

Something about the sound—or feeling, I suppose—is familiar. But that's impossible. I haven't been near any unmatched skulls since I've matched, and I don't hear the skulls of the other order members.

I nearly drop Etana's skull when I realize. I've heard this kind of murmuring before. More quietly, as if they were far away, but also in orders of magnitude. In the temple.

With shaking hands, I place Etana back carefully, silently promising to return as soon as I possibly can. I nearly run back to Dad's, my heart pounding hard, Cecelia's footsteps heavy behind me. She doesn't even have a moment to ask what's happening.

I burst in through the kitchen door, startling the others at the table. "We have to go back. Immediately."

They stare at me wide-eyed, but I can't find the words to explain. A cold, crawling fear steals my voice. The order, the temple, the high priestess—it's all wrong. Somewhere in the Temple of the Huntress is a hoard of skulls that should not exist—trapped, forgotten, abandoned. I'm the only one outside of the valley who can hear them.

I have to find them. And save them.

Chapter Thirty-One

KIAN

On the way back to Insborough, Adela and I sit in the wagon, side by side. She closes her eyes, pretending to nap but holds herself too stiffly for it to be genuine. My butt falls asleep on the unpadded wagon base. I shift, brushing against her leg. She moves ever so slightly so that we don't touch.

She's avoided me since we left the valley, not even telling me if she was able to hear Etana. I can't tell if she's angry or simply distracted by everything else. I hope the latter, but I'm afraid that it's my deception.

And she knows only the surface. How much worse it would be if I told her all of it—that I'm actively working to bring down the order, that I am the one who destroyed the matching hut and the skulls within. Yet there is a part of me that dreams of telling her. Of her seeing me. Accepting me.

Maybe even choosing to come alongside me, work with me to support my efforts.

And ultimately, to love me.

The hope stings.

Showing someone my full, unfiltered self is not something I've allowed since I was a small child. Not even for Ulric, my best friend and once lover. He wanted to be let in so badly, but I couldn't push past my fear to let him. I still can't.

When we get back to the temple courtyard, Adela practically launches herself off the wagon.

"Your skull!" Aunt Ujvala calls, holding it out.

Adela takes the phoenix skull and hurriedly threads her belt through the creature's eye socket, re-buckling it snuggly. After some warm but hasty goodbyes, she nearly runs across the cobblestone square. Bursting through the main temple doors, she stops suddenly, tilting her head as if listening.

"I think we should go change," I say, pointing toward our rooms. If anyone sees us, they'll wonder why we're not in our novitiate robes.

Apparently disagreeing, she walks briskly down a hall in the opposite direction. I follow, asking her where we're going, if she's alright, if she would like a snack or a bath. I offer everything and anything I can think of, trying to get her to engage with me. She says nothing, just follows some strange path through the temple.

Every so often she pauses and holds up a hand to be quiet.

"Where are we going?" I ask. I reach out to her and take her hand. I want to apologize. Maybe if we are touching, she will be able to feel my sincerity, to know that I am sorry for not telling her sooner about my family. "Adela, please."

"Stop!" She doesn't yell, but her voice is firm, and the force behind it lands like a weight on my chest. She pulls away, her hand slipping from mine, and for a moment, I feel like I am the phoenix, falling through the air. "Just be quiet. Stop trying."

The words are a force of cold wind blowing away the fragile hope I'd been holding so tightly. She doesn't want me. She doesn't even want me to try to repair things between us.

"We can talk later," she says.

My hope is like the phoenix in the visions, soaring over the verdant valley. Thrilled and dangerous. "Do you promise?"

She sighs at me, and I feel the weariness of it down in my very marrow. "I'm making no promises. Right now, I need to you be silent. You can come along if you'd like, or you can go away. But I need to figure out where the voices are coming from."

"Voices?"

"I've heard them since I arrived, but I didn't know what they were. They sounded different than in the valley. And then when I communed with Etana—" Her own voice softens, though the gentleness is not for me. "There are skulls here in the temple. Somewhere. But I can't tell where their voices are coming from."

Of course there are plenty of creature skulls in the temple. Every priestess, priest, and matched novitiate wears ones. But she has never said anything about hearing those. She doesn't hear my phoenix, or feel his wants, except through her own. And there can't be unmatched skulls in the temple. What use would those be for the order?

And besides, where would they even hide them? I've never seen an unmatched skull in the place, and I've been through every corner and down every aisle, up every tower and down every staircase.

Down every staircase.

Besides people's sleeping quarters, there is exactly one locked door in this entire temple. One door I have never been through. Now it's my turn to swiftly turn and walk away. Over my shoulder, I say, "I know where they are."

She follows immediately. Without sharing a word, we both begin the descent into utter darkness until we come to the door carved with symbols of the Huntress and inlaid with gold.

"How many times have you tried to pick it?" she asks.

"A dozen," I admit. "But I can try again. Maybe the thirteenth time's the charm?"

I see the small outline of a smile curve up her full lips. But there is no joy in that smile. It is pure threat. She holds out a hand over the door. I feel a pull, a building pressure, and the door is gone, just like Tani's stall wall in the barn. She is not even wearing the phoenix. It's just looped through her belt. "No need."

Her power is immense. For the first time, I am glad destruction is not mine. I would not wield it half as gracefully.

We go through the door and down more stairs. The air is frigid and stale, and Adela slows, grimacing, as if it's physically difficult to move and she must force her body forward. "They're so loud. So numerous." She covers her ears, holding her head. "They're in agony."

Down a narrow, earthen hallway, there is flickering light, and we hurry toward it. We come out into a cavern, a crypt. There's a single candle burning, with unlit candelabras beside it. We light the candles quickly, holding them up to our surroundings, illuminating horror.

Adela lets loose a wail.

On every surface—walls, insets, ceiling, even at the edges of the floor—hang creature skulls. There are not dozens, not even hundreds. But thousands. Jackalopes and gryphons. Kelpies and unicorns and pegasi. Gytrash in their sets of three. Dragons and cath palugs. Even some I don't recognize at all—a large mothlike creature and something that looks a lot like a wolf.

Adela falls to her knees, dropping her candles, holding her head. Her voice is thick with anguish. "How is this possible?" she asks.

I pick up her candelabra, not bothering to relight the candles that extinguished. The rest burn merrily, unbothered by the misery they've revealed. I set them all aside and sink down beside her. I wrap an arm around her, tugging her close. She leans in to me, but she's not there. She is consumed by grief. Her desperation and heartbreak flow through me, whether from the magic of the phoenix or simply our own connection.

Somewhere above us, I hear the soft noises of others moving through the temple, most likely heading to dinner or prayers.

"This is the reason the valley was dying." She looks around at the skulls. All hope is gone from her voice. It is utterly flat. "What have they been sending us instead of the skulls' ashes when their priestesses or priests die?"

She is so pure, her faith in the goddesses and other people, always so certain. But so much of what she believed was a lie; the proof of the deceit surrounds us.

She has been betrayed. And not just by the order.

I cannot remain silent. I can't keep hiding who I truly am from her for another moment.

I put a finger under her chin and turn her face toward mine. She is so beautiful, so precious to me, it physically hurts to look at her in pain. She has her eyes closed, blinding herself to the abomination of hoarded skulls surrounding us. "Help me destroy them. The order."

Her eyes pop open.

"I don't just pass along information to my family." I take a deep breath and tell her my truths. "My whole life, I've been working to destabilize the Order of the Huntress. They killed my parents. And my parents were smugglers, sure. For many, they were bad guys who made their livelihood through stealing and lies. But they were never malicious. They weren't greedy."

I search her, looking for any expression of her thoughts or feelings, but it's as if she wears a mask of her own face. Her expression of anguish is unchanging. She remains still. Listening.

I take her hands and she lets me, but does not clasp mine tightly.

"My parents were kind. They wanted to help those who didn't have access to the goods they needed. To bring joy. They drove Aunt Ujvala crazy with how little profit they brought in. But they didn't care. The rest of the family could make money. They wanted to do good in the world. Like you."

My hands shake. She looks down at them, but does not move to pull away, or to pull me closer. Every muscle in me cries out to be silent, to keep my secrets. But I push through. I reach down to the phoenix skull at her waist and tilt it up, running my finger across the razor-sharp beak, careful not to scratch myself.

"I always thought it was the skulls, that access to the magic, and the power that it brings over the natural world, contributed to the corruption." My voice wobbles when I admit, "But you've helped me see, it's not the skulls or the magic. You have a skull and magic. Likely the most powerful, destructive magic that exists." She flinches now. Her first reaction to anything I've said. I hurry on. "But you do good with it. You rescued Tani. You eased Etana's hopeless suffering. When used by good people, the skulls provide the means to do tremendous good.

"It's not just revenge for dead parents. It's accountability." I hold out my arms to the walls of skulls surrounding us. Surely she can see it is so much bigger than just my vengeance. My motives might be small in the larger scheme of things, but my goal is righteous. "The corruption of the order is deep and long. Generations of dishonesty, perversion, and pain."

She stands up and walks around the crypt. She reaches out to touch the skulls, but she cannot get to them. It's as if an invisible barrier protects them. But of course, it likely does. One just like the barrier around the valley, around the lock to Tani's stall.

She places her forehead against the barrier and whispers through it. Things I cannot hear. I would bet all the gold bars hidden in the walls of my family's compound that they are kind, comforting words. If the skulls feel, and I now believe that they do, they are no doubt calmed by her gentleness.

I think of the way she took out the door to this crypt and Tani's stall without blinking. The crooked building she brought down to nothing. How quickly Etana's agony was alleviated.

Adela has the power to do everything I can't manage on my own.

But will she?

"Help me," I beg. "Help me destroy the bad so there is space for good."

She turns to me, and for a moment it's almost as if I see an outline of flames and wings rise up behind her. But her face is softening. She's listening. Something deep inside me uncoils. I showed her myself and she didn't abandon me.

She is going to say yes. She is going to be my partner in this. Together we will disrupt the order, root out the corruption, and make space for good.

Before she can answer, a smooth, silky voice comes out of the darkness. "Hello, my darling little birds." High Priestess Sarai steps out of the shadows. "You are not supposed to be here. Yet."

The gems glitter in the candlelight beneath Sarai's sheer black veil. She holds up a hand, nearly as pale as the unicorn skull, and snaps her fingers. From behind her, half a dozen priestesses and priests, two from each of the orders, come forward carrying lanterns. Linden, Molvi, Ylysia, and Jasmyn are with them as well.

Their eyes are wide as they hold up their lanterns, taking in the bone crypt and the thousands of skulls that surround us. But they remain silent and steadfast.

Linden descends on me, along with two brutes of brothers whose names I don't know. One wears the red of the Spinner, one the navy of the Pupil. I had always wondered how involved the other two orders were with the actions of the Huntress. Apparently they are not innocent, as I'd hoped.

The priests grab my arms tightly, pulling so they're half-twisted behind me while Liden stands close, acting threatening.

I roll my eyes at him.

"What is this?" Adela asks. "Why are you holding him?"

"He's a traitor," Sarai says with an unamused laugh. "And he must be punished for his crimes."

"Crimes?" Adela asks.

"We have been following Kian for years as he plotted against the orders, leading his family of smugglers to the valley, even burn—"

I begin thrashing, spewing curses.

Adela can never know that I was responsible for the destruction of the matching hut. That, she could never forgive.

Sarai nods. The Pupil priest rips the phoenix skull off my face, breaking the leather strapping holding it on while Linden gags me with a length of cloth. Swift and brutal. My eyes water as my tongue is shoved too far back into my mouth, and it feels like the skin of my cheeks is cracking, it's tied so tightly.

Adela steps forward, as if she's going to come free me from the gag. I shake my head. I don't want them to hurt her. She stops ten feet from me, and I feel a tug deep inside myself and then instantly gone, along with the gag.

I spit. "You fucking—"

As if they anticipated a lost gag, Linden pulls out another length of cloth. Once again, I am silenced, this one somehow even tighter than before. But a little piece of cloth is not going to stop me from fighting. I flail against the hands that hold me, flinging my body back and forth violently. Despite my strength and size, they manage to hold me in place.

When I feel Adela's power beginning to grow again, I expect her to remove the gag a second time. Instead, she removes Linden's hands. We all just stare for one ponderous beat before the screaming begins. Blood gushes, covering Linden, me, and the priests. He turns, splattering the floor, candles, lanterns, and robes of everyone near with gore.

Ylysia collapses on the hard-packed dirt floor, knocking her gytrash skull askew as her head hits the ground. Molvi bends to help her even as Jasmyn steps over her to get to Linden. The Pupil priest is closer. He lets go of me to focus on healing Linden. His bleeding slows instantly, but the priest does not have enough magic to regrow a hand.

I could.

I turn away. Let him manage the world with no hands, and no creature skull. The fate he deserves has found him.

Taking advantage of the chaos, I pull out of the grasp of the single priest now holding me and hurry to Adela, kissing her. A desperate, hungry kiss, as if it might be the last we'll ever share.

"I wish I were you," she says softly, like a goodbye. "A healer. A creator."

"No, love. You're so much more. You're willing to do whatever is required, even if you abhor it." I think of my cowardice at not telling her about the matching hut and wish I could go back to tell her the full truth of who I am. "Embrace who you are. Exactly as you are."

"Even the part of myself that embraces destruction?"

I glance over at Linden, whimpering, and Sarai, giving instructions. They follow her orders without thinking. Or without caring, perhaps.

"Especially that part."

Once Linden is carted out of the crypt, his partners weeping behind him, Sarai's attention is back on us. "I didn't think you had it in you," she says to Adela, something like pride in her voice.

"You think I don't know the necessity of violence?" Adela laughs and does not let go of me. "I'm a keeper. To care for creatures means sometimes you mete out violence. Any animal caregiver knows you do not allow an abscess to linger. You cut it open and let the rot drain out, even if the creature flails and screams their pain."

Her eyes trace the trail of blood that stains the crypt floor.

The diamonds on Sarai's unicorn skull gleam in the flickering light. "The things we will accomplish together, you wonderful little bird."

I can feel Adela tense in my arms. She wants to argue, to fight, but she shakes her head as if trying to knock something loose. I wonder how loud this many skulls are for her, how painful it must be to have them whispering their desires, their whims, inside her mind.

"What exactly do you want?" I ask Sarai.

"Magic is failing." Sarai walks slowly over to another part of the crypt, where there is an altar similar to the one in the sanctuary above. She traces a fingertip along the edge, then lights the three candles there—one red, one navy, and one black. The three colors of the three orders. As a member of the Huntress order, she has no right to light the navy or red. Those are for the Pupil and the Spinner. They should not even be in her possession. Except obviously the other orders are also involved."

"I'm securing our futures, through the means the high priestesses established three hundred years ago."

Three hundred years of stockpiling skulls. Three hundred years of breaking their commitments to the valley. Three hundred years of deceit.

"But the reason the magic is dwindling is because you've been hoarding skulls!" Adela counters, then cringes again, pressing one ear against my shoulder, as if that could keep out some of the sounds surrounding her. "And, besides, you *have* magic. The only magic that exists. Why would you need more?"

I agree with Adela. Sarai leads the largest, most powerful order. She charges people for the privilege of helping their loved ones cross into the after. She controls the fresh fruits and vegetables of an entire city. She tells her priestesses who to heal. And who not to. What would she need with more, indeed.

"Compared to the high priestesses of old, the power I have might as well be none." Sarai takes one of the candelabras we lit and walks around part of the crypt, holding up the flickering light so we can better see the creature skulls. "I cannot bend a person's will to my own or block off a path entirely. We will match these ancient skulls with novitiates who are eager to follow the will of the Huntress." She glances at the other orders' members and acknowledges them with a nod of the head. "And the Pupil and the Spinner, too, of course."

She'll match the skulls to those eager to be puppets of herself, more like. No matter which order they belong to.

I can feel the phoenix's pressure building deep inside me as my fury grows. I cannot believe she is asking Adela to do this. To betray everything she believes in. But without a target or direction, the pressure is nothing but a suffocating frustration. After all, what am I going to do? Make a vining plant that strangles her? Put her in a box that her followers will just tear down? I stand there and seethe silently.

Sarai returns to the altar. Kneels at it. Bows her head as if ready to receive an anointment. In her dark robes and veil she looks like a pious supplicant. "The great goddess must concur. After all, she's blessed me with not only a phoenix pair to destroy whatever enemies that arise and then rebuild them to our purposes—" she turns just her head toward Adela. "But also a matcher."

"Why would I ever help you?" Adela lets go of me, and I resist reaching for her hand. If she wants to stand on her own, I will stand beside or behind her. Wherever she needs me. "You've manipulated me. You've amassed power and wealth that were not yours to keep while withholding food and other promised resources from my community. You've made it impossible for us to fulfill our destiny as keepers, and broken your covenants."

"You'll help because you want influence, of course." Sarai stands and comes closer, her arms outstretched. "As my right hand, you will have a voice in the decisions we make, the world we rebuild."

This makes Adela pause. She desperately wants to do good in the world, and I can see the temptation. If only the offer were true. But the whole room knows it's not. Surely.

Thank the goddess, it's not enough to sway Adela.

"No," Adela responds.

Sarai shrugs and immediately changes tactics. She lowers her head, as if she embodies the unicorn she wears and is going to charge. "If you don't join me, your precious valley will suffer your refusal." She raises a single finger. "First, we withdraw our aid. All three orders."

Adela does not flinch. After all, she knows the valley is healing. In addition to my family's trade, it could be enough to sustain them.

Sarai holds up a second finger and takes a small step closer to us in the center of the crypt. "Second, we prevent the smugglers from accessing the valley to provide their own version of resources. I cannot block the path in and out fully, but I can move the entrance far enough that attempting the old way in will harm them."

Damn it.

Here, I see Adela hesitate. Based on the way she spoke of going hungry in the depth of winter, I doubt the keepers have enough stores to survive without *any* food from the outside world. It will be months before the current seedlings produce enough to feed an entire village.

Sarai doesn't stop there with her threats. She holds up a third finger, stepping closer yet again. She drops her voice, and the softness of it is more chilling than yelling ever could be. "And then, when they are weak with hunger, we go into the valley. We might not have a willing dragon or a phoenix's destructive capabilities, but we still have magic. We still have power. And of course, we still have physical weapons. Most importantly, we have the will to crush our enemies."

She lowers her hand, making a fist. A promise of violence.

The air is heavy—oppressive—with Sarai's threats. Though I can't see her face, and I'm not touching her, I can practically feel a storm of emotion building up in Adela, like Lathai's storm in the valley. "You will just destroy it all with so little thought?"

Sarai doesn't flinch. Her tone is smooth and calculating. "On the contrary, I've given it great deal of thought. I don't do this lightly. You could say I'm not doing it at all. In the end, it's *your* choice. You can pledge your loyalties and power to me or you can be responsible for the destruction of your home and all the people and creatures within it."

Adela looks around the crypt's walls and ceilings, taking in the thousands of skulls stolen from her people, and I know before she speaks that she's made her decision. It was never a choice. It was a trap.

Adela's shoulders sag, her face collapses in resignation, as if the fire within her is dimming, being snuffed out. She glances at me briefly, then her gaze flicks away. As if I would judge her for what I know is coming. Her voice is barely above a whisper when she says, "I agree."

"Excellent." Sarai walks over to me, trailing a long finger across my shoulders, and smiles with no warmth, just calculating satisfaction. "As your first test of loyalty, for his crimes against both the orders and the valley, you will kill Kian."

Chapter Thirty-Two

ADELA

I feel the sharp, bitter burn of betrayal in the back of my throat.

I'm tormented by the creatures on the walls and ceiling of the crypt surrounding us. Creatures that my family has been responsible for the care and keeping of for generations. We have fed them, protected them, healed them, and when they passed, we ushered them along the path to fulfill their destiny.

A path that was supposed to be holy, blessed, meaningful. Instead they are being used. Their lives and deaths twisted for the selfish whims of greedy people.

Heat flows through me, around me. My robes and hair ripple slightly, as if I'm standing in a meadow in a strong summer breeze. The light in the crypt grows brighter, illuminating the creature skulls of the priestesses and priests. Their eyes are wide and frightened, and trace along the outline of me, but broader, beyond the bounds of my actual body.

They step back, pressing themselves up against the barriers around the skulls.

Who I am and who I want to be are in a delicate balance. I like the fear on their faces. Part of me itches to wipe them all out. I could embrace the part of myself that enjoys destruction, my seething desire to just burn it all down. Sarai. The crypt. The temple above us. The temples of the Pupil and the Spinner. A simple thought and it would all be gone. Forever.

Except the skulls.

If I could send them to their rest, I might do it. With Kian by my side and the valley safe, I could find a path forward despite the death and destruction I'd be responsible for. But I cannot get through the barrier with my magic.

I also cannot kill Kian. I love him.

"Never."

"Never say never, little bird." Sarai resembles a hawk about to snatch and devour a finch.

"I was afraid you would need extra incentive. Thankfully, my ever-faithful Sister Roberta agreed to run an errand earlier."

As if on cue, there are shuffling footsteps on the stone steps, and then Sister Roberta steps out of the shadows. Dad and Cecelia stand, bound, on either side of her, plain aspen masks covering their faces. Roberta must've followed directly in our footsteps in order to have gotten to the valley and back so soon after us.

Panic shoots through me. I know she's not lying about hurting them. I've seen the scars on Kian's body. Punishment for small disobediences. She would go so much further than lashes to be able to access the magic that surrounds us.

She begins to walk around the crypt, pulling down select skulls. "I'll begin to prepare the matching ceremony while you think, hmm?"

Before I can answer, a vision takes me.

We hear the roaring of adolescent dragons across the valley and head in their direction.

Over the cliffs where they nest, we find the two, locked in a downward spiral and screaming their rage to the sky. At this time of day, their elders are likely out hunting, or have chosen to just ignore the overly dramatic youth.

But we cannot.

The mountain spires they plummet toward are sharp and strong. If they hit one incorrectly and pierce a leathery wing, they could be severly wounded. Or worse, lose their life. They are too young to become conduits for the servants of the goddess.

Stay back, my mate communicates as he flies forward, into the fray. All he needs is to be seen, and they will cease. They always do. This is our valley to rule and protect. We keep the balance of magic in check. The other creatures revere us. And in return, we keep them safe from outsiders, and each other.

But being seen by an angry, fighting dragon can be difficult. And so I do as he says, staying away. I am our safety.

He circles the dragons, flashing his golden feathers in the sunlight. He dodges in and out. He is being dramatic himself, enjoying the wild maneuvering, which means he does not notice when one of the youth pulls its head back, collecting its breath.

Careful!

It is too late. The dragon breathes fire, which misses his rival and hits my mate. His feathers catch. In an instant, they're ash. He plummets to the rocks below.

I scream my sorrow and dive after him. At the edge of a sharp rock formation, atop a pile of rubble, he lays burnt and broken, utterly unmoving. I can do nothing for him.

He is dead.

I settle down beside him and wait for him to come back to me.

I come out of the vision, shaking. The phoenix's grief was as real as my own, as she watched her mate burn and fall to the ground.

But there was a certainty within her that I am only just beginning to understand. She mourned his pain and suffering, but knew he had not fully left her. He could not. They were two halves of a whole.

Like me and Kian.

Yet Kian is no phoenix that can rise from his own ashes. He's a mortal man. Expecting that there's any world in which he could come back to me from would be madness, and a risk beyond anything I'm willing to contemplate.

I turn and face Kian. I brace myself, terrified of what sort of judgment awaits me. He's shaken. He obviously saw the vision along with me. But he meets my gaze with a gentleness and grace I do not deserve. The light of the candles, the lanterns, reflects back in his dark stare, as if there is a fire within him that matches the one in me.

His eyes plead with me, urging me to agree with Sarai. To kill him.

As if she can sense how close I teeter on the cliff of capitulation, Sarai comes to stand before me. "What's the life of one man—who has abandoned and betrayed you—compared to everything and everyone else that you love?"

She is right and I hate it. One life compared to hundreds and only I can protect them from her violence. She's left me with no choice. I agree to do what she asks.

I will kill Kian.

Chapter Thirty-Three

KIAN

I drop to my knees before Sarai. It's ridiculously dramatic, and just the kind of thing she soaks up. And I need her to agree to what I am about to ask. "Let us say goodbye. Please."

Sarai looks over at Adela, who grits her teeth but echoes my last word. "Please."

She shrugs. "If you want to miss the feast, then that is up to you."

"The feast?" I ask.

"Of course. It's the first step of the matching ceremonies in the valley." She claps her hands like an excited child. Her delight at her twisted play for power is sickening. Especially when she threatens Adela. "But don't delay, little bird, or your father and friend will suffer."

Sarai and her followers exit the crypt, half dragging Adela's dad and Cecelia along. They're trying to get to her. You don't need to see their faces to know that they don't want her to do this, to even consider it.

I do.

The moment I'm sure they're gone, I use my magic to put back the door that Adela removed so adeptly to ensure our privacy. Then I gently remove her mask, dropping it to the earthen floor, so I can see her beautiful face in these last moments.

A crypt of creature bones isn't the most romantic of places to tell someone the deepest secrets of your heart, but whether it's by her hand or someone else's, I won't leave here alive. A few minutes alone with her to say goodbye will have to be enough.

She steps forward into my arms and kisses me gently on the lips. "It looks like you have a lot on your mind."

"Well, I am about to die," I say with a smirk.

She smiles back at me, a small, tired, hurting sort of smile. "I think it's more than that." She traces a finger along my hairline, across my ear, and down my neck. I love the way she touches me.

"I have one more betrayal to confess." She waits while I fumble with where to start. She might be the destruction half of the phoenix, but I am the one who has ruined everything. I take a deep breath and begin. "I'm the one who destroyed the matching hut—"

"I know," she interrupts.

"I truly believed it was the best way to do permanent damage to the orders . . ." I process what she's said. "What do you mean, you know?"

"Cecelia told me back in the valley."

"Cecelia *knew*?" The woman's brilliant, but how could she have possibly figured out that I was responsible?

"Sort of. She'd been researching to confirm what everyone always says—that only dragon fire can burn the skulls. We all assumed it was just a simplification. After all, it's not like another creature creates fire regularly." She pauses, looking up and to the side, thinking. "I wonder if they tested phoenix fire?"

"And?" None of that explains how she knew it was me.

"And Ulric wouldn't have destroyed them. Then I remembered how interested you were in the pyres after the funerals. And how quickly you got to me in the forest, after you felt my distress. Almost as if you'd already been halfway there."

She presses closer to me, taking both of my hands in hers. We're nose to nose. She gives me a gentle kiss.

"When I found out that you've been working to take down the order for years, it all clicked. Of course you were the one to burn down the hut." Her eyes lose focus again; then she shakes her head. "That's why you were so interested in lore about jackalopes. You couldn't get past their warrens. I take it that's what your aunt meant about Ivo's stories about the jackalopes being why Jamie wouldn't enter the valley? One of the territorial little suckers got him?"

"In the leg. I honestly thought he was going to bleed out," I reply, dumbfounded. She knew. All my secrets. I'm half-surprised she didn't just immediately agree to Sarai's demand to kill me. Or just offer me up as a sacrifice to save her valley, unprompted. "You don't seem very upset."

In fact, she is glowing. A glittering of starlight amidst the darkness of the crypt.

"Oh, I'm beyond livid," she says. "But what am I going to do? Scold you for doing a thing the order would have done themselves if they had thought of it? Make you promise to never do it again?"

"Yeah . . . there's not a lot of use squeezing promises out of a dying man."

"And there's not another hut to burn."

I reach up and take her cheek in my hand. She does not flinch from me. I close my eyes and just rub my thumb against the softness of her skin, savoring the feel of her.

"The valley has started to come back to life because you destroyed the skulls and their magic infused the valley with magic. You did what needed to be done, for a variety of reasons." She kisses me again, softly.

Her anger would have been easier to accept. I'd braced for hatred. Not . . . kindness. This forgiveness is nearly impossible to hold. Especially the hope that comes along with it.

That maybe she's being so kind because her feelings are as deep as my own.

"Hey, you," she says in the sweetest of voices. "Look at me."

I do. Of course I do. I'm not going to argue with her about doing the exact thing I long to do for the rest of my—admittedly short—life.

"I'm sorry." She wraps arms around my chest and buries her face into the nape of my neck. "I'm sorry, for what's about to happen. And I'm sorry that I revealed my face to the phoenix and set all of this in motion. Everything I touch—everything I love—gets destroyed. Even before the phoenix. I wish—" She pauses, her breathing hitches.

"What do you wish?" I ask softly. I trace a finger across her arm.

"I wish our roles were reversed." The admittance breaks a piece of me in two. All this time, I had wished our roles were reversed. That I was the one wearing the destruction phoenix. That I had her power. And now to hear her wish the same . . .

"No," I say.

Her breath is warm on my collarbone. I hear the very small hitch in her voice. "No?"

"No," I repeat. "This is how it's meant to be. This is who you are."

"You think I'm a destroyer?"

I pull back from her, stepping away. I want to see her beautiful face. The soft slope of her cheekbones, the bright blue of her eyes. We're still touching. I love the way our bodies fit so perfectly together, but now I can see her.

"I do not think you are a destroyer." I try to find the words, the nuance so she can see inside my heart. "I think you are like my parents were. They wanted to make the world better by whatever means they could. And they didn't flinch from the efforts of that work. They embraced it. Despite the costs to themselves."

"And it took them from you."

I nod. She's right. And I will be angry with them for that even into the after. "But they still did the right thing. They tried. Like you do."

I kiss her, gently at first. She kisses me back. And then her intensity grows, quickly. In an instant, there's a desperate fierceness to her kisses. I understand that desperation, that hurry.

Sarai only promised us the length of a feast, when an eternity wouldn't be enough.

Adela's starting to kiss frantically down my neck. She pulls at my tunic and unties the waistband of my trousers when I stop her. Before we get too caught up in our bodies, I have one more thing to share with her. One more thing she must know.

Something deep inside of me cracks open, and I am surprised at the joy and relief I feel at finally letting it go. "I love you."

"You love me?" she asks. It's a question, but there's no uncertainty in it. Her voice is full of awe, not doubt.

"I do. Very much."

"I love you, too," she says. I did not know how much I had hoped to hear her say that. She traces a finger down my chest. "Now show me how much."

I am exhausted down to my bones, but if these are the final moments I have with this beautiful, impossible, amazing woman, I am going to spend every single one of them showing her just how much she means to me.

I start slow, but Adela has no patience for my gentleness. Her kisses are hard, her lips and tongue and teeth insistent. I give her what she demands. I meet her frenzied pace, gripping her butt and pulling her into me, loving the way her ass cheeks overflow in my hands.

I lick and nip at her earlobe, and she twists her head to give me better access.

I see her practically melt with wanting, but she remains upright. She pushes at my shoulder, and I sink to my knees in front of her. She lifts her borrowed tunic up over her head and shimmies out of her pants until she is naked in front of me. I devour her with my eyes.

"Goddess, you are perfection. Let me worship at your altar."

She lifts up one leg and rests her knee over my shoulder, balancing on one foot with her hands on my other shoulder and head. I help brace her with my hands on her hips, and she tilts forward until the wet, hot center of her is just in front of my face.

I kiss and bite her thighs, making her moan. I love the way my teeth make small marks on her paleness. Marks to remember me by once I'm gone.

I inhale deeply, loving the smell of her. I bury my face up and into her. Making sure she is steady, I move one hand until I have two fingers hovering just at her entrance. I begin to touch her slowly, circling around. I want her to be ready. I don't want to hurt her, pushing too quickly.

But Adela is impatient. She bends her knee and sinks down onto my fingers, pushing them into herself fast and hard. She moans and grips my hair, tugging me closer, and moves her hips so I am touching her exactly where she wants, at the speed she wants.

I chuckle into her body as she writhes against my fingers and mouth, and match her urgency.

"I'm close," she moans. "So close."

I lift my face for a quick moment. "Come for me, Goddess." I return to my work, praising her body, her soul, with my tongue, lips, and fingers.

She comes, swiftly and hard. I feel her starting to ebb and scoot away from me, but I hold her leg in place over my shoulder, not letting her go. I increase my speed and intensity. She comes again, and then again.

She is panting and sweaty when she finally tugs me away from her by my hair, laughing. "Stop," she breathes. "Stop."

She drops her leg, which is shaking, and pulls me up to my feet. Eyes half-closed with satiation, she kisses me deeply. Then she kneels in front of me.

"My turn to please you, love."

I practically growl at the use of the pet name. Love. She loves me.

"What would you like?" she asks.

This brilliant, strong, powerful, perfect woman loves me. She wants to please me. But asking me what I want from her is impossible.

"I want all of you," I say.

She pulls me to the hard-packed earth of the crypt, tugging my waistband down. She straddles me, holding me in place while she sinks onto me without even a pause. She's wet, tight, fire, and I moan at how perfectly we fit. Then she slides back up, hovering ever so slightly so that I am just barely inside her. I groan, wanting her to take her pleasure. She wiggles her hips a bit, teasing. "You want me? All of me?"

"I do."

"Then take me," she demands. "All of me is yours."

I grip her hips, plant my feet for leverage and thrust up into her. She cries out, ecstatic. I continue to do exactly as she commands.

Chapter Thirty-Four

ADELA

We hold each other, chest to chest, legs tangled up together, foreheads touching.

"I love you." Kian whispers against my mouth. His voice is strong and unafraid. "I trust you."

I barely hold back my sobs when I say, "I love you, too."

After we get redressed, we can hear the merriment of a feast winding down, and sure enough, within a few moments, we are fetched. I pick up the phoenix and follow meekly. They take us upstairs, and I kiss Kian for the last time before I'm led to my own rooms by the Spinner priest.

There, Cecelia waits for me. She's changed, and I take it Sarai's assigned her the role of my assistant, since she's wearing her sister's silver and lilac robes and she has her hair up in the three, three-strand braids. She's shaking, but trying to be brave.

"A bath has been drawn," she says.

I refuse it. I don't want to wash Kian's scent from me. And besides, I'm not going to dress up for them. I don't need their pomp and ceremony. I am not a gleeful participant in Sarai's false matching ceremony.

Not that Cecelia is. She sets the things aside, and I hear her sniffle slightly. "I hate this," she whispers. "It's all so wrong."

Her eyes flick to the Spinner priest in the corner of the room. His back is to us, but no doubt he's listening. She wants to say more, to ask more. She likely has a million questions about why I'm doing this, why I would ever even consider this. I feel the weight of Cecelia's unspoken words settle like a stone on my chest.

"It is," I say, and I hope she hears my own unspoken truths: All of this is wrong—the way the temple leaders have abused their power, the hoarding of the skulls, the insistence on hurting people I love to get me to fulfill their whims. And for what? Nothing they don't already have.

Waves of helplessness, grief, rage, and fear flow through me, one after another. I push them all away. I can luxuriate in my feelings later, after I have done what needs to be done.

Until then, I cannot break.

"They had me find supplies in their pantries," she whispers and shows me to the small table in front of the fire where oils, ointments, salve, and herbs sit. "They didn't have much of quality, but I did my best."

I look over her collection. It's not bad, for how quickly she's thrown it together. "No comfrey, I see."

"Thank the goddess," she says with a genuine shiver.

"Time to go," the Spinner priest says and we collect the oils and ointments. I may not be willing to wear the raiment of the matcher, but this part of the ceremony I will gladly do to soothe these tortured skulls.

We descend back down to the crypt and the skulls that await us. We move to the altar, where Sarai has made a stack for her matching ceremony. I carry the phoenix skull, and set her down carefully beside the others. I do not need her for the work of the matcher. The skulls she's chosen consist of three dragons, a couple of kelpies, a single gytrash, and a unicorn. The dragons in particular are old and rare, and I am surprised that she would risk them since we don't know exactly how these pairings will go.

Perhaps she doesn't care.

After all, the crypt is full of backups.

Above us, the orders prepare their novitiates while we prepare the bones. I show Cecelia how to test the skulls for viability. We need to know which ones will be able to be matched and which ones won't.

Checking skulls does not come naturally to Cecelia, but that's no surprise.

Still, she helps.

One of the dragons is gone. We both check it. I even put my cheek against it, like I did with the phoenix. There is no response. I silently thank the creature on behalf of the goddess. It has done excellent work in its lifetime, and then suffered hanging in the dark long beyond. I gently set it aside.

Once we know that the others are present—though some incredibly faint—we begin the next step of the process.

I polish the bones, rubbing small swipes of scented oils and soothing ointments into the pale, craggy surfaces of the creatures' skulls. Their insistent whispered wants echo through my head. I welcome their sad, mourning voices and echo them.

I am sorry, my friends, for what I am about to ask of you, I say to them in my mind. *So sorry.*

Cecelia and I finish setting up for the ceremony. A nave of the crypt will be our matching hut; the wider, open space is where order members will wait and chant, as if they're my community of keepers in the fields of jackalope warrens.

When there is nothing else left to do, I take my phoenix skull and place it on my face. She's been quiet through this all. Whatever she feels, she is not sharing with me.

Cecelia and I ascend to the sanctuary. Their feasting complete, the three orders mingle—navy, red, and black—everyone in their finest robes. They are half-drunk on mead, and excited by the impending ceremony.

I search for Kian, expecting him to be part of the procession. When I cannot find him, I close my eyes and see if that old pull is still present. I haven't felt it much since leaving the valley, though I also haven't spent much time away from his presence.

They have already moved him back to the crypt.

"Ready?" I ask Cecelia, and wonder how much of this next process she knows.

Probably all of it, both from her research and having watched it countless times through her life. That's not the same, of course, as leading it yourself.

She's trembling slightly, but she nods. We begin to walk. Behind us, the orders take up the keeper chants. The familiar words I have grown up amongst echo around the black-marble sanctuary and grate at my ears. I hate those words, that rhythm, in their mouths. It is not made for them. It is for my people, and mine only.

I climb down into the crypt, every step reluctant.

The voices of the skulls grow enormous. They are a riot of sound, of wanting. They want release. They want life. They are confused and hurting and hopeful. I let their wants wash through me. I take them inside me. I become them.

Soon, I will give them what they want. As soon as I possibly can.

We enter the crypt, and there he is, waiting. Kian. My love.

He's kneeling in the center, his bare chest exposed, expanding with each breath. The sight of him is almost painful. He's so beautiful in this moment, so impossibly alive. His hair is tousled and loose, disheveled from our time together. He looks at me with his dark, unfathomable eyes and winks, teasing even at the end.

The wink is what breaks me. I promised myself I'd be strong, unflinching, unbreakable. But how can I be when he looks at me like that? Like he still sees me, appreciates me, forgives me.

I move before I know what I'm doing, flinging myself down in front of him. Touching his face and his neck, pushing hair out of his eyes. Tracing his collarbone as if I'm afraid he'll just disappear if he doesn't have my touch to anchor him.

And then I kiss him. Again and again. On his cheeks, his forehead, his nose, his neck. And of course, his lips. Each kiss is a promise, a plea, a protest. In the impending dark, remember me. Remember us.

"Stand up, Goddess." His smile stabs at something deep inside me.

I squeeze his hands. "I'm sorry I ruined your plans for vengeance."

"You really did." He smirks, and I want to kiss that perfect, hiding smile. Again. So I do. When I am done, he says, "Loving you is so much sweeter than any vengeance."

Sarai clears her throat, rolling her eyes with impatience. As if I should hurry to kill the love of my life.

Still, I stand.

"You are magnificent and I trust you," Kian says, quiet enough that I'm certain only I can hear him.

At first I want to shake my head and argue. I am impulsive. I react out of anger and fear and spite, but when I consider, I realize that's not always true. Cecelia, Dad, Kian—all have told me to trust myself. To believe in myself. I act quickly, even rashly sometimes, but it's not all impulse. It's not always damning. In fact, it's most often exactly in line with my values.

Perhaps, then, it's not impulse. It's intuition. I am good at seeing the world quickly, taking it all in and then deciding immediately what I want to do and how. That's not something to be ashamed of. It's something to embrace.

They're alright. I need to trust myself. And the phoenix. She's the one who showed me the path forward. But does she understand the complexity of the situation? And even if she does, can I trust myself not to completely destroy everything in my attempts to save it?

"Let's move along now," Sarai says, obviously annoyed at the time I'm taking.

I let her annoyance rush over me. I feel the buildup of pressure, expanding rapidly within me. My emotions are so close to the surface, they're easy to pull from. When there is so much pressure that I worry I might burst, I release it. The magic that pulses through the crypt is a physical presence, golden and swirling. And mine to control.

Skulls fall down from the walls surrounding us. The candles on the altar snuff out. Order members step back.

I do not pause. I do not cry. I do not even move.

I kill Kian.

One moment he is there, eyes wide and awe-filled. He is not scared. He looks . . . impressed, proud of me. The next moment, he is gone.

Not his body. That is there, a heap on the hard-packed dirt floor. But the beauty of it, the animation of him, is gone.

I love him.

Loved him.

And I have killed him. Something like a sob wrenches from me, but it is not sorrow. It is anger. Pure, luminous rage. Everything in me is aflame. Even my eyes are molten. I could blink and burn down the world.

"Well done, my little bird." Sarai steps forward. "Now let's add that phoenix skull of his to our ceremony, shall we?"

I turn to her, and I wonder if she's so used to being untouchable in her role that she is oblivious to danger. After all, no one would ever threaten a high priestess. It'd be like threatening the goddess she serves directly, and no one would risk the Huntress's ire.

I suppress the rage, hiding it behind a smile, just like Kian taught me to. "Of course." My voice is poisoned honey, but she is so excited by the possibilities of her twisted dreams being realized that she doesn't hear the threat in it.

I gesture to the crowd behind her and then to the crypt surrounding us. There are novitiates from every order standing to be matched, and only a handful of skulls.

"If you drop the barrier, we can match more of these," I say. "Drop the barrier so Cecelia and I can test and prep them as we go. Why wait?"

There's a short flicker of Sarai's intuition. A deep part of her knows she shouldn't trust me just after she's made me kill my lover, but her greed wins out. With a few movements of her hands, she drops the barriers to the skulls. The moment she does, I let my raw, monstrous rage burst forth.

How dare she.

How dare.

"I am not your little bird. I am not your anything."

"Of course you are." Either Sarai is the bravest person I have ever met or the stupidest. "You are a member of the Order of the Huntress, and I am the high priestess. You are mine to command."

"You could be the great goddess herself, and I'd still tell you to go fuck yourself." My throat is so raw that I'm surprised I don't breathe fire like Enkidus. "You want me to reshape the way things have been? To bring down the systems the orders have promised to uphold?" I direct the magic. "I am a ruinous creature. And I will destroy you."

I point at her and her unicorn skull dissolves into a pile of ashes. All of the opals and diamonds and pearls gone along with it. Sarai simply stands there, gaping. She has a small, pointed face. Pretty, with smooth, freckled skin and a little upturned nose. She looks so vulnerable without the unicorn skull.

I do not wait for her response. I turn to the other servants of the Huntress, the Pupil, and the Spinner. Nearly all of the Huntress order step back. They hold up their hands to protect their faces from the blaze of me.

It does not save them.

Everyone who steps away loses their creature skull. Gems and bones and gold fall into piles of ash at their feet.

My father steps forward, solid and true. Cecelia has moved next to him and watches carefully. I can practically see her taking notes in her head as if she were writing about this period of keeper history. I hope she will delight future scholars with the drama of her storytelling.

There are members of the other orders who are not afraid of me. They stand firm, unflinching in the face of my destruction. In front of them is Ulric. He steps forward, raising a hand to my cheek. His eyes are wet with tears. "Are you okay?"

I look down at Kian's body at my feet.

I am not certain I will ever be okay again.

"How can we help?" he asks.

I take in the people who surround me and my fallen love, who bear witness to my pain and anger and destruction and do not flinch from me. Most of them are strangers, but a few I am glad to call friends, or allies. Svena, Sister Ihi, the trio of gytrash-matched priests, and of course, Ulric. I am still aflame, but they are not afraid.

"If you trust me, I could use your help."

"Of course," Ulric replies immediately. Around him, others nod. "What do you need?"

"Half of you, go out into the community and find those who do good. People you trust. If they agree, bring them here. Quickly. They will be matched with creatures and trained to do magic. And once the crisis and chaos of this all is passed, we will revisit their bonds."

"And the other half?" Cecelia asks.

I point to the bare-faced order members with ashes at their feet. "Keep those ones out of my way."

They do.

People of all kinds come down to the crypt. Novitiates. Servants. Teachers. Smugglers. One by one, they step forward, brave despite their obvious fear.

With Ulric and Cecelia beside me, I begin to match them. From the altar, and then from the walls. I check with each of the skulls first. "Help me," I say to the old bones, "and when we are done with our work, I promise to release you back to the valley if that's what you wish."

Some refuse. And those I set aside. They have given eons to this world. I will ask them for no more. But those that agree, I match.

I begin with Cecelia. She removes her plain mask and instantly pairs with a kelpie. Then Dad with a gryphon. Svena matches with one of the oldest and strongest dragons.

Linden is there, the stumps of his arms tightly bandaged. He steps forward, hopeful.

I ignore him and turn to a young man beside him.

"I do not actually want to be a priest," a young novitiate wearing pink says, shuffling his feet.

"Then you don't have to be one," I reply. "No one has to serve a goddess, human or creature. There are no unwilling participants in this. This will be a pairing of equals, or no pairing at all."

After about an hour, I have matched fifty or so people. There are some who came to learn more but choose to remain unmatched, and I'm glad of it. This is not a path for everyone.

No path is.

But I am grateful for those who have trusted me. I look down at Kian's body. Him, especially.

I hope I have not betrayed that trust.

"What do we do next?" Cecelia asks, gently touching the kelpie skull on her face.

"The skulls will guide you," I assure her. "But basically, go out into the city. Help where you can. Prepare everyone for the changes that are to come. The world will be remade, and that could cause uncertainty. But the great goddess still protects us. We still worship and revere her. She still blesses us."

When we are done, Ulric and a few others usher the wicked, now barefaced order members back up the stairs. I don't know where they're being taken, nor do I care.

I am finally alone.

I kneel down to Kian, grateful. I take off the phoenix skull, my skin still golden with flames that reflect off the ceiling of skulls. I set her aside and lie down beside Kian's body, holding his hand. I close my eyes, and cry.

Chapter Thirty-Five

KIAN

There is a stretch of nothingness that seems both impossibly long and impossibly short. It is welcome. A bright and peaceful absence of . . . everything. The heavy weight of expectation. The gnawing hunger of want. The ache of failure and fear and hope.

I am free.

I rest inside that nothing, luxuriating in the quiet until I feel a tug deep inside me, under my breastbone, beside my heart or between my lungs. I did not think I believed in souls.

But something inside me is calling me out of the nothing. I follow that tug across what feels like an endless expanse that grows darker and darker.

I find Adela at the end. Adela, kneeling beside me, crying precious, elegant tears. I reach up and wipe one away. "Why are you crying, Goddess?"

"I killed you."

"And yet, here I am. Not even a little bit dead."

She bites her lip, uncertainty furrowing her perfect brow. I run a fingertip along one pale-blond eyebrow.

"I was so scared I was wrong," she says. "That I would destroy you and you'd be gone forever."

"But you don't destroy." I give her a small kiss on her lips.

"What do you mean?" There is a fragility of hope in her voice. "You create, I destroy. We are the two sides of life and death. The two sides of the phoenix."

I try to find the words I am looking for. I do my best. "On the natural path of things, life is not destroyed. Like when a tree falls in the valley, it doesn't just disappear. It decays. It falls apart to make room for its next stage, for new life." I reach up a shaking hand. My arm feels so heavy. "That's how your magic is, love."

I give her time to work through the thoughts. I can tell she wants to believe them. But it means letting go of ancient wounds that tell her she is impulsive or broken, that everything she touches is ruined. I can see her getting there. I can see her accepting herself, just as she is. And I don't think I've ever witnessed anything more holy.

Adela is exactly who she is meant to be. And I love her for that—in all the big feelings, the big ideas, the chaos.

"So I . . . dismantle?" She beams. She does not wait for me to confirm or deny her statement. She has come to the truth herself, and it does not matter who agrees. Not even me. "I dismantle."

"You are the first step toward healing, my love."

She leans forward on her knees, one hand braced near my waist on the hard-packed dirt floor, the other gently cupping my cheek. She kisses me. It starts off soft. She's worried I'm hurt. But I have never felt better.

I kiss her harder, stretching up to meet her, pressing my chest against her body, wrapping an arm around her, and pulling her close.

She loses her balance and falls against me. She tries to scramble aside, to move herself off me, but I don't give her a moment to readjust. I hold her firmly and deepen the kiss.

We have things to do, but I don't rush. I luxuriate in her. Eventually she pulls away and smiles down at me. Her hair is a curtain around our faces. "I'm so glad you came back," she says with a gentle smile.

"Oh, my love," I reply, "I was never gone. Just away for a bit. We are two parts of a pair. I don't think one can fully leave while the other survives."

"That is what the phoenix showed me. Her mate died. She watched him. And while it hurt her, she did not mourn or lose herself. She simply settled in. She knew he would come back to her."

I tuck a strand of hair behind one of her ears and look around the crypt of bones, and wait. She has more to say.

"But I—" she sobs out the words, overwhelmed with relief and sorrow both. "I was terrified that I was wrong. That I misunderstood. And you were gone forever, at my hand."

"As always, you saw the truth of everything, clear and bright as the morning sun." I kiss her lightly on the nose. "Now. We have some more business to take care of. Where is Sarai?"

Adela stands and holds a hand out to me, hauling me up. "What do you want with her?"

"I want her to see what the order becomes without her at the helm. I want her to live in this world with everything that she values—her magic, her power, her wealth—stripped of her. I want to take her world from her. Like she took my world from me when I was ten years old and she killed my parents. I don't just want her to suffer. Suffering would be a kindness. I want her in agony, a slow but certain ripping apart of everything she has ever wanted or loved. If she is even capable of that."

I pause, realizing I'm waiting for Adela's censure. She is so good-hearted; surely she will insist I act with more mercy, show grace. I know I am a disappointment to her in this way. I'm afraid she will hate that, even now, I seek vengeance.

But her censure does not come. When I am brave enough, I look up at Adela.

She stands up tall, the skulls of centuries' worth of creatures surrounding her. She beams at me. Her smile so wide that her eyes almost disappear behind the apples of her cheeks.

"I think that is exactly what she deserves," she says, and holds out her hand. I take it, and suddenly we are thrust into a vision.

We are nestled into our cave, surrounded by eggs that despite our best efforts, never hatched. Some are ours. Some are from a much more ancient phoenix pair. The magic in the valley has begun to dwindle, though we don't know why. But we believe it's part of why the eggs will not hatch.

We are the last of our kind. And with our death, something will shift dramatically in the creatures. We know that, and yet, we cannot do anything about it. Our time is nearly up. Hopefully in our next life, we will be able to try again.

From somewhere far off, we hear the chanting of the keepers. A goodbye ceremony is occurring, and we should go. We need to help burn the bones, return them to the valley, and usher the wild magic that flows back into the youngest creatures.

But we are so tired. We stay. We lie down together, in our beautiful nest, and after a thousand years on this earth, we finally say goodbye.

Chapter Thirty-Six

ADELA

It takes us weeks to deconstruct the bone crypt. As we work beneath the ground of the towering black-marble temple, the newly matched move through the city. They spread the news of what has happened, and provide aid to those who need it. They remove rotten, crumbling buildings and find empty places to establish gardens.

Kian helps with these, creating produce from dried seeds and rotten vines.

Others take to the river, cleaning it so it is once again potable. The most ambitious begin working on bigger-picture projects—education and housing and facilities for the very young, the very old, and those who just need extra care.

It is not perfect. Insborough will never be a utopia.

Despite occasional setbacks, the transition to new leadership in the order is not even a quarter of the chaos I expected. It turns out, for many, those in power had little effect on their day-to-day lives. And so they just continued on living, paying little mind to what was happening in or around the the temples.

Kian, Cecelia, Ulric, and I continue to work carefully on our deconstruction of the crypt. We separate the skulls. To those still present in their bones, I give a choice. They can await matching with new novitiates in time or be put to rest, finally, in the valley.

Most choose rest.

From these we pry the jewels, making a small and valuable pile on the altar. Along with much of the strange and precious art in the temple hallways above us, they will be sold. Their proceeds will be used to help fund our efforts, to buy food and necessities for the people doing the work, and to help provide support to the poorest of the city. And to support the valley.

The night we take the last skull down from the ceiling, Kian and I lie in bed atop the covers. We are damp with sweat and ecstasy, but still we curve into each other. I tuck my forehead onto his chest, and he trails a hand lazily through my hair and down my spine, sending shivers across my skin.

He kisses the gooseflesh he's created with a chuckle. "You're so beautiful, Goddess."

I open my mouth to respond, but before I can, a vision very unlike any of the others we've experienced rises up to meet us.

The world is blurry, coming to us in broad strokes of color and overwhelming emotion. Movement is different—stilted and slow, low to the ground.

I miss flying, soaring over the valley that is my home and dominion. But soon I will find my wings once again. But first, my love and I have one more essential task.

Our caretakers and others gather before a pile of our fellow creatures' bones. They have done their good work and are ready for their final rest, ready to be reabsorbed by the valley and find new life in its magic.

The caretakers begin their chanting. The pressure builds.

We are placed atop the fire as the caretakers continue their chants. The tension rises to a zenith. With a final, conjoined assent, we burst forth into a sanctifying golden light.

There is a moment of absolute nothing, and then we are flying once again.

We come out of the vision in a haze.

"I think we were just given some very clear instructions," Kian says.

"Oh, you think?" I give him a small poke to the ribs. In one burst of movement, he grabs my hand, thrusts it over my head, and shifts so he is hovering above me. His grip on my wrist is firm but gentle. His beautiful, smirking mouth just barely brushes mine as he speaks. "Do not tickle me, Goddess."

"And if I do?" I take my free hand and trace it across the bare skin of his ribs. He skirts away from my light touch.

"I will have to take revenge." He seizes that hand, too, and raises it above my head as well. He holds both of my wrists with one hand. With his other he traces up my arm, across my clavicle, and down my sternum.

"Do your worst," I urge, my voice liquid with desire.

He complies enthusiastically.

Back in the valley, we go immediately to a large meadow and unload the skulls. Everyone works together—keepers, priestesses, and priests.

All around us, Tani gambols, chasing dust motes in the sunshine and getting underfoot.

Above us, Lathai flies in lazy figure eights, watching his little one's joy.

"Are you certain I can't have a week to look through our archives for the ritual around this?" Cecelia asks, looking like she wants to cry. "What if we do it wrong and it doesn't work?"

"It will work," I reply with absolute certainty. If there's anything I've learned in the past month, it is that ritual is not nearly as necessary as intent for magic. But I like it, too. It's familiar, and it helps us feel safe and in control. "Find it for us for next time?"

"Fine." She places a gryphon skull on the pile.

Nearby, living creatures draw closer, curious as to what we're doing. The larger, flying ones make me nervous. There is still a dragon with a taste for human flesh loose in the valley.

But we have protections, including two dragon-wielders.

When they are all unloaded, I ask everyone to stay and stand witness for as long as they're able. Nearly all do.

I take a deep breath, not quite ready to take the next step. I was raised a keeper, a matcher; destroying over one thousand skulls feels fundamentally wrong. I know I must. I asked the skulls what they wanted. They have already served longer than any creature ought. These wanted rest, and I will not rob them of it.

Kian takes my hand. With a nod, Svena and Ulric light the skulls on fire, using their magic. As the bones burn, Kian harnesses their energy and magic and funnels it back into the valley.

Nearly instantly, we see the effects of magic returning even more powerfully than it had begun to show when we smuggled Tani home. Buds burst on trees we thought dead; the earth becomes a dark, rich brown; there even seems to be more birdsong. Most telling, the living creatures around us become restless. They dance and call out, run, and play-fight. They remind me of the little alicorn, pure chaotic energy. These creatures would not allow themselves to live in a house in the village like Bartholomew's pet dragons. They are wild and want to be free, not hand-fed.

When there is nothing left but ash and a few small flames, Kian and I turn to each other. Now comes the hardest and most straightforward part of this process.

It should be simple, to let the phoenix go. After all, she changed my life in a way that I wasn't prepared for, that I didn't want, but nothing about this is easy. Still, we do it.

As one, Kian and I remove our phoenix skulls. We step forward to the very edge of the fire, so close that the heat licks our feet, and we throw our skulls to the flames.

"Goodbye," I whisper to the darkening skull.

"Until the after," Kian says, his voice thick with emotion.

We turn to go, but there is a pulse of golden light. We turn back in time to see two fully formed, living phoenixes emerge. A new beginning for our wondrous creatures.

ACKNOWLEDGMENTS

These are just some the people who encouraged me over the many years it took me to develop my voice and tell this story. All my gratitude to:

My grandparents, who let me spend childhood following them through chores and showed me the beauty, heartbreak, and sometimes violence of farming.

The rest of my family, especially Mom, Kyle, N, A, and all of the other children who came into our lives through foster care and friends during the writing of this book. Thank you for loving me, and for giving me something besides stories to pour my heart into.

All of the friends who laughed and cried with me, read with me, brainstormed with me, ate with me, adventured with me, but most importantly, believed that I could do this long before I believed it myself—especially Ciara McGrane, Clay Morrell, and Emily Laclau.

The fellow writers and writing mentors who shared their knowledge, insights, and encouragement—especially Beth Revis, Claudia

Mills, Cassie Gustafson, Celesta Rimington, Delia Sherman, Isabel Sterling, James Persichetti, Rebecca Jones, Taylor Hartley, and so, so many more.

My agent, Danielle Burby, for your guidance, advocacy, and kindness. But mostly for always seeing into the heart of my stories and pushing me tell the truth of them more clearly. And to Taryn Fagerness for ensuring Adela and Kian's story would be read around the world.

Emilia Rhodes for helping me to shape this book, Elizabeth Hitti for keeping us on track, and all of the rest of the amazingly talented team at Atria. (Check out the credits for the full list of people who made this story something tangible! It truly takes a village to produce a book.)

And the many organizations and people that gave me beautiful, comfortable spaces where I could sink into writing (something infinitely necessary with small kids at home!)—especially Lindsey, Ben, Taylor, and Kelly at Starling Lounge; Amanda, George, and the rest of the team at the Highlights Foundation; Hollins University; the Toledo Metroparks Treehouse Village; and many, many, *many* coffee shops.

ABOUT THE AUTHOR

Jessi Cole Jackson's perfect day involves fresh-cut flowers, cream-filled pastries, and stories of all sorts. After a dozen years making costumes for professional theatres all over the East Coast, she moved home to rural Michigan, where she now lives with her family. If she had more time, she'd make more art. *Ruinous Creatures* is her debut novel.

ATRIA BOOKS, an imprint of Simon & Schuster, fosters an open environment where ideas flourish, bestselling authors soar to new heights, and tomorrow's finest voices are discovered and nurtured. Since its launch in 2002, Atria has published hundreds of bestsellers and extraordinary books, which would not have been possible without the invaluable support and expertise of its team and publishing partners. Thank you to the Atria Books colleagues who collaborated on *Ruinous Creatures*, as well as to the hundreds of professionals in the Simon & Schuster advertising, audio, communications, design, ebook, finance, human resources, legal, marketing, operations, production, sales, supply chain, subsidiary rights, and warehouse departments who help Atria bring great books to light.

Editorial
Emilia Rhodes
Elizabeth Hitti

Jacket Design
Amanda Hudson

Marketing
Zakiya Jamal

Managing Editorial
Paige Lytle
Sofia Echeverry
Shelby Pumphrey

Production
Abel Berriz
Vanessa Silverio
Laura Petrella
Jill Putorti

Publicity
Camila Araujo

Publishing Office
Dana Trocker
Suzanne Donahue
Abby Velasco

Subsidiary Rights
Nicole Bond
Sara Bowne
Rebecca Justiniano